USA TODAY BE~~STSELLING AUTHOR~~

Dale Mayer

SIMON SAYS...
RIDE

A KATE MORGAN NOVEL

SIMON SAYS... RIDE (KATE MORGAN, BOOK 3)
Dale Mayer
Valley Publishing

Copyright © 2021

ISBN-13: 978-1-773364-80-3
Print Edition

Books in This Series

The Kate Morgan Series
https://smarturl.it/DMSimonSaysUniversal

Simon Says… Hide, Book 1
Simon Says… Jump, Book 2
Simon Says… Ride, Book 3
Simon Says… Scream, Book 4

About This Book

Introducing a new thriller series that keeps you guessing and on your toes through every twist and unexpected turn....

USA Today Best-Selling Author Dale Mayer does it again in this mind-blowing thriller series.

The unlikely team of Detective Kate Morgan and Simon St. Laurant, an unwilling psychic, marries all the unpredictable and passionate elements of Mayer's work that readers have come to love and crave.

Detective Kate Morgan is hot on a new confusing case. A cyclist is killed at the main intersection to the University of British Columbia. At first glance it looks like a hit-and-run, but, as details emerge, it gets much more complicated.

From one day to the next, Simon is blinded by an overload of senses and noises. It's impacting his regular business day, and he seems unable to control when and how these moments occur. Angry and frustrated, he tells Kate but knows she's unable to help. How can she, when he can't help himself?

As Kate struggles to work her way through a gang of arrogant university students, reluctant parents, a defensive dean, and way too many unobservant witnesses, she finds a disturbing pattern of more "accidents" *and* more victims ...

Then finally Simon understands why his senses are on overload ... and flips the investigation around.

Sign up to be notified of all Dale's releases here!
https://smarturl.it/DaleNews

CHAPTER 1

Mid-August in Vancouver

TWO WEEKS AGO Kate Morgan had had a couple days off, and those two days she'd spent with Simon St. Laurant now seemed like a hell of a long time ago. She groaned.

Rodney looked up at her. "What's the matter now?"

"This stupid case. I'm still tracking down more of the suicides."

"I know." He nodded. "All we really can do is give the families closure at this point in time."

"At least that asshole pedophile in our other case is dead and gone."

"Exactly. And nobody will mourn Ken's death."

She sighed. "Somebody like that, I just assume we toss his file and carry on." She looked around. "Where is everybody?"

"Lilliana's running late, as she's been at the dentist all morning. Andy's off for the day. Owen's here somewhere."

Just then, Dispatch called her. "We've got a DB at the entrance to UBC. Female."

"On the walkway?"

"Sounds like it's just outside university grounds—at the intersection on one of the bike paths," the dispatcher said. "I'm sending you the exact location."

"Crap." Kate hopped to her feet. "Hey, Rodney, we've got a woman down on the bike path at the university."

"Out by UBC? Shouldn't RCMP have that?"

"This one is a homicide at the intersection leading to University Boulevard, so it's ours either way." At his look of surprise, she added, "Vehicular homicide. She's been run over. Time to rock and roll."

Rodney stood and grabbed his jacket. "Another woman was struck by a vehicle up in that area about a year ago."

She stopped and stared at him. "What do you mean?"

"Well"—he shrugged—"it's not like it's unusual, since that's a high-traffic spot."

"Isn't that also where they do bike-racing training?"

"They do some of it there. I mean, the UBC campus is full of trails and tracks, so it's perfect for a lot of this stuff. Plus, with all the jogging runs up there, it's great for fitness training."

"*Hmm*," she said. "So you're thinking it was a full year ago since the last one?"

"Yeah. Why?"

"I just want to make sure that we don't have like three in a row." She frowned. "Nothing like a serial killer coming back to mark time."

He looked at her with added respect. "I'll look it up."

"Do that. The last thing we need is another ugly story to mar the beauty of this place."

"You know that there will always be another ugly story." Rodney and Kate walked to her car, heading to the location in minutes, as he dug into his coffee and his cell, while she drove.

"I know," she said. "One of these days I keep thinking we'll have paradise here."

"Paradise is what you make it." He laughed.

By the time they drove up to the outskirts of the university campus, it was much later than she would have liked. The place was awash with law enforcement, traffic, and the always-present curious crowd. She parked near all the cruisers. The coroner was already on-site. "Looks like we're last to arrive. How did that happen?"

He looked up from his phone and frowned. "We did hit a spot of traffic on the way over. All because of that fender bender snarling things up."

"I guess." She nodded at his phone and the records he was pulling. "Did you find anything?"

"*Hmm.*" He bent his head again, while she hopped out.

She came around, leaned in through his window, and asked, "What did you find, Rodney?"

"Nothing good." His tone was grim.

She shook her head. "What do you mean?"

"You were asking about a third?"

"Yeah ..." Her heart was already sinking.

"How about a fourth and a fifth?"

"What the hell? Where?" she asked.

He replied, "All within a couple blocks of here. And ... all of them on this same weekend. One a year for the last five years."

She stared at him. "Shit." Just then her phone rang. She looked down at a text from Simon, just saying, **Call me**, her stomach dive-bombing at the timing, yet calling him. "Hey, what's up?" she asked. "I've just arrived at a crime scene."

"I know, and all I'm seeing are bikes, bikes, bikes, and more bikes."

"Yeah, how many of them?"

"Right now, I'd say five."

She swore. "*Great.*" She sighed heavily. "Apparently I'm at a crime scene in an area where crimes of the same kind occurred every year for the last five years, on this very weekend."

Dead silence came first on the other end, and then she heard Simon's weary voice. "You'll track this one down, I presume?"

"I won't have a choice," she said.

He whispered, "Neither do I."

"Any help you can give me?" she asked.

"No," he murmured, "not yet. But it'll come. Don't worry. It'll come."

At that, she hung up, nodding, a grim expression on her face.

CHAPTER 2

KATE WASN'T SURE what to think of Simon's message. Even Rodney didn't know what to make of it, even though he'd heard part of it. She looked down at him, still seated in her car. "Can you send that search to me, please?"

He nodded. As soon as he was done, he hopped from the vehicle, and they both stared at the people everywhere, on both sides of the street, in the street, and generally getting in the way. Cops were moving everyone back, but it took some work.

"Of course we've got a massive crowd." She pushed her hair off her forehead. "I'll start with the body." She headed to the coroner, who already leaned over the dead woman's body. He had pulled back a sheet, covering her to her waist. "Well, Dr. Smidge?"

He looked up at her and glared. She glared right back. He sighed and sat back on his heels. "You know that I'm not quite adjusted to seeing your face at all these scenes yet."

"I'm in homicide now." She shrugged. "I'll be on most of them, so get used to it."

"It's like you're a harbinger of bad news. You and the other members of the team—and I see a lot of them around too," he snapped, "but somehow they don't give me that same ugly feeling."

Her eyebrows shot up. "Thanks, Doc. You don't really

think I've got anything to do with this, do you?"

"No, of course not." He shook his head. "That would be stupid. But it seems like you have a nose for trouble. The kind of trouble that doesn't solve easily."

"I'm not so sure. This one could be easier. Although—" She stopped and shook her head. "No, we, … we don't know that."

"No, you don't, and the minute you start getting cocky about it—"

"I'm not cocky," she interrupted, speaking quietly, wondering why all the doctors in the coroner's office were so cranky. "But according to a search that Rodney just did, several other vehicular homicides have occurred annually in this area over the last few years."

"I wouldn't put more into that than it will carry. University students ride bikes, a lot of them, faculty too. So there is bound to be a higher occurrence of accidents than in other areas. Plus, many ride their bikes while under the influence."

At that, she winced. "That's not a smart idea."

"No, it's not," he snapped. "I've seen way-too-many kids do stupid shit. I can't even count the number of times I've thought about wringing their necks. But I'd like to do it before they end up on my slab."

"That would be nice, but it never seems to work that way."

"No, it doesn't. They do what they think is a great idea at the time, and then, when they wake up—or don't wake up—the family is left pondering the choices they made. And so many times it was either while under the influence or otherwise having fun with their friends on a dare. Then it's left to the rest of us to clean up the mess they made." A tone of belligerence filled his words.

She wondered how many that he'd had to deal with lately. Her job was tough sometimes, and she hadn't been on the job all that long. She'd been a cop for a long time, but she had only been a homicide detective for about five months now. She looked down at the body. She found it easier than looking at the doctor's face and seeing all the lines and creases this job had put there. He was a good man, and he worked damn hard, but, at some point in time, the job got to you. She studied the dead young woman and understood his mood. "What is she, eighteen?"

"The older I get, the more I can't tell age, but, as we ID her, we'll nail that down. Probably a student here at the university."

"And what? Just riding her bike and not looking?"

"That would make it an accident, and you and your partner wouldn't be here."

"That depends." She stared at the coroner, waiting for more information.

"Hey, I'm not here to argue about what the charges will end up being, if any even are, but I'm telling you that just because other people died from bike wrecks around here doesn't mean there is some great mystery."

"Meaning that I shouldn't make too much of the five-year annual repeat within these few blocks?"

"Exactly. All kinds of problems, all kinds of things can go wrong, and it's got nothing to do with murder."

"We got called in for some reason," she noted. "We don't generally catch traffic cases, even the bad ones."

"Well now, young lady, that could be because of this." He tilted the young woman's head ever-so-slightly.

Kate leaned over so she could see it better, and she stared, shocked. "Is that a bullet hole?"

He nodded grimly. "Yes. She was shot first. And I bet the other cases don't match that."

"I have no idea. I have yet to look at them, but this is definitely not what I expected."

"No one ever does. This is definitely your case now," he muttered. "God help you."

"Why? Do you think it'll be ugly?"

"Anything to do with a young person is tough," he explained, "and the university is pretty protective of their people, and you'll have to deal with that bureaucracy as well. Although this isn't on campus grounds, so you won't have to bring the RCMP into it."

"Can't say I'm too worried about that aspect. I'll get answers no matter who's in my way."

He let out a short bark. "That's always your attitude, isn't it?"

"I don't mean it to be, but I do tend to get in trouble for being on the short-tempered side."

"Yeah, well, maybe you'll get some answers, and that is what we need right now. Good luck with it." He sat back on his heels and glared down at the young woman.

Kate knew Dr. Smidge wasn't seeing the actual body in front of him. He was viewing the devastation and the wastefulness caused by whoever had chosen to take this young woman's life. Kate reached down, gently pulled the soft red hair off the victim's face, and whispered, "Such a waste."

"Indeed," he said, with regret. "I'm taking her now. I'll look after her." And, with that, he stood and went over to talk to his team.

She stepped back, looked around at the crowd, and found Rodney, talking with a group of young women. Kate joined them to hear him asking about anything they might have seen. And, of course, they hadn't seen anything. She moved through the crowd herself, asking questions, taking names and contact information, getting explanations as to why people were here.

More often than not, they were just gawkers, interested in something different that had happened, something that added a bit of dash and verve to their monotonous lives, even though it was terrible news for somebody else. Like always, as long as it wasn't bad news for them, everybody was fascinated. Murder had a way of doing that to people. Something was horrifically mesmerizing about it.

As Kate moved through the throng, she hoped the crowd would dissipate—but not before she took photographs of the bystanders and potential witnesses. She had noted street cameras here, but there was also construction going on which could complicate things. What she really needed was to find out if anybody had heard or seen the shooter—without mentioning the shooter first. She had to be careful with her questioning of witnesses, so as not to influence their recollection.

The bullet hole already made this case something very unusual. The question now was, did the vehicle kill her, or had she died from the gunshot and then swerved off into the oncoming traffic? Had she been hit because she was already down on the ground?

Kate knew the coroner would have to help them sort some of that out. The roads were freshly rained on, and she saw no tire tracks, although she took several photographs of the roadway for her own use as well. As she stood here, turning in a slow circle, studying the remnants of the crowd definitely shifting away, Rodney joined her.

"Nobody saw nothing," he said in disgust.

"Was she alone?"

"Nobody's stepping up to say they were with her."

"No, of course not."

"You okay?" he asked.

"Yeah, I am. Listen. What you need to know is that she was shot."

He stared at her, shocked. She pointed to the back of her own head, where the bullet had gone in. "It's tiny, so probably a .22. Or"—thinking about it—"it could even be one of those new BB guns. You know? The air guns or whatever they are."

"Whatever it was, it certainly changes things, doesn't it?"

"Maybe," she murmured. "Though it cements our role. Somebody targeted her, and, whether the vehicle was a part of it or not, I don't know."

"I wonder if the other cases have anything to do with this?"

"I have no idea." She turned to look at him. "We're a little short on information. Yet we can't ask anybody about hearing gunfire, without giving that tidbit away." She paused. "Unless the killer used a silencer."

He nodded. "Yeah, but what we aren't short on is bodies." He looked down at his witness notes. "One of the women said that a group of young men and women—five or six, she thought—were here, and they had all been there before her death and headed over to the pizza parlor for lunch."

Kate stared at him. "So, you watch somebody die, hang around to look at the body, and you get hungry?"

"Hey, absolutely no way you'll bring me into that discussion. You know it takes all kinds of people."

"That it does. That it does. We'll have to hit them when we're finished with all these people here."

"It's just amazing," he muttered, "how observant some people are. Somebody said that they came upon her, saw her on the ground, and called it in."

"We had four different 9-1-1 calls, I think," she muttered, "if I remember that right. I'll run it, so we can make sure we catch everybody."

"And, of course, so many people don't like to give any information at all."

"I've never understood that," she said.

"They don't want to get involved. It's easy enough to understand, I guess. All these questions. It's ... an unfamiliar experience for most everybody, so nobody wants to bother."

"Maybe. If we don't go over to the pizza parlor pretty quickly, they'll be gone too," she said. "I think I'll go there first, if only I knew which one."

"Probably the one everybody talks about. It's been popular for a long time."

Something about his tone got her attention, and her eyebrows raised. "Don't even tell me that you attended UBC."

"Sure did," he said, with a big grin. "The go-to pizza place is just across the street and on the corner over there."

She looked where he pointed and nodded. With that, she bolted across the road, holding up her badge as she darted through traffic. As she approached the pizza parlor, she saw a group of five or six young people, stepping outside, laughing and joking. She immediately intercepted them, stopping their progress.

One of the men said, "Hey, what's with the pushy attitude?"

"I presume you're the group I'm looking for." Kate held up her badge.

They frowned, looked at each other, then shifted uneasily. "We don't even know what you're talking about."

"Are you sure about that?" she asked. "I understand from other witnesses that you were one of the first on the scene to see that poor young woman on the pavement over there."

"We don't know anything about it," one of the two women protested.

Kate turned to her. "I'll be the judge of that, and I'm really hoping you didn't have anything to do with it."

"Everybody else got there, so no reason for us to stay," the woman argued, sticking out her chin.

"Interesting," Kate said. "You didn't stop to answer any questions though, did you?"

"No," the first man said. "We knew it would take forever, and we didn't want to get stuck over there."

"No, of course not, you'd rather eat." Kate shook her head.

"It was our lunch hour," the same woman protested. "It's not like we could do anything to help her, so why shouldn't we enjoy our life?"

"Absolutely," she murmured. "What did you see?"

At that, the men stopped, glanced at each other, and looked at the first woman who had spoken. Still, one male and one female had not said anything.

Kate turned and asked the silent female directly, "What is your name? What are you studying at the university? When did you arrive at the scene, and what did you do when you got there?"

The woman's jaw dropped, and she looked frantically from one to the other of her group.

"Hey, she's really shy. Don't. ... You'll kick her over the edge and make her all stressed," the other woman said crossly.

"I have questions. I need answers. You can either answer them now," Kate said patiently, "or you can all come down to the station and talk to our team of detectives down there."

"Are they any different than talking to you now?" asked one of the men.

She shook her head. "No, not at all. So, what will it be?"

"We could just walk away," said the first, more belligerent male. "It's not like you can stop all of us."

"No, absolutely I can't, but the cameras here have caught you already, so we will have somebody at your house, your dorm, your family's home, your classroom, or anywhere else we need to go, depending on what we find out. We'll find you one way or another. So, is that really how you want to play this?"

The young woman who had been silent said, "No, no, no. We weren't doing anything. Why are you being like this?"

"I asked you some very basic questions. Why are *you* being like this?" Kate asked in a hard tone, looking straight at her. "A young woman is dead, and we need to find out what happened and who saw what."

"I didn't see anything," she said quietly. "We had just arrived. We were all talking, laughing, and joking. We were coming down University Boulevard. It's quite a walk. We were planning on making a fast trip for pizza, then turn around and go back again."

"How fast will it be when it's *quite a walk?*" Kate asked, her head tilted, eyeing the nervous woman.

She flushed. "Okay, so we weren't planning on going

back," she murmured.

"So, already the lot of you have been uncooperative. And now you've lied."

"She didn't lie," one of the men said quickly. "We weren't really sure what we would do, and she got quite upset when we came upon the scene. We called 9-1-1."

"Who did?" Kate interrupted. "I need the name and the number, so I can verify it."

He hesitated. "Well, it was my phone."

"Your phone but not you calling?"

"No. Yes." He shook his head. "I phoned."

"Interesting phrase." She stared at him with a narrowed gaze.

"You make me feel like I did something wrong," he protested. "It's making me nervous."

"*Did* you do something wrong?" she asked him flatly.

"No."

"Then just answer the questions and give me the information I need, so we all can move on."

After that, with the thought that maybe they could walk away from this quicker if they gave her what she was looking for, they settled down. She was only after their contact information, the reasons why they were where they were, and exactly what they saw. It ended up being not a whole lot.

As she stepped back, she asked, "Was this really that hard? Just being reasonable and cooperating makes a whole lot of difference in our world."

"Sure, but you were harassing us," one of the men said.

She snorted. "Really? We are trying to gather information on a death, before everybody scattered and disappeared, *especially* the ones who didn't want to talk to us because they seem guilty right from the get-go. The first groups that arrive at a scene and call it in are really important. And, by the way, you're not allowed to leave the scene of a crime, particularly after you have called 9-1-1, and here you guys not only left the scene but you're off having pizza."

"You make it sound worse than it is," one of the women said.

"Maybe so. I wonder how the dead woman's family would think of it though. What if it was your body lying there, and your friends treated you that way?"

"We don't even know her though," one of the men said.

She nodded. "No, you didn't. At least you're telling me that you didn't. Easily one hundred thousand students are on this campus, but she was a student there. So it'll be interesting to cross-reference your classes with hers."

"Why would you do that?" The first woman reared back slightly.

"I have to," Kate said flatly. "The woman is dead. We'll conduct a full investigation to find out how and why that is."

"She was hit by a car," the first guy roared. "How hard is that to understand, even for you?"

She looked at him, raised an eyebrow. "Watch it."

He snorted. "What? So you're allowed to insult us, but we're not allowed to insult you?"

"Pretty much." She nodded. "Yeah, I'd say so." She looked at each of them. "Are you all living on campus or do any of you live at home?"

"We already told you. You asked for our addresses, and we gave them to you."

"Yes, you did." She smirked. "*But*, according to what you've given me, which appear to be family addresses, none of you live on campus. Is that correct?"

One of the women hesitated.

Kate looked at her. "But you do?"

"I do, yes."

"And what address did you give me?"

She hesitated again. "I gave you my family address."

"And why did you do that?"

"Because that is my permanent address."

In a way that made sense, but it also made it much harder to contact her immediately. "So, where are you staying on campus?" And, with that, she had to go back through all six of them again and write down their student housing addresses.

"We don't want you coming up to our rooms," one of the guys grumbled.

"I don't want to, and, if your information checks out, then it's not a problem, is it?"

"I still don't understand what you'll check out," said the first woman, puzzled.

"Just to make sure your stories line up."

"But we didn't kill her."

"Yeah, you say that, and yet somebody did. And it's my job to find out who did. However inconvenient that may be." With that, she gave them a cheerful smile. "Have a nice day." As she took off, she heard them muttering behind her. She walked across the street again to talk to Rodney.

He asked, "Did you piss them off?"

"What a bunch of smart-asses. They didn't figure they had to answer any questions and don't understand what they could possibly have done wrong."

"They could have stayed at the damn scene of the crime and told us about what they'd seen," he muttered.

"They could have, but, you know, they were busy, with

pizza on their minds, and they didn't want to waste any of their time on something so minor." He shook his head at that. She sighed. "And honestly, I don't know if it was anything more than that. People handle stress very differently, and they were further proof."

"Did you get any vibes off them?"

"You mean, ugly vibes? Yeah, a couple. One of the females had been pretty aggressive, and one of the males—Brandon—was definitely somebody I'd like to knock down a peg or two."

Rodney snorted at that. "Remember. You're not supposed to be fighting or getting in trouble."

"So you say." She smiled. "That doesn't mean they didn't need it."

"No, it probably doesn't. That doesn't change the fact that it doesn't progress our case though."

"And that part pisses me off," she muttered.

"Of course nobody saw anything. And, if it happened fast, and a silencer or whatever was used, you can understand it."

"I can." She studied the building across the street. "I'll head back over there and check to see if anybody has security cameras. I can't see anything specifically, but I'm hoping maybe somebody does."

"You go do that. I'll stick around and see who's still hanging around, watching the proceedings."

"Which is another reason I wanted to get names of everybody who was here," she said.

"And we probably didn't get everybody."

"No, I'm sure we didn't. And, if anybody here was watching the results of his handiwork, he's probably long gone, but you never know," she muttered. She had seen it

17

happen time and time again. And still, only so much one could do about it.

———∽∼∼∽———

MEANWHILE SIMON ST. Laurant had started his day early, as usual, and knocked on the door. He was down in one of the alleys he knew well. Although he'd been here several times, knocking on this door made him feel odd. When it opened, just barely a crack, he smiled and handed over a roll of bills. A smile lit up the face on the other side.

"Simon, thank you," she said quietly.

He shrugged. "Maybe it will keep somebody safe for a little bit longer."

"It will," she said. "It seems, right now, donations are hard come by."

He nodded. "It's not an easy time for anybody these days."

"And yet Vancouver is so wealthy." She shook her head.

"Wealthy in many ways, yet profoundly destitute in others. Take it and use it." With that, he turned to walk away.

"You never seem to want anything in return," she said.

He looked at her in surprise. "No, of course not. Why would I?"

She laughed. "A lot of people would."

"I'm not a lot of people." He turned and walked away from the very private entrance to the women's shelter. A shelter where women, who had escaped from an abusive situation, were in hiding.

The trouble was, like she had said, donations were hard to come by, and it was run by the charity and the goodwill of others. He did what he could, when he could. Too often he had forgotten to drop by and had felt terrible. But, when he remembered, he would walk down here and give them something. The few thousand he had given her today would go a long way to help, but it certainly wouldn't solve all the problems. Some things would just never get solved.

As he walked forward, he smiled, sniffing the fresh air. A coffee was what he would like. A nice fresh Americano perhaps. He stopped by a small food cart and waited his turn, then ordered. As he paid, he left them a generous tip and kept on walking. A small park was up ahead, a favorite spot, so he walked over and sat down. He lived in the False Creek area, one of the nicer areas of town, as far as he was concerned. He liked being close to the harbor and to the markets, and the whole atmosphere there made him feel at peace. But it was also close to some of the hardest, poorest, darkest areas of town—talking just about Vancouver proper, at least.

With his pockets still full of cash, he headed to the home of a woman he knew, who kept taking in street kids. She had everything from fifteen-year-olds, trying to get out of the cycle of prostitution they had found themself in, to a couple newborn babies and everything in between. He tried not to ask too many questions, as long as she was helping them and wasn't doing anything illegal. When he stepped onto her front porch, the door opened, and one of the fifteen-year-olds leaned against the doorjamb.

Her arms were wrapped over her chest, as she eyed him suspiciously. "What do you want?"

"Is Sybil here?" She just shrugged. "In that case, tell her that I'd like to see her," he said, his tone mild. From the doorway he saw the chaos of all the children's toys and heard the noises from gaming systems and televisions. When a harried and frustrated Sybil came toward the front door,

Simon was almost sorry he had stopped in. She carried a young child in her arms. Stepping outside, she took one look at him, and her face lit up.

He grinned. "Well, it's nice to be welcomed."

"Absolutely. It's just chaos here, as usual."

"Good chaos or bad?"

"Good. In addition to the regulars, I have two kids going home to their families—runaways. And I've been fostering this little guy, after he was picked up not far from here."

"Lost?"

"More like deserted," she said quietly.

"As in abandoned? Has the government stepped in yet?"

"Since he's happy here at the moment, we're keeping him for now, but, yes, they know he's here."

He nodded. "You know I can't support anything that isn't legal."

"I do, and you know the finer points of legality can be somewhat capricious at times."

He burst out laughing. "Always, and, of course, ultimately it's all about the children." With that, he handed her a roll of bills, which she accepted gratefully.

"Thank you. Sometimes it's tough."

"I can imagine," he said. "You've got a full house here."

"It's quite something." She nodded. "I can't handle any more right now."

"Until somebody calls, and then you find a way."

"And I hate it," she murmured, "but I can't say no."

"Got it. That's what life is."

"I know. … Sometimes it's rough. Sometimes, in the middle of the night, I wonder how I'll even get up in the morning. I get so tired."

"Can anybody help you?"

"Not really," she said.

"What about the older kids?"

"Well, you get some, who really want to help because they're grateful to be here, and then others think the world owes them a favor—so to be asked to do anything is too much for them."

He winced at that. "I guess it's the age, isn't it?"

She laughed. "It absolutely is"—she gave Simon a big grin—"and I don't blame them one bit."

"No, but this isn't where you expected to be right now, correct?"

"No, not at all."

"Hopefully it will ease up soon."

As he turned and walked away, she called out, "Thank you again."

He nodded and kept on going. If it wasn't for the fact that some of those kids looked like they would take the money and run, he would have left it in the mailbox. But he'd also learned that it was that extra step of stopping by and visiting for a few minutes that added humanity to the money and put that much more of a smile on Sybil's face. These impromptu visits also gave Simon a chance to take a closer look at what was going on in there. With that behind him, he headed to a couple more spots that needed help.

One was a small community church, surviving on donations, which were pretty darn thin. As he dropped the money into the donation box, the priest lifted a hand in thanks. They didn't talk today since the priest was surrounded by various others now, but Simon and the priest had met many a time before. Simon turned and kept on walking.

At the food center, he found Johan in the back, muttering over bills. Simon dropped a big thick roll on the stack.

"Maybe that'll help."

When Simon walked away, Johan called out, "God bless you."

Simon laughed. "He already has." As he headed out, he smiled because he meant it.

He was alive, and, after a really shitty start to his life, he was doing just fine. And, even though the last few months had given him some awakenings that he'd hoped to never have—and nightmares he'd never thought could be so bad—he was finally starting to recover from both. He headed toward one of his rehabilitation building projects, calling out to his project manager, who stood there, muttering over a clipboard. "A good day or a bad day?"

The project manager looked at him and glared. "Are there any good days?"

But it was hard to keep Simon's good humor down. "Today is definitely a good day."

Johnny shook his head. "I don't know what the hell you're sipping from that cup, but I sure as hell wish you'd give me some."

"Got it. I should have remembered to bring you a coffee. Next time."

"Don't bother," he said. "With my luck, on the day you bring coffee, it would be the one day I'm not here."

At that, the two men smiled at each other.

"Sorry." Johnny chuckled. "It's been a shit day."

"Ah," Simon said.

"It's the usual problems, nothing major, nothing new, just a continuation of all of the above."

"Which, in itself, gets to be very worrying."

"It does, but it is what it is." He looked at Simon. "How come you're in such a good mood?"

"I'm not exactly sure, but you know what? It—well, it is what it is, and, if you don't need me here, I'll go home early."

"What's the matter? Gotta hot date?"

"I'd like to think so, but she caught a new case, so that's out."

"You're dating a cop?" Johnny looked at him in surprise. "Really?"

"Why not?" Simon asked. "It's an experience."

"Yeah, I'm not exactly sure it's a good one though."

"The jury's out. I haven't found any reason to stop, but there are many compelling reasons to continue."

"Well, that's interesting. In that case, see where it goes."

"That's the plan." And, with that, Simon waved his hand, turned, and headed in the direction of home. On the way, he stopped, picked up a newspaper, and then popped into his favorite little Italian restaurant for lunch. Then his sense of smell overrode his desire to eat. So he stopped eating and brought his leftovers home, before he continued the rest of his day. Thankfully his overactive sense of smell retreated on the way. As he returned to his apartment building, the doorman met him with an open door. "Hey, Harry, how you doing today?"

"Good. Sorry I didn't see you this morning, sir."

"I was up and out early, not an issue."

"Glad to hear that." Harry looked at the bag and smiled. "Had a good lunch, I see. The finest Italian in town."

"It is, indeed, and my favorite." And, with that, he headed to the elevator and upstairs.

As he dropped the newspaper on the dining table, along with the lunchtime leftovers, a headline caught his attention. "Another Hit-and-Run at UBC." When was it time to change the road rules and protect these young people from the actions of poor drivers? He wondered if that was the case that Kate had just picked up, though it didn't seem a traditional homicide case. As he stared at the headline, his fingers retraced some of the letters of the first couple words.

"Traffic," he muttered.

He stared out the huge expanse of windows in his living room that overlooked the beautiful city of Vancouver. Somehow, from the back of his head, came a scream, from a long distance away; it was faint and indiscriminate. He couldn't even tell if it was a scream of joy or one of horror. Then came a *thud*, as somebody was hit.

He couldn't see anything, yet he felt the blow. He bowed at his midsection and slammed down onto the kitchen chair, his breath gusting out in shock. He shook his head, turned, and looked around. "What in the hell was that?"

But, of course, nobody answered at all.

CHAPTER 3

K ATE WALKED SEVERAL blocks of the neighboring area, her phone in hand. She mentally noted where the other accidents had happened, as she reached each one, even though—according to the coroner—the cases had no connection. True enough, no apparent relation had emerged, but it was early days yet. The crime scenes were all within a span of probably four or five blocks, and, given that a lot of heavy traffic was here—from the students and the rest of the traffic coming out of the university—this intersection itself had a bad history. Plenty of small pizza places, sandwich shops, little delis—all to tempt the college crowd—also contributed to quite a traffic jam in itself.

With that being mapped out, Kate walked back to the scene of the current death to find that everything had been cleaned up, except for the smear of blood on the road. The fire truck had just arrived to do something with that. She always wondered what that substance was that they put all over the pavement. She walked down the long boulevard, heading toward the main part of the campus, golf courses on both sides. Beautiful, stunning, peaceful, elegant, and yet such a killer.

She shook her head as she walked a good hundred yards, wondering if anybody could have been over here watching. Obviously, if they had been playing golf or walking through any of the grounds, they could have. So far, she hadn't spoken to anybody but those who had been walking on the streets and who had seen the accident from that vantage point. She pondered the location, and, when Rodney texted her and asked where she was, she answered by calling him. "I just walked around the five crime scene areas along the boulevard."

"It's quite something, isn't it?"

"The grounds are gorgeous and amazingly open for people to walk and to take advantage of the countryside. Where are you?"

"I just finished with another group who arrived. Sounds like they'd been here earlier and came back. I'm on my way to you."

When he met up with her, she guessed, "So, as usual, nobody really saw anything."

"One thought he saw her riding on a bike—or saw *someone* riding a bike. He did describe the red hoodie though."

"So beforehand."

"Yes."

"Did they have anything to say that was helpful?"

He shook his head. "Not really. They crossed there." Rodney pointed, facing the intersection and using his left hand. "They were walking from here over to the other side. One guy glanced this way and saw the cyclist coming, so he was past the viewing point when she was hit."

"Yes, but," Kate said thoughtfully, "that means she was riding the bike then."

He stopped, frowned, and nodded.

"So we know that the bullet hit somewhere after she cut out of his view, right? Could he explain how close?"

"He said it was down a way. Close enough that he could

see she had on a red jacket, but too far away to determine that she was a she."

"Okay, so what are we talking about then? Thirty or forty meters?" Kate asked.

He nodded. "Walk backward."

She immediately stepped backward until she got closer to the point of impact with the car. "What about here?" she yelled.

"I can see your jacket, but I can't see any details."

As she walked closer, he stopped her. "You know what? Right about there is maybe one hundred feet out. I can see that your jacket is black. I can see that you've got the hood up, and surely I could see that you're on a bike at that point, right? At a quick glance that's probably as close as I get with these parameters."

She nodded and continued to walk forward. She looked around. "This area has no cameras of course. Absolutely nothing here for any security. It's wide-open grounds. Other people could have been walking here, but that didn't mean they paid any attention either." Kate shook her head. "Not only didn't they pay any attention but they might not have had any clue that something was wrong with her. And the car wouldn't have hit her necessarily until the intersection."

"That's what we're trying to figure out. Was she shot before and went down, then got hit by a car? What does the driver say?"

"*Right.*" She rolled her eyes. "No driver because he took off."

"Well, he's probably afraid that he killed her."

"He might have, but, if he'd stayed in place, it would have gone much better for him, and we would have had a hell of a lot more information," she snapped. She ran her fingers through her hair. "It's just so frustrating that people can't do what they're supposed to do."

"If they'll get in trouble, nobody will do it," Rodney said, with a weary smile.

"I know. I know." She waved her hand dismissively. "It's still just pissy."

"Pissy it is." He nodded. "A good word for it."

She sighed. "I get it. Nothing really to fuss about."

"It is frustrating, particularly in this case, because we might have found out that she was already dead before she made contact with the vehicle. So right now, our driver is probably hiding at home, terrified to be sent up for vehicular manslaughter."

"Or worse." She nodded, with a roll of her head to loosen her tightening neck and shoulder muscles. "Reese can check city cameras here, to see if we have anything that gives us a clear view."

"Yeah, should be waiting on us, as soon as we arrive at the station. I've already put in a request."

"Okay. I guess it's back to the office then, huh?" Kate stopped, looked around, and swore. "Still seems like such a waste."

"It's always a waste," he said. "No other way to describe it."

"I know." She looked back at him and smiled. "You driving?"

"I can if you like," he said. "You drove here."

"I did, but I'm feeling a little on the tired side."

"It's all good," Rodney said. "Let's go."

HE WATCHED THE vehicle pull out and away. He didn't

know who they were, but he had taken several photographs of their vehicle and the two people wandering around who had gotten out of that vehicle. They had been flashing badges early enough, but he didn't think they realized they were being observed. Or, if they did, they didn't care. That always fascinated him. Everybody always thought that they were in charge, that somebody out there was beneath them.

In this case, the woman fascinated him. Tall, sparse, and lean, she walked with a clip to her step and strode around with a no-nonsense demeanor. The guy was slower, more comfortable, not as young, and walked with an easier gait. That guy was okay if it took him an extra couple minutes to get somewhere. His stride was more of a shuffle, although he covered a lot of ground at the same time, but he didn't have that same tension that the woman had.

He'd watched her as soon as she had arrived. It was fascinating. The whole thing was fascinating. It was always the best part; he knew that. He'd certainly been told that, and, right now, it was ... sheer fun. But the fun was beginning to wane. He felt the adrenaline—that had been so high and had spiked earlier—now dissipating, and he missed it.

He missed that high. He missed that sense of being in control, that feeling of living on the edge. Somewhat like crossing a wire with no safety rope or net to catch you. That sense of danger, that sense of purpose, that goal that you needed to accomplish before everything blew up in your face.

When he reached that goal, this euphoric moment washed over him, this sense of *Oh my God, I did it*, along with the panic, the fear, and the complete chaos running through his mind. But he was here. He was done with his earlier deed. He was good, and the investigators had no freaking clue. He smiled, took a sip of his coffee, and watched as the rest of the details played out.

All of the action was long gone, and he thought that was interesting too. He figured it would take hours and hours for sure, but it didn't. They had been beyond efficient. But, to them, there was absolutely nothing to this. And here he was, already looking at a completely normal traffic pattern.

That was a disappointment.

And even now the two investigators pulled away in the small Jeep that she had driven in, yet he had driven out. He wondered if they were partners in life as well or if there even was such a thing. They were dressed in plain clothes, so they couldn't be street cops. Had been plenty of uniforms on the scene earlier; still were a couple. But any motor vehicle accident involving a fatality would bring more than the average patrolman, since an investigation would have to be done.

And that was very true. It was all good and definitely something he wanted to keep feeling. But he also didn't want to lose his focus—or his reason for doing this. With a smile he turned and poured himself another cup of coffee.

CHAPTER 4

K ATE WALKED INTO the bullpen, sat down at her desk, and downloaded the photos off her phone into her computer. After printing those out, she put them all into a physical file, setting up a new one for this latest UBC case.

"What's the matter?" Rodney asked.

She looked over at him, shrugged. "I'm ... not sure. I—I just—something's wrong about that bullet."

"What do you mean?" he said.

"Based on the entry wound, it had to be super-small, like a BB or a pellet."

He frowned at that. "If the shot happened from a distance, regardless of the size of the ammo, wouldn't she have completely collapsed from the force alone?"

She replied, "I don't know. I mean, do people continue to walk or to ride a bike after that? Could she have been disoriented enough that she rode into an intersection, where she was hit by a car? What was the sequence of events? What are the chances that somebody came up after the motor vehicle collided with her, carrying a small BB gun, and shot her behind the ear, even though she was down and potentially already dead?"

Rodney looked at her in shock.

Kate shrugged. "I'm just tossing out ideas and various concepts as to what could be going on here because it doesn't make sense to me."

"So, you're taking something that looks like a pretty normal shooting, where the person is shot in the head, and circumstances propel her forward into traffic, where she also gets hit by a vehicle, but now you're wondering if that's how it really happened?"

"Yes, I am. You didn't see the size of that hole."

"I'll wait for the autopsy report, thanks."

"And I get that. I know it's not your thing to stand beside the dead, whereas it fascinates me. I could easily have gone into that field myself."

"Why didn't you?" She just gave him that look. His gaze caught sight of the folders beside her, and he winced. "Sorry. Okay, so we obviously know why you didn't, and I applaud you for the dedication that took you down this pathway because we obviously need your help," he said, with a smile.

She rolled her eyes at that. "I don't know about that, but this case?" She shook her head. "Just ... something feels off."

"Definitely something is off in the sense that she was killed for no apparent reason. She was picked out as a victim, targeted, and brought down. But why?"

"That's what we have to find out," she said, turning to her computer.

"Where will you start with that?" he asked curiously.

She smiled. "First, I'll go through these faces at the crime scene because there's always that—that feeling that somebody out there is watching what we're doing. Watching however long we're out there doing it."

"I'm sure there is." Rodney nodded. "The press is always looking to hunt down whatever it is that we've found and to tear us apart for our methods, and the general public is right there with them."

"When you say it that way, why would anyone even want to do this job, since everybody is out there working against us?" she asked, looking at him sideways.

"I've asked myself that a hundred times," he said, with a grimace.

"Did you ever get an answer?"

"Not a good one." He laughed. "I mean, when you think about it, what's a good answer?"

"I don't know." She shook her head, then pulled up all the images she'd taken, and slowly sorted through them. A couple that were really terrible she deleted, since she had better ones. "I have got to get a better camera phone," she muttered.

"Yeah? Will you learn to use it properly?"

"I sure need to," she said. "Some of these are great, and some of these are shitty. I mean, like, why? Why is one better than the other?" She shook her head again.

"Usually it's because you moved, or you didn't give it a chance to lock on to whatever it was supposed to focus on," he muttered.

"I can see that in some of these. When you look at them, it's pretty obvious that I was either still in motion or hadn't stopped long enough because they're blurry."

"Exactly, but, if they're not any good, you took another one."

"I took a lot from every position. I took hundreds of them. I think I was just snapping, afraid whoever would be out there was already leaving."

He looked at her. "We often talk about having that feeling that somebody committed a crime and stood around to watch. But why would they in a case like this?"

"I don't know. Maybe just for the chaos. Or maybe to

make sure she was dead because they didn't get the chance to confirm it."

He frowned at that, as he turned back to his desk. "It could be any number of things, and the problem is, … they all suck," he snapped.

"Yep, they all do, but it doesn't change the facts."

Sergeant Colby Stevens walked in just then. "What are we looking at?" he asked, one eyebrow lifted.

She shrugged. "We had what we initially thought wouldn't be a case for us, but, as it turned out, it is."

"Okay, try again, and this time tell me something," he said.

"Aren't you supposed to be off doing paperwork or schmoozing with the brass?" Kate asked.

He glared at her. "Come on. Spill it. As you just pointed out, some of my tasks aren't that enjoyable. So I'm looking for a distraction." He added, "I don't like what I have to do next, so you can take my mind off it."

"Fine, that's way too much information. We have a woman struck by a vehicle."

"Okay. So why did it end up on our desk?"

"We had an unidentified body, which is why we got the call in the first place," Rodney said.

"It looked like a vehicular accident, but we weren't sure," she interrupted, "and, when the coroner took a look, we found a small hole of some kind behind the ear."

"*Bullet* hole? She was shot?" he asked, his eyebrows rising.

"Well, we said shot, but I'm not exactly sure with what just yet. It was an extremely small caliber."

"So, an air gun?"

"We don't know. Maybe a BB gun or something smaller

than a .22." She scrunched up her face. "I'm not exactly sure what's out there when it comes to something that small."

"The coroner will be on it," Colby said. "As soon as it's pulled, we can get the forensics people on it."

She nodded. "Whatever it is, it still means that she was murdered. We're just at the beginning of the investigation."

"Good, that's a good thing."

"Why?" she asked.

"To keep you busy," he said cheerfully. "I'm sure an awful lot of people were there watching."

"There was, and there wasn't. A lot of people but nobody saw anything."

"They didn't see anything because they didn't comprehend anything," Colby said. "You have to jog their memories, so that they can remember something."

"I think we talked to about thirty-seven potential witnesses, and then you had how many more?" Rodney asked Kate.

She said, "I talked to another twelve, I think."

"There will be people who saw things but didn't realize that they saw something." Colby tilted his head at her.

In that moment, she realized what he was talking about. "You want me to go back and talk to them?"

"Leave it for a couple days. And then go."

She nodded.

"Did anybody catch your suspicion?" he asked, turning to look at her, then Rodney and back to her.

"Yeah, six of them left the scene, after supposedly calling it in, and went to have pizza."

"Pizza?" He stared at her, then shook his head. "So seeing death made them hungry?"

Her face cracked into a smirk. "That's what I said. ...

But they were all about not wanting to hang around and not wanting to wait for the whole investigation to happen. They figured that, if anybody wanted to talk to them, it would take hours anyway."

"And it might have. But presumably you did talk to them?"

She nodded. "I did, and all of them very helpfully provided their parents' addresses instead of where they're living right now."

At that, his eyebrows went up again. Then he thought about it, shrugged. "I'm not sure that was deliberate as much as instinctive. *Where do you live? Well, I live in Burnaby.*"

"In this case they lived all around the province, which is how I knew that they were all living in the residence housing."

"Did you get those addresses too?"

She nodded. "Of course. And the cell phones."

"Good, then I guess we better check to see if any of the cell phone numbers given belong to them."

"Those six, you mean?"

He smiled. "If you were talking to all university students, I wouldn't put it past them to offer somebody else's cell phone number."

"Thinking this is a joke or with ill intent? What are you thinking?"

"I had one case, and it taught me a lesson I never forgot. Somebody on campus was strangled to death at a party, and everybody at the party gave somebody else's number. So, we had all these wrong numbers, and, in fact, we even had a couple duplicates, but we didn't know that until we sat down and compared our notes."

"Right, and was it done to confuse the issue?"

"Nope, they thought it was a lark. They didn't really seem to get the seriousness of the fact that somebody had died."

"Jesus," she said.

"It's not that they were being foolish or stupid or intentionally difficult. It was just their mind-set at the time. They were all half high on drugs, alcohol, and sex. Half high on college life, living the dream, and pushing aside their responsibilities." He sighed. "They weren't even thinking about anything real going on in their world, beyond enjoying that moment. And, once somebody lied, and they all figured out what was going on, they all did it."

"Did you haul them all back in again?"

"Oh, yeah," he said, with a big fat grin. "Hauled them all in, contacted all the parents. Yep, that was fun. Now it's your turn."

"I don't think that's the case here, although one or two of them were completely belligerent."

"But you get that all the time, don't you?"

"Yes, and I've never quite understood it. We often get the shock, the denial, those who are curious, and then others who are very worried and afraid that something they might have done will surface, even though they probably haven't done anything at all. But belligerence? Not so much. And, in this case, there was an arrogance, an attitude of entitlement, like, 'Hey, you know who I am? I'm somebody special, and you shouldn't be talking to me,' or the like," she muttered.

"Yeah, he's probably got a wealthy family. Don't forget. BC is full of wealthy families, and we have a lot of international students. Was he from Canada?"

She grabbed her notebook, checked, and shook her head. "No, he wasn't. I think he was from Germany."

"I don't know about Germany, but we have a lot of—"

"No, wait. He was from South Africa," she corrected immediately.

"That could explain it too. Check in with him in a few days. See how his attitude is then."

She nodded. "One of the females was really quiet, like hiding, trying to blend into the furniture to avoid getting involved."

"You definitely need to follow up with her then." Colby gave her a knowing smile.

Rodney glanced at her, his fingers still working on his keyboard. "You're usually pretty good at reading people."

"I would think so," she said. "Something was off about that young woman for sure."

"Off in what way?" he asked.

"I don't think it was a fear of being interviewed. It might have been fear of the others in the group."

At that, he slowly turned to face her.

"I don't know what it was," she said. "I'll follow up."

"Maybe you better not wait a few days for that one then."

"I know. I'm wondering if they saw something or were involved somehow, and they're worried about her speaking up."

"I hope not," he said quietly. "Because, if that's the case, and they've already killed once, they could quickly decide she's a liability and needs to be terminated too."

❧

AFTER HIS MIDDAY stopover at home, Simon walked through the alleyway, heading toward the next project he was looking at doing. He'd planned to stay in for the afternoon but had felt cooped up so was back out looking at properties. He had tried to buy the property a month ago, and the Realtor had gotten snippy and had refused to place a second offer, so he had walked. As it was, it was still for sale. He wandered through it yet again. These old buildings were never locked up. They should be because the homeless would move in, but, in this case, it appeared to still be empty and still livable, which just increased the chances that the homeless would find it sooner or later.

Although ... maybe not. He got an odd feeling from it, like a really odd feeling.

He frowned as he walked through, having remembered that same odd sensation from before. As he took several more steps inside, he stopped and sniffed the air, then immediately retreated. However, realizing that nobody would listen to him if he didn't see the proof of what it was, what he thought he was sensing, he would have to go in and take another look.

Sighing, he strode quickly and confidently through the main floor. Seeing nothing, he moved up to the second floor, and, with the same result, on up to the third, only to find nothing again. Stunned, and not knowing what the hell was going on with his senses, he turned and looked around. "Thank God I didn't call the cops," he muttered to himself. "But what the hell is going on?"

Normally the smell of something dead was easily recognizable and definable. But now, he had no doubt that the smell remained. He turned slowly, did a more thorough search of the empty building, then headed back down to the main entranceway, eager for fresh air. As he walked out the front door, the Realtor appeared with another set of clients. She glared at him. He just shrugged and walked away.

"I can always put in another offer," she said.

"I wouldn't add any money to it," he said calmly, as he carried on. He heard them talking behind him.

He turned as he went around the corner and cast a glance back, watching them heading into the building. Good. Maybe they would smell something. Of course, if they did find something dead in there, he'd be placed at the scene of the crime, and that would cause him no end of hell. He wasn't sure what was going on there, but something was definitely weird. His sense of smell remained heightened, as he carried forward.

Unnerved and put off, he finished his day and walked toward the little coffee shop. Even though he had a date with the good detective tonight, it could be later in the evening before he caught up with her, so he upped his interrupted lunch with a sandwich now to tide him over. Then he went in, hit immediately by the incredible smell of coffee. With his olfactory senses on high alert, he ordered coffee and a sandwich, then sat in the outside section of the restaurant and enjoyed his dinner thoroughly. Something was refreshing about the scent of the day and about the air around him. He didn't know what it was, but something was just off today.

When his phone rang, he smiled to see it was the beautiful Kate Morgan. "Good afternoon, Detective Morgan," he said, his voice silky.

"Oh no, you don't," her voice was testy. "No fair using that sexy voice on me right now."

"You're working still, I presume." His smile widened.

"Yes, I'm working. We had plans for tonight, but I've got to push them off."

"Push them off or push them back?" he asked calmly,

checking his watch. "It's only four-thirty now."

"I know, but it won't get any better. I've got a lot of testimonies and camera images here to go through."

He hesitated and asked, "You'll work at home?"

"I'm still at the office, so I'm not sure."

It was obvious that she was really distracted by whatever was going on in her world. He immediately decided to let her off the hook. "Tomorrow then?"

"Yes, as long as this case doesn't run over and take over tomorrow too."

"A little bit of help might keep it under control for you."

"Maybe. Rodney is on the case with me."

Simon vaguely remembered Rodney. More of a big hulking teddy-bear type than anything. "I'm sure that'll be helpful," he said quietly.

"It will be. Rodney's good. And he's not very *in my face* about anything, so that's always welcome."

"He's obviously not at your side either." Simon laughed.

"No, he stepped out."

"Is he going home?"

"No, I don't think so, but he'll be back. Oh, I know. I think he was just grabbing some food."

"Have you got anything with you?"

"No," she said quietly. "I'll get something in a bit."

"If you would accept a delivery, I'd send something over."

"I'm not quite ready. Maybe in an hour or two I can leave this place for a bit and go home. The change of pace might clear my head."

"It probably would. I'll check in with you in a little bit, and we'll see how you're doing." With that, he rang off, placed his phone on the table beside him, and polished off his light dinner.

He stared out at the humming bustling street around him. That was the problem with being with a cop. She would always be busy, and there would always be another case. It's funny that it had never concerned him before. It wasn't anything he'd ever bothered with. He had always tried to stay clear of the police. He didn't get into anything that was too shady or would involve an investigation, so he had managed to spend the bulk of his life without having any contact with them. But now he could think of nothing else. Well, with one detective anyway.

He'd like to have contact with her anytime, anyplace. He smiled, pocketed his phone, and picked up his coffee. He took another big sip, closing his eyes at the absolutely stunning aroma, as it drifted through his nostrils.

Shaking his head and wondering what was going on with his senses, he got up from the table and moved off down the street. Absolutely everything looked, seemed, and smelled far better and stronger than before. When a vehicle went by, shooting out a black cloud of exhaust, he frowned because the scent, the smoke, just assailed his senses, making him wince. Not only were the good things amplified but so were the bad ones.

Deciding that home would be better than this, he turned and headed back in the direction of his own place.

CHAPTER 5

KATE PUT DOWN her phone and turned toward her monitors. From behind her, Lilliana said, "You know that you do get to leave. You get to have a life."

Kate turned to look at her. "I didn't realize you were still here."

"Absolutely. We've also got a case that's driving us nuts."

"Right, you caught that downtown hotel shooting case, didn't you?"

"Yeah, and it's crazy," she said.

Kate knew she looked just as tired as she felt, nowhere near as perfect as Lilliana always seemed to appear. And that said something about how Kate felt about her case. "I'm sorry. That has to be rough."

"Hey, you know how it is. We're all in the same boat here." Lilliana gave her a one-arm shrug. "It's always a juggling act between our professional and personal lives."

Kate sighed, leaned back, rotated her neck and head a little, then added, "Simon's a bit of a different case."

"I'm quite surprised to see that you're still dating him."

At that, Kate studied Lilliana, wondering what she was getting at. She didn't feel any animosity or any nastiness and hadn't since the first few days, where it was more a case of being avoided than being negative. "And why is that?"

"It's the whole psychic-connection thing," Lilliana said,

giving a little shiver. "I'd be worried he knew things about me that I'd just as soon keep to myself."

"Nothing to hide really. Although I think Rodney said something about him reading my mind."

At that, Lilliana looked horrified.

Kate laughed. "I don't even think that's possible to do."

"Yeah, but you don't know—like, you *really* don't know. There could be all kinds of things that he can do."

"So far it's just numbers and connecting with victims, and I think that's enough for him. He's not happy about any of this as it is."

"Do you believe him?"

Lilliana's questions seemed to show a sincere curiosity, and, as such, Kate treated it that way. After a moment's thought, she said, "As much as I hate to, and as hard as I've tried to negate everything he's come up with, I've found myself believing him. I don't think I believe anybody else, and it would take an awful lot for me to get there, but I really am at the point of concluding that the information he's provided is true."

"It's been helpful, right?" Lilliana questioned.

"Yeah," Kate said, "that's the problem. I haven't found a way to dismiss it, and that's made it very difficult."

"Of course." Lilliana nodded. "It's one thing to disbelieve. It's another thing to have the proof presented and then still disbelieve—since it makes you sound like you're just being difficult and don't want to look at the evidence."

"And it's always about evidence for me." Kate gave a quick nod, as she turned to face her monitors. "But that still doesn't mean that I'll automatically believe everything he says going forward."

Lilliana burst out laughing. "You don't ever want to do

that in a relationship anyway, right?"

She smiled to herself. "Isn't that the truth." She laughed and turned to look at Lilliana. "What about you? Do you have a partner?"

Lilliana smiled. "Well, I did. I was married for twenty-plus years," she said. "Then about eighteen months ago, we had an amicable split."

"Is there such a thing?" Kate asked in wonder.

Lilliana burst out laughing. "Yes. The last few years we were together mostly for the kids, and then it was like, okay, this isn't even working for the kids now. So, it was time to shift. The kids go back and forth, and I honestly think they're happier. We're happier. It's all good." She shrugged. "Besides, I have so many late nights, this way they have a little more stability."

"Yeah, I'm surprised that so many cops even have relationships. When you think about it, we're a bad bet."

"We are, indeed, but look at perfect-family-man Owen. Plus, I do have another partner now, who's a better fit. He's also a cop, and you'll see him around every once in a while, if we stay together." She gave another shrug. "I'm not so sure about that, but it's good right now, and it keeps me grounded, and that's really important."

"The grounding?"

"Yes. Having somebody to go home to at the end of the day really matters. Like what Owen has. Cops who are happily married handle the job stress better, and they last longer in this job. They don't burn out as quickly. But only if they can keep the marriage together of course."

"That's good to know," Kate said. "There's got to be something, some redeeming reason, to keep these guys in our world."

And again, Lilliana burst out laughing. "You really have a great sense of humor. I'm sorry that I haven't allowed myself to recognize it until now."

"Not a problem. I wasn't terribly popular or chatty when I first came on board." Of course she still wasn't either of those things, but she wouldn't say that right now.

"It wasn't you. You know that, right?"

"I know," she said. "It was the fact that I wasn't Chet."

Lilliana nodded. "He was a good guy, and we'd gotten to know his wife and his kids really well. It's hard because we'd become a family, an imperfect and slightly dysfunctional family, but a family just the same."

"I get that, and I'm really happy you guys had that." Kate frowned, pausing. "It's nothing I've ever really had a chance to experience. I've been close with my former partner, but it's not the same thing. I didn't do anything with him and his family. I didn't have that kind of relationship."

"No, but it was respectful, right?" she asked, with a questioning note.

"Very." She smiled. "We had broken up before I made this move. He was happy for me when I made detective, even more so when I got this job."

"Good. Yet how would he have been if you two were still together? He might not have been so happy. All too often, some of these guys don't really like it when you move on and up."

"I don't think they consider it *on and up*. It was definitely a shift. It's not like it's a promotion."

"No, but it's not easy to get, and, then when you make it, it is something to be celebrated. We didn't do that for you, and I'm sorry about that."

Kate shrugged. "Don't worry about that. It's not like

school, and I don't need a reward every time I achieve something in life. It was enough to know that I'd made it."

Lilliana smiled. "One of these days we'll have to go to the pub and have a beer, at least take a few minutes and connect a bit more. We need to celebrate the wins that we do have." She followed her words with a yawn. At that point she groaned. "We were here late last night. I may have to go home after all. I was really hoping to stay and to get through some more of this, but it might have to wait."

"Take it home and see how you feel when you get there," Kate said.

"I could, but I'm supposed to be meeting that partner later tonight."

"Ah. That's the thing about partners," she said. "They tend to screw up your plans."

At that, Lilliana chuckled, stood, and grabbed her jacket. "You know that tomorrow will be another day."

"I know," Kate said, "but how do you reconcile that with the reality that tomorrow somebody else will be dead too?"

Lilliana stopped at the doorway, looked at her seriously. "Because that person will be dead whether we do anything about it or not. We can't save them all, Kate. We can't even save most of them," she replied, her tone dropping painfully. "All we can do is the best we can, and that means being sharp and on target ourselves. The quicker you burn out, the harder it'll be to handle some of these jobs, and there won't be *any* tomorrow for them."

"I know." Kate caught Lilliana's glare directed at her. "No, I really do."

Lilliana added, "Ignoring that advice and working yourself to an early grave won't help anybody."

"So? You think I should go home too?"

"Absolutely. Call Simon back and tell him that you'll see him. Reconnect with life and find the reason why we're doing this. Because we can't keep doing it if we don't have that passion and that goal anymore."

"You're right. … It's too hard without that purpose and goal and passion," Kate said.

"Yes, it is. There's got to be that purpose in life, but it can't overtake your whole existence. It's all about balance." And, with that, Lilliana turned and walked out of the bullpen and the building.

Knowing Rodney was coming back, Kate sat here and waited. But, when Rodney called her instead, she said, "Does this mean you're not coming back?"

"No, I'm not actually. I headed out to get food, but I'm not feeling all that great."

"I was thinking about going home myself," she confessed.

"Do it. I know this case is sitting there, and it's bothering you. It's bothering me too, but the odds of somebody else dying because of it tonight are extremely low."

"Maybe so, but that doesn't feel like a good enough reason."

"You're not walking away from the case, and you're not doing anything more beneficial than anybody else could be doing right now. Remember. We're part of a team, and part of our mandate is to look after ourselves, so we can come in and do the job again another day."

"Got it. I heard the same lecture from Lilliana."

"Then listen to your team." He laughed. "I'll see you in the morning." And, with that, Rodney rang off.

Kate sat here at her desk for a long moment, then got

up, closed down everything that needed to be closed down, and walked outside. An ever-so-slight drizzle of rain fell. She tilted her face to the sky and let the drops fall on her, absorbing the freshness, the moisture, the cleanliness.

Even though she was in a big city, and the world sucked sometimes, it was important for her to stand here and to just reconnect. She was a water baby and absolutely adored Mother Nature, even at her shittiest. Standing here, right now, in the pouring rain, many people would probably say that this was an example of a crappy time when Mother Nature was not being her best, but Kate loved it; she absolutely loved it. She turned toward her vehicle and drove home, wondering if she should do a workout. She probably should, but she was also tired. The trouble was, she also knew a workout would invigorate her. She checked the time and winced when she saw how late it was. She better just go straight home. As she neared her apartment, almost there, her phone rang.

"Where are you?" Simon asked.

"I'm almost home. I was thinking about going for a workout, but trying to convince myself isn't exactly making it happen."

"Sometimes you just need a break and the chance to rest and relax."

"That's why I'm thinking of walking in the rain." She smiled about that. "How are you doing? Sorry I canceled earlier."

"It's okay."

But something was off in his voice. "What's the matter, Simon?" Her voice sharpened, as she stopped, parked, and locked up her vehicle. "Did something happen?"

"Yeah, what else?" His tone was hard. "Shit's always

happening in my world."

She froze. "Have you connected with something?"

"I don't know what I'm connecting with, but it's like my sense of smell is on overdrive."

"That could be a good thing," she said lightly.

"Holding a beer in my hand right now is a good thing. I can smell the hops like it's ten times the strength of what I was thinking it was. But, on the other hand, going to the washroom, walking in back alleys, the traffic with its carbon monoxide, and the smog, not so good."

"Are you at home then?"

"Yeah. I was at the coffee shop when I talked to you earlier. I stayed for a little bit longer, realized my nose was acting up, and I headed home. By the time I got here, honest to God, it was all I could do to get into the apartment and to shut the door to keep out all the scents of the city."

"And did it work?"

"No," he snapped. "The Italian food I ate for lunch became this overwhelming aroma that I wanted to just dive into, but, after three or four bites, it's like I couldn't handle it anymore. So I brought the rest of it home, hoping I can handle the leftovers later." Maybe just some smells hit him harder than others.

"Is this like a psychic thing?" she asked, cautiously looking around to make sure nobody was within earshot.

"And I love how you probably checked to make sure nobody heard what you were saying," he said in a dry tone.

"Hey, it'll be a hell of a long time before I'm comfortable with anything along that line. I managed to get the word *psychic* out, so be happy with that."

"Oh, I am, and I don't know what this newfound ability of mine is. So I don't have an answer for you."

"And I'm always looking for answers, right?"

"Answers I can't give."

"Which just makes me really frustrated and fed up," she said.

"I know, and yet somehow we still work." She could hear the smile in his voice.

"No." Her voice had a hard tone to it. "It's worked for a little bit."

"Hey, don't even go there. I'll hang up right now if you think you'll be breaking up."

"Do we have anything to break up?"

He laughed. "Oh, God, it's one of those nights, is it?"

"Yeah, a young woman died today at the university. I thought she'd been hit by a vehicle, but it turns out she's got a small bullet wound in her head."

"Interesting."

"Yeah, maybe, but, at the same time, what the hell does any of this have to do with anything? And why did this young woman, only eighteen years old, have to die today? For what reason? Did some asshole do it because she wouldn't date him? Or just targeted her because she's a redhead?"

"Do they often pick redheads?"

"I don't know," she muttered. "I'm just depressed and upset that some asshole could do this to her. She had her whole life ahead of her, and it's gone in the blink of an eye."

"So the vehicle didn't kill her then?"

"I don't have the—no." She stopped, gathered her thoughts. "I shouldn't even be talking about this. Nothing has been released to the public yet."

"It's not like I'll be calling the media with an exposé."

"They probably wouldn't believe it anyway. I'm not sure

I believe it. Look. I'm almost inside. I'll have a shower and grab some sleep. I'll talk to you later." And, with that, she hung up.

She stared up at the sky all around her, shaking her head. "It's such a messed-up world. We really need to do something about that." Maybe, just maybe, a hot shower and an early bedtime would reset her attitude. She doubted it.

———✦✦✦———

SIMON DIDN'T LIKE to hear the defeat in Kate's voice, that negativity. He also had not been invited over, which made him a little worried because of the tone of her voice. Giving her a bit of space to get over whatever was bothering her was one thing, but giving her the space to decide that she didn't need him in her life was something completely different. Grabbing leftovers from his lunch today and checking the fridge, finding a bottle of wine, he grabbed that too, strolled to his penthouse elevator and took it all the way to the lobby. As he walked toward the front entrance, he saw that Edgar, on nightshift, was manning the front door and immediately opened it for him.

"Have a good evening, sir."

"I hope so," he said.

"Hey, you're bringing wine and food. What every woman needs tonight is to be looked after."

Simon stopped and stared out, realized it was pouring down rain. He swore.

"You want a cab? Do you want to drive? I can get your car brought around."

Simon looked at Edgar. "Grab me a cab, will you?"

After that, as he waited a few minutes for the cab to pull up, Edgar said, "What about the Ubers? Are you happy with them?"

"They're fine, and, if they're faster than cabs, that's good too. Normally I'd just take the Aquabus."

"At least she's worth it," Edgar said, with a beaming smile.

There was some truth to that. When Simon said good night to Edgar and walked out, he got into the back of the cab, gave the address to the driver, and was there in no time. "Too wet to walk tonight."

The cab driver laughed.

Simon nodded, then dropped in the fare and a tip, and headed up to Kate's apartment. When he knocked on the door, there was no answer. He swore at that, realizing he should have checked to see if she would stay home or would go for that workout. When it opened suddenly a few moments later, he was startled.

She looked at him in surprise. "What are you doing here?"

He held up the food and the wine and watched as her eyes lit up. "That's all it takes, is it?" he said, with a smile.

"Nope, not at all." She reached for both and snatched them from his hands. "I'm not that easy of a lay."

"Hell, there's nothing easy about you." She was already walking back into the kitchen, but she turned and tossed him a grin. He checked her out carefully. "You sounded despondent earlier."

She stopped, looked at him, and shrugged, and he almost felt bad for bringing it up. "Sometimes I just hate the senselessness of what's out in the world right now," she said quietly. "People should have every moment of joy coming to them, not get cut down in the prime of life over nothing. Less than nothing. It's like a whim of some asshole who deems at that moment in time that a person shouldn't be allowed to exist anymore. Who gives them the right?" She grabbed a dinner plate and slammed shut the cupboard.

"Nobody, which is why it's so important that you're there."

She stilled, looked over at him, and finally nodded. "I was depressed and upset today, so thanks for this." She held up the silverware she had grabbed. "I haven't eaten." With her dish and knife and fork, she sat at the kitchen table.

"Maybe that's partly why you were depressed." He took a seat across from her.

"Maybe." She had the bag open, reaching in without looking. "I also interviewed this kid at a pizza place today, and his attitude bothered me and hung with me all day. He was just one in a group of six, and it shouldn't have really been a problem, but it seemed like, the longer the day went on, his attitude just got to me more and more. So that it's all I can think about."

"You need to get him out of your head because you know that guys like him exist everywhere."

"I know, but it's like he felt he didn't have to answer my questions. He didn't have to talk to me at all. Like, he was *somebody*, and I should damn well know it. He didn't need to stay at the crime scene, much less answer my questions or give me the straight truth." She snorted, then shook her head, dumping whatever food she had retrieved onto her plate.

"That just means that, one of these days, he'll get his comeuppance, whether it's from you or somebody else," he said.

"Maybe, and maybe not. It seems like these kids born with a silver spoon in their mouths always get an easy pathway ahead of them." She took a big bite of whatever.

"Did you ever have an easy pathway?"

She stopped, looked at him. "I told you about my brother, right?"

He nodded. "A little bit."

"Right, well, I'm sure you can fill in the rest."

"Sure, I probably can, but it's not the same thing as hearing it from you."

"And that is one of the topics I really don't want to discuss tonight." For added emphasis, she pointed her fork at him. "Talk about a life cut short."

"I'm sorry."

She shrugged. "You see? That's why I didn't invite you over. ... I'm in a shitty mood. I get moments of clarity— where I'm okay for, you know, ten or fifteen minutes, like now," she said, lifting another forkful of her food. "And then everything just comes back down again, and I crash."

"You know that you don't always have to be on. You don't always have to be perfect."

She stopped, stared. "It's a damn good thing, since I'm a far cry from being perfect." Her tone was harsh. She narrowed her gaze at him, and he shook his head.

"You can't scare me off. I've seen way worse than you," he said.

At that, she burst out laughing. "I don't know what it is about you, but that sense of humor gets me every time."

"And here I wouldn't have said I even had one."

She chuckled again. "See? It's shit like that. And you don't shoot me down for being in a pissy mood, but neither will you indulge it either, so that works."

"Yeah, we work."

She glared at him. With some heat this time. And not

the good kind.

"Oh no, you don't. I get that it's not a conversation for right now, but neither is this a conversation about shutting us down."

"It was part of my earlier mood," she snapped. "And it's something I have to consider."

"No, you don't. Remember that part about we're all good?"

"We're good, but that doesn't mean it's healthy."

He stared, the anger inside him growing. "What the hell is unhealthy about it? What the hell are you even talking about?"

"I don't know. I told you it's a shitty day. Just leave me alone."

"Happily." He stood now. "Absolutely. But stop getting inside my head then too."

She stared at him. "You mean that literally?"

"No, I don't mean it literally." He groaned, sat back down. "Why are we arguing?"

"I don't know. Maybe because you didn't bring enough food."

He stopped and stared, and, sure enough, she had almost all of it on her plate. And for some reason it struck him as completely funny. When he stopped laughing, he said. "Oh my God. You know what? I didn't even think about it. It was my leftovers. So I just grabbed it and came over."

"And it was leftovers, and it was good," she mumbled, as she shoveled another forkful in her mouth. "But now I feel like shit because I'm eating your food, and there isn't enough for you."

"Do you have anything here to eat?" he asked her.

She shrugged. "Nothing up to your standards."

At that, he turned to her, glared. "Enough of that BS too."

She shrugged. "I'm serious. I mean, there's like bread and peanut butter."

"You got any jam?" he asked, with a raised eyebrow. She stopped and stared, and he shrugged. "You think I didn't have peanut butter to get through the days when I was young? Lot of times I was damn happy to have peanut butter. And sometimes there was no bread to go with it."

She winced at that.

"Yeah, not all of us had the silver spoon."

"We haven't talked about our history much, have we?" she said quietly.

"Who wants to?" He walked into the kitchen, found a loaf of bread, the butter, and the peanut butter. Then took it all back to the kitchen table and sat down. She looked at him in astonishment, as he slathered four slices of bread with both butter and peanut butter.

"Do you want honey with that?" She continued to eat the leftovers he had brought.

He stopped, looked at his sandwiches. "I don't. I really like peanut butter," he said. And he put two pieces together, even though he had peanut-buttered both sides, then started to munch.

"And you're right about talking about our pasts. Who the hell wants to?"

"Exactly, they're over, and that's the way they'll stay."

She smiled, and then her smile dropped.

"Now what?"

"The problem is, that young woman's life is over too. She can't ever add to it. She can't ever have another day of fulfilling a dream or ... or doing something, anything that she wanted to do … all because of this guy."

"So get angry. I don't have a problem with that. Get angry, but get angry at the right person, not me."

She looked at him in surprise. "I'm not angry at you."

"Good, then don't go trying to break up with me."

She stared at him. Her lips quirked. "Is that what the food is for?"

"Is it working?" He checked her out, with interest.

She rolled her eyes at him. "You bring me leftover pasta, meatballs, and whatever else this is, including the garlic bread. I eat it all without a thought, and you're sitting there eating peanut butter."

"Right, and there's only one damn reason why I'm here and tolerating that," he said in a deadpan voice.

She leaned forward. "I know why too."

His eyebrows shot up. "And why is that?"

She grinned. "Because it's absolutely great fucking sex right afterward."

He had to admit her words shocked him, but what she did next sent delighted thrills up and down his body. She had crawled across the table they shared, grabbed him by the tie, stood him up on his feet, wrapped her arms around him, and kissed him until he felt it everywhere.

By the time they made it to her bed, he was already out of his jacket and his shirt. He still had the tie hanging around his neck, and he was tripping over himself, trying to get his pants off his feet. The damn shoes had to be forcefully kicked off, and, by the time he made it to her bed, she was laughing like a crazy woman, stripping off her clothes every step of the way.

When she jumped onto the bed, and he jumped after her to land on top, his temperature was through the roof, and he couldn't have been happier. This woman tormented him, shocked him, and, at every turn, delighted him. His head came down, his lips matching hers with an ardor that he'd rarely seen matched in another, as they quickly fed the fire, until it burned hot and bright.

She flipped over, sat up on top of him, and whispered, "Let me ride."

He immediately relaxed underneath her and whispered, "You go, girl."

She laughed and slowly lowered herself onto his erection, and she stopped, almost shuddering in delight, as he filled her to the brim. When he reached up to cup her breasts, she was left to wonder at how something so small could hold so many damn nerve endings. Just his touch sent a moan rippling up her chest to exhale on a heated breath.

He shook his head. "You're so damn perfect."

"I'm scrawny," she said.

"And that's all right too."

She slowly raised herself up onto her knees and then sank back down again. He shuddered and whispered, "You'll push it too far."

"Oh, I don't know," she whispered. "I think there's a lot of room for all of this."

He smiled and agreed. "If you say so."

"Sit back and relax."

He shook his head. "Not a hope in hell." He slid his hands down to her hips, gently stroking the soft curls and the plump lips below.

She shuddered, reaching for his hands, and held them there close to her, as she rose and sank, feeling his fingers against her flesh, as she went up and down his shaft. She rose, fell, and then leaned forward, placing her hands on his shoulders, as she started to ride. Thrust for thrust, he met her oncoming passion, driving them forward, driving them both closer and closer to the edge.

When she finally came apart, he grabbed her hips, holding her tight as he ground upward, plunging to his own climax, until he groaned, his body shuddering in delight.

When she collapsed on top of him, she whispered, "I don't know what that was, but it was fabulous."

And, with a heavy sigh, she closed her eyes and, like a child, fell asleep in his arms. He lay here, exhausted, delighted, winded, and, at the same time, completely entranced. It's not that he hadn't had wild and crazy sex before because, of course, he had.

He was a man with a lot of years of experience, but nothing so completely natural as her. She was 100 percent—all the time, one way or another—whether she was cranky, whether she was happy, whether she was making love, or whether she was giving somebody, like him, a dressing down. Usually it was all her, and she was all in. It was glorious to watch and even better to experience.

He closed his eyes, then wrapped her up tighter in his arms, ignoring her murmurs, as she tried to shift more comfortably, then stretched down to grab a blanket and awkwardly pulled it over the top of them. His boxers were on his thighs, his socks still on his feet, yet she had somehow managed to strip herself right to the bone.

He shook his head. "Efficient, aren't you?" he murmured, as he pulled the covers up to her shoulders.

She gave a happy sigh and wiggled in his arms.

He shifted her to her side, curled up with their thighs entwined, and whispered, "Just sleep."

She closed her eyes again, tucked her head up against his

shoulder, and was off.

He marveled at her ability to drop like a child, to just live in the moment, and to move on as need be. He wished he had that ability. Nightmares kept him awake most nights. And right now he was dealing with that weird sense of smell, which he hadn't had a chance to tell her more about. But it was here. He could smell her elemental female essence. Also the heavy smell of sex permeating the room. But, if there were two smells that he could handle quite nicely being amplified, they were those.

He nuzzled her hair, loving that he had her near him. He sighed happily and shifted again, wondering if he'd sleep. No question that he was struggling with what she obviously wasn't struggling with. He did doze for a little bit, woke for a while, and dozed for a bit more. When she shifted out of his arms and rolled over, only to sprawl out, taking up three-quarters of the bed, leaving him just a few bare inches along the side, he burst out laughing and got up, quickly stripped off the rest of his clothes, and used the bathroom.

He rarely slept long anyway, but, in this moment, it was so much more fun to just be here with her and watch. Not that he wanted to watch while she slept but to just experience having her here. Too often their time together was short, rushed, and then over. He wanted more but knew she wouldn't accept it. They hadn't even talked of this, but he already knew that he wanted her in his life, a whole lot more than what she would likely be willing to give him right now.

He also knew that, if he did anything other than give her space, she would probably walk away completely. And, for the first time, he admitted that such an outcome would incapacitate him. He couldn't stand the thought of losing her, and that's what he was facing right now. It was hard to admit that a man who had so few attachments in life was now hook, line, and sinker aligned with this one.

"Dear God," he whispered, knowing it was the one thing he could say that would adequately cover all his conflicting feelings, ranging from joy to terror, all at once. Yet he wouldn't change it for the world.

He crawled back into bed. Kate had shifted just enough so there was room for him to crawl up beside her. He tucked under the blankets, wrapped his arms around her, pulled her up spoon-style, and whispered, "I don't know what I'll do with you."

She shifted her head, looking at him bleary-eyed.

He just smiled and whispered, "Go back to sleep."

Her head dropped like a rock, as if she hadn't even been awake. Just like that, she was out again. He marveled at that. But, happily tucked up where he wanted to be, he closed his eyes, and, this time, he slept.

CHAPTER 6

K ATE WOKE THAT morning, calm and at peace, everything inside her completely loose and relaxed. She lay
here boneless on the bed, Simon's arms still wrapped around
her, holding her close. She smiled, even as she felt his body
jerk and shift in sleep. She rolled over ever-so-slightly to look
at him. His facial expression kept changing, not so much in
fear but as if going from one experience to another, different
reactions affecting him every time. She reached up a hand
and gently stroked his forehead.

At her touch, he calmed down and drifted into a deeper
sleep. She smiled, got up, and went in to shower.

It was 7:00 a.m. already, and she had to go to work. He
might work from home to a degree, but she needed to be
there in person. After her shower, she wrapped up in a towel
and came out to find him watching her. She smiled. "I half
expected you to come into the shower with me."

"Don't worry. I had to fight a battle for it too."

An eyebrow shot up. "I'm surprised you did."

"I knew you had to go to work, and I didn't really want
to rush it."

She laughed. "What you mean is, you knew I also needed to make coffee and to get some food because I can get
very cranky when I don't get both of those."

"I do know that." His eyes twinkled, as he hopped up

from her bed. "Are you okay if I have a quick shower?"

She nodded. "Absolutely."

With that, he headed into the bathroom, and she quickly dressed in clean clothes. In the kitchen, she put on coffee and searched the fridge for food. They'd left all the dishes out last night. She smiled at that because she wouldn't have missed it for the world. But, as it was, she had already pretty well cleaned up the leftovers, and he'd had the peanut butter and bread. She had a couple slabs of bread left but not a whole lot else. As she stood here in the kitchen, doing an inventory of what they could eat, he came out, stuffing his shirt into his pants.

"Is there anything left to eat?" he asked her.

She shook her head. "Honestly, no."

He gave a roar of laughter at that. "I can always grab something to eat on my way home or cook some eggs even, but what about you?"

She frowned and looked at the two slices of bread in the bag on the table. "Well, there is still a little bit of peanut butter," she said.

His eyebrows shot up. "Can you really do a day's work on that?"

"Doesn't look like I'll have much choice." She quickly slathered up the two slabs. She looked at him. "I'll pick up some muffins on my way in. What about you?"

"I can get breakfast at home."

"I thought you had meetings today?"

He nodded. "I do. And I'll get to them."

She wasn't very good at this whole relationship thing. It wasn't … it wasn't her thing. People always expected too much of her, and then she felt terribly guilty because she couldn't give it to them. It was part of the reason she hated relationships because she always ended up feeling like shit. It wasn't supposed to be like that, but somehow she always ended up feeling that way.

He stepped forward, grabbed her by the chin, then gently tilted her head and gave her a hard kiss. "No frowns. I'm fine. You go to work."

She picked up the sandwich in her hand, checked the clock, and groaned. "I have to go." She reached out, gave him a quick kiss goodbye, raced out the door, and called back, "Can you lock up?"

"I got it," he said.

She laughed and boogied down the stairways. She met one of her neighbors as she went, an older woman who always seemed quite friendly, if maybe even a little too lively at times. She stared at her and smiled. "Good morning."

"Good morning. Aren't you bright and cheerful?"

"Yep, I had a good night."

"I'm sure you did, and I'm jealous. I haven't had a good night like that in a long time."

Embarrassed that the woman had guessed what Kate had been doing for most of the night, she quickly hurried outside and raced to the station. She found a nearby vendor with pretzels again, and she quickly paid for one and took it into the station, as she walked in right beside Rodney.

He took a look at the pretzel. "Damn, they always look so good."

"Couldn't resist it this morning. I haven't had a chance to get any shopping done. I've got to pick up some groceries tonight."

He nodded. "Cases are like that. Some more than others, of course, but they can dominate your world, until you can't think of anything else."

"That's for sure."

He smiled. "You'll get there."

"*I'll* get there?" she asked, with a laugh. "It's *we*, isn't it? As in, *we'll* get there."

"Yep, that's what I meant to say," he said, but he flushed.

"But you aren't feeling like it's a *we*, are you?" She frowned.

"Of course it is," he immediately backtracked.

She thought about that and then shook her head. "No, I think your wording was deliberate. What's going on, Rodney?"

"Nothing," he said.

She frowned and would not let it go. "Am I taking too much of the case?"

He looked at her in surprise. "Don't you ever hide your light or try to not do as much because you're afraid of how other people will view it?"

"No. I don't really think about how others perceive my work. I'm in competition with myself." She shrugged. "I just know that it seemed like, for the longest time, that I couldn't do anything right, and that was really bothersome. I feel much more in my element here."

"And that's a good thing. You're really good for the team, and you've got a hell of a brain on you."

She looked at him, pleased. "And that is another odd thing for you to say." She frowned. "So I'm not sure what's going on, but are you okay? I mean it. Are you?"

"I'm okay. I'm just in one of those *rethinks*."

"You're not thinking about quitting, are you?" she said in alarm.

"No, no, not thinking about that," he said, with a smile.

"Just, you know, life."

"I get it. Life can be a bitch sometimes."

"That's for sure."

She worried about him throughout the day, as she collated all the statements they'd taken. She started to organize an investigation on anything and everything she could, while she waited for the video camera footage to show up on the university death. And, of course, there was the autopsy. When they didn't get any word this morning on the uni victim's autopsy report, Kate phoned and heard it wasn't even on schedule for the day. But she did get a bit of information. She groaned, sat back, and looked at Rodney. "Her name is Sally Hardgens. She was only twenty-one and a full-time biochemistry student at the university. If the coroner can't get to the autopsy today, we'll be walking blind on this one."

"I think we already are. Not a whole lot to go on."

"There's always something though," she said.

"Yeah, always something, but I'm not seeing a whole lot yet."

"Forensics would be nice," she grumbled.

"Forensics would always be nice," he pointed out. "But it doesn't change the fact that it always takes time to get it."

She nodded. "I still don't like it."

He burst out laughing. "Get some more coffee. It's time for the staff meeting anyway."

Colby stepped from his office and addressed his team in the bullpen. "Meet up, people."

Kate grabbed coffee and walked into the larger room, where her team all took a spot.

"Why don't you start, Owen?" Colby said.

Together, the five of them all went over the various cases

that they had and shared any progress.

"And now you've got this cyclist," Lilliana said to Kate.

She nodded. "Yeah, last night before I left, I was able to run through all the witness statements. Absolutely nothing of interest though."

"Do you have anyone worth following up on?" Lilliana asked.

"I'll definitely check out two students I want to talk to again. But I can't really say that anything was there, outside of the fact that, honestly, they just pissed me off."

Colby agreed. "Sometimes that's all we get. It's an impression we have, in the absence of any actual facts."

"Sure, but we also have to walk a fine line." Owen sat back, tossing down his pencil. "We don't need any more accusations of police harassment."

"*More* accusations?" Kate turned to him.

He nodded. "Apparently we've been hit by a couple recently. It depends on what the cases are and how much of a headache they are to crack. It tends to happen when we think people are holding back on us, and we put the pressure on. But, when it gets to be too much, don't worry, the litigation starts, and we'll get smacked for it."

Colby agreed. "Just something to keep in the back of your minds."

She frowned, as she thought about it. "I guess that's viable though, isn't it? Just because we think they're guilty or have something to do with it or know something, if we can't find anything, it makes us look stupid. Yet, at the same time, we can't let it go because we know it's there. Except we're not always right."

"Not only are we not always right, sometimes we're completely out in left field," Rodney added. "Look at our cyclist at the university. I mean, up until we arrived, you and I thought it was just an accident, right, Kate?"

She nodded. "Yeah, I was wondering why we were called."

"It was a dead body on the scene," Colby explained, "so you can expect to get called for that."

"Sure." And she thought about it. "It was the hole in the head that got me though."

"Cases are like that," Lilliana added. "You have to go with the flow and adjust as the evidence changes."

"The problem is," Kate asked her team, "what to do when there is no evidence—when we don't have anything to go on, and it seems like absolutely everything has been done, and we still can't find anything."

"And unfortunately that happens way too often too." Andy shrugged.

They all nodded at that.

"That's why we end up with so many cold cases," Lilliana said. "They're a nightmare for everybody. We don't want them. We want all of these families to have closure. We want everybody to get the answers they need to move on and for the dead to be recognized and to be honored at an appropriate time after their death, instead of being held in the morgue, which is very offensive and troubling for families."

"Right." Kate sighed. "I'll talk to these two witnesses because I definitely still have a few questions that need answered, but, other than that, it's camera footage for me today."

"Remember," Colby told her. "You can always ask Reese if she has some free time."

Kate nodded. "I just automatically think she doesn't have room for something else on her desk."

"That's why she's here," Colby replied.

"Will do," Kate said.

"Good." Colby nodded.

"And let us know if you get anything to pop and if you need an extra hand or two," Andy told her.

She looked over at Rodney. "You okay to help go through all those camera feeds?"

"Yeah, we need to."

She nodded. "Yes, exactly." After the meeting broke up, she refilled her coffee mug and headed back to her desk. Rodney was already logging in to see the camera footage. "I'll take half of them," she said.

He nodded.

And they spent the rest of the morning, right up until the lunch hour, checking out all the cameras in the area of the cyclist's death, looking for anything that would pinpoint their redheaded victim, but every camera seemed to be angled the wrong way. Finally they did catch sight of the victim, riding her bike forward, but saw nothing untoward. She just plopped over, almost crashing with the car. Instead it seemed as if the young woman on the bike had a haphazard fall in front of the vehicle—a small black car, which they were currently running potential makes and models of to see if anyone could match it.

From this feed, Kate couldn't confirm that the car had even made contact with the woman on the bike.

But, at the same time, it wasn't clear enough to get a license plate or an image of the driver, who had most definitely backed up and driven away very quickly. The way the redhead had fallen had also been so slow that Kate wouldn't have expected the woman to have been hurt by the sheer fall either.

So Kate didn't really blame the driver for leaving, yet she did blame him for leaving a crime scene, leaving a potentially injured person down on the street. He should have stopped and reached out to see if the woman needed anything. That her accident didn't appear to be something major didn't mean that it wasn't.

She pointed out this section of video to Rodney, and he agreed. "But now we know she's fallen, as if it's not a major bike-car crash at all. She just went down, and the driver didn't stick around to see if she got up again."

"Finding out she's dead, if he has by now," she murmured, "must have come as a shock, and now he probably doesn't know what to do."

Just then, Kate got a call from the in-take desk out in the front. "We have a man here saying that he killed your cyclist at the university."

She stared at the phone in her hand, then turned toward Rodney. She bolted to her feet. "Take him into Interview A, please."

At that, Rodney hopped up, and the two of them walked over. As they entered the interrogation room, a young man, maybe twenty years old, stood nervously.

"You've got something to tell us?" she asked quietly. "Please have a seat."

He nodded. "I don't know how it happened. I was so careful."

"How what happened?" she asked, motioning at the chair. "Sit down, please, and identify yourself."

"My name is Matt, Matt Powell. And I was just driving toward the university. I know I was distracted. I had a really bad exam, and I was struggling. I went by the pizza place but decided against pizza. I went to the corner store, but I

71

couldn't find anything to eat, so I ended up just going around the block and coming back up, thinking I would head back to the university. And then *boom!* This woman was right there. I didn't even think I'd hit her. Honestly, it just looked like she collapsed sideways. There was no braking. I mean, obviously I braked, but there was no speed. There was no need to brake. There was no—"

He stopped talking, completely overwhelmed, and then he burst into tears. "I heard later that I'd killed her." He was shaking. "I didn't mean to. I didn't mean to have anything to do with it."

Kate sighed, looked over Rodney, and he nodded. "First, the problem is, you took off. You should have waited to make sure that she was okay."

He looked at her, tears in his eyes. "But she didn't even look like, ... like anything was wrong with her. It looked like she was just falling. I pulled around and left. I didn't do anything to help her."

"Did you look back through your rearview mirror?" Kate asked.

"No." Matt shook his head. "I didn't even think of it. I just thought she'd had an accident, and then I heard ... No, I saw her arm hit the street, and I didn't think anything of it." He stopped, looked at her. "I should have though, shouldn't I?"

Kate nodded. "Yeah, that would have been the right thing to do."

"But I couldn't have helped her, could I?"

"Probably not, though I can't say what condition she was in when you were there at the accident."

"What do you mean?" He was obviously a little confused.

"How did she appear before you hit her?"

"I didn't hit her. That's the thing. I don't think she touched the car. I think she just fell in front of me, so I pulled around her."

"You didn't wonder when she didn't get back up again?"

"I thought I saw her there, as I went around, but she was on the other side of my car. Vehicles were everywhere, and I was trying to get out of the way. People were behind me." Running his hands through his hair, he said, "I waited for some people to go by, then I pulled out and left. I didn't even think she was hurt." He stopped, shook his head. "My parents will kill me."

Kate wanted to laugh because that was certainly one of the problems he was facing, but another problem was the fact that he had left the scene of an accident, though he hadn't killed her. Unless they could prove he'd even hit her. She frowned as she thought about that. "When you saw her, how did she look?"

He looked at her in surprise. "Her head was down, and she was leaning over the handlebars. Honestly, I wondered if she was drunk. So many parties and stuff are going on at the university that it's not uncommon. She didn't look all that great."

"So she was leaning over the handlebars?"

He nodded. "Yes, but she kept on going. I hit the horn, and she jolted and then collapsed. So I went around and took off." He let out a long breath. "How much trouble am I in?"

She looked at Rodney, who picked up the interrogation from there and explained what happened. Matt looked at him in shock. His voice sounded like a tiny-mouse squeak. "She was shot?"

Rodney nodded.

"Oh my God, oh my God, oh my God." He shook his hands. "I didn't shoot her. I didn't shoot her. I don't have a gun. I don't know anything about guns."

"No," Rodney said, "and I'm glad to hear that because that makes things a little bit easier."

"Not for me it doesn't. Oh my God, that poor woman."

There. That's what Kate had been waiting for, that sense of empathy, that sense of understanding of what had happened to the victim. "Did you recognize her?"

He shook his head. "No, when she jolted, I saw her face, some of it, and, of course, saw the red hoodie. I mean, so many people wear those hoodies, and then you can't see much. Everybody's so rushed, so busy, so stressed right now, that, I mean, I just expected her to be another stressed-out student, like me. We're all just trying to complete our studies, get a degree, and get ahead in life."

"And I get that," she said quietly. "So you have no idea who she is or who did this, but you definitely saw her go down in front of you."

He went over it again, this time hopping up, explaining where he was and where she was. It jived with what they'd seen from the cameras.

She got his contact information and the other details she needed, then told him that he was free to go.

He asked, "Will I get charged with anything?"

"I don't think so, but I'll be talking to the prosecutor, and we'll follow up."

He nodded slowly. "Honest, it seemed like she just fell over in front of me. I should have stopped. That was an asshole move on my part. I should have stopped and helped her. She might—I will live with that regret forever. I should have stopped."

Kate nodded. "I get it. So next time, remember that there are more people in the world than just you, and plenty of them have problems too."

He winced at that. "And she'd been shot. Jesus, what kind of a shitty day did she have?"

"She's dead, so I rather imagine it was the worst." He stared at her, his bottom lip trembling. She hopped to her feet. "You can go home now. And remember—"

He bolted to his feet. "Got it." He hesitated. "When do you ... When will I hear?"

She shook her head. "I have no idea. I'll let you know."

With that, he nodded and raced out.

"You could have let him off the hook."

"Maybe, but he did drive away from somebody who collapsed in front of him."

"Being an asshole is not a crime."

"Leaving the scene of a crime too. But I know, and I'll let him off the hook tomorrow."

He shook his head. "Are you trying to make his today worse or his tomorrow better?"

"I just want him to remember that this selfish attitude doesn't work in this world, and, if we don't help each other, things can get pretty ugly."

"I get it. You keep thinking about your brother, don't you?"

She shrugged. "Sure. It would have been nice if somebody had seen Timmy, if they had stepped up to the plate to help him. It didn't happen."

"Did you ever wonder if maybe he was kidnapped, and he's living another life somewhere?"

"Absolutely. I keep hoping for that. You hear of cases

like that. As you know, we've seen it, where various girls have been held captive for ten-plus, even twenty, years, and all of a sudden they surface—after living horrific lives in captivity somewhere. Some of the cases aren't that bad, and others are something you don't ever want to contemplate.

"In my case, this was my brother. So it's a little different, since most of those cases are about girls, but it's not impossible. There's always that sense, that bit of hope that maybe Timmy's alive out there somehow. But hope is scary because there's absolutely no guarantee that it will come true. And so you wait, and you wait some more, and then you wait even more."

"In the meantime," he reminded her, "you're checking out every lead that comes, every time we get a boy or a child's body."

She nodded. "And those are the worst," she said quietly. "Because, even though you hope, every time a body is found, you know it could be the one you don't want it to be."

He nodded in understanding, got up, and they left the interview room. As they walked back to their desks, Rodney said. "Now what?"

"Now let's look into those other cases you pointed out at the very beginning of this case, the ones you emailed me, and also I want to phone those two pizza-eating kids."

"Did they really say something that triggered a lead, or did they just upset you?"

"Both. I just don't know what it was. For all I know, they didn't want to talk to me because they had joints on them or something stupid like that."

"And yet it's legal."

"It's legal, but maybe they have a reason that it's not allowed in their world. Maybe they're on a sports team or something. Maybe they don't want their parents to know. Let me put it this way. They definitely acted guilty about something."

"Good enough. Sometimes all we have to go on is that instinct."

She nodded. "In this case something's there. I just don't know what it is."

"Let me know how it comes out."

She laughed. "Yep, will do." And, with that, she headed back to her desk and had an afternoon that just wouldn't quit. "I'll start with those two kids," she muttered to herself. She began with the male, the one who really got to her with his arrogance and his entitled attitude. She looked up his name, and, when she called the number he had given her, he answered but sounded distracted. "This is Detective Kate Morgan. I spoke with you yesterday ... about the accident."

"What about it?" he asked, his voice immediately surly.

"It seemed to me like you weren't saying something," she said calmly. "So I'd like to go over some of these questions again."

"And maybe I should phone my lawyer."

"That's fine. In that case, I'll expect you both down here tomorrow at one o'clock. Okay?"

"Wait, wait. What are you talking about?"

"If you're calling your lawyer, you may as well come in and give a formal statement and be done with it," she said, her tone hard.

He hesitated. "Fine. What questions?"

"The same ones. I just want to go over some of these because it doesn't jive with what other people were saying."

"What do you mean, it doesn't jive?" he said in disgust. "Who the hell were you asking?"

"Everyone who was there." She calmly went over the questions again, what he'd seen, who he'd seen, and basically he didn't have anything to say. "*Hmm.*" She tried to make it sound like she was unimpressed.

"What? Did I get something wrong?" He sounded stressed. "Nothing was there. Honest."

"So, what are you hiding then?" she asked quietly.

"Nothing, and, if you say that again, then we will be talking to my lawyer."

"Okay, give me his name, please."

He hesitated and then gave her the name of a local legal counsel that she was familiar with.

"Your own personal lawyer?"

"My family's."

His pompous tone made her eyebrows go up. "Perfect. I'll give him a call. Thank you." And, with that, she hung up. Rodney happened to look over at her. She shrugged. "He pulled the lawyer card."

"Interesting. You bringing him in for questioning?"

"We'll see. He gave the same answers to the same questions as before. Thus, so far, nothing necessarily to get antsy about, but he's definitely hiding something."

"He's a kid. He's in college, away from the folks. Who the hell knows what shit he's up to?"

"Exactly, and it is what it is."

"It's probably more than that, but it's probably not criminal."

"Maybe. You know what? The quiet young woman was the weakest link." She thought about that for a moment. "I think I'll go to the university and talk to her myself."

"Not call?"

"No, if anything's there, she's the one who'll spit it out."

"Do you want me to come?"

She laughed. "No, it's all good. I'll go take a look. I want to return to that scene anyway." He frowned at that. "You can come if you want. It's really not a big deal. I just want to double-check something."

"You're trying to catch her in a lie?"

"I want to find out what the hell she's hiding. That's the part that bugs me. And I want to do a search on this other guy and see what the hell's going on in his world that requires lawyers primed for his phone calls."

"What do you want to bet the kid's got a record?"

"You're right. That's something else I need to do—pull all these names, everybody on that witness list. We need to run their names through the database and see if anything pops."

"Why don't you run up to the university and talk to her, and, while you're doing that, I'll input everything here and see if we can come up with anything interesting."

"That would be great. Thank you. And add that kid who came in and confessed."

He nodded and added Matt Powell's name to the list. "Okay, give me an hour and check back in," he said.

With that, she walked out of the station and headed for the university. At least she had something concrete to do, and sometimes getting away from the computer and talking to people through legwork, the good old-fashioned style of police work, was still the best way to go. She hoped it made something pop. No guarantee, but she was running out of time.

SIMON MADE IT through most of the rest of his day with

absolutely none of the enhanced sense of smell symptoms he had experienced the day before. He even stood at the harbor and spent a long time just inhaling the sea air, wondering at the absolute lack of saltiness. It made no sense that yesterday he would be so hypersensitive and that today it would be so bland. Not really caring either way, he was just a little perturbed at the quirkiness of his "gift" when so much else was going on in his world. Still, he was grateful to not be connected with the crazy psychic scenarios he'd been through twice with Kate and her cases.

He walked to the market, picked up an apple, and, since they had fresh coffee, grabbed one of those too. Back outside he wandered along until he found a bench, where he sat down and just watched the world go by, as he enjoyed a snack. He rotated his shoulders, gently easing back the stress. It was one of those days where he was dealing with multiple people, usually with problems associated with his rehabs. As much as Simon could be a people person, he also found that it used up a lot of his energy.

The psychologists had a million names for it, but Simon considered himself more of a social introvert. That didn't quite fit either though; it wasn't totally correct. He knew people who fed on crowds and just got louder and lighter and brighter. While Simon could be social in a crowd, the interaction with too many people drained him. Then he had to leave and go recharge somewhere else. That was just the way he was built, and it worked for him.

He wasn't an introvert. He could socialize if he needed to, but he didn't want to be around people all the time. Maybe that had something to do with his upbringing. He'd been hidden away for so long and had traveled such a rough road that it was hard to learn to trust.

He had encountered people who gave this superficial public appearance to everybody that seemed normal but hid everything that was real about them, and that was exhausting to Simon, sifting through the masks. It had to be equally draining for those to be fake all the time, to deny who they really were. For him, he was who he was in any setting, but periodically he needed time to get away and to recharge— mostly to just be alone and relax. Still, relaxing as he was right now, wasn't hard to deal with either.

He pulled out his phone, while he ate the apple, and ran through his emails, wincing at a few of them. A couple invoices had come in. One in particular was a good 20 percent over what was expected. He quickly sent off a terse message about that one. He only employed people who kept their invoices within 10 percent. If they couldn't manage costs properly, then that was their fault, and he would not be working with them in the future. When people gave him estimates, he expected quotes that mattered. True professionals could meet that standard, and anyone who couldn't wasn't someone he would do business with.

Sure, as a businessman, he understood that supplies went up and that shipyard workers went on strike. That meant there would be extra expenses at various times, but Simon didn't expect to pay all those costs himself. These guys were in business for a reason, and they charged enough to cover a lot of it themselves. By the time Simon finished going through his emails, the apple was gone, and so was the coffee.

He hopped to his feet, heading to the bank. He would spend a couple hours in there at this rate. He could do an awful lot of his banking business online, but a lot he couldn't. He still dealt with cash from a few of his clients, a few of his contractors. Some of them preferred money orders, and some were just straight bank transfers.

Seeing the long afternoon ahead of him, he yawned and walked beside the harbor as long as he could, before heading back into town. When he realized he would be late for his appointment at the bank, he hopped the next Aquabus, catching a ride up the waterway until the next stop, bringing him ten blocks or so over. When he hopped off, he checked his watch—perfectly on time. He grinned at that, enjoying the precision.

As he walked in, he lifted a hand to Ben, sitting in the back room, clearly visible since the rooms were all glass. Ben immediately hopped up, walked over, and opened the door to let him in.

"Right on time as usual."

"Thought I would be late today," he said.

"Not likely. You keep such a perfect attendance record that it makes the rest of us look like shit."

"You look like shit anyway," Simon said, flashing a grin.

Ben immediately smiled, appreciating the wit.

They had a professional relationship that worked, as long as people did what Simon needed them to do, and they did it efficiently.

Ben knew that, and, as long as everybody could work together, he was all about keeping the relationship at this level. As he sat down, Ben asked, "So, what's on the list today?"

"Too much." Simon handed over the list of transfers and other transactions that he needed.

Ben shook his head, as he looked it over. "Man, I almost feel like we should get you your own private teller."

"You're not kidding, It's a long list this time. It'll take a while."

As he started in on the payments in their various forms, Ben immediately brought up the computers and sorted through Simon's list. By the time he was done, Simon had already gone through another cup of coffee, and now it was an hour and a half later. When Ben turned to face him, Simon stood to leave. "Thank you."

Ben replied, "Moving money around is always good for the economy, and, therefore, the bank, no matter where it's going."

"Glad to hear that." Simon waved and headed back outside again.

Almost as soon as he stepped outside again, the scent of the city hit him like a ton of bricks. He frowned at that. "From nothing to this again?"

He looked around but nothing to see. He studied his surroundings now with his psychic senses but picked up absolutely nothing. It was bizarre to have this particular "gift" ebb and flow, and, because he didn't have any answers for it, it unnerved him. He liked to have his *T*s crossed and his *I*s dotted to ensure the world knew who he was before he ever got there. But that wasn't happening right now. This uncontrollable sense of smell was something completely different. It wasn't comfortable, and he didn't like anything about it.

As he shuffled toward Hastings again, everything wrong in the city got sharper and sharper in his nose. Like sulfur from somewhere, and gas leaks from somewhere else. Natural gas too. He wasn't even sure what he was smelling in some places. He shook his head, as he picked up the pace, getting there as fast as he could. He wanted to take a shortcut through an alley, but, as soon as he stepped in, the smell of urine slammed him, and he immediately backed up, bending over double because of the intense rank smell. At that, he stopped, then leaned against the wall, giving himself a chance to just digest whatever the hell was going on. His world was all about balance, and, when there was none, life was that much harder.

As soon as he could breathe again, he headed down the main pathway, avoiding all unsavory places that normally wouldn't be an issue, but something today made them a serious problem. He was late for his next appointment. By the time his project manager gave him the lowdown on the rehab—now at 30 percent over budget—Simon got frustrated and angry again.

"This will be the job to keep an eye on," his project manager muttered.

"Yeah, there's always one, isn't there?" Simon tried to remember that. Some projects, no matter how well he and his crew prepared for it, turned into money pits. Thankfully the overall majority of his projects made money, so the offset could be absorbed without affecting his bottom line too much. However, dealing with the daily headaches sometimes made Simon question his desire to revive the original beauty of the Vancouver buildings here.

"There's always one, and honestly, we've done the best we can."

"And yet it doesn't seem to be doing a damn bit of good."

"That's because you're caught up in the daily drudge of it all right now. And I get that, I really do. I mean a ton of your money is involved in this."

"We're 200K over budget," Simon said in exasperation. "What the hell? We weren't supposed to get anywhere close to that figure."

The project manager nodded. "Yet you've okayed all these changes."

"Sure, but those change orders are bullshit," he snapped. "Especially at this level."

"Part of that was the supplies. We had to source out new suppliers, and that meant we had to do other changes because we couldn't get some of what we needed."

Simon shrugged. "It's bad right now. I get it."

"I do too."

"Whatever, come on. Let's just get this job done. Completion is the only way to get out of this hole, the only way to stop the bleeding."

"When I hear that from others, it always makes me wonder. How do you spend your way out of a financial holes? Yet it seems like sometimes it's the only answer."

"I agree," Simon said. "We have to spend to get out of it. So let's get the spending done, so I know what the bottom line is, and we can go forward from there." With that, he turned and walked away.

It had been all he could do to not say something more. That aftershave, cologne, or whatever the hell his project manager used was pungent. However, Simon had never noticed it before. So today he had decided to overwhelm himself in it? Like that white noise you suddenly notice and now can no longer ignore? Or was it that crazy psychic olfactory sense of his? Considering that everything else was also on steroids, it was probably that.

It was irritating as hell. Plus, now a weird rumbling appeared in the back of his head. He swatted at it, shaking his head. It sounded like a washing machine running in the back of the house. He stood in silence for a few moments before saying, "Screw this."

He needed this day to be over, and, if he was lucky, he'd get his work done first. If not, then to hell with it. Maybe Kate's day was going better. And, with that, he pulled out his phone and checked it, intending to send a text to Kate, but hesitated. It was still relatively early in the day, and she'd be busy at work, what with her long hours. Groaning, he shoved his cell back into his pocket and headed home. It was definitely a day to shut down early.

CHAPTER 7

A S KATE GOT close to the university, she deliberately drove around the block, taking a look at the area, wondering if the previous accidents had anything to do with this one. They were hardly accidents, but that's what she would call them for the moment. *Incidents*, maybe that was better. She didn't have the history on the previous four at this time of year in the same area, beyond a quick report, but she'd rather go home and study the written details in full later.

As it was, she took a quick look around, wondering what the problem was with this corner. Apparently the city had been lobbying for a change of traffic patterns here, in order to make it safer, but she didn't really notice any difference. She shrugged, turned the corner again and then again. The traffic was steady, but it wasn't overly slow, and, by the time she headed down the boulevard toward the campus center, the opposing traffic flowed smoothly at her side in the other direction—not a problem whatsoever.

Then again, most traffic wasn't a problem if people kept to the rules and to their own side of the road. As soon as everybody accepted that they couldn't go as fast as they wanted, they should just calm down and allow for more time. What really chapped her butt was those who didn't want to listen to the rules—because the rules weren't made for them, because they were *special*. The number of people who thought they were special just blew her away.

Shaking her head, she pulled into the student housing parking, then exited her vehicle and walked to the steps of the building. Groups of people stood around talking here and there. It was exam time, and summer session was almost over. Exams were hanging over the heads of some. As she almost reached the steps accessing the building, somebody called out, "Hey, do you have permission to go up there?"

She turned, looked at the young woman, and smiled. "Will this do?" She held up her badge.

Immediately the other woman recoiled. "Ah, is there a problem?"

"I need to talk to somebody. Is that a problem?"

She shook her head. "No, we're just trying to keep security on the place a little tighter."

"Have you had problems?" Kate asked.

"No, not really. It's just, you know, sometimes breakups aren't all that pleasant. And, when there are breakups between friends on campus, and everybody knows everybody, it's really easy to get in and out of buildings, even if you didn't really want them getting in and out."

It was stated very cryptically, but Kate understood perfectly. "So, somebody had a bad breakup. He's made some threats, and now you guys are all worried that he'll come in here and cause chaos for his ex-girlfriend, is that it?"

Her eyebrows shot up, and she nodded. "Wow, that was quick. I guess you are a cop."

"Yeah, that's what the badge is for." Kate looked around at the crowd. "I'm looking for Candy."

"Oh, Candy is upstairs, studying," she said, with relief.

"Good, I'll just go on up and talk to her."

"Is she in any trouble?"

"Nope, not at all."

"Of course she isn't. She's not the type."

"Not the type?"

"To get into trouble."

"Interesting phrase," Kate said, with a bright smile. "Who are the types to get into trouble?"

"Actually quite a few of us," she said, in a half-joking manner. "It goes along with the territory, you know? Freedom from home for the first time. A chance to make our own decisions—without anybody looking over our shoulder and judging us for it."

"Oh, so you mean, sex, drugs, and alcohol. And all that at the same time?"

The young woman flushed. "Well, it's not that bad," she said.

Kate laughed. "Relax. I'm not here to tend to anybody's love life. I'm just here to talk to Candy."

"Okay," she said, in a much more cheerful tone of voice. "Just be nice to her. She's having a rough day."

"Why?" Kate asked, not having made it any farther than two steps toward the door.

"I'm not sure. A breakup, I think."

"Ah, that's tough."

"Yeah, it's a good thing though," said one of the other females, stepping up and joining the conversation.

"Why is that?"

"He's an asshat." Her words were succinct and clear.

"At this age, lots of them are," Kate said, with a knowing smile.

The two young women thought that was the funniest thing ever and howled with laughter. "Oh my God, that's perfect."

Not sure what was so perfect about guys being asshats, but Kate was happy to go along with whatever the hell this was. "Anything else to say about this guy? Is he a problem?"

"Nah, he's just one of those rich guys. So, when you have a problem with him, you have a problem with the whole group."

"Interesting that she got hooked up with him in the first place, isn't it?"

"You know what? That's exactly what I said," replied the first woman. "I mean, I'm much more their type than she is."

"Their type?"

"You know? Plenty of money and willing to do whatever for that fun evening." She shrugged. "I'm not as limited by morals and ethics as Candy is."

"Yeah, it's quite a handicap sometimes, isn't it?"

"It really is," she said seriously. "Think about it. I mean, if you don't worry about the rules, then you're not hung up with guilt over them all. And Candy is definitely hung up in guilt."

"Yeah," the second young woman agreed. "Something about she wouldn't do something with them, and they made her do it anyway, and now she's up there, bawling her eyes out, thinking her world is over."

"Sounds like I need to go talk to her then." Kate smiled and pulled out her card and handed it to the two women. "If you think of anything else, or if this guy—whoever it is who could cause trouble—causes some trouble, give me a shout."

Looking at the card, one of the young women said, "Wow, you're a homicide cop?"

"A detective, yes. That's what I do."

"Did you always want to do something like that?" she asked.

"Yep, pretty much." She cheerfully pulled the door open. She stopped, looked back at the pair, still standing there, staring at her card, and wondered. It seemed like a hell of a long time since Kate had been that innocent. And the years didn't lie; it *was* a long time ago. Shaking her head, she strode inside, letting the door close behind her.

It always blew her away that the badge made such a difference. And she got it; she really did. Everybody wanted to believe in authority, but what if somebody else had grabbed that badge? What if somebody else was using it for nefarious purposes? These women weren't even calling it in and checking it out any further. Instead just wondering in delight that they got to talk to a detective. Kate worried about that.

Given that same level of innocence, it's no wonder her brother had gotten into trouble so easily. He'd only been a child, and whoever had taken him had been wiser in the ways of the world than Timmy was. He'd been easy pickings, and it had been over so fast. Even two years older, Kate hadn't been any smarter; she'd gone inside and left her brother alone. She shook her head at that. It shouldn't have been her problem. It shouldn't have been her responsibility, and it definitely sure as hell shouldn't be her guilt. But it was, and that was just something she never got over.

As she raced up the stairs, taking two at a time, she passed several other young women heading down to go out. Nobody asked her anything; nobody questioned her presence, but why would they? It was broad daylight, and everybody knew predators came out at nighttime. She shook her head at that. She'd learned very early on that predators were there every hour of the day, just looking for that split second of opportunity.

Reaching the door she was looking for, she knocked. There was absolute silence. She called out and knocked again, then waited. When there was no answer, she immediately rapped harder. "Police, Candy. Let me in."

A gasp came from inside, but she was on the fourth floor, and the chances of Candy bolting out the window were not good. And, if that's the route she chose, then a hell of a lot more was going on here than anybody suspected. When the door opened ever-so-slightly, with a chain still across it, Candy looked out through the crack, saw Kate, and immediately started to cry.

"Yeah," Kate said, "time to talk to me."

The woman opened up the door and let her in. With tears running down her face, Candy slammed it shut behind her and immediately put the chain back again.

"So, you want to tell me what's going on?" Kate gave the small dorm room a quick look around. It was barely big enough for one person let alone a live-in student, but it was pretty normal college quarters—a bed, a desk, what looked like a bathroom attached, which meant Candy had a private room. Kate turned and looked at the young woman, and Candy collapsed on the bed, bawling. "Come on. Talk to me." Kate pulled out the chair from the desk and sat down.

"I can't. They'll kill me."

Kate heard that phrase, and yet, knowing who she was talking to, she said, "I presume you're not being literal with that phrase."

The young woman looked at her, as if her world had collapsed. "I really love him," she said.

Kate's heart sank. The last thing she wanted was to have a heart-to-heart discussion over a schoolgirl crush. "I can see that. I get it." When Candy didn't show any signs of calming down, Kate sighed, got up, and grabbed a box of Kleenex off the desk, then sat down beside her. "Here. Start with this."

Candy snatched several out of the box, shoved them against her face, and proceeded to bawl into them.

"If you're not talking to me here," Kate said, "I'll have to take you down to the station."

At that, the woman bolted to her feet, and, the tears still streaming down her face, she stared at Kate, as if her world had completely cracked apart.

"So, sit yourself back down, get a grip, and talk to me."

With that, she sagged into the bed and sobbed a few more times, but it was obvious the onslaught was slowing down. "They wanted me to do it. I didn't want to."

"They wanted you to do what?"

"Push her over."

At that, Kate stopped and stared at the young woman. "Push who over?"

"A woman on a bike," she said. At that point, she bawled again.

Kate reached over, grabbed her hands, and pulled them away, along with the balls of Kleenex, all pressed against her eyeballs. "Before you do damage to your eyes, talk to me," she said, her voice sharp.

Candy took several long deep breaths. "I'm not like them," she cried out. "They do things, and they don't care. They don't seem to feel any guilt. They don't care about anybody else. I just don't know what to do."

"Did you push somebody over?"

She nodded. "Yes. But not the one they wanted me to."

"I don't know if that's good or bad," Kate said, "but you pushed somebody over?"

At that, she started to cry. "And I feel terrible about it."

"So, why did you do it?"

"They wanted me to."

"Why did they want you to?" she asked.

"Just a lark. They like picking on people. Particularly on those not perfect, like them."

"So, why are you even with them?" Kate asked, looking at her. "That's hardly your style."

"No, it really isn't. But, when you get into a group like that, it just seems like there's no other choice. They get you all twisted up, so, if you want to be with them—be one of them—you have to do what they say. And he was my boyfriend. They were all doing it, so it seemed like you have to do it too."

"So, what are they all doing then?"

She frowned. "They were pushing people."

"What people?"

At that, she winced. "Disadvantaged people. Disabled or whatever you call them."

Kate sagged in her chair. "So, you're talking about people in wheelchairs or like on crutches?"

She nodded. "Yes, and some with diseases or tumors or not smart or whatever."

"So these people, who already have enough of a challenge getting through the day, now have to deal with shitheads like you guys deliberately making it harder?"

Candy just stared, her bottom lip trembling.

"Yeah, I'm including you in that group," Kate said, "if you're doing it with them."

"I don't want to be a shithead," she said.

"Did you push one of them?"

She started to bawl. "I did, but not one of them."

"Why not?"

"I couldn't. They wanted me to pick on a blind woman."

"Wow, really nice friends you have." Kate shook her head. "Did they hurt anybody seriously when they did this?"

She nodded. "They pushed one woman down some stairs. She broke a leg, but, of course, they got away with it."

"And what about the others they picked on and pushed?"

"I don't know about all of them, but they really like to do things like that."

"I don't care if they really like to do shit like that or not. That's really not cool, not allowed, and it's assault. And, if somebody broke their leg, that's even worse." Kate thought about the woman at the corner on the bike. "Did you see the woman hit by the vehicle recently at the intersection?"

She shook her head. "No, we really didn't."

"Yeah, right. Not sure I believe you. After all, I can imagine you didn't want me to find out about all the bullying your little group does around campus." Kate was completely exasperated. "That just goes to show what shitty people you all are."

The other woman gasped at the hard insult.

But Kate wouldn't hold back. "Seriously? They wanted you to push a blind woman? Who won't even have the chance to know where that blow comes from? Do you think she hasn't grown up with other little shitheads just like that? But that would have been years ago, like grade school, possibly even high school. But this is the university. This is about being an adult, in an adult world—or not. You get to make that choice now. Every day, it's your choice to be a good person or a shithead," she snapped. "Congratulations for proving yourself to be in the shithead category."

The other woman looked at her, shocked.

"Yeah, don't even go there. Why should I take any pity on you? You pushed somebody, didn't you?"

She nodded. "But she was healthy at least."

Kate snorted, totally disgusted. "And that makes it better, right?" Candy just bawled again. Kate shook her head. "Wow, now I have all that shit to get through, as well."

"What will you do?"

"*You'll* talk to your dean for one thing."

"No, no, no. You don't understand. They'll kill me."

"And so, do you mean *kill me* as in *fear for your life* kill me?" she asked. "Because now I have to wonder just what kind of shitheads these guys really are. I mean, for all I know, they're into murder."

"No, no, no," she cried out. "They're not that bad. At least I don't think so, but I'm not sure."

"It's just a matter of degrees," Kate said. "Once you go down the pathway that you're talking about, it is a very simple step to cross that line."

"No, they wouldn't do that."

Kate snorted at that. "You know something, Candy? Anybody who'll deliberately attack disadvantaged people or people with disabilities, or someone suffering with injuries already, yeah, they absolutely will. It's a very thin line between acting that way to somebody and participating in their deaths."

At that, the other woman stopped and stared. "I didn't think of it that way."

"What do you think happens when one of these accidents goes wrong?"

"I think it already did. They're really secretive about one

of them."

"Yeah? What happened?"

"I don't know. I don't know any of the details. They won't tell me."

Kate sighed and stared at the young woman. "And did you break up with him now?"

"Well, supposedly." She sat here, with her shoulders sagged, as if the whole world was over.

"Okay, clue me in on this relationship stuff. As much as I don't want to go there, I don't get what you're talking about right now."

"We've broken up several times. And honestly, I usually come crawling back," she admitted shamefully.

"Why?"

"Partly because I have to live here too. And I'm afraid that I'll become one of the people who they decide to knock over one day."

"That would be justice, wouldn't it? Some would call it karma."

"I get that. I really do, and, if I thought that would be my punishment, and then I could be free of all this guilt, then I'd take it. I really would. I'd take it and be happy to move on. But, like I said, I'm not so sure that something else hasn't gotten much worse."

"So you think they killed somebody?"

"I don't know," she whispered, "but I think one of their jokes backfired or something, and somebody got seriously hurt."

"In that case, I'll need more information."

"And I can't give it to you. You don't understand. These guys are really dangerous."

"Yeah, I get that," Kate said, "but the question is, what

will we do about it?" She pondered that for a moment. "I'm also here about that accident you saw."

"But we didn't see anything," she said.

"What about the blind woman?"

"She was at the intersection. I think a man was escorting her," She nodded. "But I don't know how close she was to that accident."

Kate frowned at that. "I'm waiting for the autopsy report on her now."

At that, Candy gasped. "That would be terrible."

"Why would that be any more terrible than what they wanted you to do to her? Or knocking someone down the stairs?"

"It wasn't supposed to involve the stairs. She was just supposed to fall over, but instead she tripped, stumbled, fell forward, and ended up falling down the stairs."

"Even picking a place that's dangerous where she could fall down the stairs is stupid. Are you really making excuses for this? You're all lucky she only broke her leg and not her neck."

"If I don't make excuses," Candy whispered, "I have to face up to the fact of what I did."

"News flash," Kate said in a hard voice, "you have to do that anyway."

INTERESTING, HE THOUGHT. Maybe that was the female detective again. He recognized the car. He was just sitting here, having coffee, watching her go around and around the block. Either she was well and truly lost or she was checking out the block. But really, how much checking out could you do from a vehicle? That's just lazy. Sloppy and lazy. She should get out of the vehicle and walk the area, and, even then, she wasn't likely to pick up on anything. It was all over with. Nothing to see. He'd been sitting here, perusing the people coming and going, wondering if anybody even realized that somebody just died. Did anybody even care?

It was such a fake world, where people could do whatever they wanted, and nobody seemed to give a damn. It often amazed him how callous everybody else was out there, as if it was literally just a worldly life outside. It used to bother him, but now it was an advantage. It made life so much easier and simpler. With a smile, he got up, put his money and a tip down for the coffee, then walked toward the corner light. Another day in paradise. But he had things to do, plans to make.

Victims to pick.

Everything had to be just right.

CHAPTER 8

FUMING, KATE CONTACTED Rodney, not too long after she'd left the university, as she drove back to the office, and just spilled everything this woman had shared.

"Jesus," Rodney said. "They're targeting people with disabilities?"

"Disabilities, diseases, those obviously sick, broken legs, whatever. Anybody considered as weaker or more vulnerable than them," she spat out. She quickly shifted down 12th Ave, loving the traffic that flowed smoothly. She knew it was too much to ask that it be smooth traveling the whole way, but she'd take it while she could. She shifted over onto South Grandview Highway and continued on toward the station.

"I don't know how, but we've got to do something about this." Unseen by him, she shook her head, while he was still talking about it. "There's got to be something we can charge them with."

"Absolutely there is, but it's not a homicide. And these crimes happened on campus, so you know that's the RCMP's jurisdiction. If we have any evidence of this, in the pursuit of our case, we hand it off to them."

"It's also just her story."

"I don't suppose you got that on tape, did you?"

"I did get a statement from her, and she signed it. She didn't even know all the victims' names, just a few of them.

Apparently one of them fell down the stairs and broke a leg from this group's actions."

"That's definitely assault."

"And I think the one guy in their group—who I can't stand, *Brandon*, the one entitled student with the family lawyer—is probably the ringleader. That's exactly the shit he would pull, thinking he's untouchable."

"We can bring them in and can ask them about our case, how it led us to this other crap, but it'll let them know we're on to them."

"We want to hold off on that as long as we can." She pounded her steering wheel. "I'm about fifteen minutes out."

"Forget about that bullying report for a bit and get back here safe and sound, so we can go see how these punks hold up to somebody their own size," he snapped. "This whole thing just pisses me off."

"You and me both," she said.

She hung up and continued downtown to the station. When she pulled into the rear parking lot, she was a little bit calmer but knew she'd get riled up as soon as she saw Rodney. Some things were just too shitty to even think of people doing, and then they surprised you and did something even worse.

As she walked in, Rodney was busy talking with the others in the team. He looked up at her, smiled. "You seem a little bit calmer."

"Not really. I still can't believe they think they can do that to people. It totally pisses me off."

"I wonder if their dean knows anything about it," Colby said, as he joined in.

"I don't know yet," Kate noted. "If you've got any pull with him, maybe give him a call and see if he has any idea what the hell's happening on his own damn campus. Otherwise we'll need to talk to RCMP."

"True." He frowned at that. "I do know the man. Dr. Paul Agress," he admitted. "He's the Dean of the Faculty of Arts. We've attended multiple functions together, but, as you know, it's not our jurisdiction."

"Doesn't matter," she said hotly. "It needs to stop today. And you know it'll be that rich kid Brandon behind most of these."

"Oh, I agree with you there, but he might not know he's even got a problem. Depending on how closely this group of bullies has been holding their cards and how well they're keeping this under wraps, nobody may even know. And for anybody who reported that they'd been pushed or whatever, you know there'll be plenty of people in Brandon's sphere ready to not believe them or for Brandon's crew to shut them down."

"Of course. Particularly if they're naming names now. I think these rich-kid bullies are fairly well-known on campus. They're the wealthy group." She rolled her eyes.

"You don't understand the power that kind of group has," Colby said, "particularly in a peer group like that. Let me talk to him."

Colby headed off, and Kate turned to Rodney. "We can still investigate it though, can't we?"

"No. That's RCMP's job. If it's part of our case, that's a different story, but we can get their assistance, if necessary. That's how this shit works."

"Candy said that it went wrong one time."

That got the attention of Kate's other team members, who all stopped what they were doing and turned toward her. She pulled out the USB key she had in her pocket. "This is her statement. Let me pull it up."

After pulling it up, she printed off copies for everyone and handed them out. "This is what we've got to go on, and, of course, the last thing we need is more work, but these bullies must be stopped."

"It may be more work," Rodney said, "but this is all about the job. Because, if they've killed somebody, that's a whole different story. I'll contact the RCMP and bring them in on this. I have a friend in the unit."

Lilliana added, "And I'll call Reese. Some jobs take priority over others."

"Good." Kate sighed loudly. "I'm not convinced it's not the same story."

Her team looked at her in surprise.

She explained further. "I don't know that it's connected to the bike that went down with Sally Hardgens at that intersection recently. Candy said that she had seen a bunch of people gathered there, but she couldn't really remember about our red-hoodie student. Yet Candy was honestly rattled. I told her that I would talk to her later, but she said her group, the six of them, didn't have anything to do with the killing of our latest victim."

"And you believe her?"

"I don't know who to believe anymore"—Kate raised both hands in frustration—"because I can so see that entitled asshole pulling a stunt like this with injured or disabled people. He would consider it a complete lark, and Candy was very convincing. As to the rest of it, I don't know. And where is the motive?"

"Power," Lilliana said. "The *perfect race* mentality. Also an abusive personality."

Kate nodded. "Ah, … that works for me. If that gives us

the right to get in there and to dig a little deeper into his life, I'm all for it. I sure as hell hope we find some dirt too." At that, she sat down at her computer. "Rodney, did you run any of those witness names we had for priors?"

"Reese pulled them. Found a couple parking tickets. One student was picked up for possession of drugs, and another one had a couple workplace accidents about four years ago. But nothing that really sparks in terms of killing the cyclist."

"Right. So, with five annual deaths, same place, same weekend yearly, why would somebody wait a long time to kill?"

"Because it's not about the time," Owen offered. "Opportunity maybe? They didn't have access or because they didn't know what to do or how to do it, and it took him that long to plan it?"

She nodded. "All of those work, I guess. The question really is, was this premeditated, or was it just an off-the-cuff decision?"

"Well," Andy added, "if it weren't for the bullet hole in her head, I would say it was an accident. Short of the coroner saying something about it, we don't really have any reason to think that the car did anything more than bump her, if it made any contact with her at all. And it's looking more like she bumped him."

Kate nodded at that. "You know what? This one, Candy, she was supposed to attack a blind woman," she said, with a frown. "This group of *upstanding* college students picked out that victim for her."

At that, Lilliana stepped forward and stared at Kate, incredulous.

"Maybe that unintended victim was protecting herself

from them. You know? Like fighting back. Candy attacked somebody healthy instead of that blind woman, made it look like an accident. Candy was bawling her head off over the whole thing. Did she knock somebody over? Yes, I think so. Did she help them up and apologize afterward? Maybe. Was all of this because this group was pressuring Candy to be as bad as them? Possibly. I have no idea. They're all entitled rich kids, all a brick short of a load."

"They're creepy for sure. It comes with that upper-class-privilege personality," Owen said quietly from the side.

She looked over at him and smiled. "And you're right there—the privilege, the lifestyle, the wealth. They just ooze arrogance."

"We've all met that kind," Owen agreed. "But we can't afford to piss them off and their rich parents with fancy attorneys, until we get some corroborating information. Plus, we don't want to tip off this group of bullies, or they'll be lawyered up so damn fast that you'll have a hard time getting anything out of them."

Kate nodded. "Absolutely, he's already threatened that over routine witness questions."

Just then, Colby returned to the bullpen, a frown on his face. "I spoke to Paul. They have had a couple complaints about a gang of kids from his Faculty of Arts, running around and knocking people over, but, when nobody would come forward to make any definitive statements about it, it was pushed to the side. Nobody seemed to get seriously hurt, and no one wanted to talk to the UBC Legal Department or to the RCMP, so it was never reported beyond Paul." They all just silently looked at him. Colby shrugged. "It's a university campus, full of kids, plenty of them drunk or loaded half the time. A lot of them make poor decisions.

We'll need a whole lot more to go on, if we're to get very far before they're tipped off."

Lilliana said quietly from behind them, "So, we all agree that we need to stop this."

"But we also can't forget about everything else on our docket," Colby said. "These guys are shitty. I agree. But we also have a killer out there."

"We have more than one this team is working on," Owen said. "We need to keep focused on what's hot and move when we can. This is a great sideline and something that we all really want to work on, but just because these guys are shits doesn't mean they get to take our priority and divert our attention."

Colby shook his head. "Don't forget that we have Reese and two assistants." He raised a hand before he heard the usual comments. "Yeah, yeah, yeah. We're shorthanded. We all need more help. Keep your priorities, people."

It was a hard truth, but one that Kate had to listen to nonetheless, because they were right. Only so much anybody could do at any one time, and, although she had intimated that these guys may have killed someone with their bullying, she didn't have any proof. And that was bothersome in itself. She didn't want these guys to get away with anything—rich daddies and rich attorneys notwithstanding—but she didn't have anything on them at this point that would do anything but get their knuckles rapped.

Kate looked over at the others and nodded. "What I don't want is to see Brandon's group just get a suspension for a few days. It should be much more serious than that, or it's not worth doing."

"She's right," Rodney said. "A slap on the wrist will just empower entitled assholes like this. We'll have to work that angle as we can."

Kate agreed. "Let me get back to the accident on the corner."

"Accident?" Rodney asked, with a wry smile.

She frowned. "I don't know why I keep thinking of it that way."

"Maybe it is an accident, as far as the auto collision is concerned. But did somebody *accidentally* shoot her in the head?" he asked. "Unless somebody was out shooting for fun, not intending to hit anyone, in that case, it's possible that it could have been an accident."

She frowned. "Let's wait until we get the forensics for that."

He said, "It doesn't feel like an accident to me."

"No, but it doesn't really feel like a regular murder either." She frowned, thought more about that, then shook her head. "I don't even know what I'm saying at this point. Right now there's too much going on in my head."

"Focus." Rodney dropped off the report that he had printed for her. "This has the police histories on all the people on the scene. Take a look, and see if anything pops for you."

She sat here with her coffee and perused the reports. Like Rodney had said, a few small hits but nothing major, nothing that even showed any older trauma that could account for this. That didn't mean that one of these bullies didn't have something else going on in their world or that they hadn't waited all this time to get back at somebody, but nothing really got her attention. She kept reading and noted there wasn't a report on the victim herself. With that, she turned on her computer and brought it up.

Sally Hardgens had lived in Vancouver for over twenty-one years. *Wow,* Kate thought. *Either college kids look five years younger than their age or maybe this was a sign that Kate was growing ever older.* She shook her head at that. Sally was in the first year of her master's program in chemistry, and she apparently wanted to be a biochemist. At that, Kate gave a silent whistle, thinking, what a shame she was killed because anybody with the brains to pursue that field could really do some good in the world. And this woman was in the prime of her life.

Checking further, Kate couldn't find any campus records to indicate any black marks against Sally. Everything indicated she was a model student. Of course being a model student came with its own perils too because not everybody was a fan.

Of course killing them wasn't exactly the most common way of snubbing them.

Kate kept going through everything she had on the victim, then tossed the report on her desk in disgust. "Nothing on our victim to speak of either. At least nothing that's showing up."

"Good," Rodney acknowledged. "I mean, it's not good in the sense that random killings are much harder to solve. But what if somebody was just going after anybody who happened to be at that corner?"

"So, wrong time, wrong place. Not about the victim but about the location. If so, then we go back to the history of that particular spot." With that, she brought up all the reports on the other accidents in the area. "Here are those other four cases you mentioned."

"But they weren't all in the same block," Rodney said. "So does our killer think it would be okay to move it to a new location?"

"I don't know. Somebody is doing something here, and we just haven't figured out how or why … just yet."

"No."

"But we have to consider these other cases"—Kate tapped her monitor—"because at least this one was very similar."

"Which one? In what way?" Owen asked.

"Listen to this, from an earlier death in that area. According to observers, this woman just collapsed in front of the car. The driver wasn't charged because there was absolutely no evidence that his vehicle caused mortal injuries, and it was an *undetermined* cause of death. She died at the scene—no signs of obvious trauma. It was initially thought the car itself had been the weapon, but no forensic evidence was found there. No hair. No blood. No skin cells. No nothing. The coroner also said that, due to the circumstances, he couldn't confirm natural causes either. In the end, he had no way to say how she died. He did run a tox screen, and it came back negative. No drugs. No alcohol."

The others looked at Kate, and she shrugged.

Andy returned to the bullpen, with a hot cup of coffee, catching the last part. "That makes no sense. If they're connected, how did she die?"

"That's the thing." Lilliana frowned, looking over Kate's shoulder at this earlier report. "Her heart just stopped, or it was stopped for her, and we don't know how. They examined her on scene and ran a tox screen, but no autopsy was done."

At that, Kate whistled. "So if no autopsy was done, and she died at the scene, it should have been just put down to natural causes." She shook her head. "But they didn't do that either." Noting Smidge had signed the report, she picked up the phone and called his office. When he answered, as cranky and as testy as always, she smiled because that was a man after her own heart. Being bitchy just made her happy. "It's Kate Morgan," she said in a snappy voice.

"I've got nothing for you. If you'd stop sending bodies down here, I could actually get to them."

"I hear you. Five years ago was another vehicular accident with a bike rider. Not the same block, just down a little bit farther."

"Yeah, what about it?"

"No cause of death," she said.

"What the hell has that got to do with me?"

"At the time, the investigators initially thought it was impact with the vehicle, but you found no obvious trauma to the body, right?"

"Right. I remember that case. That one puzzled me too."

"So you could pull up nothing for it?"

"Well, if I said that, I said that," he said in a cranky tone.

"Right, I get it. So, how is it that somebody dies from absolutely no sign of death?"

"The heart stops," he snapped. "It happens."

"But it wasn't a heart attack?"

"No, and sometimes it happens like that. For one reason or another, we just don't really know."

"She had no underlying condition, but her heart stopped, and she just keeled over for no reason. That's the best we could come up with?" Kate asked.

"It's an open case, I believe."

"It's not closed in the sense that no cause of death was identified, so it hasn't been closed because you didn't decide if it was from *unnatural* causes."

"I couldn't say either way. When I was pressured to put something down, that's what I chose to put down."

"Interesting," she murmured.

"Don't go calling me on that one," he snapped. "On this one, however, I found a cause of death."

"So, do we know that the hole in the back of her head caused her death?"

"Yes. It goes right into her brain."

"So, theoretically, could she have ridden a little bit forward, even with that in her head?"

"Yes," he said.

"How far?"

"I don't know. Probably up to fifty, sixty, even seventy meters. I mean, we've had people walk into the hospital with knives sticking out of their skulls. So the self-preservation ability of the human body is amazing. Our cyclist could easily have been shot way down the road, and, not knowing what the hell happened to her, she faded more and more as she got to that intersection."

"Do you know for sure that the vehicle did not cause her death?"

"Yes," he said, without hesitation. "It did not cause her death."

"Fine, because we have the driver. He came in and confessed."

"Confessed to what? Hitting her?"

"Well, no, not quite hitting her. He said he was at the intersection, stopped, and she was there in front of him and just kind of collapsed."

"And of course, the fine upstanding citizen that he was, he hopped out and immediately administered aid and called 9-1-1."

"No, of course not. He took off, citing the line of traffic behind him."

"Sometimes I hate people," Smidge said.

"I think our job gives us a little more license to hate people," she said quietly.

"Nah, I'd probably still hate people anyway." Then he hung up.

She chuckled. "He's in fine form today."

"He doesn't like being called out on an old case, never has," Rodney said. "He gets quite snarky about it, but you seem to get along with him just fine. Why is that?"

She turned to him. "Why not?"

He shrugged. "Can't say that he and I ever hit it off that well."

"Nothing to hit off. He's the guy you got to hit against."

He looked at her, his gaze narrowing, as he studied her. "Seriously? You go in there aggressive?"

She shrugged. "He'll be that way regardless. If you can't give as good as you get, he'll walk all over you."

"*Great.* Here I've been trying to be a nice guy and tiptoe around him, while you go in there, like a bowling ball."

"Yep," she said cheerfully, "knock him right over. He talks to me. We talk to each other. We don't have any bullshit back and forth, and he appreciates it."

"Well, I'll be damned. I've been handling all those grouchy assholes over there wrong this whole time. Who knew?" He shook his head and returned to his computer screen, while she sat here, chuckling beside him.

"Doesn't help much though on that one earlier case." Kate got up and started two separate whiteboards, one with the bullies and one with this accident and, at the bottom of that one, she added the other accidents annually for the past five years. She put up pictures and reports and a summary of all the dates. Then she looked at it, shrugged. "Not a whole lot here."

"You've got multiple cases there and nothing to even begin to fill the board," Lilliana said. "That's how these cases end up cold in the first place."

"Yeah, I hear you. I'm doing my best to make sure it doesn't happen to this one."

Colby walked in again, took one look at the empty second board and frowned.

She raised one hand. "Don't say it. I know nothing's up there."

"A few things are. I remember a couple of those accidents," he muttered. "There was some consternation among us because we didn't end up with a definitive cause of death. Families really struggle with that. They need to know what happened, so they can work through it and move on. When you can't do that, it's really hard on them."

"So what do you do?" Kate asked.

Colby shrugged. "You make it a little more general, a little less easy to deal with, but you give them closure."

She frowned. "In this current case, the young woman has a hole from some projectile. Smidge didn't say bullet, and he didn't find it in her head. As a matter of fact, it's not there at all."

"What? It went in and didn't come back out?"

She shook her head. "No, it didn't."

"Ice," Owen said immediately.

She turned, looked at him, and frowned.

He continued. "We had a case like that not too long ago. This guy was making ice bullets, and they can kill people. By the time we got to the autopsy, the ice bullets had, of course, dissolved, and nobody could find anything. Maybe run it and see if there's a history somewhere with it."

Inspired by even the thought of having something to check out, Kate sat back down again at her desk and immediately searched for murder cases involving ice bullets.

Meanwhile Colby walked over and studied the boards. "I see you got the bullying kids up here."

"Yep." She spoke to him, not even turning to face him. "As long as I've got the kids up there, I won't forget about them."

"You've got a long-ass memory. I can't imagine you forgetting about anything."

"You'd be surprised. I try not to, but, once in a while, I mess up."

With that, he turned and walked out.

When she came up with two cases, one was caused by dry ice, she turned to the other one. She whistled. "Look at that. Owen, you're right on target."

"What did you find?" he asked.

"About ten years ago, a kid on campus was killed. They were all making ice pellets and using BB guns. This one ended up shooting himself in the head and dying."

"He shot himself? That's in the report?" Rodney asked Kate.

"According to the eyewitnesses, yes."

"I wonder if those eyewitnesses would change their story now." Rodney looked over at her.

Her eyebrows shot up. "It is at the university again."

"Which brings it back to a connection that we can't ignore. And that's not our jurisdiction."

She tapped her fingers on the keyboard aimlessly, as she thought about it. "It was a long time ago though, ten years.

So, why now?" She turned to face her team. "If we're working on a revenge theory, why so long afterward?"

"Maybe our fictional killer was a younger brother, or maybe it was a family member who didn't live here, or maybe it has absolutely no connection," Lilliana said, trying to bring their musings back to ground zero.

Kate looked over at her. "A serial killer is motivated by something known though—at least to him. And we need to find that motivation. *And* we have five annual deaths, which is suspicious, and, if murders, done by the same person, is the definition of a serial killer."

"Maybe," Lilliana said, "and we'll follow the leads, but let's make sure we stick to the line of truth and not fiction."

"But fiction is so much more normal," Kate said. "All this reality, it's way worse than fiction. Nobody can make this shit up."

And, with that, she turned around and did some more research.

IF SIMON THOUGHT the damn enhanced sense of smell was bad, the noise in the back of his ears was driving him nuts. He had cut his usual day short and, once home, started right away on a heavy weights workout in his spare bedroom, burning his muscles, until he was in a hard-core sweat in an effort to ignore the white noise in his ears. But it seemed like the more he tried to ignore the background noise, the more he focused on it. And the more he focused on it, the louder it got.

Finally he cried out, "Stop! For crying out loud, stop. Stop."

When a knock came on the door, he groaned and looked

through the tiny window to see it was the doorman. "Harry, what's the matter?" he asked, as he opened the penthouse elevator door.

Harry gave him a smile. "Parcel came for you." He handed it over.

"You could have called me. I would have come down."

"I considered it, but I saw you come up, so I was afraid that you might not be feeling so well."

"I've got this damn ringing in my ears. It's pissing me off."

"Oh, my dad had tinnitus. It was really, really a terrible thing. It drove him crazy."

"Yeah, that's what it feels like, but it just started today, so I don't know what it could be. But it's got me spun out very quickly." He stood here in his sweatshirt and track pants, heaving, as he accepted the parcel from him. "I didn't order anything."

"I didn't know that, but it's got your name on it."

"*Great.* I sure as hell hope it's not from Caitlyn."

Harry frowned, as he looked at it.

Of course it's from Caitlyn. "Did she pay you to bring it up?"

"No, no, no, no." Harry held up his hands and backed farther into the elevator, the only place he could go. "Sorry, sir. If you want me to take it away, I will."

Simon shook his head. "I'll deal with it. I've told her to leave me alone, but she's been pretty insistent."

"You were quite the number for a while. She probably wants to rekindle it."

"Yeah, well, what she pulled after we were done means I'm not at all interested in rekindling that craziness."

Harry gave him a conspiratorial grin. "Got it. Did you

get any food, or do you need me to order something for you? You'll need some protein after a workout."

"Yeah, I was just going to have a shake. This ear thing is really bugging me."

"There's a really good little Portuguese place that just opened a couple blocks from here."

"Portuguese?" He stopped, looked at Harry. "I don't know that I even would recognize Portuguese food."

"It's good. They've got some great dishes there."

"Like what?" he asked.

"It's hard to even describe, but lots of seafood, sausage, rice. Some great pastries. You could order in, if you didn't want to go anywhere."

"Yeah, but I should get out more, and who knows? That might help my ears."

"Think about it. Then come on downstairs. If you're interested, I'll give you the address. It's good. Trust me on that."

"You haven't steered me wrong on food yet," he said, with a smile.

"Nope, not when it comes to food." Harry patted his very ample belly. "And don't let my wife see you working out. She'll never leave me alone."

At that, Simon burst out laughing. "I hear you. The good news is, you're already safely married, so nobody else can nab you."

"She would probably say that she'll put me up for sale, if I don't start listening to her."

"Nah, you're too precious, and I know without a doubt that she believes that."

"Hey, we're twenty-four years now this weekend." His smile beamed.

"Good for you," Simon said. "Not many can say that. Congrats." He waved, closed the elevator door, headed back inside, then dropped the parcel on the kitchen counter.

"What the hell are you up to, Caitlyn?" he said out loud.

And he was sincerely happy to hear Harry's news about his anniversary because he really liked the guy. Ever since Simon had moved into the place, Harry had been polite, not overly subservient, yet not too familiar. Just the perfect balance so Simon could be friendly, yet not feel like he had to put himself out and be overly so, especially if he was in a shitty mood. It was simple enough to give him a hand wave. It's not like Harry would take offense, as some of Simon's friends would.

Grabbing a knife, Simon slashed open the tape on the side of the package, and, when he opened the box, he found a very expensive bottle of wine nestled inside. "What the hell?" He noted it was the same wine they had shared on one of their more intimate evenings, when they were celebrating, probably like six months together or something. Then he stopped, frowned for a moment, and winced.

"The night I asked her to marry me." He stared at it. The last thing he wanted was to touch it. He groaned and sent her a text. **Thanks for the gift, but no thanks.**

She immediately called him. "Hey, it was just a *thank you*, for finding my nephew."

He hesitated at that. "You're welcome for that, but you don't have to send expensive gifts like this."

"I just wanted to remind you of a better day," she said quietly. "I know I was shitty to you. I wasn't thinking of how it would feel."

"Yeah. It doesn't bring back happy memories because you gave me six months of shit afterward. Thank you. That's enough now. So leave off, will you?"

"Hey, what if I want to see you again and just be friends, instead of this nastiness between us?"

He sighed, loud enough for her to hear it.

She said, "Come on. I'm not trying to get back into a relationship with you or anything. It just, it feels wrong to have this animosity between us."

He snorted.

"I know. I know," she cried out. "It's my fault. I did this. I get it, but I'm trying to undo it."

"Some things you can't undo," he said quietly.

She groaned. "You don't have to be so literal. Obviously I can't go back and erase everything that I did. I wish I could, dammit. I really wish I could. But I can't, so I'm doing the next best thing and trying to make amends. Just let me make amends."

"Fine. You've already thanked me. You've now sent a gift, and that's enough, okay?"

"Seriously, you really don't even want to hear my voice anymore?"

"Do you remember the shit you pulled? My keys that you gave away and the tapes? The tapes you have not returned."

"I told you that I deleted them."

"Yeah, you told me a lot of things, but how am I supposed to believe you?" She hesitated, and he went on. "You blackmailed me into helping find your nephew with those tapes, and then you told me that you didn't have them anymore."

"I never took any. It seemed wrong."

"At what point in time did you think it was wrong?" he asked. "We were in my house, in my bed, and you were taping my nightmares. Thanks for that. I can never trust you again. So, if I can't trust you, I don't want you in my world."

"Oh," she whispered. "I never thought of it like that."

"No, of course not."

She said, "I would have done anything to help get my nephew home."

"Yeah, have you looked after him since?"

"No. My sister won't even let him out of her sight for a minute."

"I wonder why?"

"It wasn't my fault," she said.

He just waited for reality to seep in.

"Look. Okay, I didn't keep as close an eye on him as I should have. I get that, and, believe me, I'll be trying to convince my sister that I'm sorry for the rest of my life. But, at the same time, I don't want to be punished for it forever."

"Nobody wants to be punished forever," he said quietly, "but what you also have to understand is that some things are forgivable, and some things are not. And, sure, all the shit you pulled on me since we split up, it's forgivable, but I can't trust you, and I don't want people I can't trust in my world." And, with that, he hung up.

Of course it made him feel like shit afterward, but how else was he supposed to get the idea across that she wasn't coming back into his life—no matter what? It didn't make him feel any better to know that he was being a shit about it, but the message did seem to finally get through to Caitlyn.

Plus, what he'd said was true. If he couldn't trust someone, they wouldn't be invited into his world. And, after what she'd said about the tapes, yet another version, he still wasn't sure she was being truthful.

But he wasn't certain how the hell he was supposed to

find out. It's not like he could ask her for the tapes again, since she'd just say she didn't have them. And again, that just reinforced the fact that he couldn't trust her. The simple act of speaking to her would be seen as, *Let's get back together.*

He sighed, as he sat here for a long moment, staring at the bottle of wine. Then he brightened. He quickly changed and decided he'd have a shower later. For now, he would walk downstairs, maybe go for a run, and stop for takeout at the new little place around the corner after all.

With that in mind, he grabbed the bottle of wine, still beautifully dressed up with ribbons, and carried it downstairs. When he saw Harry, Simon walked over, put the expensive bottle of wine on the desk in front of him. "Harry, this is for you and your wife. Happy anniversary to you both."

Harry looked at him in shock, staring at the wine in awe. "Oh, my God, that's got to be a couple hundred bucks."

Simon snorted. "It's a hell of a lot more than that, but wine is only good for drinking. Please don't just put it in the cupboard and admire it. I want you and your wife to enjoy it, every last drop." And, with that, Simon lifted his hand in a wave and headed out. In the distance, he could still hear Harry's profuse thanks ringing in his ears, which was a nice change compared to the noise that had been driving him batty earlier. But thankfully that seemed to have stopped, and he felt so much better.

As he raced outside, he picked up the pace and dashed off into the night. Almost immediately his sense of smell came alive, like a wave of some strong sweat or body odor slamming into his brain. Shuddering, he ran faster and faster, and the smell just seemed to chase him down the street. He ran until the demons could no longer get him.

CHAPTER 9

KATE WENT FOR judo practice after work. It's almost as if her instructor had seen that she had been playing it safe each and every time, and tonight he decided to kick it up a notch. But he hadn't forewarned her, and, by the time she was done, she laid on the mat, gasping for air.

He reached a hand down and pulled her to her feet. "That was much better."

She shook her head. "That was deadly."

But she felt like a million bucks by the time she'd made it home. Exhausted, worn out, and basically brain-dead, but her heart hummed with joy, her muscles were pumped with power, and even her skin had cooled down and felt enlivened. She didn't know how the hell it worked, but she felt better than she had in a very long time. It didn't make a whole lot of sense, but she'd take it because, dammit, something good must be found in all this.

As she walked in, she headed straight for the shower and, when she came back out with a towel wrapped around her, she was hungry. Except she had yet to go grocery shopping. No food was in her house, and, although she could pick up food, the last thing she wanted to do was even get dressed, much less leave again. So ordering in was her only option.

When her phone buzzed, she groaned, then looked at it to see a message from Simon, saying he was on his way over.

She shook her head at that. "What if I don't want to see you?"

The trouble was, she did want to see him. She hated to say it—but she had this fear of starting something she would end up getting hurt over. A fear of starting something she couldn't even begin to open up enough to complete. And he had the ability to affect her on a very deep level.

Grabbing a sports bra, a pair of leggings, and a sweatshirt, she dressed quickly. That was as far as she would go. She put her hair into a braid. She padded barefoot to the door, opening it just as he arrived there, preparing to knock. He looked at her attire in surprise. "I just came back from a workout. I'd barely gotten out of the shower when you texted."

"Good, at least *you* got a shower. I feel like I'm running from demons."

"You and me both." She shook her head at not only the synchronicity of his visit but of his wording. "Come on in." Then she stopped, sniffed the air. "Oh, my God, food. What is that?"

"I'm not even sure," he said half apologetically. She frowned at him. He shrugged. "My doorman said that a new Portuguese restaurant had opened around the corner, just a few blocks from my place. So I went for a run and stopped to pick up some takeout, and somehow I ended up here."

She smiled. "And you know what? *Somehow* you ending up here works for me too. After my workout, I needed to eat, but I still haven't bought groceries—and the last thing I wanted to do was go shopping tonight. So takeout delivered by you is perfect."

"It seems so, but, in this case, I had no idea what to order, so it will be an experience," he said, stepping in. "Grab the plates. I'm starving."

She laughed and raced into the kitchen and pulled out a couple plates, while he put the bag on the counter. As he opened it, she watched him rear back. "Is it hot?" she asked, raising an eyebrow.

"Yeah, it's hot, but I've had the weirdest set of symptoms these last few days."

"Are you sick?" She stopped where she was.

He looked over at her. "No, and I'm not contagious."

She shrugged. "It's probably too damn late if you are anyway," she muttered. "That night was probably still within your infectious period, if it's a contagious thing ..."

He snorted at that. "If that's what you call it."

"It is what I call it, but, if you're not sick, all the better."

"I'm not sick at all. When I said *symptoms*, I just meant—" He stopped, hesitated. "Never mind. Just more weirdness."

"So normal for you, so go ahead," she said, bugging him good-naturedly.

He just rolled his eyes at her.

"Come on. Tell me what's up." She pulled out the containers. They had cardboard tops on them, so she had no idea what was inside, and, when she pulled out more, she sniffed the air appreciatively. "Whoa, what an aroma. So what is this anyway?"

"I am not sure, but I think it's chicken in some curry sauce or I don't know." He raised both hands. "All kinds of unknown food is here."

She found an interesting potato dish and an interesting vegetable dish and then meat on skewers, maybe deep-fried. She wasn't even sure, but she quickly loaded up two plates and still quite a bit was left in the containers. "I don't know how much you ordered, but it looks like they were generous."

He nodded. "Honestly, there was a language issue, so we made do with pointing."

She laughed at that. "At least you can probably count on it being authentic."

He shrugged. "I was so damn hungry that it didn't seem to matter."

She nodded. "I hear you there." As she sat down and picked up a forkful, she watched as he leaned over hesitantly and sniffed it. "So tell me. What's going on? You don't normally look like that, when you're about to try new foods."

"My sense of smell is off the wall, as in seriously powerful. And it makes no sense."

"What? Like just suddenly? I don't think that's a symptom of being sick, at least not of anything I've ever heard of before."

"I know it doesn't make any sense."

"I got it." She shrugged. "Sometimes these things don't make any sense."

"Yeah, I know. This one is particularly bizarre." But he dove into the food, forking up the first bite.

"Is your sense of taste affected?" she asked, wondering at the look on his face.

"It's heightened. Everything tastes better."

"But in a good sense?"

"Exactly." He pointed his fork at her. "But my sense of smell is making things worse. Like, I would go down an alleyway and cut through to the other side to save myself going around a block, but the scent of urine just wrecked me, so I had to take the longer route to avoid it."

"Ha. You have a fair bit of experience with alleyways, so your olfactory senses should be used to it."

"I thought so, but, honest to God, the smell was so intense, I couldn't handle it."

She frowned. "Did anything happen? Did you get hit over the head or fall and hit your head? Has anything weird happened that could have caused it somehow?"

He shook his head. "Nothing that I know of."

She hesitated, wondered about asking, and then finally decided to do it. "I might as well ask, since I don't know jack shit about this stuff," she said in her typical style, "but is it psychic?"

He looked at her and then laughed. "Is what psychic?"

"I don't know." Feeling stupid, she glared at him because it was his fault she felt that way. "You're not allowed to laugh at me when I ask questions like that. Remember?"

He smiled. "Right, I forgot that golden rule."

She shrugged. "I don't know about that, but, when you think about it, if I don't ask, I won't get an answer."

"No, you're quite right. Sorry, I shouldn't have laughed at you."

She nodded with grace, even though he continued to grin at her. "So I'm not asking if your nose is psychic but if it could be a symptom of a psychic session or some vision or something."

"I have no idea." He looked surprised. "I didn't even consider that because there's no connection to a person that I can see."

"Right, and I guess that connection thing is what you're all about, isn't it?"

"Well, that and numbers. I keep telling the victims out there in the world that I don't want anything to do with them," he said in a harsh voice.

Her eyebrows went up, as she listened to the tone of his voice. Quietly she spoke. "It's really getting to you, isn't it?"

He slowly put down his fork. "Think about it. You know you can't do anything but sit there and watch as other people suffer in the most terrible ways, and you don't have any way to stop it. You have absolutely no way to get the word out that this unidentified person needs help, and you're just supposed to watch it, like it's a movie or something. Who the hell wants that shit?"

"Yeah, I was pondering that the other night, wondering how you can remain sane with all that going on."

"Who says I'm sane?" He waggled his eyebrows at her.

She rolled her eyes at him. "I already know that you're half crocked, but apparently we're half crocked together," she said, with a sigh.

"So tell me," he wanted to know, "how come you had to go for such a hard workout tonight?"

"This shitty case at work. It's out of our jurisdiction likely but borders on another of our cases. We're stretched kind of thin, what with missing three team members—or at least two for sure." She took a bite, pointing with her fork as she chewed and swallowed. "Although we sort of have an analyst and two assistants, it never seems to be enough. So you know what that means." She sighed.

"Yeah, everybody wants their time. The VPD needs more staff, more detectives, in my opinion, just from watching you putting in the long hours, working on your supposed days off. And this city is big, and you have how many murders on a regular basis?"

"I think there's been, like, what? Twenty-nine already this year." She shook her head. "You'd think we were

Chicago or something."

He smiled. "I get that this is probably more than you're used to, but is there anything you can do about these cases, any leads to follow?"

"If I can prove that they're murders, then maybe, and I've got a witness who said these bullies were involved in something that went terribly wrong. She thinks that the person died, but I don't have any proof of it, and neither does she."

"So it's all hearsay?"

"Even worse, it's hearsay from somebody who's now basically turning on her own group."

"So she's trying to defend herself."

"I think she's trying to protect herself. She says she didn't do anything terrible, but she did do something bad enough, and she's now suffering from the guilt of it."

"I just love the human condition."

"Right." She tilted her head. "We're all so screwed up."

"Hey, speak for yourself," he said.

She smiled. "If you're not screwed up, neither am I, but I'm pretty sure the rest of the world would definitely consider both of us well over the mark."

He shrugged. "No, you're right. You're absolutely right. So there's no hope for us whatever then."

She smiled. "They're attacking people on the campus, innocent and already disadvantaged people. And they're not so much directly attacking, they're more subtle, making it look like an *accident*," she said, with a strong emphasis on the word.

"So what are they doing?"

"Knocking them down. One apparently sent somebody down a set of stairs, and she broke her leg."

"That's pretty shitty."

"Hearsay though, and I'm not even sure who that person is. The campus is saying that nobody ever came forward to report or to complain about that, and I don't know if that's because of being pressured or because these guys are so good at making it all look accidental. You know? Like, it wasn't really them, or the suspicion is there but no proof, so it becomes a case of, 'Gee, I must have tripped and fallen.' She was apparently on crutches already because she had some injury, but I don't even know what that was." She raised both hands in frustration. "It sucks. So this one female was supposed to be part of the group ..."

By the time she finished telling him the rest, he stared at her in shock.

She nodded. "And, on top of that, I'm looking at this death at the intersection, where this one young woman on a bicycle dies in what appears to be an *accident*, except evidence shows some projectile in her head. The autopsy is in progress, but nothing showed up on the scans."

"Wow." Simon sat back, staring at her, as he munched on his dinner. "I'd forgotten what an interesting life you have."

She glared at him. "If it involves standing knee-deep in blood and gore and motives and hate and revenge and shitty people, yeah, it's *interesting* all right."

"It's complicated *and* interesting. I deal with a lot of that too, but in a way that you probably wouldn't expect."

"You've never told me much about what you are involved in." She studied him. "I get that you're rehabbing buildings, but that's all I know about it."

"I do rehab lots of buildings, and all of them have stories." She looked at him in surprise, and he shrugged. "I'm kind of partial to buildings, and the ones I buy—versus the ones I don't—is a combination of a business decision and a heart decision. Sometimes I feel like I have to rescue these buildings."

She stopped and stared, slowly putting down her fork. "Say what?"

He shrugged. "Nobody said I had to be completely logical all the time. Anybody who tells you that these kinds of business decisions aren't also emotional at some level is lying. Whether they lock down that emotion and make it fit some parameter, or whatever they're doing, they're still using their emotions to buy properties. Either because they think they can make money, and that makes them happy, or because they think they can turn it around and steal it from somebody else, also making them happy. In my case, I like to turn them around and make them useful again after years of abuse. And that makes me happy. So it's emotional." And, with that, he picked up a chunk of meat on a skewer and pulled off a piece. "Do you know what this is?"

She looked at it and shrugged. "No, I was waiting for you to try it."

He laughed. "Here goes nothing." And he took a bite off the end of the piece in his hand. His eyebrows shot up immediately, and he smiled at the piece remaining. "I think it's chicken, but, wow, is it ever flavorful."

She immediately picked up her skewer and took a bite. She looked over at him, nodding. "I don't know where you got this from, but it needs to go on my Redial list."

He grinned. "That's only if you're nice to me. Otherwise I'm not telling you where it is."

"That's okay. I'll go talk to Harry myself." His jaw dropped, and she laughed. "Do you really think I'm not on a first-name basis with him by now?"

"Are you bribing my doorman?" He leaned forward, waggling his eyebrows. "And, if you are, maybe it's me you should be bribing."

"I don't have to bribe you, and you should always be friendly with the doorman because they know a lot. People treat servants and staff and the hired help like their slaves, but they don't consider who these people are with at the end of the day and what they have to deal with. You should treat them better than your own family because already they're doing a job for you that they probably didn't want to do in the first place." She pointed her fork at him for added emphasis.

"Hey, I treat mine great," he said.

She glared at him suspiciously.

"I'll have you know that I gave Harry a wonderful bottle of wine today for his anniversary."

"Yeah?" She suspiciously gazed at him. "Why'd you do that?"

"Because it's his anniversary." He looked at her in astonishment.

"Yeah, I get that, but why that bottle of wine?"

He frowned, and then he chuckled. "Because it made me happy?"

She looked at him sideways. "Feels like there's more to it than that."

"And here you go being the detective again. Can't you just leave it as the simple fact that I wanted to give it to him?"

She hesitated and then shrugged. "Since you brought me dinner tonight, I guess I can limit the questioning."

"I'll tell you anyway. Caitlyn sent it to me."

At that, she chewed on her mouthful, as she studied him. He picked up another skewer of meat and eyed it, as if it were a specimen. Or maybe it was Caitlyn he was eyeing. Kate knew of her and knew a bit about that prior relationship of Simon's but not a whole lot. She wasn't sure if jealousy was supposed to come into this or if it was a nonissue, but she felt her heart sinking a little bit. That made her realize that, as much as she tried to appear disaffected, he really was affecting her, and that wasn't necessarily a good thing. She frowned, as she studied her own plate, for lack of anything to say.

He looked over at her, smiled. "She's trying to get back into my life, and I'm avoiding it in a big way."

"Why is that?" She tried to detach her own emotions from this discussion.

"I can't trust her," he said.

She stopped, looked at him, and nodded. "I guess that's a big one for you."

He looked at her in a challenging way. "Isn't it for you?"

She stopped, thought about it. "It's kind of everything, isn't it?"

"It is," he said simply. "If you can't trust people to do the best for you when they can and to not blackmail you or to cheat or to lie or to do all kinds of other shit that Caitlyn has pulled," he said flatly, "nothing is there. If you can't close your eyes and trust that you'll be safe, there's really nothing left."

"And yet this is a new phenomenon for you, isn't it?"

"What do you mean?" he asked, frowning at her.

"Was she not your fiancée?"

He frowned, then nodded. "Did I tell you about that?"

"It came up somewhere along the line," she said.

"Yeah, so that was another part of it. I could no longer trust my judgment either. But she has pulled some pretty ugly shit after we broke up, and I just couldn't let her off the hook on it. As much as I've forgiven her for a lot of it, I can't forgive her for all of it. A part of me wonders if she still thinks she's got some hold over me, though she tells me she doesn't."

"Is she blackmailing you?" Kate stared at him in shock.

"Maybe, she certainly did over her nephew."

"On that point, if it was about saving my brother, and you had the ability to help me, I might blackmail you too," she said succinctly. "Love will do that to us."

He looked at her and slowly nodded. "You know what? That I could accept. And see? You're right upfront about it."

"Hands down, if that had been my brother, I'd have killed for him. If I could have answers anywhere along the line for what happened to him and to find the asshole who did it, I would do whatever it took."

He nodded. "That at least lets me know where you stand. I would never do it unnecessarily. I would never do it for money. I would never do it for power. But ... I would do it for love."

She said quietly, "So, I guess that tells me where we both stand. So the question is, is that a deal breaker?"

He looked at her thoughtfully. "The thing is, in your case—and in the case of Caitlyn's nephew back then—I could understand it because you're right. For love, we do things like that. If I could have blackmailed somebody into saving me all those years ago, I would have done it myself," he said quietly. "It's love, but it's also to save someone who you care about. Even if it's yourself."

She nodded. "That's the thing really. The human psyche

is pretty basic. It's called survival."

THAT WAS THE one thing about Kate that Simon never had to wonder about. She was as direct and as clear-cut as anyone could be. But he also had heard the tremor in her voice when she had talked about her brother. "Just for the record"—he reached across the table and picked up her hand—"I've never yet connected to anything about your brother."

She looked up at him, her gaze searching, and he realized that she probably had wanted to ask that question many times, but it wasn't in her to do so.

He squeezed her fingers gently. "And, yes, if I had anything at all I could tell you, I would, and I promise that, if it ever happens, I will definitely pass on the word."

"Good, not that I believe in any of that stuff."

He smiled as she tossed it off, but he also heard the relief in her voice and saw it on her face. "I get that," he said comfortably, as he settled back. "And I love the fact that you're very direct. It saves time."

"It does, indeed, but most people aren't that way, and many don't appreciate it."

"That's because most people are idiots."

She laughed. "No argument there. So, are you going to tell me what she was blackmailing you about?"

He hesitated and then shrugged. "It's not exactly something that you don't already know."

She frowned. "If I already know, then what's to blackmail?"

"That's the thing. I don't know."

"Meaning?" She looked at him. "You're talking in puzzles."

"Okay. Have I ever had nightmares when I'm sleeping with you?"

"Yep. Have I ever had nightmares when I'm sleeping with you?"

He looked at her in surprise. "Well, yeah."

"It's the life we live. The nightmares catch us when we're subconsciously weak and get in through our lowered defenses, then attack us to the point that we don't even know if we're coming or going."

He sat here and stared.

Kate asked him, "What? Did I say something wrong?"

"No, it's just that forthright honesty that I love so much."

"Good. So what's the blackmail thing?"

"She says that she made recordings of when I was having nightmares. She said she would release them to the public, and that some pretty horrific things were on them."

She stared at him in shock. "Jesus, that's a pretty mean and lowlife thing to do, isn't it?"

"That's Caitlyn for you."

"Did she really record them?"

"See? That's where the confusion comes in. She says she didn't *now*."

"Oh, but she said she did when she needed you to find her nephew?"

"Exactly. She was looking for leverage. I would have helped her anyway, and I did, in fact, try to help her. As it happened, I did connect with him down the road. I didn't do it because of the blackmail, but she thinks I did. So now she's using it. I think she's keeping that in the back of her mind as a weapon."

"Wow, I really don't like this person. It's pretty interesting that she was your choice of a partner."

"Don't even go there. Sometimes you look back on your history, and you wonder what the hell you were thinking." He looked at her. "Isn't there a relationship somewhere in your background where you now wonder what the hell you were doing?"

"Yep, another cop. I knew better—*Don't do it, bad news, stay away*—but, no. Hormones got the best of us. We were jumping in the sack every chance we could get. It wasn't until later that I found out he was married."

At that, Simon winced. "Ah, shit."

"Yep, guess how I found out."

He stared at her and waited.

"The wife came to me. That was a pretty ugly scene. Not doing that again, and I wouldn't have done it in the first place if I'd known. But I also didn't check it out, so it's my bad."

He agreed. "Back to that *people can be people* thing, huh?"

"That's the lesson, isn't it? That people will be people, and it's up to you to protect yourself."

He winced. "And we both learned that the hard way."

"And that's one of the reasons we're good together. But it's also damn scary."

He reached across, grabbed her hand. "But I trust you."

She looked up at him, her thoughts shattered, as she said, "And I trust you. But are we sure this is a good idea?"

He studied her for a long moment, seeing the insecurity and the doubt in her face, and nodded. "Yes, it is."

CHAPTER 10

KATE WOKE IN the middle of the wee hours of the morning to the sound of her phone, the incessant drumbeat rolling through her brain, bringing her exhausted and yet happily humming body to full awareness. She groaned, as she turned over and reached for her phone, noting Simon was still here, had even slept through the buzzing of her cell.

When she answered the call, Rodney said, "Sorry, kiddo. We've got another body."

"*Great.*" She yawned. "Where is it this time?"

He hesitated before answering. "At the university. At one of the off-campus residences."

She bolted upright. "Please tell me that it's not Candy."

"I don't know anything about it. All I got was that we have a body. I'll pick you up in ten."

"*Great,*" she muttered again, and she tossed her phone on the bedside table.

She quickly got dressed, wishing she had time for a shower, but that wasn't to be. Multitasking—brushing her teeth while running a comb through her hair—got her out the door quicker, aware that it would be a very long day. She and Simon had shared one of those nights. They had talked, made love, talked some more, but no talk of plans, no talk of tomorrow, because, for both of them, there was only just today.

She shook her head, as she stepped outside her building, feeling the chill, as a whistling watery breeze came in off the ocean. Rodney arrived five minutes later. She hopped in, shivering, and he immediately reached to turn on the heat.

She shook her head. "I'll be fine." But her teeth were chattering. "Besides it's August for Christ's sake."

He turned and headed out to the university. "These middle-of-the-night calls always get to me."

"Yeah, me too, especially when you said it was close to the university."

"You really think it could be her?"

"If it is, I know who we'll focus on."

He shook his head. "We can't do that."

"I know, but I really want to," she said.

"That's if it's her, and we don't even know that yet. We won't know until we get there. Was she concerned?"

"Not really." Kate shook her head. "She didn't appear to be. She was concerned at some level because she didn't want to tell me anything and said how they'd 'kill her,' but, when I asked her specifically if I should take that wording literally, she shook her head, said she just meant they would be furious. But later Candy had wondered if they'd crossed that line another time. She suggested that she already got blamed for everything because she was the odd man out. She was trying to be somebody she wasn't, somehow just trying to belong, which is why she did what she did. And, when they found out she was quite traumatized over it all, they thought it was hilarious, and that's one of the reasons they were going for pizza that day."

"So they saw the latest accident, or they didn't?"

"No. Candy said they saw the cyclist but just like a casual glance and didn't realize what had happened, until they turned around, and she was on the ground in front of the vehicle."

"Did they say anything about hearing a scream or a thud?"

She paused, looked at him. "I don't think she mentioned anything like that. Those would be things you'd think would be automatic, right? I mean, if you get hit, there'll be a scream of pain, the sound of a crunched bike, so there should be noise. At least the sound of people hitting their brakes."

"Yet the driver said he was already basically stopped, so there wasn't any squealing of *his* brakes." Rodney turned off Valiant Street and headed up East 1st Ave.

"You always like going this way, don't you?"

"Yeah, I just like the road better. You can move along at a decent clip here."

She shrugged. "We'll get there soon enough." She closed her eyes.

"Did you get any sleep last night?"

"Hell no." She yawned. "But don't go bugging me about it because, if you're not bugging me to get laid, you're bugging me to get some sleep."

"You could try both."

"If we didn't have all these midnight calls"—she glared at him—"I would."

He nodded. "Got it."

"What about you?" she asked.

"I slept for a bit."

"You realize that's what the rest of the world is doing, while we're out here running around, looking like idiots."

"Hopefully we don't look like idiots. That would ruin my stellar reputation."

She snorted at that. "Just keep thinking that."

He glanced at her. "Grumpy much?"

"No, I've just been doing a lot of thinking."

"Nothing wrong with thinking, as long as you keep it reasonable and in perspective."

"Whatever the hell that means." She yawned again.

As they approached the boulevard, she looked at the intersection and sighed.

"I know it'll be hard every time you drive past this now," Rodney said.

"I do that already at a bunch of places in town," she said quietly. "It seems like, when you've already seen so much violence at one particular spot, you approach it gently."

He nodded. "I do the same thing."

"We know the city so well because we're in it constantly, and we're driving around, dealing with the aftereffects of shitty people. I'm still struggling to believe these kids are out there, picking on people who already have enough challenges, just because they can. Whatever happened to helping people just because they can instead? Why is that not a thing?"

"I don't know. When we get them in for questioning, you can ask."

"I don't think they'll give a crap." She shook her head.

"These rich kids, I'm sure they'll probably grow up one day. Or ... do they ever grow up, you think?"

"I don't think so. They probably just become arrogant rich entitled adults."

As he pulled up outside the apartment building they'd been dispatched to, she stared at the big building in front of her, and she just knew. "Damn. It just had to be this one."

"Is this the apartment where Candy lives?"

"Yeah. It'll be her. I just know it."

"Hey, don't go there. Lots of people live in a building this size, so it might not be her. Remember that."

She nodded. "I know. I know. I'm trying to be objective."

They got out to find cops everywhere already, hanging around, making sure that nobody came or went.

When Kate questioned one, the cop shook his head. "No, everybody is still sleeping, so we were told to leave them be."

"Good. We might get a little privacy for a bit."

"Not likely. Somebody knows, and the word will spread like wildfire. Not to mention these emergency vehicles and all."

He was right. She just didn't want to deal with it. She opted for the stairs, even though Rodney had been looking for the elevator, but she shook her head. "I need to wake up and to get sharp in a hurry, and exercise will do it."

"It'll kill me." He groaned, as he patted his stomach. "Too much pizza for dinner."

"You had pizza?" she said enviously.

"I live for pizza. When did you last have any?"

"Not for way too long. Simon keeps insisting on all these weird and wonderful foods, but somehow a good old-fashioned pizza never seems to make his list. Of course when I'm alone, I could get pizza, but then I'd feel guilty, since it's hardly a healthy food group."

"Hey, don't go knocking my pizza," he protested. "I live for that shit."

"Ha, we're too cliché."

As they finally got to the fourth floor landing, and she opened the door, he asked, "How did you know it was on this floor?"

She stopped, looked at him. "Is it?"

He nodded slowly.

She turned her grim face down the hallway. "This is also Candy's floor."

They headed down the hall; a security detail stood outside one of the doors. She walked past them into Candy's room and looked, but it wasn't Candy. She shook her head in shock. "That's an interesting twist."

At her side, Rodney whispered, "What's the matter?"

"It's the other female from the bully group. It's not Candy." He looked at her, startled, and she nodded.

"So this is her apartment? This is Candy's place?" he asked.

Kate nodded, then stopped, hesitated. "You know something. I'm not so sure about that. This is where I interviewed Candy yesterday though."

She walked over to the desk, looking to see if anything there identified it as Candy's. But nothing was here. As a matter of fact, it looked like it had been completely cleaned out. She turned toward Rodney. "It looks like Candy has left. Everything is missing."

"Everything except her friend," Rodney said in a hard tone.

Kate frowned at the crumpled body on the floor, facedown. The woman's hands were to the side, as if to break her fall as she'd fallen forward. Only she hadn't broken anything.

Smidge walked in, took one look at Kate, and groaned. "You again?"

"Yep, it's me. You don't have too many choices when it comes to detectives."

"Nope, and you keep bringing me the best cases."

"Glad you think so because I have a hunch this will be another one."

He sat back on his haunches, before he looked down at the woman. "What do you mean?"

Kate explained the little bit she knew.

"Oh, shit, well, this will be a fun one. So she's part of the wealthy group then?"

"Potentially, yes. I'm not exactly sure because my understanding yesterday was that this was Candy's room. But, if it was, then she should be here at this hour of the night. So I don't know where Candy has gone." She turned, walked through the little bit of a room to the bathroom, then came back and shook her head. "Everything is cleaned out."

"Exams are potentially over, depending on their schedule," Smidge said.

"I know, but she didn't make any mention of leaving, and this is not what her place looked like when I was here yesterday."

"You were just here?"

"Technically yesterday at this point, I guess. I was looking for more information on the woman killed at the intersection."

"Right, so this is one of the witnesses?"

"Yeah. She was part of the group who went on to the pizza parlor, instead of waiting around for questioning." He looked at her sideways, but she shrugged. "They didn't seem to think they would be needed right away, so why waste time with some fatal accident scene, when they could be sitting inside and enjoying life."

He shook his head, as if to say, *What the hell?*

A sentiment she completely agreed with. She waited and

watched, as he did a quick visual on their victim.

"No obvious cause of death. We'll get her on the table, and we'll find out what's up."

Kate stepped back to give him space and then asked, "Anything on that projectile in the head on Sally Hardgens?"

"Yeah, what about it?" He turned to face her.

"Ice?"

Looking surprised, he replied, "Yeah, that's what we're looking at. Water in the brain cavity. How'd you know?"

"A case about ten years ago. Something similar."

"Interesting. I'll look it up."

"Good, thanks." As the coroner went about his work, she turned to look at Rodney and the rest of the room and asked, "Do you see anything here?"

"Nothing but an empty room, which in itself is suspicious, given that you just spoke with her."

"She surely couldn't have taken everything," she said.

"I don't know," he murmured, swinging his arm around the room. "If not, she's sure given it a good old college try."

Even she winced at the unfortunate phrasing. "What the hell is going on here?" she asked quietly.

"You didn't want it to be Candy, and that's what you got, but the problem now is that it's somebody else."

"It is, indeed," she whispered, then shook her head. "And now we still need to track down Candy." She stopped and hesitated; then she looked intently at the floor where the dead woman was. "I know forensics will get to all this, but look." She pointed at the carpet.

"What about it?" Rodney asked, Smidge listening in.

"It looks like a double stain," she said quietly.

Rodney bent beside her. "What do you mean?"

"It looks like old blood atop new blood."

"Not necessarily old on new, but they are definitely both pretty fresh."

"Yeah, we need to check Paula's room." She stopped, hesitated, and looked back at him. "What if—" She winced, hating to even say this. "What if it's two separate bloodstains?"

SIMON WOKE UP, then rolled over and reached out an arm to tuck Kate up close against him, only to find the bed was empty. He groaned, as he sat up and stared around. "Kate?" he called out.

But the empty hollowness to the room meant she was gone. He didn't even remember hearing her leave, and just that lack of awareness drove him nuts. He used to be extremely alert, always aware, and wary of being woken up. He was always the first to leave somebody's apartment, often sneaking out on them. But he sure as hell wasn't used to being snuck out on himself.

Disgruntled, he got up, had a quick shower, intentionally avoiding the soaps and shampoos, but wondering, he opened one of the bottles and sniffed it, then the others, but each was a neutral scent. He smiled at that because it was so Kate; no time for fripperies, as she would call it. Yet most women would say that it was something in the shampoo, so why not? But, no, not Kate. She was all about getting to work and about forgetting all that feminine stuff.

He smiled because it was just so her, and that again brought him back to the fact that she was incredibly honest, whether he liked what came out of her mouth or not. She was there 100 percent, and that just meant that she must have been called into work. He got dressed, looking around for a shaver or razor, and saw absolutely nothing here he could even borrow. "We'll have to fix that," he said.

Then he wondered how she'd handle it if he moved in a razor at least. Probably not well but then it was also way the hell more comfortable at his place, so he should just move her over there. At that thought he almost froze. It's not that he was getting old, but he did like his comforts, and his bed versus her place was a hell of a different story. He wasn't a snob by any means, but his body certainly appreciated his high-end mattress, and his bones appreciated that hot shower with double sprays and the rain showerhead.

But was it fair to ask her to move in with him? He figured that he would probably get a pretty damn fast answer of *hell no*. Because it would be a commitment that she didn't want anything to do with. He wasn't sure if it was commitment or fear of the future that would get to her. She had this notion that she didn't do relationships, and she was constantly mumbling about it too. He'd heard her and had ignored it because what was he supposed to say to something like that?

If this were just a quick lay for immediate gratification, well, he didn't find anything quick about it. He didn't want there to be anything quick. He wanted it to be a whole lot more than that; yet sometimes he didn't know quite what the hell he wanted either. Groaning, he walked into the kitchen and winced, when he saw the instant coffee on the counter.

"Hell no." He stared at it. Shaking his head, he put away the food they had left out in a disarray last night, when things got more than a little interesting. He quickly cleaned up, then walked out the door, locking up behind him.

As he headed downstairs, an older woman looked at

him, saw where he had come from, and her face lit up. "So, you're her new boyfriend, are you?"

"Who?" he asked, as if not understanding what she was asking. Old busybodies were not his favorite people.

"It's a good thing. Kate is a good person, and she needs somebody."

"Oh? And why is that?" He studied her quietly.

"Because she does so much for everybody else."

"Do you know her well?"

"Oh, I know her, though not as well as I'd like to, but only because she keeps everybody at arm's length. People who do that are just afraid to get hurt more than they already have been."

The truth struck him in the gut, and he thought about the older woman's words, well after he'd left and started his day, because it was true. After loving her brother and her mother, only to be abandoned by one and then blamed for the loss of the other, Kate had kept herself behind a wall. Even in the relationship with the married cop, she took the blame. Now she preferred to keep herself safely away from everybody. So, in that way, the old lady was quite correct, and it spoke to how well she knew Kate.

Kate would want time and space and everything that was her own.

In all of his previous relationships, they'd all been very willing to move into his place, as it was obviously high-end, secure, peaceful, private, and gorgeous, with a view to match. There had never been any discussions about it. Kate's place, while clean and neat, was a cramped little dump by his standards, but it was hers, and that mattered.

CHAPTER 11

B ACK AT THE office, tired and worn out, Kate sat at her desk, huddled over a cup of coffee. The others in the team came in bright and cheerful soon afterward. Rodney walked in and smiled at her. "Anything back from forensics on Candy's and Paula's rooms? At least we found Candy's stuff. But having Candy's boxes of her things in Paula's room just adds to the mystery."

Kate wondered about that. "Looks like a setup, pinning Paula's death on Candy." Kate hesitated, then added, "And preemptively pinning Candy's death on Paula."

"Uh-oh, looks like you guys got a call last night, huh?" Andy asked.

"Yeah." Kate sighed, shook her head to wake up. "I'll go over the related deaths as soon as everyone's settled. You've got five to grab a coffee."

When the rest of the team had their coffee and gathered around the bullpen, Kate stood and gave them all a rundown on the case they had caught overnight.

"So it wasn't the woman you had spoken with, but it was her room?" Lilliana confirmed.

"Yes, not Candy's body, although Candy's room had been cleared of personal possessions—but we found them in the dead woman's room. Compliments of assistance from the RCMP, as Paula's dorm is on the campus."

"Interesting," Lilliana said.

"Yeah, that's one word for it. I don't know if Candy has skipped town, but I'm having forensics go over that carpet stain with a fine-tooth comb." Kate hesitated and looked at her partner. "I don't know if I'm projecting and seeing something I want to see—which, in this case, would be really sick—but it seemed to me that the bloodstains could potentially be from two different victims. Or at least spilled at different times. And given Candy's possessions were in the dead woman's room, … Paula could quite possibly have killed Candy. I expect we'll get notice of her body soon."

"So, you're thinking the other female, Candy, was killed first?" Owen asked Kate.

"I suspect so, yes. I hope not. I really hope I'm wrong. But what are the chances that she was killed first, and then Paula was killed right afterward?"

Lilliana frowned. "But this known DB is one of the long-term members of the group of bullies though, right?"

"Yes," Kate said, "but that doesn't mean she wasn't disposable as well."

At that, Lilliana winced. "Hard to imagine people thinking like that about another person."

"Maybe so, but remember. These are the same bullies who are knocking over disabled people for kicks."

"Does any of this have to do with the cyclist killed on the street?" Lilliana asked her quietly.

"I don't think so. I haven't been able to tie any of it in yet. At any rate, I've barely even gotten through all the witness statements, and we've got nothing back from forensics yet. I did talk to the coroner about ice bullets though."

"Right." Lilliana nodded. "That was a good catch."

"And I told Smidge about another similar case that happened ten years ago around the same area." Her team stopped, looked at each other, and she nodded. "He'll check into it."

"He's good," Owen stated. "A bit like a terrier with a bone, honestly. So at least you can rest easy with that part in his hands."

"I know. It's just frustrating. As soon as I found out where the crime scene was, all I could think was that it was Candy. And even when the DB was found in the same room, where I found Candy earlier to interview her, something was wrong with the entire picture."

"That's because you were convinced it was Candy," Rodney said.

"I know, and I get that, but it still feels wrong. And, yes, another young woman is dead, and we need to look after her and find out what the hell happened to Paula, but still, I was really expecting it to be Candy."

"And now you're afraid that both of them are dead?" Andy asked her.

"Yes, that's exactly what I'm afraid of. It was stunning to discover Candy's room had been stripped. I doubt she packed it all up herself, as she made no mention of that when I was interviewing her. In fact, she wanted to go back to her douchebag boyfriend Brandon, so why would she leave college and her access to him? So, who did pack up Candy's stuff and put it in Paula's dorm room?" She looked to her team members. "And now where are Paula's possessions?"

"Between RCMP and Forensics, their teams will find out what they can and will share it with us. Then we'll go from there," Lilliana said.

Kate nodded, and just then Colby came in and called

everybody into a meeting that included discussions about vacations and overtime. Taking a vacation was something she couldn't even begin to contemplate, when she was working all these cases.

When Colby's meeting with the team was finally over, and everybody was back at their desks, Kate turned to Rodney. "How do you handle leaving for a holiday, when you know so much shit is going on?"

"Easy. Because I accept that it'll still be here when I get back, along with a whole pile of new stuff too." He gazed at her. "Remember. We have to be rested, nourished, and ready to fight the good fight, or we're no good to anybody else. You have to take these breaks when you can. Vacation time is also to remember that you have a family and a larger reason for your existence. More is out there that's worth fighting for."

She nodded. "I get that in theory. I guess I'm still struggling with figuring out how to solve all these cases."

"One at a time and we'll get there." Rodney patted her arm. "Actually this case is moving along at a good clip. We might get this sorted and closed in ten days, a week even." At her snort, he continued, "Faster than the pedophile case, for sure. Even faster than the jumper case. Remember how long it took us to see those were assisted suicides? We're farther along here in a matter of three days than one week into the jumpers' cases." When she remained quiet, Rodney said, "Right?"

"Okay, I'll give you that, but ..."

"No buts. You care, and that's good, but you must keep it in check. Otherwise you'll burn out." She frowned, but he shook his head. "Don't even look at me like that. We all care. Don't think we don't," he muttered. "But, at the same time, you also have to understand that there'll always be another case."

She sagged in place. "I know. I just don't want there to be."

He nodded and smiled. "That's what makes you a good cop. You come from the heart, but remember that everyone here does. And the bad guys will eat you alive if they find out you've got that weakness."

"I've been told that a time or two," she said quietly, "but never at work."

"That's because you don't ever let people get close to you. Here, things are raw, and, when they go bad, they go bad in a big way. We all feel it, and that's what happened with Chet. We cared. We cared a lot, and we were a strong team. We worked well together, and he was my friend, even the godfather to my son." Rodney turned his head to look away.

"He also had a huge heart, and he's missed, and it's important that he's missed. It's important that his existence isn't ignored and that we find reasons to say his name once in a while and to honor his memory and to believe in the good Chet did while he was here because the reality is that it could be one of us tomorrow. Unfortunately the reality is, it could even be one of us today."

His words were harsh, but they also rang true. She wasn't a workaholic. She winced at that. Okay, so she was a workaholic. But only because she was working for the people.

What Rodney spoke of was the need for balance. There had to be a time when you backed off and gave yourself a break, so that you come back the next day and could do this all over again. Something she was coming to understand all on her own. When she came on the job as a detective, she was fired up to solve everything right now. But there was no such thing as solving everything, much less solving anything right now. It took days to find and to interview witnesses, to scout crime scenes, to read reports from assisting units. It took days to get information from forensics; it took days to get an autopsy done. Even longer to get certain information back from the crime lab, like tox screens and DNA runs.

There seemed to be a constant lineup of traffic down at the morgue, so you had to wait on autopsies. She couldn't even bear to think about all the DBs that went through the system without one. An autopsy was rare, probably less than two percent of the cases that went through the morgue, in fact. And that was just the reality of it.

Still, it was frustrating, because, as much as Kate had more access and more time and more tools available to her, there was also a time lag in areas that she just couldn't get away from. Even though she tried hard, she found a bottleneck at every turn. That's because, in a big city like this, there were too many cases, too many murders. She slowly rotated her head, realizing that she'd bolted out of bed too fast this morning, and even now a kink in her neck started to ache. Tired was one thing, but she was still functioning, so, with that in mind, she turned to her computer and dug in again.

EVEN BEFORE DAWN, Simon had returned to his home from spending the night at Kate's, then had a nap, which was unusual, so he woke up late to start his day. For a disorienting moment he tried to figure out what was going on, then bolted, racing for the bathroom. He leaned over the toilet, just as contents of his stomach spewed out. It was followed by waves of anger and guilt. Then more anger. Then more guilt.

Since he'd had no food in at least twelve hours, it was mostly bile and acid. He groaned, as he sat on the side of the bathtub and heaved again. With his hand on his stomach, he looked blearily around his huge bathroom, wondering what the hell had just happened.

When everything calmed down to the point that the cramping had stopped, he got himself a drink of water and rinsed out his mouth, then grabbed his toothbrush and scrubbed hard. He couldn't even remember the last time he had puked but was pretty sure it had to do with alcohol, which wasn't the case today—or yesterday. He didn't feel sick either, but the reaction to waking up and darting for the bathroom had been instantaneous, and it had been all he could do to make it there in a timely fashion. He slowly made his way back to bed and sat on the edge, staring out the massive windows at the view of Vancouver.

"What the hell was that?" He ran a hand through his hair.

He could smell the vomit in here. "Oh no. No, no, no," he cried out. "This is not a good time to have that olfactory sense on overdrive again. I don't know what the hell is going on, but that is not the odor I want in my nostrils all day long."

He got up and headed to the bathroom again, hoping he could do something to ease the odor, but it was not cooperating. No matter where he went in his apartment, the smell of vomit followed, even though it had long since been flushed away, and no residue was left on him.

He dressed quickly and raced from the building, lifting a

hand in greeting for Harry. Just to make sure the doorman didn't stop and talk, Simon kept up his pace all the way through the front lobby. As soon as he got outside, he inhaled several times in great gasping breaths, as if he had been poisoned inside the building. But still he fought that familiar and overwhelming smell, with apparently no way to get rid of it. Stumbling toward his favorite little coffee cart, he ordered a coffee and noticed they had fresh buns.

Hoping that something would settle his stomach, he ordered one of each and sat down at a small bench off to the side. A beautiful little garden was beside it, where the aromatic scent of the roses should have been overwhelmingly strong, but instead all he could smell was the vomit from his bathroom, a bathroom he was no longer in. His gaze wide, he stared at the surroundings, wondering what the hell was going on and how he could stop it. Was it a psychic thing? Like Kate had asked earlier?

If he connected psychically with live people, why the hell couldn't he connect with dead people? That would be the best thing. Then at least maybe he could talk to his grandmother. Although, if she hadn't wanted anything to do with his own psychic visions on this side, Simon highly doubted she would want to deal with it there on the other side either. But then why should she get a choice, when he apparently wasn't getting one?

Realizing he sounded like a whiny little bitch, he groaned and focused on the coffee, trying hard to bring the aroma of the fresh ground brew into his nostrils and into his system. But it was not to be.

All he could smell was vomit.

Thankfully it seemed to ease up the longer he sat there, so he waited a little bit, hoping something would completely remove the horrid vomit odor, but, even though that didn't happen, it was reduced enough that he could breathe again. By the time his coffee was gone, it was safe to stand up and to walk around a little bit. He did so gently, in case it all came rushing back, but it seemed like whatever it was had passed. He glanced around him and realized the coffee guy was looking at him sideways.

Simon walked back over, smiled. "I'll take a second one of those."

"You okay, man?"

"Yeah. Bad night."

The cart owner snorted. "You know what? If you're drinking hard, those nights just never get any better."

Realizing that almost everybody who saw him during one of these psychic events would think he was completely hungover, he just shrugged, accepting that as the better reaction. "Sometimes it's hard to get out of it."

"Looks like it's time for you to kick a bad habit."

He agreed, but no way Simon could explain to this guy that the bad habit was this nightmare of smells.

With his second coffee in hand, he slowly turned and walked to one of the buildings he had to check on today. He didn't have his notes with him; he didn't have anything. He'd left it all on his dining table at home. Thank God he had his phone.

Still, as he wandered through his morning's visits of his properties, nobody seemed to make any comment about his appearance or his actions, so he figured maybe it was fine. Only as he headed toward a sandwich shop around the corner did that overwhelming sense of smell came on again. He stopped warily at the edge of an alley, but it wasn't too bad, at least it didn't seem to be too bad. He crossed the alleyway and moved forward. And then the wind seemed to pick up and race around him, but he stopped because nobody else's jackets were blowing. Nobody else was leaning into the wind, like he was.

He realized just how bizarre this new sensory issue was. He leaned up against the wall, trying to brace himself, as if buffeted by a hurricane. It was weird. He ducked into the nearby sandwich shop, but the psychic assault didn't stop. Seeing a full crowd inside, he ducked back out again, using that as an excuse for his actions. He sat down on a bench around the corner. Thank God benches were everywhere. Convenient places to sit and hopefully to look a little less of an idiot. Or at least an idiot who blended into the rest of the world who strode quickly by.

When his phone rang, he looked down to see it was Kate.

"Hey," he answered, his voice strained.

"What's up?" she asked, her tone sharp. Of course she noticed. It was pretty damn hard to get anything past her.

"Just another weird symptom," he said quietly.

"And you can handle it or no?"

"Do I have a choice?" he asked, his voice stronger.

"No, I don't think so."

He had to love that about her. There was empathy but not an overly large dose of sympathy. As if he would figure out how to handle it. As he thought about it, maybe he would. Hell, maybe he had somehow brought all this on himself, and it wouldn't stop until he'd paid a penance for whatever it was that he'd done. Again his grandmother's voice came to mind. What the hell had she ever done that she'd had such a rough life herself? Because, damn, some things in the world shouldn't have happened, but they did, ... right before his eyes. It drove him nuts to think about it.

"Is it anything you can stop?" she asked, surprising him that she was still on the line.

"Nothing has worked so far," he said.

"What reaction?"

He explained quietly.

"Oh. Okay, that's gross." He burst out laughing. "At least you're laughing about it."

"Only since you called," he said quietly.

"Is it somebody? Are you connecting with somebody who might have gone out, like, was partying too hard last night?"

"I don't know. I feel pain now, like a deep pain. I don't know what it is."

"Maybe that's the problem." Then she said something else that completely blew him away. "Maybe you need to sink into this instead of fight it. Sorry. I would talk, but I've got to go."

With that she hung up, and he stared down at the phone in surprise. First, he wondered why she called him to begin with. Could she feel him in distress? He chuckled. Boy, he would not want to entertain that thought. Secondly, was she worried about him? That's what it sounded like. As long as she was thinking about him. ... He knew she cared, but it made him feel infinitely less worried to see evidence of her feelings for him.

But, third, that was a very interesting comment on her part at the end of her for-whatever-reason phone call. *Sink into it instead of fight it.* Interesting. Nothing that he would have expected, and yet she continuously surprised him. Just when he thought he understood some of this stuff, she said something that blew him away. It was fascinating; it was troubling, and it was also enlivening because she was probably right.

Maybe he needed to stop resisting it and to sink into it. Maybe a message was in this somewhere. Maybe a person was at the end of this, just like there had been the children who had needed help. He hadn't seen any of the dead women cyclists so far in Kate's current cases, but, then again, he'd done his best to block everything out, so no more dying people were in his world.

"How is that working for you?" he said out loud, with a note of bitterness. Because, while he wasn't seeing kids in pedophile rings needing saving or suicidal folks standing on bridges, definitely something was going on.

CHAPTER 12

K ATE PICKED UP the phone as it rang under her hand. "Hello?"

"It's Dr. Smidge," said the coroner, his voice gruff. "I just sent you the autopsy report on your bike accident victim."

"Good enough. I'll go over it now. What about the dead UBC student?"

"Don't get greedy. We had a four-car pileup last night."

"I get it. I've also got murders happening."

"I know, but unfortunately there is always one of those."

She winced at that.

"Anyway, I've taken a preliminary look. Cause of death is blunt force trauma. She was hit over the head at the front temple."

"Interesting, so by somebody facing her."

"Yes, with a blunt object, but we didn't find anything at the scene." He gave her a TOD estimate, which put it somewhere around four o'clock in the morning.

"That's interesting," she murmured.

"Not really. It's student life, all kinds of activity, all night long."

"I get that. I guess I think more in terms of sleep at that hour."

"You and me both, but, at her age, not so much."

"Anything on the bloodstains?"

"Hang on a minute. I did ask them to rush that." And he hung up. He called back almost immediately. "I just got the email in on it, and you should have a copy too. Just as you thought, they confirmed two different blood types."

She whistled at that. "Please tell me that they're both female."

"Do you have any DNA from the missing woman?"

"No, but I'll contact the family. I'll get on that today."

"We don't know for sure that it's her. Remember that," he noted.

"No, we don't, but she's missing, and it's her place."

"But it's been cleaned up," he said.

"Yes, but the question is, by whom?"

"I suspect by the dead woman whose body we have," he said. "There was blood on her fingernails, skin. And no defensive wounds."

"What? You think that she did the cleanup after Candy was killed, and then the bullies killed her? Though it's also possible that somebody caught her in the act and murdered her where she stood."

"Possible," he said thoughtfully.

"What if she was involved with the first murder with somebody else? The easy way to get rid of any witness—"

"I hear you. Now all you have to do is prove it." With that, he hung up.

She brought up the reports in her email and quickly read through them. Not a whole lot of surprises. The woman in the apartment, her last name was Mallow.

She shook her head at that. "Isn't that some baking ingredient?" she wondered. But her first name was Paula, and that's where she got confused with the other one, Candy.

Okay, so she had a Paula Mallow, and every time she thought of that name, it tripped her up. She quickly pulled up the details on her. She was twenty-four and had been at the university for just one year, after transferring from the University of Toronto. That transfer didn't allow all her former college credits to carry over, so she was taking more classes to count toward her English degree. Her family was back there, and, with that, Kate picked up the phone. The parents should have already been notified by the Toronto police. When she reached the mother on the other end, she quickly identified herself. The woman bawled immediately.

Kate winced. "I'm very sorry for your loss, but I do have a few questions I need to ask you."

"No," she sobbed, "I can't answer anything."

"Nothing about your daughter's life here?"

"No. She insisted on transferring over there because of that guy. And she hadn't been the same ever since."

"Not the same in what way?"

"She just became really snooty, as if she was too good for us all the sudden. She didn't have time to visit with her father or me. She didn't have time to even say hello to her grandparents. She was completely wrapped up in her own life. She was never like that beforehand."

"Before what?"

"Before she transferred. She was happy here, and we were delighted to have her close by."

Kate winced at that because so many parents lost their kids when they ventured out into the brave new world and became somebody else. Usually that somebody else was indicative of how honest they were being when they were at home, compared to finding out who they really were when they were loose. Sometimes they connected with the wrong people and became someone nobody recognized. Really no way to know if independence and freedom were something that they would handle.

Kate asked a few more questions, but the mom really didn't seem to know much about Paula's friends. Her parents hadn't spoken to her in the last couple months. They had tried to send texts, but their daughter basically ignored them.

When Kate mentioned Candy's name, Paula's mother said, "I remember something about her."

"What about her?"

"My daughter didn't like her."

"Okay, any idea why?"

"It was the boyfriend. I think it had to do with Paula's boyfriend."

"Would that be the one she met back in Toronto?"

"Yes, she went away on some workshop, and he was there. They hit it off and kept in touch. He's the one who convinced her to head out west. When she got the transfer, we were all devastated but more so because of him. I never did trust anybody who would do something like that."

"Do something like what?" Kate asked, not sure she was getting all the story here.

"Deliberately try to separate her from her family." The mom sobbed loudly. "We were really close before that."

"I hear you. Does she have other family? Any family out west? Did she have a job? Did she have any friends she stayed in touch with?"

"Not since that man," she said.

"We're talking about Brandon here, right?"

"Yes, that was his name, Brandon."

"Fine, and what about friends from back home? Did she

stay in touch?"

"You know what? I saw her friend Bethany here not very long ago, and she was asking me if we had heard from Paula because she hadn't. Bethany was pretty heartbroken because Paula had completely ignored her since she moved."

"Which is too bad," Kate said. "And she didn't make any other friends here in Vancouver?"

"Just that one group," the mother said. "I think they were all the same in that group."

"I do know the group you're talking about, but I was hoping that maybe she had somebody special."

"No, but, if you're looking for who killed her, I would look at him first. Look at Brandon first."

"Had they broken up? Was there any reason why he would try to kill her?"

"I don't know except maybe to get rid of her," she said in a vicious tone.

Kate winced at that. "I mean, I get that's a possible answer, but we can't make an assumption like that. She traveled a long way to come here to be with him."

"And yet, when she got there, she was pretty upset about him. Something about another woman coming to university for him, I think."

"So Paula made the move, thinking she would have a serious relationship with Brandon, and they didn't have one because he had another girlfriend?"

"Yes, exactly. She called me in tears. I tried to get her to come home again, but she was determined to win him back."

Kate frowned at that. "So, it sounds like a love triangle gone wrong then ... in many ways."

"It was wrong right from the beginning. I don't know what he said to get her to go there, but he had no intention of being her boyfriend ever."

"Yet she didn't seem to know that, right?"

"No, she didn't at all. My girl used to be naive, but I doubt she is now."

Ouch, that was an ironic statement, but Kate wouldn't remind the poor woman that her daughter was dead. That was hardly fair, given the circumstances. At the same time, it was obvious that the mother was overwhelmed and looking for somebody to blame. "I may have to get a hold of you again. In the meantime, just know that we're working on your daughter's case."

"Please find who did this," she bawled. "My Paula was a beautiful person, and she didn't deserve this."

With that, Kate hung up and sat here, frowning at the phone.

"What's the matter?" Rodney asked from beside her.

"I just talked to the mother of our latest victim. And honestly it's almost like I was talking about Candy, the one whose room it was, not Paula, not the one who died."

"Why is that?"

"Just the way the mother described her daughter. Either she really didn't have a clue about who her daughter was or hadn't seen the changes she had made after moving here."

"What do you mean?" Rodney asked.

"She made it sound like her daughter was a complete innocent, with no idea what was going on in the world, until Brandon, the rich kid with his lawyer on tap, lured her into coming out west, like she had no idea what she was getting into."

"Ah, so Mom isn't ready to accept her daughter as an adult capable of making choices that she didn't agree with?"

"Something like that, yeah. I guess all parents get surprised by the decisions of their adult children, don't they?"

"I think they like to think they know who their children are. But then, when they hook up with other people, and, sometimes under that influence, they become somebody else."

"Scary thought," she said.

"Not really. I think it's part of being a parent. You have to love them enough to let them go, then hope that, over time, they come back again." Rodney sighed. "And I mean that geographically as well as morally."

"Yeah, I guess, but I wonder how many actually do."

"It's easier than ever to stay in touch with each other now," he said.

"But it's also easier to hide. People's lives are crazy busy in some cases. Thus it's much easier to just, you know, pretend to be too busy to have anything to do with people."

"You're right there too, but, considering that we have all these things—like, cell phones that are basically hand-held computers in our pockets, plus FaceTime and social media groups and other apps to stay in touch—I think that most people would say that they're more connected now than they ever were."

"I wonder," she said.

"Aren't you?" he asked.

"I don't have anybody to connect with." She looked at Rodney. "My mother is in a home, and she's not quite all there, and, when she sees me, she goes into a screaming fit anyway."

He winced. "Still because of your brother?"

"Absolutely. She was married to that huckster who took all her money, and I think, in her mind, I'm probably to blame for that too."

"Wow, you're really a terrible human being, aren't you?"

"In a way I am. At least for thinking that losing her mind was the easiest answer for her because that way she didn't have to own up to her own behavior. But it left another bad memory for me."

"Your stepfather, where is he?"

"He died in a car accident," she said absentmindedly. "And, yeah, more proof that I'm a horrible person when I say, *Good riddance.*" He stared at her in surprise, and she shrugged. "He was not a good man. He beat the crap out of her, stole all her money, and left her behind, broke and devastated, for someone else to take care of."

"Wow, nice family."

"Yeah. The best part of the family disappeared when I was seven, and it was all downhill from there."

"Sorry, I know all that is hard for you."

"I don't talk about it much. But you asked, so it's fine." With a shrug and a smile, she said, "Now we need to talk to the rest of that uni gang."

"That should be fun."

"Yeah, Paula's mom says arrogant Brandon's responsible for her daughter's death."

"It's not as if we're against the idea."

"He's a jerk, so, if it is him, I would be delighted. However, despite my glee, we can't project it."

"Right, but we're sure not getting any further on whoever killed our cyclist," he said.

"No, which is another odd thing."

Rodney nodded.

"And, if it's once a year, and there's a pattern, then, in theory, there won't be another killing for another year. Yet we have Paula Mallow's dead body. And potentially Candy's, still to be found."

"Are you saying there's no connection?"

"No, not necessarily. We can't assume that. It would just mean that something triggered a change in the pattern."

"Right." Rodney's smile was grim. "So let's hope we don't get another one."

Just then both their phones went off. They shared a look, and both groaned.

"I think you spoke too soon." Kate grimaced.

"I shouldn't have spoken at all," he said.

They both answered to find out about yet another victim. As Kate stood, she looked over at him. "Now you need to bite your tongue."

"The DB's up in the same area too."

"I know." Her voice was soft. "I'm just hoping it's not connected."

He nodded. "Let's go."

"You driving?" she asked.

"Yeah, I'm driving."

As they headed to his car, she thought about the odds of yet another victim in that area *not* being connected. "I wonder how many traffic fatalities we have up in that area."

"We can pull the stats later, if you think it's important," he said.

"It's not that I think it's important. I'm just wondering what the odds are that this guy has done it again."

"We'll find out soon enough," he said.

"I wish we could deal with one case at a damn time."

"Not enough hands, not enough hours. We're assigned the first one, and, because of your connection, we're assigned the other. Don't forget. The rest of the team has other cases of their own."

"I know, and it's great that we share notes, but I'd really like the time to dig fully into one for once, with all my focus there," she said.

"In this case, you don't have that option, and you get to dig into more than one."

She sighed. "I get that. I really do. It just sucks."

"You just clear off your plate and compartmentalize, so you only have one on your plate at a time and can give it 100 percent of your focus while you can."

She looked at him, then frowned. "You know, in theory—"

"Let's just go with it," he interrupted, before she could get too far.

She laughed. "Let's just hope this one is open-and-shut."

"Are they ever?"

"Yes, just not very often."

As soon as they arrived at the scene, a crowd had already gathered.

She groaned. "Is this the exact same corner?"

He nodded as he stood here, grim faced, looking out at the crowd. "I wonder how many people are duplicates."

"Let's start getting photos, and then we can at least match interviews to the photos."

And that's what they did. While everybody was still shuffling around, Kate and Rodney walked around the crowd themselves and took photos of everybody standing here, watching. When somebody protested, Kate looked at him. "Really? You're standing here, gawking at a crime scene, and you're complaining that we want to know who you are?"

The kid immediately backed up. "I just didn't know what was going on."

"In that case, give me your name and phone number,"

she said, immediately pulling out her notepad. He glared at her, and she patiently waited, until he finally mumbled it out and then took off.

She noted who he was and why he was here for future reference. As she walked over to join her partner, Rodney put a hand on her shoulder. "You need to come see this."

Kate walked over to where Dr. Smidge was crouched in front of the victim. He looked up at her. "You need to get on this."

"What do you mean?"

"Because this is the second one." He pulled back the victim's hair, so Kate could see the hole behind the ear.

"Good God," she whispered. She couldn't see the victim's face. "Give me a look at the face, will you, Doc?"

Quickly he brushed the victim's hair to the other side, so Kate could see, and she stared in shock.

"I gather from your expression that you know her?"

She nodded. "We were in Candy's apartment last night with Paula's body," she said in a low tone. "This is Candy."

He stared at her, then at the victim. "I'm thinking your cases just collided."

She grimly focused on the scene before her eyes. She turned, looked over at her partner. "We need to get that whole group back in. That's two of their numbers gone. Both of the females. That leaves the four males."

He pulled out his phone. "I'll start setting it up. You want to talk to them individually?"

"I do, but I want them all down at the station."

He nodded. "We'll be a while, checking into everybody here."

"That's all right. I'm sure we can get some help, maybe from the local beat cops. We need to get statements from everybody. We need to know what the hell happened and how this happened twice without anybody seeing anything."

"Oh, somebody saw something," the coroner said. "You can be sure of that. But getting them to talk now? That's a whole different story."

She hated to admit it, but he was probably right. Still, she'd do the job and work the case, and, at the end of the day, she'd catch this asshole one way or another. She didn't know what the hell was going on or what the motive was, but when two cases combined into one, things could get very interesting.

AT THE END of the day Simon felt a whole lot better, at least he hoped so. Some weird images were knocking on his brain, but he found a way to successfully put out the door knocker that read Nobody Home.

He wasn't sure if it would work or not, but he had to control where and when. Now that he was home, a glass of wine in his hand, lying on the couch in front of the big bay windows that overlooked the beauty of Vancouver, he opened up that same internal door. "Who are you, and what do you want?"

At that time nothing was there, and he took another sip of his wine and just relaxed, thinking that maybe it had been all for naught. Maybe that whole *sink into it and allow it to happen* thing was bullshit. Just as he considered that, a floodgate of images—or maybe not images but blacks and grays, like shadows, passed through his head. All accompanied by his damn magnified smell again. This time though, the wine aroma was amplified. He bolted upright on his couch, almost spilling it. But he sniffed the aroma and breathed the bouquet that slammed into his senses, once again on overload.

He slowly leaned back into his couch again. "What the hell is going on?"

And he noted more images, more of everything really, and all at the same time. Including good smells and bad smells. He cried out, "What does this mean? What is it you want? I don't understand how to interpret this."

Then he heard tears and that weird noise in the background, that almost worrying sound again. The sound that had driven him crazy earlier. Here it was once again, driving through the back of his brain. He groaned. "That I don't need," he muttered. But apparently nobody was listening to him.

As he sunk down into his couch again, all he could do was witness everything flooding through his mind, which circled back around and dashed in again for a second viewing. Yet nothing, absolutely nothing, made any sense. Through it all, he heard this sad weeping, and that crying was amplified so much more inside his head that he felt sick with the sadness of it. He shook his head, wondering who it was and what made her so distraught.

"Can I help you somehow?" he whispered ever-so-softly.

What came back nearly broke his heart.

"No."

CHAPTER 13

ATER THAT DAY Kate walked into an interview room, a
grim smile on her face. Brandon was here with his
lawyer. Rodney sat beside her and turned on the recorder.
The two of them introduced themselves. Rodney added,
"Interview with Brandon Frost and his lawyer in Interview
A." Rodney stated the date and time.

The kid crossed his arms, then leaned back and crossed
his legs, a smirk on his face.

"Tell us the last time you saw Paula Mallow." Kate
stared at him.

"Ms. Paula." He sneered. "A couple days ago."

"Can you be more specific, please?"

"I don't know that I can be. Why?"

"Answer the question, please."

"I can't. I don't know when I last saw her." And then he
stopped. "Oh, wait. She might have been at the party last
night."

"She *might have been* at the party last night," Kate re-
peated for clarity's sake. "And when might she have been at
this party?"

He shrugged. "We were there for hours."

"So when and where was this party?"

"At the dorms." He named the student residence building, where Paula's body had been found.

"So this party just went from room to room?"

He sneered again. "It covered a bunch of rooms, a bunch of floors. A really good time was had by all."

"Drugs, sex, booze?"

He nodded. "All of the above. That's what university life is all about, isn't it?"

"A lot of kids try to go to class."

"Sure, but, when classes are over, a whole new experience happens." He chuckled, looking smug.

"For some people, yes," she said.

"For me, I don't have to worry about grades. I don't need to study, like these other suckers."

"So who are these other suckers?"

"Paula and the others." He waved his hand. "Not a one of them can hold a candle to my brains."

"Too bad they apparently can't hold a candle to your personality either."

"Exactly," he said complacently. "They hang around me because they want to be like me." He grinned. "That it will never happen isn't the point. In the meantime, we have a little fun, while we go through our years at the university, that's all. A good time was had by all, so what's your problem with it?"

"When did you last see Paula?"

"She was at the party last night. I already told you."

"What time was the party?"

"We went up there about eight o'clock, and I think we were there most of the night. I don't remember a whole lot after four in the morning."

"And what happened at four in the morning?"

"I think I probably collapsed in my bed." He chuckled.

"Anybody see you?"

"I'm sure they did, anybody who was at the party, at least."

"And who did you go with?"

"My buddies. You know? The same ones you hassled over that stupid car accident."

Kate said, "Please state their names."

He quickly named the other three men in the group.

"And when you saw Paula the last time, how was she?"

"She and Candy were having a hell of a fight," he said gleefully.

"Over what?"

"Over me. I walked away from both of them and found somebody else to have a good time with." He chuckled at the thought. "They can fight all they want, but I still make my own decisions."

"Of course you do. Pay your own bills, do you?"

He laughed. "Just because you're broke and have to live on a stupid cop salary doesn't mean I have to live the same way."

"That's got nothing to do with it. But, with that attitude of yours, it will be interesting retelling the tale."

"I didn't do anything wrong," he said in that lazy voice that she really hated.

"So, when you last saw Paula, she was doing fine, just arguing with Candy?"

"Yep, and, man, when those two go at it, they can fight. Really they were much better off when they had sex instead."

At that, Kate stopped, looked at him. "The two of them were in a relationship?"

"If it wasn't the three of us, yes. It happens all the time there, chickie."

"You may call me Detective Morgan. And is that the

relationship you had with both of them?"

"I just said that."

"Not necessarily. Were you not in a relationship with Candy?"

"Sure I was. I was also in a relationship with Paula. I went with whoever I wanted, whenever I wanted, and sometimes I wanted them both." Now he was balancing on just the back two legs of his chair.

"I see, and they were happy to do that?"

"No, they didn't want to be in bed together, which made it a lot more fun for me. If they wouldn't play nice, I told them to get the hell out. I don't have to take shit like that."

"What shit like that?"

"Chicks only pretending to have fun. Tons of them are out there. I don't need any spoilsports."

The complacency of this guy just blew her away. "I see, and how is it that you don't remember what happened afterward?"

"Because I was with some other chick," he said.

"And what was her name?"

"I don't know. She was somewhere around 36DD, as I recall."

"Wow. I see that your brains are shrinking as you age too."

"No need to insult my client," his lawyer said testily.

She gave him a lazy smile. "No, apparently there's enough money to keep even you happy though, huh?"

"Again, no need for insults. We're here, cooperating."

"Yes, you are, to a certain extent." She turned toward Brandon. "Did you see either of those young women again afterward?"

He shook his head. "Like I said, I don't remember a whole lot."

"So you might have."

"Yeah, sure. I might have. I was only with that chick for a while. I mean, we had a good bang, and that was it. Then later on they came back for another toke and another drink, but I don't remember if they were still fighting then or not."

"They?"

"Candy and Paula."

"But you saw them again?"

"Yeah, I saw them again," he said, with another wave of his hand. "What the hell is the big deal anyway?"

"Considering that you were the last one to see Paula alive," she said, with emphasis, "I think it's a big deal."

He stopped and stared at her. "What the hell are you talking about?"

"You heard me. Paula was found deceased early this morning."

"Probably choked on her own vomit," he said in disgust.

"Meaning that she was intoxicated last night."

"Did you hear me?" He came down hard on his chair legs. "We were all intoxicated."

"You were for sure, but did you see Paula drinking?"

"Of course. They always drank. It was a steady thing between them."

"Between who?"

"Have you been listening? Between Paula and Candy. Honestly, I think they both really cared for each other, but the whole situation made them pretty ugly."

"You mean, the situation with you?"

He shrugged. "Yeah, they didn't seem to like being caught up in the middle."

"Why would they? It sounds like you were just pulling a power play."

"Sure, it's fun to manipulate people." He yawned, then looked over at his lawyer. "Can we leave now? I really need to catch some sleep."

"Why is that?" she asked. "Do you have a job to go to?"

"No, don't need to." He looked back at her, with that same irritating lazy smile. "Independently wealthy."

"You mean, your family is."

"Same thing in my world. My family sticks together."

"Even when you're in trouble?"

He glared at her. "Particularly if I'm in trouble."

She smiled over at the lawyer. "Is that right?"

"His family has always been very supportive," the lawyer said stiffly.

"Right." She looked back at Brandon. "And when did you last see Candy?"

He looked over at his lawyer, back at her, and rolled his eyes. "You really don't listen, do you?"

"I'm waiting," she said.

"Somewhere around the same time."

"And about what time was that?"

"I would say maybe about three or four o'clock this morning," Brandon said. "I can't believe Paula is dead. What a son of a bitch."

"Son of a bitch?"

"Yeah. Paula."

"Okay, that turn of phrase usually refers to men. And Paula's mother had been clear that Paula was a female."

"Paula was a transvestite. That's why it was fun to have him around. He made me look good, but, when I really needed to fuck somebody, it would be Candy. Sometimes."

Then he smirked again, topped off by a laugh. "If you could only see the look on your face, Detective. You didn't know, did you?"

"The autopsy isn't back yet." She stared at him. "So how would I? Was he transitioning to a she, or was she transferring to a he? Or are you making up the whole thing?"

"I don't think he was transitioning at all." He laughed, enjoying this whole tale. "I think he just liked to play the part."

"So, he was a cross-dresser then? Do you think that had anything to do with him getting killed?"

"A lot of guys expect to see something under the hood, and, when you present them with something completely different, I don't imagine it makes them very happy."

"And yet that was part of the relationship between her and Candy?"

"Yeah, but Candy really didn't like multiples at the same time. I told her that it was no big deal and that she should just take it and swallow it, like a good girl. Other than that, she would cry every once in a while, which got really damn irritating."

"Really? So tell me about the case on campus here of someone you guys threw down the stairs?"

He glared at her. "That's just bullshit. I had a talk with that girl, and she changed her tune pretty damn fast."

"Threatening a witness is a crime in and of itself," she said.

"I didn't have to threaten her. She saw me coming and just bawled her eyes out."

"Maybe that's because you had already helped her down the stairs in the first place."

"I didn't help her at all. We just laughed and kept on

going. It's not our fault she went tumbling down the stairs, ass over teakettle. She was the clumsy idiot. We didn't even have to help her."

The lawyer studied the cocky young man, as if he were something beyond recognition, but, when he caught Kate looking at him, his poker face immediately returned.

"There have been a couple other complaints about you and your little posse on campus."

"Whatever." He shrugged. "This is a boring place to put my time in, until we get out in the real world."

"What is it you plan on doing when you get out in that real world?" she asked.

"I'll be a lawyer," he said casually. "Everybody in my family becomes a lawyer."

"Great, so they're all here to help you stay out of jail, huh?"

"Absolutely." He smiled smugly.

"So you think you can do anything and just get away with it?"

"Sure, why not?" he said. "It's not like I've been caught for anything yet." At that, he laughed. "Of course I haven't done anything serious, just stupid childish pranks. Right?" He looked over at his lawyer.

The lawyer immediately nodded. "That's correct. My client is high-spirited and doesn't always make the best decisions, but that, in itself, is not a criminal act."

"We need to confirm things with your buddies. Please stay here for now."

She stood, about to exit. "Should you pull out your phone and send a text, make a phone call, or communicate by any means, in an attempt to warn your friends, we will take the device as evidence, and you will forfeit your phone."

"You can't take my fucking phone," he said.

She smiled. "If you try to collude with your friends to align your stories, that is also a criminal act." She focused on the lawyer. "It's up to you to try to keep him on the straight and narrow." As soon as she went out the door, she heard the lawyer talking to him.

She didn't know what kind of lawyer would want to be on this family's payroll if the whole group of them were lawyers. She shook her head at Rodney.

"I'll go make some phone calls," he said.

"I'll stand in the observation room and see what the idiot does."

"We probably should have taken his phone away from him in the first place," Rodney said.

"We should have, but he wouldn't have handed it over easily. And we didn't have legal cause."

"No, he wouldn't have given it up. All you can do is hope that he texts his buddies."

"Even if he does, we'll have a hard time proving it was anything other than stupid childish talk, like his previous tale."

"Do you believe his story?"

"Parts of it. As you know, the best liars always weave in a little truth. That whole transvestite mess was BS, just trying to divert our attention, I'm sure. I already talked to Paula's mother."

"What a jerk," Rodney said.

"I know, right?" she said. "Is he stupid enough? Yes? But is he also smart enough, laughing at us for this whole thing? Yes. I really don't like his attitude. I don't like the lawyer either."

"I feel sorry for the lawyer." Rodney dialed a number on

his phone. "Must be a royal pain dealing with guys like this all the time."

"If the family is full of lawyers, why do they need him anyway?" she asked.

"Oh, because they're not criminal lawyers. They're all corporate."

"Interesting. So they're all about business deals, right?"

He nodded. As soon as somebody came on to the call, he took a few steps away from her. She looked back to see the others in the interrogation room. The lawyer and Brandon were arguing over possession of the phone. She smiled when the phone flew out of his hand and came toward the door. He bolted to his feet, but she quickly opened the door, picked up the phone. "I'll take that off your hands for now."

"You can't touch that."

"I wouldn't be able to, except that, right here, on your screen, is a text to your buddy saying …"

"I didn't get a chance to send it."

"I see that." With her own phone, she took a picture of it. "And now I'll get a warrant for your phone and your laptop and everything else in your room." She waved his phone before his face. "I'll be back in a moment." And, with that, she walked out again. She immediately called the local prosecutor. "I need a warrant." When she explained the situation, he whistled. "An arrogant smart-ass of a kid, huh?"

"Yep."

"So he was really trying to set up a story?"

"Trying to shut them up at least, but he didn't get a chance to send it. That'll make it dicey. And apparently he comes from a family of corporate lawyers."

"He'll get off with just a rap on his knuckles. You know that, right?"

"Not if we get him for murder."

"Is this about murder?" he asked in surprise.

"According to the one woman who had gone missing but just died in an intersection, the answer to that question is yes."

"You lost me there," he said.

"Somebody they hassled earlier may have died, after they went a little too far."

"May have?"

"Yeah," she said sadly. "Until I can get a chance to get deeper into this whole mess, it's a maybe. A warrant would help a hell of a lot. The witness is now dead."

"I don't know if I can get that far," he said. "Nothing you've given me is enough to get what you want."

———〜〜〜———

WITH NOTHING ELSE to do, Simon picked up one of his journals, then sat and wrote down everything he could remember about this last set of visions. As he did this, he shook his head. He should have done that every other time as well. When he was done with this latest rendering of his current visions, he would go back and write down what he could remember from the earlier ones. It was the only way to track whatever the hell was happening. To the best of his ability, he noted the dates and times when his senses went crazy and when the whirling rumbling noise interrupted him.

The woman crying really got to him. He couldn't tell if she was a prisoner or what. He presumed she was blindfolded or in complete darkness because of the shadows, the quiet. However, nothing gave him any sign as to where she was. To make this record was completely defeating in that way, but it helped drain it all from his brain, so he could think again. After a hot shower, as he collapsed down for bed, he whispered to the woman in the darkness, "Calm down, just take it easy. I'm here. I'm not sure how much help I can be, but I'm here."

Almost a sense of peace filled him, as he reached out to her. Only he got no answer.

He frowned because it seemed there was this wall between them now. He couldn't see a door to walk through, and, given the hour, he wondered if he even wanted to walk through one anyway. He frowned at that because he generally liked to help the underdog. If she was a victim, he wanted to help her, but was she being held against her will, a prisoner somewhere? Or was she just somebody who was overcome by a bad scenario in her world?

That meant something completely different. Because, if she was just having a bad time, well, he could understand that, and he could send her a virtual hug. Not that he had any clue if that was even possible or not, but it was about how he felt. Trying to help, as he lay here in the darkness, all he could do was close his eyes, trying to remember his grandmother's lessons, sending waves of comforting energy in the direction of the crying sad woman. He didn't know why it was so different this time.

With the abused children, Simon had seen visions of them being collected and held captive, yet Simon had only connected with the one child. He thought at the time that maybe it was because the others were dead. He didn't know about this psychic stuff; it wasn't his thing, and he had no idea what he was capable of. Unfortunately it was apparently becoming his thing, and that was a whole different story.

When it came to the woman on the bridge, he had probably connected with her because she was so emotionally overwrought. He didn't really know why that one had connected. It could have been because Simon had felt so bad about his friend David's suicide. Perhaps it was because he wanted to help, and so he picked up that same suicidal energy of that one woman, which the asshole had been fostering in her, pushing her to do the deed.

But what did any of those jumpers from the bridge have to do with this woman? Who was this crying woman? And why was she so haunted? Not only haunted but so devastated and broken by the life around her? It drove him crazy. He couldn't seem to help, so what was he supposed to do? That helplessness, that hopeless inability to make a change in one's own life, which seemed to be happening all around him, was driving him nuts.

Yes, he knew he couldn't force others to act. Yet he wished he could at least talk to them, get them to open up, maybe see the fallacy in their thinking.

It wasn't fair; it really wasn't. What was the point of having a gift like this? People called it a gift, but he thought it a curse, since he couldn't do anything to change the outcome. As he lay here in the darkness, he heard his grandmother's voice rolling through him. *You can only observe. You cannot change.*

He remembered yelling at her back then, hearing this in real time, saying he didn't want anything to do with it. What was the point of seeing things if you couldn't affect the outcome? She'd given him a sad smile, saying, "It's just the way it is."

"I don't like it," he yelled back at her.

She nodded slowly. "In time, you will learn to live with it."

"No." He backed up, heading outside to play with his friends. "I'm not going to," he'd snapped. It was pretty rough just hearing and even observing some of the things his grandmother had gone through. He could do nothing to help her, even as such a young child already with this "gift," even when growing into a teen with more confirmation of his "gift." All he could do was avoid these discussions with his grandmother. She never called him back, never told him how to help those in the visions, or what he could do to stop anything like that from filling his mind.

Now he wished that he had stuck around and had had her take him under her wing, tutoring him in the ways of this craziness. At one point in time, she had just given him a sad smile. "You will find your way. No one can help you, but you will find your way."

He had to wonder if that was even possible. Sitting in this craziness and listening to a woman gently sob, he couldn't even find out the reason for it. He reached across the divide and whispered to her, "Tell me what's wrong."

But there was no answer.

He wasn't even sure that she heard him. It was quite possible that her earlier response was to something completely different. How egotistical of him to think that it was a reply to his question, but, given the circumstances, he hadn't known how else to deal with it.

Frustrated and almost on the verge of anger again, he lay here quietly in the darkness and listened to her sob. When she finally stopped and fell asleep, he followed her into dreamland, wishing with all his might that this could go away and never come back.

CHAPTER 14

WHEN KATE WOKE up the next morning, her eyes opened, and her brain clicked on. To think that the two recent murders of Candy and Paula were connected to the death of Sally on her bike was something completely different. And it surprised Kate that the killer had positioned Candy's body near Sally's crime scene. Was that deliberate or accidental? Were there two killers?

At the same time, Kate wondered how much of Candy's death scene was a copycat of Sally's, and how much might be that the killer had seen Candy and Paula at Sally's crime scene and had chosen his next victim then. Just so many options. She bolted out of bed and dressed quickly, realizing again that she still didn't have any groceries and couldn't keep existing on the leftovers from Simon.

She walked to work, her steps rapid and purposeful. Her mind buzzed with possible connections, possible links. But she needed to track them down and see if she could toss some of them out. Maybe if she got lucky, another autopsy would have been completed by now.

She thought about turning around, grabbing her vehicle, and heading up to the morgue, but changed her mind, as she should wait until the coroner came back with his reports for her. She stopped, picked up one more of those absolutely lovely pretzels that she really shouldn't be eating all the time, and carried it into the station, still warm and steaming.

Grabbing some coffee, she sat down at her desk and brought up her emails. No autopsy report. It wasn't even eight o'clock, so it was early yet. With her notepad, she wrote down all the possible scenarios she could come up with. Then she set up some searches. Way more computing power should be here than there was, but she would do what she could. She wondered if their analyst, Reese, had bigger and better tools at her disposal. Kate needed to remember to ask that of someone later.

Right now she started searching for more history on these bullying kids and then brought up anything that looked like UBC complaints in the local media. She was still trying to sort through the last cyclist-related accidents that had happened in the previous ten years in that same area, then widened the search to include a ten-block radius.

She wasn't even sure what she was looking for, just a connection. The fact that she had a second ice-bullet victim now at the same intersection within four days—not one year later—meant something different was going on. That it was connected to these students was something else again. She just didn't know quite what it was. Her computer hummed along steadily, as she wrote down notes.

When Rodney walked in, he stopped and looked at her. "Stop being so damn early all the time."

"I woke up with my mind buzzing. I need to get some of this down on paper and rule out some of these scenarios."

"Run them past me because I'm feeling like my brain is dead." He went and got coffee, then sat beside her, as she went over her notes. "Yeah." He contemplated her list of potential scenarios in front of her. "The connects are just pretty slim, don't you think?"

"It's possible the killer was watching the chaos after Sally, the first woman, died at that intersection recently. Maybe he saw Candy there. Maybe he saw the whole group of bullies, and they did something that pissed him off. I mean, they're the kind of people who piss everyone off. They are callous and inconsiderate. They don't give a damn about anyone else. For all we know, they may have laughed at our killer or something." She was warming to the theory now. "Given the bullies penchant for pushing and hurting the disabled, what if our potential killer is in that group?"

Rodney turned and looked at her with respect. "Interesting notion." He nodded.

"Not impossible, anyway," she said.

"Sure, it's a bit of a reach, but this kind of a killing is also distant. Or is this true for these ice-bullet pistols?" He swung over to his desk and punched in a speed-dial number. "Hey, Reese. Quick question. Are ice-bullet pistols long range or short?" He waited while keys clicked in the, background then nodded. "Thanks."

"Wait," Kate called out. "Ask her what her workload looks like?"

Rodney laughed. "Did you hear that?" he asked Reese. He paused. "Got it." He hung up and swung around in his chair to face Kate. "She says heaped. If it's important, she'll get to your stuff fast. If not ..."

Kate grimaced. "By that time, I'll have slogged through it myself."

"Impatient little devil, aren't you?" Rodney laughed.

Kate waved him off. "What about the range of the ice-bullet gun?"

"Depends on the delivery mechanism used."

"Of course," Kate groaned, then motioned him over to

her and her list again.

He pointed at one of her items. "But why are the dead cyclists always women?"

"I don't know, unless of course a woman disabled our killer, our fictional killer, and put him on this revenge path."

"It's possible." He nodded. "But … *hmm*. Let me check those witness photographs and see if anybody was obviously disabled. Like crutches, walkers, canes. Do you remember talking to anybody with a limp? Was anybody there missing a limb? Or had an obvious facial deformity?"

Kate shook her head. "Nobody immediately comes to mind, but I was more interested in their faces for ID confirmation purposes. You look at the photos, while I keep running this down."

He nodded and swung his chair over to his computer. "I guess we don't have anything on that kid Brandon, do we?"

"No, he's at home, promising to stay in town."

"Do we believe that?"

"Yes."

"He probably will. He can't take a chance of getting kicked out of the university."

"I'm sure his parents could buy his way back in again," she said.

"Probably so, but they might be getting pretty damn tired of it. This is his third university."

She jerked her head up, looked at him. "What? Why?"

"I contacted the Committee of Student Affairs at the University of Toronto, and let's say they were more than happy he was moving."

"Wow, same shit?"

He shrugged. "They wouldn't go into any detail."

"Of course not," she said.

"He did say that the kid had little respect for life."

"We've already seen that he's just a sheer troublemaker. A spoiled punk-ass troublemaker." She shook her head. "He needs to be knocked down a peg or two."

"Maybe, but we have to make sure it sticks. Otherwise the family will get him off, and he'll be laughing all the way out of the station, as he continues to pull more stunts like this."

She agreed with him, but it just made her even angrier. The onus was always on them to prove their case, but it didn't make it any easier when they were up against guys like this because they could always find ways to wiggle out of everything. An open-and-shut case was what she needed. But, so far, she didn't have jack shit to make anything happen.

But she would, no way she wouldn't.

"We've got the other three to deal with this morning?" Rodney asked her.

"Right. Tell me about that."

"We did talk to them over conference calls yesterday. That was the best we could get at the time."

"I wish we could have gotten them down here, so we could make sure Brandon didn't talk to them."

"We did get short statements from them, so they couldn't change their tune, and they're all coming in person this morning."

"Good enough. What time are they starting?"

"Nine is the first one," he said. Silence ensued for the next little bit, as they worked their way through the research, and then he went "*Huh.*"

She turned, looked at him. "What does that mean?"

"This vehicle here on the side of the road."

"And?"

"I'd have to run the plates to see, but it looks like it's been modified. It's a convertible, and the gearshift has been extended up to the front dash."

"And that would only happen why?"

He shrugged. "Somebody has a deformed arm maybe? There could be other modifications made on it too."

"You've got the license plate?"

He shook his head. "No, but I have the make and model of the car. Let me work on that."

He dove into that, while she sat back, with all her theories running. When she came to Brandon's case history, it was clean. It was way too clean. As in scary clean. She realized that some history here had been secreted away, and somebody had gone to a lot of trouble to make sure that nobody ever found it. And most likely he had a juvie record as well, but good luck getting that unsealed.

"Belongs to a student with a disability. According to the records, he has half a right arm. So makes sense on the gear shift."

"Good catch." Returning to her keyboard, while shaking her head, she pulled up an email and sent off a request. It would come back saying the records were sealed, but maybe that would be enough. That fact alone would give her a little ammunition. People had gone to great lengths to make sure nobody ever found out what the hell Brandon had been up to. Maybe the suggestion of a court order would be enough.

With that, she went back to her research on Paula. That was a whole different story. She was not the angel her mother had said she was, but her mother probably didn't know about the depth of her problems since she'd hit the university. Drunk in class, drugs, misdemeanors, theft from other students, generally raising chaos and raising Cain. She'd been put on suspension once and had a second one written up. Kate frowned at that. "Looks like Paula was in trouble a lot," she murmured.

"While hanging out with that crowd, I'm not surprised."

She nodded. "I doubt the mother knew anything about any of this."

"Paula would have done everything she could to keep that from them, just to stay here with her perfect boyfriend Brandon."

"Of course, but she had to be pretty damn close to getting her ass kicked out," Kate said, "and she didn't have an attorney on retainer or someone standing by to make a nice big donation."

"I'm sure the mother would blame this group."

"I'm not sure that it wasn't them either, but people still have to own their own decisions. You can't just blame everybody else in life."

"No, but obviously this Brandon kid had some weird control over the others."

"We've seen it before." Kate shook her head, ending with a sigh. "It's like a weird mesmerizing personality that gets people to do what they wouldn't do in any other circumstance. In this case, we've got two young women, vying for the same guy potentially, but, according to Brandon, having some attraction to each other, caught up in this triangle. The whole transvestite angle was definitely to derail us but also to soothe his ego. Can you imagine how Brandon would handle it if some hot girl dumped him for another girl?" Kate chuckled at that. "What a fragile sense of self. And neither of the women really fit into the bullying rich-guy group, but they sure were desperately trying, yet not succeeding."

"And is there anything worse than failure in college?" he asked, looking at her. "Worse than high school. If you don't make the popular group, they feel doomed forever."

"Especially in a case like this," she murmured. "Failure is not an option because, if you aren't part of *that* group, what are you?"

"Pretty sad that they think that way," he muttered.

"Right. You'd think they would have figured that out in high school," she said.

"Nobody gets past that need. Human nature has an innate desire to belong to something, even if it's the wrong group."

SIMON LAY ON his bed in the early morning, as he tried to figure out if it was safe to get up or not. For some reason he had a sense of impending pain. He hated that concept. There was absolutely no reason for it, as he looked around his bedroom, everything was suspect at the moment. His gaze narrowed, as he wondered where this information was coming from. Whenever something bizarre like that filtered through his brain, he had to stop and wonder if it was him or if it was a vision. The fact that he was even contemplating such things was enough to drive him crazy because it shouldn't be visions. That was of his grandmother's world, not his own. At least as far as he was concerned. But it didn't seem to matter what he wanted these days.

As he rolled over to get out of bed, he banged his head against something. His night stand was where it always sat, out of the way and up against the wall. He should easily have gotten out of bed without hitting it. But he hadn't seen it.

He slowly got up and realized that he was struggling to see anything. He shook his head, and clarity came back again.

He kept on moving, got to the bathroom, turned on the hot water, and stepped in for a shower. Not for the first time, he wished he could talk to somebody. And though the time and opportunity had long past, his grandmother would have been the perfect person.

He stepped out, feeling better, yet these weird little cloudy wisps of another person's life seemed attached to him. It filtered in and filtered out, so sometimes he thought it was his world, when it really wasn't, and vice versa. It added chaos and confusion to his world. It was something he would have to work on. If he could get them to stop or could get the connection to that veil to strengthen, so that the visions or thoughts couldn't cross so easily, it would help.

Not that he blamed whoever it was because he highly doubted they had a clue what they were doing either. If, in fact, they had done anything. Somebody was just calling out in need. Unfortunately Simon was picking it up, as a receiver. And that just brought back memories of his grandmother because, of course, she'd been a receiver and had been able to do a lot.

His grandmother would flat-out say that it didn't matter what he wanted; it mattered what the spirit wanted. She was a firm believer that this was all spirits at work. And, in her case, she believed in God.

He was on the fence about that. He couldn't understand that a God was out there who would allow a child, like Simon at four years old, to be hurt the way he was, with nobody to give a damn. That had really bothered him growing up, especially when the church types had repeatedly told Simon that God was looking out for him because Simon knew in his heart of hearts that, after his grandmother's death, there hadn't been anybody looking out for him.

As an adult, he could now see why there had been so much belief in the world, especially for those whose faith had not yet been tested, but it didn't make him ready to listen to it. His grandmother had just said it was the Great Spirit around them. That they were all part of the same. He'd never told her about what happened to him, but she seemed to have known, though not at the time it was happening, only later when they reconnected. It had taken a long time for him to make that connection happen, but, as soon as he'd seen her, he'd instinctively known who she was, and, being as special as she was, she had seen it too.

That's when she'd also become worried about him, worried about the path already presenting itself in his life. Even though he told her that he didn't want anything to do with his "gift" and that he didn't even believe in it, there had been just enough psychic happenings where he couldn't *not* believe. Whether she had shown him those things on purpose or not, he didn't know, but she was certainly capable of such deceit, all in the name of giving him the facts of life.

Mostly because she had seen so much herself, and she didn't want him to be unprepared. But how did one prepare for having one's life put under a microscope like this and then be tormented to the extent that Simon had?

It made no sense that such a thing was even possible, and yet, here he was, still tormented, while being connected to some woman crying her heart out. He didn't know if she was physically hurt. It seemed like she was emotionally traumatized. In the background with her tears, although right now she wasn't sobbing, it was more of a heartfelt disquiet on the inside. He wanted to poke it and make it bleed because, if it festered and didn't bleed, then it would never heal. But that emotional ball inside wasn't something he seemed to be able to access. It was more of an emotional window into her soul, and that was hard to take in.

Shrugging, he turned his head, as he got dressed, looking out at the city around him. It would be a gorgeous day. He really loved this area and especially enjoyed walking along the harbor, sitting down with a coffee. It also reminded him that he was behind on his workouts, something he rarely let happen. He enjoyed his workouts, but, at the same time, he also found a lot of things were keeping him off balance right now. Things that he probably shouldn't let have that much power over him.

On that note, he stopped and frowned because that's exactly what he was doing. He was letting this "gift" have power over him, and that was something he couldn't afford. He quickly changed into his jogging shorts and a muscle shirt. He picked up a key he kept on a wristband, put it into his pocket, leaving his wallet and full set of keys behind, then headed downstairs.

He didn't let himself think about it, but he just raised a hand to the doorman as he plowed through the stairwell door into the lobby and kept on going outside, intent on a hard morning run. He heard Harry in the background, telling him to have a good time. Simon wasn't sure anybody had a good time running, although, at times, it was good to run and to get away. As he ran, he let the voices disappear inside his head. He let them drift out what he considered the back door to his mind, as he was breathing really hard.

He exerted himself right now, waiting for the oxygen to kick his brain into gear, for his nerves to fire up, and for his heart to come alive and to make all this seem like it was his world—not somebody else's. Being caught between two worlds was the oddest feeling ever, and he just wanted to be in his world, not theirs. He wanted to feel alive, not half dead with these other ghostly impressions. He ran down the blocks for a good mile, before swinging down around the harbor and coming up along one of the paths.

And here, he picked up the pace and raced faster and faster. The area was mostly empty; the world was just waking up. The sun had risen but just barely crested over the horizon. The rays landed on the water at his side, as he ran harder and faster, until finally he felt his heart slamming against his chest, and his brain lit up like a Christmas tree. His body pulsed with energy, as he slowed to a walk and cooled down.

When he circled back around again, coming up on the same walkway, an old man sitting on the bench smiled at him. "That was a hell of a run."

Simon looked at him, grinned. "Some days you just need to make sure that everything is alive, even when they feel half dead."

The old man cackled. "Hey, in my world, half dead is still a good thing."

"Not mine." Simon smiled. "I needed to know it was still my world."

"Hey, I get you. Sometimes we're pulled in so many different directions that you wonder if it's even worth trying to fight it anymore."

"Yet it has to be," he murmured. "Because, otherwise, there's nothing."

"Haven't you figured out that nothing's there anyway?" he asked, with a quirky smile.

"I hope you're wrong," Simon murmured.

"You just got to decide what it is that you'll do in your life."

He stopped, looked at the old guy. "In what way?"

"Will you listen to the voices in your head, or will you do what *you* want to do?" And, with that, he lifted a hand and stood. "Have a good day." And he turned and walked away.

The old man's words were uncannily prophetic because the words in Simon's head weren't what anybody would have expected to be there. It was definitely a case of listening to them or listening to his own words. Is that why he was out of sorts? Because he was listening to other people? Of course he was listening to other people, but why?

It hit him just then—because this crying woman needed help. He didn't know how to help her, but there had to be a way. And because he didn't know what that was, he was the one feeling pressured and powerless.

"It's all about finding the pathway forward," he muttered to himself, as he walked back to his penthouse. "So how do I find out what to do? I've already tried to track this woman, and I'm not getting a response. I've tried to figure out who she is and where she is, but, for all I know, she's not even in the damn country." And that thought posed its own problems.

According to his grandmother, geography didn't necessarily matter. As far as he was concerned, that made no sense because surely a signal should be stronger if it were closer, but his grandmother had said it had nothing to do with distance and everything to do with emotional connection. That wasn't what he wanted to hear, but, in a twisted way, it made some sense. Except this woman was breaking his heart with her tears and that ingrained sadness, that loneliness overwhelming her. It impacted his life because he couldn't find a way to reach out to help her.

There was no way for him to tell her that it would be okay because, hell, half the time in life, things weren't okay, and there was no way to make them that way. And he wasn't somebody who would lie just to make her feel better. It was one thing to tell her that she was strong enough to handle whatever this was and to offer support, but it was another thing entirely to tell her it would magically be okay.

As he walked back up to his building, he saw Harry, a big grin on his face.

"Now you look better. Earlier you looked as if you were running from something hellish."

"I do feel much better."

"Good, glad to hear it."

When Simon walked inside his penthouse, he brought out his blender and snagged a couple fresh oranges, made orange juice, and then added bananas, protein powder, his oils, and some greens to it. With a beautiful shake in front of him, and, feeling like he might be getting back a little more to normal, he sat down and enjoyed his breakfast.

CHAPTER 15

K ATE WAS FRUSTRATED that, with rundowns on all the suspects and all the observers they had managed to locate and to talk to, nobody saw anything on the second killing at the intersection. Even when they had gone through as many of the faces as they could, they still saw no sign of anybody with a disability or even someone at Candy's crime scene that seemed to have been at Sally's crime scene just days earlier. It was well-known in the industry how other criminals stayed at a crime scene to watch the chaos they caused—arsonists, for example.

Back for yet another visit, Kate stood at the intersection, her hands in her pockets, and studied the surroundings. A pizza shop was on one side, and she and Rodney had checked its surveillance cameras, but they weren't working. She walked over to see if they sold pizza by the slice because her stomach was growling; it was lunchtime, after all.

As Kate entered the front door, several people left. She noted a couple empty tables, and one was tucked into the far side. She walked over on a hunch and considered, if somebody had been sitting here, they would have a perfect view of what was going on at Kate's intersection in question. She sat to confirm.

With a nod, she stood, heading to the front counter, reading the menu. They did have pizza by the slice, and, not caring what they gave her, she just had the guy behind the counter choose whatever was hot out of the oven. He served her immediately, and she stood off to the side to eat, while she continued her conversation with him. "Do you ever get people who sit here for a while?"

He nodded. "Sure, lots of students. They bring in their laptops, and sometimes we get locals, who stop by, waiting for the fresh pizza to come out."

"Do you ever get some people who just come in for coffee?"

He shrugged. "It's not as common, but we do have a group of customers who like to sit around and have coffee."

"Is the coffee that good?" she joked.

"Actually, it is." The guy smiled. "One of the best-kept secrets around. My boss invested in a really good espresso machine, so it's something you can count on. The locals all know about it. Here. I'll give you a cup to try for yourself."

"Interesting. Anybody in that group that's been enlightening?" He frowned, not quite sure how to answer that question. She shrugged, pointing out the storefront windows. "We've had so many accidents out there, we're just trying to see if anybody around here may have seen something."

"You should talk to Bill."

"Who is Bill?" she asked.

"One of the regulars and he sits over in one of those chairs." He pointed to a couple seats by the big picture window.

"When does he usually come in?"

"Every couple days. I haven't seen him today yet, but I wouldn't be surprised if he shows. I think he was here yesterday. Yeah, when the police were all here. We were talking about it. He's the one who told me that it was the second one in just a short time."

"You didn't know about that?"

"No, I was off that day." He shrugged.

"So, you wouldn't know if he was here when the other accident happened then?"

"No. He'd heard about it for sure, but almost everybody here had. You don't hear something like that without everybody talking about it."

"What are you hearing?"

He started to speak, then looked uncomfortable for a moment. "Mostly, like, wondering why the cops aren't doing something about it."

She winced at that. "Right. That's always a topic of interest."

"You're a cop, aren't you?" he asked.

"A detective, but it's amazing how many people don't see anything, even though it's information we need to solve some of these crimes."

"Right, nobody ever wants to get involved, I suppose. Bill is like that, so, even if you were to talk to him, I don't know if he'd tell you anything."

"Why is that?"

"He says, he *doesn't like no coppers.*" The kid shook his head, grinning.

Chuckling, she replied, "Sounds like quite a character."

"If you could ever convince him to talk, he'd probably have a lot to say."

"How old is he?"

"Oh, he's not that old, I suppose. He's got to be forty."

Kate stared at the kid behind the counter. "You're calling forty old? When did that happen?"

"I mean, for here, he is. We see mostly university students, so, as far as our customers go, he is old."

She'd accept that as an excuse, but still it smarted. But it was more irritating when she realized that younger people, like him, thought life over and done at forty. Old age sets in then. "Did he ever say anything else?"

"Nah. He doesn't talk a whole lot," he said.

"Interesting."

Pointing at her empty plate, he asked, "Want another?"

"Not now. Do you have any other regulars around here?"

He shook his head. "Not really, although a couple come in every once in a while." He shrugged. "Bill comes in more often. The other day he came in and wasn't happy when somebody was sitting in his chair, so I guess he comes in enough that he considers it his spot." The kid gave her a one-arm shrug. "In fact, when the other guy up and left, Bill moved over and sat in the same damn spot."

"Oh, that's too funny. But people get comfortable in their habits, even proprietary, though they don't always have any reason to."

"Yeah, that's Bill." He shifted his gaze, then nodded behind her. "That's him coming in now."

And, sure enough, as she turned, a man maybe in his forties walked in and headed to the counter. She stepped off to the side slightly.

Bill moved into place. "Morning. I'll take the usual."

"Sure, no problem, I was just talking to this lady about you."

At that, Bill turned to look at her. "Cop?"

"Yeah, detective, good eye."

"You can smell them all a mile away."

"You were on the force, huh?"

He looked at her in surprise, then nodded slowly. "Yep, I was actually. How'd you know?"

"I can smell an ex-copper a mile away." She gave him a knowing grin.

He looked at her with respect. "Not too many people know that."

"Maybe not, but it's all good."

He snorted. "It depends. You getting anywhere in this damn case here?" he asked. "People are dropping like flies around this place."

"I hear you were here the day of the latest accident."

"Both days. I was here early enough to see the one, while I was sitting here, but I didn't see the other one though."

"Yeah?" she said. "Did you see anything helpful?"

"Sure took you guys long enough to get around to this place. It's got a bird's-eye view."

"I know. That's why I'm here. I also needed coffee and some more food." At that, her stomach rumbled.

He shook his head. "I remember that on the job. Seemed like we never had any time to get a meal in."

"True enough. So, did you see anything?"

She studied him, as he turned and looked over at the kid behind the counter, watching as he made up the coffee for him. "Not really. Nothing I could count on, at least."

"Anything you can't count on?"

He turned toward her. "You really got nothing, huh?"

"Not a whole lot," she said cheerfully. "Of course everybody is pretty thin when it comes to having any information."

"That's normal. What about the cameras?"

"The cameras here are broken," she said.

Bill looked at the guy behind the counter. "Really, kid?"

"Yeah, we had a break-in a while back, and they damaged the cameras. The boss never got them fixed."

"You probably need to get on that," Bill said. "Otherwise, if it happens again, the insurance company will be all over him."

"I think that's partly why he didn't bother getting it fixed. The insurance wouldn't cover it in the first place, so then he figured, why bother? They wouldn't cover it anyway, so it was just more money out the window for nothing."

At that, Bill nodded. "Once you start getting into a scenario like that, it's pretty damn hard to convince yourself that it's worth the money."

She watched the two talk. "So, back to the accident."

Bill snatched up the pizza the kid held out for him, grabbed his coffee, and walked over to his preferred table. "As you can see, I had a good view. But, when I came in that day, I wasn't looking out the window. I was studying the newspaper."

"So you didn't see anything?" Her heart sank.

He nodded. "Exactly. I saw it afterward, when the woman was already on the ground."

"Did you rush out to help her?" she asked curiously.

"Nope, I'm not doing that shit no more. Besides, a crowd had already gathered."

"How quickly? Too quickly?"

"Now that's a good question." He stopped to consider her. "That's a really good question." He thought about it and shook his head. "I don't think you're right though. It happened fast, and the driver of the car got out. But he took off soon enough, and she didn't look like she was all that badly hurt."

"So he did get out?"

He frowned, thought about it. "The second one, not the first one."

"You saw the first one?"

"I did but not for long. And I didn't hang around. A ton of people were gathering fast. I knew the cops were on the way, and it would just be chaos."

"And you didn't want to get questioned, I suppose," she said in a dry tone.

"Hell no," he muttered. "I know how long that takes."

"And you don't want to be a good citizen now, huh?"

"Nope, don't feel any incentive for that at all, nothing in it for me."

"You only do what's in it for you now?"

"Yep, pretty much."

"What happened to you?" she asked, frowning.

"Not all cops end up retiring, being all good ex-cops." He sneered. "I didn't leave on good terms, so I don't really have a whole lot of fond memories."

She winced at that. "I guess that's everybody's worst-case scenario. When you put in that many years, you do want to get your pension and hope there's something else to do when you leave."

"There is. You rot at home. You can't get other jobs."

"You're still young," she said.

"Yeah, but with a disability."

"On the job?"

He shook his head. "No, that was the worst part because I would have gotten a better pension if it had been."

"Yeah." She grimaced, then shrugged. "Life is a bitch no matter what, it seems."

"It is, indeed." He gave a startled laugh. "Anyway, I

didn't see anything I could help with. Otherwise I would have called somebody," he said. But he appeared to be dismissive of it.

"Did you see the vehicle?"

"Which one?"

"So, they weren't the same?"

He stopped, looked at her, and shook his head. "No, they weren't."

She nodded. "It was a thin hope anyway. Anybody hanging around the same crime scene twice?"

"Not that I noticed, but it did occur to me. When it happened the second time, that just seemed like way too much of a coincidence."

"My thought exactly. Anyway, if you do hear something …" She pulled out her card and handed it to him.

He nodded. "I can do that. Particularly if you're paying for my pizza."

She rolled her eyes at that one but paid for his pizza, ordered herself a coffee to go, and walked outside. She didn't know whether she believed Bill or not, but it was interesting that he sat here all the time. Did he have any attachment to this place, or did it just happen to be a cheap place to get food on a limited budget? Despite his disability claim, he looked very healthy, so she didn't know what the hell was going on. She didn't even know his full name and considered whether she should interview Bill further at the station. She frowned at that, and, as she walked back inside and looked around to find Bill, he wasn't here. She looked at the kid. "Where'd he go?"

"As you went out the front, he went out the back. Bill muttered something about the air no longer being as fresh and clean."

"Interesting. I don't suppose you know his last name."

"*Huh.*" The kid frowned. "You know what? I don't think I do." He paused, as if thinking. "No, I don't think I've ever heard it mentioned. Bill is all I know."

She nodded. "Any idea where he lives?"

He shrugged. "Nope. He just shows up and buys stuff and sits here a while, then leaves. Just the way we like it."

She nodded and headed out the rear exit. She went outside, seeing that the back of the pizza place connected to an alley that went around the corner and came out at the block again. She kept walking down the same direction, wondering where Bill had gone and why he'd left so suddenly. Was it really because he didn't like cops and had a bad taste from all of it? Or was it something else?

Instinctively she felt like something else was going on, but she had no idea what it could possibly be. She wanted it to be connected, but just because she wanted it to be didn't mean it was. She kept on walking, until she saw him up ahead. He turned to look back, saw her, froze for a moment, then bolted. She tossed her coffee and raced after him.

Now she really wanted to have a talk with him.

Then lost him around the next corner.

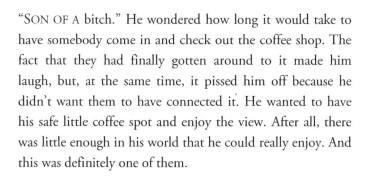

"SON OF A bitch." He wondered how long it would take to have somebody come in and check out the coffee shop. The fact that they had finally gotten around to it made him laugh, but, at the same time, it pissed him off because he didn't want them to have connected it. He wanted to have his safe little coffee spot and enjoy the view. After all, there was little enough in his world that he could really enjoy. And this was definitely one of them.

After the cop had left, he'd laughed because it seemed like all he could do was play games with the coppers, and that suited him and the other guy, fleeing her now; the police were kind of boring and stupid. But when she came after the other guy, he realized she must have suspicions. He'd been looking after this for a long time now, and he wouldn't let them get in his way, not when he was finally down to the wire. He needed to finish this, and, as soon as he did, he would stop. That was the plan.

He hoped he could stop; it had at least been something he had looked forward to every year. The fact that things were off this year wasn't his fault. It was the damn rich kid's fault. If he and his crew hadn't done what they had done, then he wouldn't have done what he'd done. At least that was the theory, but a part of him, that tiny sneaky part of him, was staring at him sideways, reminding him that he was enjoying it a little too much.

He didn't think anything could be a *little too much*. Yet it was too risky to keep this up, so he couldn't. He had to finish. But *knowing* he should versus *doing* what he should was like getting a gym membership because he knew it was good for him, yet, at the same time, he hated it. So he found any excuse to not go. Thus he was now finding any excuse to *not* stop because it really was far too much fun. Something about the control and regaining a sense of purpose in his life and the sensation of not being a victim to the world around him anymore.

That was an inescapable pleasure.

Putting it on other people, letting them be the victims, made it even better and was something he really wanted to pursue. But, if he didn't stop doing what he was doing, he knew that, at some point in time, the cops would catch him. They might be stupid now, but they wouldn't be stupid forever. And the thought of having to go to jail for this and to be a victim all over again made him sick to his stomach.

If he continued this—and here he was, already trying to set up alternate plans in order to give himself permission—then he would have to find a way to get out of it permanently at some point. Whether that meant killing himself before the cops found him or suicide by cop was something else; it would have to be an all-or-nothing deal.

So what the hell would he do about it?

He had pondered his options, as the day had turned from morning to afternoon. And finally he shrugged and parked it.

"We'll finish this. That was my original plan. That was my initial commitment. *That was my promise.* Then after that," he muttered, "we'll see."

He still had a couple more to do, a couple more years, although he wasn't sure that would happen, considering that he'd already killed this year. But, when they said that practice made perfect, they weren't kidding. It also made it so much easier in that he stopped thinking about the consequences. And that was the dangerous part because, if there were no consequences, what the hell was stopping him from taking out any asshole who he didn't like in the world?

Nothing.

Still, that was not today's problem. Today's issue was getting rid of the cop who was hanging around this corner, wondering what the hell was going on. He knew something was in her head, something a little more than he wanted her thinking about. Did he need to do something about it now? That was the question.

Then he realized he was talking about killing a cop for the first time, and, instead of fear, all he felt was a buzz of pure pleasure.

CHAPTER 16

TWO DAYS LATER Kate sat at her desk. Reams of paper were in front of her, plus her screens. Her whiteboards were beside her. Each day was a repeat of the previous one. If not for the fire in her belly, Kate would have given up long ago.

"What are you doing now?" Rodney asked.

"I'm going back over the previous incidents at this intersection or nearby to see if I can find any similarities, any connections."

"And you're thinking they have something to do with these two recent deaths of Candy and Paula now?"

"I don't know if they do or not. I'm grasping at straws. We have very little in the way of forensics. We're still waiting on the autopsies on Candy and Paula, and, so far, no witnesses saw anything. And, of course, spoiled-brat bully Brandon is at home, smug as a cat in front of the fire, thinking he can completely walk free. Again. As soon as I've done this, I'm hoping to talk to Dr. Paul Agress myself to ask him about these previous victims."

"You think he'll know any of them?"

"I looked it up, and he has been there for fifteen years." She eyed Rodney over her sheath of papers. "So, in theory, if he wanted to cooperate, the answer to that question would be yes."

"And if he doesn't?"

"Then I suspect he's protecting the university."

"Which would be his position anyway," he said.

"True, but we have to do something here. I should reach out to the RCMP and see if they have any similar reported cases. I've been trying to search these victims' names to see if anything comes up that could connect any of them, but I haven't had a whole lot of success."

"Give me the names again. I'll sit down and work on that."

"Or maybe try one of Reese's assistants?"

"I've got the time."

She ran off the names. When he had them in front of him, she asked, "What are the chances it was just luck? What if it was just somebody testing his prowess for staging deaths as accidents and deciding if this game was worthwhile? I just … I don't get it. Are people so bored in life that this becomes something new for them?"

"I don't know." He shrugged, turned, as he started running through searches. He frowned. "There really isn't a whole lot on these cases, is there?"

She shook her head. "Not on the internet anyway. There's the odd mention and that group of locals trying to get that whole traffic pattern changed because of the accidents, but they never really got anywhere with it."

"No, because you'd have to prove that the traffic pattern is causing the accidents, which, in this case, I agree with the city, and it isn't."

"Maybe, but you know what we do have? Five cyclist accidents, one a year for the last five years."

"But that's the problem. It's been one a year there until recently but also probably fifteen over the last ten years in that same area."

"Do we think any of them are connected?" she asked.

"I don't know. We'll have to run through the database and see just how many there are, see if it's the same vehicle, same drivers, same anything."

"I doubt it will be," she said.

"You're not really thinking more than one person is involved, are you?"

"I don't know," she said. "But think about it. Five annually at the same time at or near the same place seems like a revenge thing. So someone died six years ago—or, hell, ten years ago for all we know—that meant a lot to someone who got no closure, so he's doing this. Then we've got Brandon. I can't make a connection between the possible revenge thing and the sheer bullying thing gone wrong. None of this is making any sense. I can't help thinking that Candy was killed because she knew something about what Brandon and his gang had done."

"Knew something or saw something." Rodney nodded, sitting back.

She stood. "I think I'd like to go back to the scene."

He agreed. "That's fine. I'll come with you, if you want."

She shook her head. "Better if you keep running through these to see if you see anything that links them. Fresh eyes and all that."

"I can do that," he said.

She took related stacks of paper and shoved them into a big envelope. "I'll take these with me too."

"Good enough. You're sure spending a lot of time up there."

"I know. It's as if I feel like somehow I'll be on the spot

when the next one happens." She almost laughed at her own statement, sounding like Simon, with the jumpers. "It's just that weird sensation that I should see something that I'm not otherwise seeing."

He nodded. "Just don't get obsessed over it."

"Of course I will." She gave him a half smile. "It's an open case. *Obsessed* is what I do best."

He snorted. "I get it, but it's also not a good way to live."

"Neither is not having any answers," she said quietly. "For us or for the families."

And, on that note, she headed to her vehicle, thankful she had driven in today. The drive across town wasn't too bad, but it was still about forty minutes before she pulled into the pizza place. As she hopped out, she walked into the place, studying the intersection through the big front windows and ordered coffee. The same kid was behind the counter.

He looked at her in surprise, and she shrugged. "I'm back, just looking at the intersection again."

"I don't know what you'll see. It's not like it's changed much in the last few days."

"How long have you worked here?"

"A couple years." He shrugged.

"You've seen any other accidents around here?"

"Sure, but nothing where anybody got badly hurt. The one with a couple pedestrians. One where they were playing around, and she got pushed into the road. She was lightly tapped by a car, but that was it."

She nodded. "Did you know any of the victims?"

"Nope, I stay away from the university crowd. Not that the people in the accidents were all students—or maybe they were. I don't know."

"Why is that?"

"Partly because it's not my scene. Another part is because I don't think they see me as part of their scene."

"I can understand that. Thanks for the coffee." She paid and turned to walk out.

"You haven't found anything yet, have you?"

"Not yet," she said sadly, "but we're on it."

"Yeah, it must be hard to figure out though."

"Trouble is, it takes time to get forensics. It takes time to get anything. So, as much as it might look like we're not doing anything, we are."

He nodded. "I didn't mean that the wrong way."

"Not a problem. It's a misconception that we deal with all the time."

"Yeah, good point. Sorry about that."

She walked outside and stood in front of the pizza parlor. It was empty at the time, but, as she took a sip of her coffee, she wondered. Stepping back inside, she asked, "Hey, have you seen that guy again. Bill?"

"Now that you mention it, no. I haven't seen him since that day you both were here last."

She nodded and stepped back outside again. If the ice-bullet shooter was Bill, he didn't want to show up in his same spot, and, if the five annual deaths at this intersection wasn't about Bill either, he was doing his best to keep a low profile.

While she stood here, Rodney called. "Did you find anything?" she asked.

"The only thing I could confirm was that they were all students."

"Which I was assuming, so I didn't take time to verify it,

but I'm glad you did."

"Why would you assume that?"

"I don't know, but they were all on bikes, and it seemed like a student thing to do."

"No, you'll find a lot of the faculty and staff there ride bikes as well. And there is a lot of staff. Don't kid yourself. That university is a small city."

"My bad, but our victims were all students, huh?"

"Yes. And these ones in particular are from the Faculty of Arts."

"Okay," she said, "thanks for covering me on that then."

"What are you up to now?"

"I just stopped in at that pizza parlor, grabbing a coffee and asking if that Bill guy had been back again, but he hasn't been in."

"Either way, if he's involved in this, he won't want you to see him, and, if he's not involved, you probably chased him away from his favorite haunt for now."

"I know. I'm heading over to get answers now," she muttered, "still looking for a connection, still looking for something that would tell us what the hell is going on."

"And yet, we have connections. It's just not close enough to pin anything on."

"I know. Track any of those victims against Brandon and his crew, will you? Cross-reference everything from previous schools, parents, siblings, charges, if there are any. Look at anywhere they might have crossed paths."

"You're still thinking they're connected, these repeat anniversary killings and Brandon?"

"Yeah, I know. Brandon wasn't around five or six years ago and would have made for a younger suspect. But, the trouble is, because of the way Candy was killed, either it's a copycat of Sally's death or it's a connection."

"Either way, it's a connection. It's just whether it's ... Yeah, got it," he said.

And, with that, she hung up. She walked around to her vehicle, hopped in, and went around the block, so she could hit the intersection the right way, then turned the corner and drove down to the boulevard.

As she got close to the admin building, she parked and walked in to find the Executive Assistant for the Dean, Faculty of the Arts, on the phone. Kate waited until she got off her call, held out her badge, and said that she needed to see her boss for a few moments. The woman immediately looked worried. Kate tried to reassure her. "I just need a few moments to ask him a couple questions about this trouble on campus."

"I know he's pretty booked, but let me go see." She hopped up and disappeared into the room behind her. When she came back out a few minutes later, she looked more relieved. "He'll see you now," she said, with a bright smile to Kate.

Kate muttered, "Thanks," as she walked past and inside the office to find Dr. Agress, sitting behind a huge desk.

He looked up, frowned. "Sorry, I don't have very long. Hope this can be fast."

"That's fine. Even a few minutes for a few questions will help."

"How can I help you?" He crossed his hands, resting them in front of him. "I have to admit I'm more accustomed to working with students. Surely this is for the UBC Legal Department to handle or maybe the Committee of Student Affairs. At least the RCMP over the VPD."

"Both law enforcement departments work together as

needed. I can bring them in on this, if necessary. Have you heard about Candy yet?"

"Did you find her?" His face lit up. "I really hate it when we can't keep track of the students, but they're all expected to be adults."

"In this case, it's a little bit different."

He looked at her, a frown forming. "Oh, dear, what do you mean?"

"She was found dead at the intersection at the entrance to the boulevard."

He winced at that. "That intersection, most of the time I don't even think about it. Then we have an accident, and it brings back every other accident that's happened there."

"I understand there have been quite a few."

"Yes, over the years, there definitely have been. I was part of a group who tried to get the traffic pattern there changed, so we could minimize the accidents—at least get a bike path over the top or something. Unfortunately it's such a small intersection compared to some of the bigger ones in the actual downtown core that it didn't make sense for the city to put that kind of money into it."

"I think they would have, if you could prove that the accidents were caused by the traffic pattern."

"What else would they be caused by?" he asked, with a wry smile. "I know people are idiots sometimes, but not everyone is all the time."

She chuckled at that. "No, that's very true, but, in this case, they're all different people."

He nodded. "Every time you hear of a new one, it just brings back the pain of the old ones."

"It does, and that's been a real hard cross for you to bear, I'm sure."

"When you try to get a pattern like that changed, hoping to save lives, and you fail ..." He shrugged. "Let's just say a failure that's once in a while is one thing, but a failure that you're constantly reminded of? That's a different thing entirely."

"In this case," she said gently, "it's a different story."

"How so?" He looked down at his cell phone, and she could see him checking the time.

"Actually, sir, she was murdered."

He froze, his gaze widening, and he stared at her. "Good Lord, are you sure?"

"Yes, I am. The other accident at the same location, just days earlier, involving Sally Hardgens, it was also a murder."

He leaned back in his chair, stunned. He shook his head. "No, no, no, that is not good news." Then he straightened. "But it's not on university property, so the negative impact should be minimal in terms of fallout for us."

"I get that's really *your* priority," she said, with heavy emphasis on *your*, "but *my* priority is the victims."

He had the grace to flush at that. "I'm not trying to be insensitive, Detective, but we do need to try to keep that conversation out of the media. Public confidence in keeping our students safe is paramount."

"And yet, two have been murdered. And I don't know, but there may have been many others over the years."

At that, his expression changed to a frown, and he looked quite puzzled. "I don't understand. Has there been any suggestion that—that the others were—that there were other murders I don't know about?"

"Not confirmed. We're looking at connecting a few scenarios that we thought were accidents that may not be."

"It's still very disturbing." He put on a very fatherly concerned expression.

"It is, indeed, but do you have files on anybody who complained about other students' behavior? Any accusations? Not just Brandon."

"Brandon, yes." Dr. Agress automatically looked at the file cabinet beside him. "He certainly has been a bit of a challenge. The RCMP opened a file on him after the last set of complaints."

"I'm sure he has been problematic," she said smoothly. "I understand he was removed from other universities before he came to you."

"We don't usually get the problem-child students. We're considered a much better bet than that. But, every once in a while, when the parents have run out of any other options, they'll come our way. Brandon's brilliant, you know that, right?"

"That's what he told me. That he doesn't have to worry about exams, doesn't have to study at all. Schoolwork is easy for him."

"Yes, and that's often a problem." Dr. Agress sighed. "Students need to work and accomplish something. Otherwise life becomes boring, and they go looking for a challenge in other ways. That is exactly what's happened to Brandon, and that's not good news."

"No, and he also has this group of other young people with him."

"Yes. And guys, like Brandon, they tend to collect people he would consider beneath him, people who won't challenge him in any way."

"But that just perpetuates the same issue, doesn't it?" She went on. "Still no challenge and completely bored, so he gets them into trouble with him."

"Perhaps because it's more fun that way because he can watch the downfall of their careers," he said quietly.

"It really sounds like Brandon needs to talk with somebody about his life goals and his methods of handling the challenges of life."

"Not all kids from rich families are useless, but all too often we get those who have had a far-too-easy pathway in life. In this case, because he's already very smart—which is something that money didn't buy him—but it goes right along with it."

"Right, so, if he applied himself, he could really be a huge asset to the family and to the university—and to the world in fact—but why bother, since he'll never have to work for a living anyway."

He nodded slowly. "Exactly."

"So, about that complaint file?"

He looked at his file cabinet again. "I know we've had a few," he said cautiously. "I just can't have any of this become public."

"We are the police, and I am looking into multiple problems on this campus."

"That's what concerns me. If I were to let you have that information, what are the chances that it would get out into the public or that you'd be questioning people, after this was done in confidence?"

She responded, "Whenever people write letters complaining about others and hand them over, it's not in confidence. I can get a warrant, but it would be much better if I didn't have to." She quietly studied him. "I get that you're all about trying to be effective and about protecting privacy and the reputation of the university, but what about protecting everybody else? What about protecting the ones at risk, but who don't even know about all these problems?"

"Let me go through them, and I'll hand you any that appear to be possibly relevant."

She winced at that. "The trouble with that is, something you think I should look at and my own interpretation are likely to be very different."

"I still need to go through them first," he said firmly. "I can't just hand over this information blindly."

"That's fine. I want it by tomorrow close of business then, or do you want me to go through the RCMP and have them process this through official channels?" He stared at her, and she stared back. "It's that important," she said quietly. "We don't want to lose any more students."

He swallowed hard at that. "You're serious? Is that a possibility?"

She nodded. "Yes, I'm serious. I am concerned that there could be more deaths."

He swore. "Fine." He picked up the phone. "Noreen, please reschedule my afternoon. I've got some things I need to do here." With that, he hung up, then, turning back to Kate, he said, "You can expect a call from me."

"It's an email I want, with attachments. Scan in the information and email it all to me by tomorrow at six p.m." Then she stood, laying her card on his desk, and nodded to him. "Thank you very much."

And she turned and walked out.

───※───

HIS DAY HAD been pretty decent. Simon appreciated a break from all his weird psychic symptoms. Today he had grabbed the tools of the trade and had worked on the roof of one of his buildings, with the rest of his rehab crew. Then he came down, nodded at the foreman, who looked at him with added respect, and headed home.

As he walked toward his penthouse, he heard the sound of a bicycle. He was now finally able to pinpoint what that weird background noise had been—the sound of somebody pedaling a bike—and he heard the faintest of whirs as the wheels turned. Even now he wasn't sure why that's what he'd been hearing, but it had gone on and on in his head, like somebody doing miles and miles. He felt the breathing, the hard breathing of somebody moving on a bike. Yet no sound of gravel or wheels on pavement. No slowing down or stops and starts. Yet maybe not someone on a bicycle outside. He frowned at that. It was just odd. So maybe it was a stationary bike? Then he realized it was likely her. "Hello?"

But he got no answer. What did he expect? It's not like anybody was listening to him just because he was listening to them. That was always the trick, realizing when you heard somebody versus somebody who heard him. Still, he was walking and listening, and then he heard the hard breathing and the harder breathing yet again. And finally a heavy sigh, almost a groan in his mind. And he knew how she felt. Whatever it was she was doing was really exhausting. He smiled, mentally gave her a high five. "Good job."

Then more heavy breathing came, as if she were slowing, yet out of breath. She never talked—well, except for one word earlier. That was the thing he found odd. And, even now, he had no vision to go with the sounds, with her feelings. He had connected with her emotions, but he couldn't see anything, just that shadowy world out there again. He struggled with that because, at least with the boy from the pedophile case, Simon could see something clearly.

With this, the longer he tried to peer into the darkness,

the less he saw. It was frustrating as hell. He just kept sending her positive thoughts and happy affirmations. And finally she calmed down, drifted away. He wasn't even sure that she knew what she was doing—projecting psychically—and suspected that she had no clue she was transmitting or that he was receiving.

The longer he was connected to her, the more he started to connect with her literally. He didn't think that was terribly healthy, but, hey, it was what it was, so he had no choice but to take whatever he got and carry on. As soon as he returned to his apartment building, he walked inside, and, sure enough, there was Harry again. "Hey, how are you doing, Harry?"

"I'm good, but how are you? That was a hell of a run you had the other day."

"Yep, like the devil was after me." He gave Harry a big grin.

"Hey, I don't—I don't joke about the devil," Harry said. "A little too scary for my liking."

Simon chuckled at that. "Isn't that the truth? Sometimes it makes you wonder if the devil isn't in us."

"I know it is," Harry said. "I've seen some bad shit in my life, and trying to be a good person doesn't always work out."

"No, it doesn't. And sometimes we have really shitty starts, and we spend the rest of our lives trying to earn forgiveness."

At that, Harry looked at him in surprise. "We always tend to think of the people in this building as born with a silver spoon in their mouths and having perfect lives."

"And you would be wrong," Simon said quietly. "Some of us came from the bottom and worked our way up."

"See? I knew I liked you for all the good reasons," Harry said. "I'd much rather know a man who did that than somebody who stepped out of his daddy's home into a fancy car his daddy bought for him to hang with the beautiful people, and everything else was just handed to him."

"That's definitely not my story." Simon grinned and waved, as he headed to the elevator.

Harry called out, "By the way, the wife loved the wine. Thanks again."

"You are welcome," Simon called back. As he entered the elevator car alone, that weird sense of smell showed up again. He froze; then he realized it smelled like curry. As the door shut, he asked the mystery woman in his head, "Did you ride to get curry? You want to pick me up some?" he joked. "I didn't bring any food home."

He didn't think he'd grocery-shopped at all this week. Then he remembered Kate had said she was still out of groceries too and probably still was. Hell, she always was. He pulled out his phone and typed a text message and sent it off. **I'm home, about to have a shower, get changed, and then maybe go grocery shopping. Dinner?**

He could only hope she'd say yes. But he also knew the current case she was working on was driving her a little bit bonkers. But he couldn't imagine any case not doing that. She wasn't the kind to sit back and to let the world go by; she wanted to do something and to make an effective change. He just wasn't sure that was always possible in her line of work. Hell, in his line of work too. By the time he hopped into and out of the shower and got changed, he found a text message from Kate.

Pick me up. I need groceries too, and it's a deal.

In response, he called her. "I'll meet you outside your

place, unless you are still at work. Or, if you've got any idea what you need, I'll go shop for both of us."

"Coffee for one thing."

When she yawned, that made him happy that he had offered.

"Other than that, groceries. Something fast and easy to pick up and eat on the run."

"One of these days, you'll have to get real food."

"I'll see what I can come up with," she said.

"I'll see you in about an hour." And he hung up.

He didn't really give her a chance to back out. He also knew that, if he gave her an inch, she'd take a mile, and she'd probably find a way to avoid meeting him. And that was something he wasn't prepared to let happen. There were so many good things about her that he couldn't walk away from her. Hence the state of their relationship as it stood right now—her fighting it every step of the way, and him not giving an inch and ignoring all her efforts at sabotage.

One of these days she would say that he mattered. He wouldn't wait for it, but he knew it would happen. He might have to wait a hell of a long time for it, but, if there was one thing he had, it was patience. At least where Kate was concerned.

Good things came to those who wait. And even better things came to those who made it happen. He'd be damned if he would let her walk away from this. One of these days she had to give in and had to realize just how important she was to him.

And how important he was to her.

CHAPTER 17

WHEN KATE GOT home, exhausted after her workout, Simon stood in front of her apartment, juggling multiple bags, as he tried to open the door.

"I'll get that." She walked rapidly toward him.

"Good." He held up a bobby pin. "I was about to unlock the door and let myself in."

"Not a good idea. We detectives have words for that."

"We haven't discussed *exchanging keys*." He put added emphasis on the last two words. She completely ignored it because that was the last thing she was ready to talk about. If she gave him access to her place, he would want to give her access to his, and his place was beautiful and made her feel so uncomfortable.

As she opened the door and let him into her cramped one-bedroom apartment, she scooped up a couple bags of food from the floor and brought them in with her. With all the groceries now sitting on top of the kitchen counter, she looked at it in wonder. "I didn't mean for you to buy out the store. I meant just a few things."

"Yeah, well, *just a few things* ended up being more than just a few. And every time we're here, we don't have any food to eat."

"I know. It's a fact of life, isn't it?"

"Short of having a chef who delivers or living on a property where we have somebody cook our meals, we are responsible for putting food on the table."

"I guess we could do takeout every night." She tilted her head, gave him a one-arm shrug. "Lord knows, sometimes I can go weeks and weeks that way."

"Not the healthiest of diets," he noted in admonishment.

"No, and you're also used to having whatever you want. I'm just not in that league."

"You might not be, but that doesn't mean you're not capable of doing more than you are."

She snorted. "Go ahead and criticize me," she snapped, "and see how much food you'll get."

He shrugged. "I brought pretty-easy-to-fix stuff. If nothing else, I'll slap together a sandwich. Go have a shower and an attitude change, and, when you're done, you'll probably feel better."

Glaring, she stomped off to the bathroom, muttering, "Who needs an attitude change?"

She did, clearly, but she wasn't about to acknowledge that. She quickly stripped down, stepped into the hot water, and stood here for a long moment, trying to figure out why she was so cranky, tired, and irritable. Well, from the looks of it, he had just spent hundreds of dollars on groceries, so now she felt beholden to him. If she tried to pay him, he'd be insulted, but she would give it a good shot anyway. She had asked him to pick up a few things, although he had picked up way-the-hell more than a few.

And yet he had also done it out of kindness, plus the fact that he too wanted to eat, which had turned her back around to being cranky.

When she stepped out of the shower, she quickly toweled off her hair, then ran a comb through it. Walking back into her bedroom, the towel wrapped around her chest, she found some clothes. Just a pair of jeans and a T-shirt. Dressed again, she padded out to the kitchen in bare feet to find that he had already put away most of the groceries.

"How much do I owe you for today's haul?" she asked in a crisp voice.

"Nothing."

Exactly what she had expected him to say, yet it didn't make her feel any better. "I'm happy to pay for the groceries. You know that."

He waved a hand. "And I'm happy to bring some groceries and have a meal with you. If I were to go to a high-end restaurant, it would take a couple hundred dollars to do a couple meals. This way, we've got lots of meals here."

"Are you cooking then?" she teased, something about his words hitting her funny bone.

"I can cook"—he turned to look at her—"in case you didn't think I could."

She shrugged. "I can cook too. That doesn't mean I make a big fancy meal out of it though."

"I don't do five-star-restaurant stuff by any means, but I can throw a steak on the barbecue, steam some vegetables, and make a salad."

Her stomach growled at the mention of food.

Hearing that, he laughed. "The trouble is, you don't even have a barbecue, do you?"

She shook her head. "The best I have to offer is a cast-iron skillet."

He frowned and considered the idea. "You know what? A cast-iron skillet does a hell of a job on a steak." He rummaged around in her cupboards, while she put on coffee, and, when she turned around, he had pulled out a large cast-iron pan, looking at it approvingly.

"Don't know where you got this, but it's exactly what we'll use." He put it on the burner, while he unwrapped steaks.

Those, to her, looked like they probably cost thirty dollars apiece. "Those are very expensive-looking steaks."

"And?" he asked smoothly. "Do you think I'll ask you to eat chopped liver? I bought the groceries, so just say, *Thank you*, and we'll eat."

"Thank you." As she watched him at work in her kitchen, she asked, "Do you want me to do anything?"

"What do you want to go with it?" He raised an eyebrow.

"I'm hungry enough that I'll need some starch."

"Rice, potatoes, or pasta?" he asked, tossing her a package of a mix of rice with quinoa.

She looked at it in surprise. "What are those funny little yellow things?"

"That's the quinoa."

She shrugged. "I recognize the rice part."

"Quinoa's good. We'll have that with it."

"In that case, why ask me?" she grumbled.

He chuckled. "You can pick the veggie."

But, as she looked at the vegetables he had put in her fridge, she wasn't even sure which would go best.

"It's not rocket science. Whatever you like goes best."

She laughed at that, then quickly picked up the broccoli and showed it to him.

He nodded. "Sounds good. Do you want to prep it, or shall I?"

She shrugged, took a small paring knife, and had it in

even size florets within seconds.

"Perfect. Now you can take your coffee and go sit and relax."

Her eyebrows shot up at that. "Did you not work today?"

"I did, but it wasn't as stressful a day, like some of them have been."

"Good for you. My cases are getting to be a nightmare."

"Sorry," he muttered, as he turned up the heat on the cast-iron pan. He already had the water for the rice mix coming to a boil. "Go take a break."

Following his orders and realizing that she was just cranky enough to make more trouble, she poured herself a coffee, walked over, and slumped onto the couch.

"You want to tell me about the case?"

"Not really. Unless you have any insights, I don't really want to discuss it."

"And how could I possibly have any insights," he noted in a reasonable tone of voice, "if you don't tell me what it's about?"

"I've told you a lot of it, but now my two cases have dovetailed." She shook her head. "I'm trying to figure out what these bullies at the university have been doing, but, so far, I haven't had any luck. I'm waiting on Dr. Agress's executive assistant to send me a list of complaints from other students, but he wanted to go through them first."

"Of course he did, so any complaints against rich donor-family kids won't be allowed to come your way."

She opened her eyes and stared at him. "Do you really think he'll censor them?"

He turned and gave her a hard look.

She nodded slowly. "In that case, I'll need a warrant. I

shouldn't have to do that."

"Send him an email and remind him that you want full access or you'll bring in a warrant."

She quickly sent off an email to Dr. Agress. She hated to, but, if he wouldn't be cooperative, it would just cost valuable time. "And that's only part of it. I don't know that these kids, the bullying gang, have anything to do with these murders at all."

"Murders?" He frowned. "Are we talking plural now?"

She nodded. "Yes, plural."

"Interesting, so you have a serial killer."

"I don't know that the definition of a serial killer would apply in this case. We have two deaths, both with similarities, and I'm really hoping we won't have any more victims."

"But didn't you also say you had another murder on the campus?"

"Well, fine, okay, so I have three murders. And you're right. I do, and this one, I ... I can't see that they *aren't* connected, but I haven't figured out how they are yet either."

"Which is very typical anyway, so that's hardly the issue."

"I'm still running comparisons, and it's taking so long."

"Comparisons of what?"

"It's a long shot," she explained, sitting up, grabbing her coffee, and pacing her living room. "But there have been a lot of accidents in that block over the last ten years."

"Similar?"

"Very similar, too similar for comfort."

"As in what similarity?"

"Running down cyclists."

"Well"—he stopped and shrugged—"that's a hard one because, with those kinds of accidents, there's only so much similarity possible. Cyclists are hit by vehicles all the time, unfortunately."

"I know, and that's the problem."

"Are these fatalities?"

"In all cases, yes."

"Did you check the relatives?"

"That's in progress. There are still about a good dozen people, depending on which case we're looking at, to be contacted. So far everybody we've contacted has talked about how horrible it was and how much it affected their lives, but I didn't get any ring of leftover anger or need for revenge or anything. To them it was just a straight-up accident. Something that was terrible and that people should be punished for, but there wasn't anything that anybody could do."

"Got it," he said.

She watched as he checked the rice, and then, adding the olive oil in the preheated cast-iron skillet, he tossed in the two big steaks. She was amazed that they even fit. He had cut off the edges of fat and had sprinkled some spices all over the top. "Where did you get the spices from?"

"I bought them." With a wave of his hand, he said, "Go back to the case."

"Well, and then, when we had a fatality at the intersection, it wasn't supposed to be my case, but a projectile penetrated the back of the cyclist's head, right above the ear."

He turned, looked at her. "So it was murder."

She nodded. "Yes, but whether the projectile was some kid on the golf course with an errant golf ball or someone on purpose with an ice bullet, we don't know yet. However, she managed to move forward after that hit to her head. The blow would have been stunning, but ... I don't know. I get the feeling that the projectile angle just kept pushing her into the intersection. It was timed very well, right at the intersection."

"So afterward she was hit by a car?"

"Yes, but the blow from the vehicle didn't cause very much damage. There would have been some bruising, but she had no broken bones, and she didn't hit the pavement with a horrific force. Obviously all of it together kills her, but the driver swears to God that he was stopped and didn't hit anybody, but he took off anyway."

"So he panics, and now you're looking at him."

"It's hard not to. But then we had the second murder at the off-campus student housing."

He nodded. "I remember you said something about that."

"Yeah, but it was in another woman's room."

"Right, but they were all partying that night."

"Exactly, but the woman who belonged in that room was missing."

He turned and looked at her. "Did you find her?"

"I did. In the intersection, the same intersection, with the same projectile hole behind her ear."

He stared at her in shock, his jaw dropping. "Seriously?"

She nodded. "Yes, so now our most recent cases, all within one week, are linked—the murder of Paula in student housing and the two others, shot by the same type of projectile, Candy and Sally, both found at the same intersection. Things are bad, and I'm worried there will be more victims. The only thing I have is this group of six people, of which two are now dead, the only two females. But get this. Both women had a sexual relationship with this rich-ass Brandon kid, and there was some fighting between the two females, but there is also talk that they may have had a relationship of their own."

"As in?" He looked at her, clearly puzzled.

"Apparently they often did threesomes with this puke Brandon, and then the two females would go off and have a twosome. That's according to Brandon though, and I don't believe jack shit that comes out of his mouth."

"Because he's the kid with the silver spoon, is that what you mean?"

She nodded. "He's also arrogant and slimy."

"Meaning, you find it hard to trust anything about him."

"And he has a lawyer on speed dial. He also earned himself an ugly reputation at several other universities, before he ended up at this one. I did speak to Dr. Agress, who acknowledged that Brandon came with a checkered past, but they didn't have any real proof because nobody at the previous institutions would go on record, saying he was a bad apple, so no one saw any reason not to allow him in UBC."

"Wonder how these decision makers will feel about that when this is all over."

"When I was there, asking him for any and all complaints against this group of bullies or any others on campus, Dr. Agress told me that he was part of a movement to get the city to change the traffic pattern so that these cyclist accidents could be avoided."

"And was the traffic pattern determined to be at fault?"

"According to the city of Vancouver, no, so their request was denied."

"That in itself could make people angry," he said.

"I hadn't considered Dr. Agress a suspect."

"No, and I don't suppose that he would make a good one anyway," Simon said. "I'm just pointing out the fact that, when you go through a lot of effort to affect change, and then it doesn't happen, it can leave people with an ugly taste in their mouths."

"Maybe." She groaned. "There's just nothing that I can lock down. I found a strange guy at a nearby pizza parlor, who likes to watch that intersection a little too much, so I wondered if he was watching the results of his actions."

"But he couldn't be shooting somebody and watching them get hit in the intersection at the same time, right?"

She looked at him and slowly shook her head. "No, which is another reason why occasionally our discussions in the bullpen have suggested there could potentially be two of them, working together."

He gave a low whistle. "Wow, these are brain twisters."

"Sometimes cases are simple. Sometimes people think that they're really smart and that we won't figure anything out, but then we get the evidence we need, and it all falls in place quickly. And then there are cases, like this, where you just sit there and stare at it, wondering if it's just too much of a coincidence to have all this stuff happening, and yet none of it even be related."

"That's the problem though, isn't it? If it's not related, then you have multiple separate incidents."

"Exactly."

"Now, why the second woman in the intersection with the same projectile from an angle behind her?"

"Right." Kate frowned. "So those are connected. But maybe the killer saw Candy at the first crime scene with Sally and picked out Candy randomly."

"Which then links Brandon the bully, as Candy was part

of his crew."

"And I really like that idea too," she said.

"Rich assholes will never be my favorite topic, so I like him as the killer."

"But this one has a lot of lawyer power, so we need to make sure that we have everything locked up tight. Therefore, they can't pull a random string and unravel the whole thing."

"And I get that." Simon shook his head. "Except for the projectiles, I would say it was just another random bike accident."

"Exactly, but it's the projectiles that make the bike accidents happen."

He stopped, turned around, looked at her. "And do you think that's what he's trying to do?"

"The thing is, I don't know. We're really struggling on the whole motive here for Brandon. Which is part of the problem anyway. For bullies, it's just because they can. Yet we have five annual bike accidents at or near that one intersection."

"It sounds like it all surrounds that traffic pattern somehow."

"And who kills over that?" she asked, with a wry look.

"Someone who lost a loved one there. Maybe that Brandon kid is just piggybacking on that." Simon blinked several times, as he thought about it. "That's just bizarre."

"Yeah, which part?" she asked, followed by a short laugh. "When you think about it, so much of this just doesn't make any sense."

"No, but if it's to make it look like a traffic accident, then you have to look back at the histories of all these other ones."

"Which is what I've been doing." She turned and looked at him. "I'm not exactly sitting around doing nothing."

"Whoa, believe me. I know that you're working your ass off on this. I just find it fascinating that, in this case, the traffic pattern matters."

"But it'll only matter because somebody is legitimately affected somehow by the traffic pattern."

He nodded. "So somebody connected to the deaths? The first one you dug up from ten years ago?"

"That was my thought, but, so far, we haven't found anything. But, like I said, I've still got a dozen family members and friends of the prior victims to connect with. I've left an incredible number of messages. Two are out of country, and I don't know about some of the others. We've got two who are missing persons, but the family of one said that the husband of one of the female victims just up and disappeared. They don't know where that husband is, but, because he was overwhelmed from the shock of what happened to his wife, they think he basically took a step back out of life—or committed suicide. And you know we have an awful lot of suicides across the country and a not very easily updatable database to try to track them down with."

"Or he's gone underground, and he's trying to get re-venge."

She stopped cold, looked at him. "That's another op-tion. It just depends on who this person is. Of course, in this case, I do have a name, but names can be changed, and people don't necessarily use their real names. I've asked for credit card records, phone records, anything and everything, and the family has given me any known forwarding address-es. They even asked that, if I get in touch with him, to let them know so they can reach out as well. They said they all had a hard time back then, and it would have been nice if they could have stayed in touch to support each other, but he was not in great shape."

"Oh, I like him for it now. Because people who are strong and emotional like that make all kinds of decisions, like finding a way to get back at the world."

"It was an accident, according to the records."

"An accident?"

"Yes, but also it was a young driver, and the roads were bad. It was winter, and, for whatever reason, his wife had decided to go cycling, figuring that, by the end of the day, since this is Vancouver, not like it's up north, the snow would be gone, and she'd be clear to go do her stuff. She was a fanatical cyclist. He didn't want her to go, and that's part of the reason why he's had so much trouble dealing with the loss because they had a fight on her way out the door."

"Oh, crap, and that changes the motivation then too, and it could just be that he's feeling guilty."

"Exactly. So, none of this is pulling together as a viable suspect."

"I still like him."

"And he's on my list. But he hasn't had anything to do with anybody in a long time."

"Right, so you have to find him first in order to even question him."

She nodded. "Exactly."

"What about kids?"

"There were a couple, a son and a daughter, and the extended family, her sister, has them."

"Hang on a minute. You mean, he walked away from his children too?"

She nodded. "Yes."

He frowned. "In that case, it doesn't play out the way I thought."

"That's what I mean. None of these theories are necessarily looking solid."

"What about any of the other victims' families?"

"There was one son from another family and two daughters from yet another victim's family. The rest had no children."

"Well, that's good. It's one thing to recover from a loss. It's another thing to recover from a loss when you still have children to raise."

"And, in many cases, in several of these, the spouses went on to remarry and have somewhat normal lives."

"Which is the healthy thing to do because focusing on what you've lost will never get you that same scenario back again."

"No, and it just gives you something to dwell on instead of picking up from the loss and moving on," she said quietly.

He looked at her and winced. "Hey, I didn't mean to bring up bad memories."

"They are always there, but I do understand loss in a way that a lot of people don't. So I empathize with some of these people. I certainly empathize with the father who turned and walked away because of what happened, but to leave the kids behind? No way."

"Yet, at the same time you can't judge him because you really don't understand."

"No, I don't. And that's another problem."

He nodded. "I get it."

At that, her phone rang. She looked at it, frowned. "I'll have to take this."

"You've got two minutes," Simon said on a note of

warning. "After that, I'll be pissed if you aren't here ready to eat a hot meal."

She nodded and answered her phone. "Detective Morgan speaking." She listened to the voice on the other end.

"Hey, I'm not sure why you were calling me, but I presume it has to do with my wife's accident because I haven't had a reason to be involved with the police otherwise," said a man with a gruff voice on the phone.

"Who are you?" she asked.

"I'm Jack, Jack Wellington. My wife died in a cycling accident at the university years ago."

"Ah, I'm sorry about your loss."

"Me too," he said, with a heavy sigh. "It was probably the roughest time in my life. But the kids and I, well, we got through it."

She nodded. "And what are you doing now?"

"I'm living in Saskatchewan. My son's at the university, and I'm dating a pretty professor."

"It's nice to see that life has picked up and moved on for you somewhat." She smiled at the thought.

"But your call was a blast from the past, and one I would just as soon not deal with."

"Right, I understand. Listen. I have calls out to several other victims of similar accidents, and we're going on a hunch with a current case. I would just like to confirm whether you know any of these people." And she ran through the list of prior victim names.

"Honestly, Detective, I don't know any of those," he said in astonishment. "Are you thinking that somebody other than the person who hit my wife is connected to another murder?"

"It was vehicular homicide. Yes, she died by another

hand, but ..."

He said, "I know. I know. I know. I don't want to get into the logistics. I went through a lot of anger and hours and hours of torment trying to figure out how to get revenge. And then I finally realized there wasn't any such thing. He's already in jail, and that's just the way life is." He stopped for a second. "He is still in jail, isn't he?"

"Yes, the person who hit your wife is still in jail."

"Good. In that case I'm the one who's blessed. My wife had her life cut short, and there's nothing I can do to change that. But at least that asshole isn't going free. Now, if you don't mind, I'd just as soon get off the phone and forget that I had any calls to make on this matter." And, with that, he hung up.

She frowned, as she looked down at her phone.

"Problems?"

"No." She shook her head. "Just another husband who didn't want to have all the painful past brought up again," she said quietly.

"It's got to be painful for sure."

"I know. I know, but what else am I supposed to do?"

"You do your job, the same as you do every other time," he said gently. "But, right now, your job is to sit down and eat."

And, with that, he put their plates on the table with a hard *bang*.

VERY EARLY THE next morning, long before the sun would rise, after Simon dressed, tiptoed out of Kate's bedroom, and left her apartment in the dark, when he was heading down to his car, an overpowering scent once again hit him. He stopped outside in the fresh air, took several deep long breaths, smelling the same sweaty body odor. "Why body odor?" he murmured. "Makes no sense."

He had yet to tell Kate about it. Mostly because he didn't know what he was experiencing and didn't want to be questioned about it. Like her and her cases. He was interested in everything going on in her world, and her cases fascinated him. But, at the same time, there didn't appear to be anything he could do to help her. It wasn't something that he could ask about on the streets. It didn't appear to be anything up his alley at all. And the scents certainly weren't connected to the nightmare going on in her world. It was fascinating; it just wasn't relevant.

As he got into his car, it was like the leather in his vehicle ... was just like that new-car fresh-leather smell. He inhaled deeply, smiled, and started up the engine. He could even smell the gas from outside. He shook his head and drove home slowly, even though at this sleepy time of the wee hours of the morning, not much traffic was on the road to hinder Simon.

Everything out here was highlighted, exasperating in a way. It made no sense, and yet here he was, outside of his penthouse in his parking spot underground, hopping into the elevator, which had a less-than-pleasant smell.

As he made his way up to his penthouse and into his living room, he tossed his wallet and keys on the countertop, putting away the few grocery items he'd picked up for his place. Hating the stuffy air, he walked over to the balcony, opened up the double doors and stepped outside, just smelling the city. The fresh air, the early morning, the coolness.

Everything from gas to sweat to fast food to flowers to

the sea. He turned to face the harbor and just took a deep breath of the fresh salty air coming in off the water. It was stunning; then it was weird when he heard the sobbing. He groaned, as he stood here, his head bowed. "I don't know what's the matter," he whispered, "but I wish you would stop crying."

And, for the first time, he heard words, words that seemed to be directed outward.

"Why?" this woman raged. "Why me?"

Something was there, and he strained to see through the shadows. But nothing he could actually discern. "*Why you what? Why? What's going on?*" he replied, in an effort to communicate.

She answered, but it wasn't to his question. "Of course it's me. It's not like I ever had anything good happen to me. And this is just another cross to bear." And, with that, it's like she shifted somewhat, like the shadows around her became more ... they just became different. They weren't new; they weren't old. They were just different shadows. Something that struck him as odd because how many shadows could there be? Was she a prisoner? That was the thing that bothered him the most. What if she were being held captive? He frowned and whispered again, "Where are you?"

Silence came from the other end, and then she called out, "Hello? Hello? Is somebody there?"

He froze. "I'm here," he said urgently. "Talk to me."

"Who are you?" the woman asked, clearly puzzled. "And where are you?"

He felt and heard the pain and terror in her words. "Oh, God. Don't be afraid. I'm not trying to hurt you. I'm not here to hurt you," he cried out again and again.

"Who's there?" she cried out. "Who's there?" she

screamed. "Go away. Go away." And then she burst into tears yet again.

He closed his eyes, and thankfully he slowly withdrew from the scenario. And again it wasn't by his own hand. If it had been by his hand, he'd be a happy person because he could control something, but it wasn't his to control. The vision just shifted and changed, and it wasn't the same mixture of grays anymore.

Instead he was staring out at the city around him, studying all that was going on. Yet, at the same time, all he could sense was the deep, dark sadness inside her. Whatever it was, it terrified her, whether it was his voice or somebody else's, he didn't know, but the thought of her being a victim, hidden in the dark somewhere, incapable of getting out, was breaking his heart.

And just when he thought that it couldn't get any weirder, he heard that bicycle again, just the sound of the wheels turning and turning, again and again. Was she using it for stress relief? Was it even her? That was another thing that got him. What if, … what if the bike sound was not related to her at all? Maybe it was somebody else out there in this weird, wonderful world he had opened up in his mind.

Wonderful? Right. He was being facetious about that. He groaned and whispered, "If I can't help, I don't want any of this."

And then the thought slammed into his head. *It's happening, and, therefore, you need to help.*

"What are you talking about?" A part of him suddenly understood these people were coming to him because he could help. And, with that stunned realization, he turned to face the living room. "But, if I'm supposed to help, how? What is it I'm supposed to do?"

Silence was his only answer.

CHAPTER 18

K ATE WOKE IN the middle of the early morning hours and lay here, disappointed that she was alone. She'd heard Simon get up and leave, but she'd been so exhausted that she hadn't murmured a dissent. She just knew that he was up; sensing something going on around her, she'd come awake, but, realizing it was him, she had let him go. But now she lay here, wondering what was wrong. Frowning, she reached for her phone, ignoring the time, and texted him. **What's the matter?**

She immediately got a question mark back.

I woke up, and all I can think of is something's wrong. And you're the first person who came to mind. Her phone rang.

"I don't know." His voice was distracted, worried. "Something's happening with me, and I haven't really been telling you about it. It's just getting to me."

"You're talking about that weird sense of smell and all that?"

"Yes. And sometimes I get this sense of wheels turning."

"Wheels turning?" she asked, confused, rubbing the sleep from her eyes.

"Yeah, like somebody's on a bike."

She pushed her pillows together and sat up and leaned against the headboard. "No, you haven't told me about that." Damn it, why did it have to involve bikes?

"She's crying. Often she's just crying, bawling her eyes out. Tonight she spoke. She asked, 'Why me?'"

"Spoke? Did you see anything?"

"Nothing, absolutely nothing, just shadows."

"You think she's a prisoner?"

"Of course that's what instinctively comes to mind, but I really don't know."

"*Hmm.*" She didn't know what to say to that. To any of it. On the surface there wasn't much to go on.

"I know. I'm nuts."

"No," she said immediately, "not nuts. But you do have a track record that makes me wonder what this is all about."

"Oh, I have a track record now," he said with sarcasm. "Funny, that's not quite what you were saying to me the other day."

"You know I struggle with this," she admitted, "but it's obviously bothering you, so, if there are any answers that we can come up with, then we need to."

"*Great idea.*" And there was that tone again. "You think I haven't been trying?"

"I know you have. Like me working my cases, huh?"

"That's why I haven't told you. This is a sensitive area of my life that I'm not very comfortable with."

"I get that. So do you want me to hang up?"

"I want somebody to tell me what the fuck's going on," he roared.

"So tell me everything, as far back as you can remember, when this started."

"I don't know when it started exactly. A few days ago, a week maybe. I don't even know. I don't think it's been that long. It's just, it's dominant."

"So it's every day then?"

"Yes, it's every day. Some are better than others. But my experiences could be different, from her crying in the background to wheels turning to that exasperating sense of smell. Sometimes it's even just incredible hearing."

"Interesting." She thought about it for a long moment. "Do you have a first name?"

"No, not at all."

"And no sign of a location or landmark or anything to help identify her?"

"No. The only thing that I can tell you is that I hear her crying, sobbing, saying things like, 'Why me? Why does this have to happen?' It's not so much a sense of self-pity as that of great sadness, grief almost."

"Like maybe she's lost somebody, or she's been caught up in something she can't change?"

"Caught up in something she can't change," he said thoughtfully. "That feels about right."

"Feels?"

"Yeah, and that's all I can tell you. It feels like that." Again that defensiveness came into his voice.

She didn't blame him because they had no guidebook to anything that he was experiencing, and it had to be frustrating for him to not get any answers, to not get a say in anything one way or another. In order for any of this to come to a happy conclusion, he needed to find a way to get out of this. "How does that work, in terms of you shutting it off?"

"I've tried and succeeded a couple times, and then, out of the blue, suddenly I'm back in it again."

"And usually it's just the really strong sense of smell. Any theories on why it's that?"

"I think because I can't see through her eyes. There are just shadows."

"Because she's in darkness?"

"Maybe, that's why I was thinking captivity."

"And that makes a certain kind of rational sense. Do you think she has a message for you?"

"I don't know," he said bluntly. "I did come to the conclusion that I needed to do something to help her."

"Okay," she replied slowly. "Do you know what you can do?"

"No," he said, his voice heavy. "I just feel like the only reason I'm connecting with her is because there is something I can do. Just like with the jumpers, just like with the kids."

"And, in both cases, you gave information to me and between us—"

Excitedly he interrupted her. "Yes! *Between us*, we helped. Why didn't I think of that?"

"Think of what?" Kate asked. "You haven't given me anything to help you with, and I don't have anything to give you."

At that, he stopped. "Then I'm not sure what I'm supposed to do with any of it."

"If you do find something that's usable, then please let me know. If you figure out why or where she is, or if you figure out even something about the source of her grief, tell me. So, that bike, is it a stationary bike?"

"I—I don't know," he said.

"Right."

There was a long silence between them, and he finally said, "Go back to sleep."

"I'd love to. Why did you leave tonight? Why didn't you just stay until I had to go to work?"

"I don't know," he murmured. "If I figure it out, I'll let you know." And, with that, he hung up.

She lay back on her bed, staring at the ceiling above her. Without the lights on, the room was full of shadows and darkness. She looked around, feeling a sense of comfort in what was the usual, the normal. How would she feel if this were not her normal, if this wasn't usual?

Of course it would be scary, and she would feel fear, depression, anger, grief—not the same things that this woman was feeling apparently, if Simon was connecting in any way that could be believed. She winced at that because there was a lot of belief required in this. A lot of trust and an acceptance that what he was doing was something he felt he needed to do. And a belief that there was no other way out of it. She'd seen him; she had heard the same nightmares that his ex had witnessed and had taken videos of, something Kate could never do. It surprised her that, after that scenario, Simon was comfortable enough to sleep beside her.

Then again, she had worn him out.

With a tiny smile playing at the corners of her mouth, she rolled over, punched the pillow a couple times, and closed her eyes. As she slid into a deep sleep, the answer came hurtling into her brain. She bolted upright, reached for the phone, and called him.

His voice was groggy and disoriented when he answered. "What's the matter?"

"Simon, is she blind?"

There was dead silence on the other end of the phone, and then he said, "Good Lord, I don't know."

"It would explain why the other senses were heightened," she murmured. "And why ... why the hearing is so amplified, and so is the sense of smell. And maybe that blindness is the source of her tears. Maybe that's the grief and the sadness."

"It's possible," he said slowly. "I hadn't considered that."

"I know. Neither did I. I was just sleeping, when it hit me."

"Wow, when things hit me in the middle of the night, they rarely wake me up. I wake up in the morning with the answers."

"Apparently I needed to have this answer now."

"It's possible. Let me think about it." And, with that, he hung up.

But she knew she was right. She didn't know how it connected to her cases, but it felt right. It would explain the shadows too. Maybe she was going blind; maybe she had been going blind for a while. Kate didn't know, but, as she checked the time, it was five o'clock already. She groaned. She would have to be up at 6:30 a.m. anyway. What were the chances of getting some sleep now? Not much, she realized. She hopped up, had a hot shower, and got dressed, then sat in the kitchen and had a cup of coffee, staring out into the early morning light. Full of pent-up energy. She realized she wanted to go for a run. She should have done that before her shower.

Groaning, she quickly changed into her running gear and raced from her apartment. She lived downtown, so not a whole lot of enlivening areas to run in, but, at this hour, it was just too gorgeous to stay inside. As she hit the pavement hard and fast, she realized it would be more of a sprint than a jog. Probably the stress inside her, the tension that was always coiled up there, waiting for her to find an answer. That feeling of desperation that she needed to get this case closed, before it became buried under fresher, newer cases that had information and threads that she could follow up on. How was one supposed to work with basically nothing, knowing that victims' families, friends, people were out there, waiting for answers?

She shook her head, trying to pull back the shadows, and ran harder and harder and harder. When her feet slowly calmed down, she turned around, only a few blocks away from home. And that was a damn good thing because now she was very tired.

She rubbed her eyes, feeling the sweat collect in the corners, burning and stinging her tear ducts, flushing them out. That was what she thought anyway, since she wasn't the teary type. But, as she slowly walked back to her apartment, swinging her arms and trying to loosen up her joints, she realized that this blind woman, whoever she was, *could* be connected to her case. Maybe she was alone now because of one of these accidents. Maybe she had been in one of the accidents. Kate didn't know. Maybe it had nothing to do with these cases at all. Maybe it was a case Simon had yet to spring on her.

She didn't like the idea of that.

Kate shook her head, walked up to her apartment, and stepped right back into the shower, and this time she stood under there, enjoying the hot water as it hit her shaky body, soothing some of her muscles that would pound and ache for the rest of the day. When she stepped out for the second time, she quickly braided her damp hair, wishing she'd found time to get it cut, then dressed in a no-nonsense black T-shirt and black jeans once again. She put on her holster, grabbed her jacket, and headed out. By the time she walked into the station, even without the time-saving efficiency of driving her vehicle, she was still early.

She put on the coffee, and, when nobody showed up to grab the first cup, she happily took it and headed to her desk. And, with that, she opened up a blank document and started to write, letting the information in her brain pour out. She recorded the ideas she had talked about with Simon, added the information about the woman Simon was dealing with, and then realized there wasn't a whole lot else. She grabbed the list of numbers they had been trying to call and checked the list of victims' family and friends.

Instead of the dozen there, the last time she looked, she found a few notes added, saying that Rodney had connected with four and found nothing of interest. She quickly added notes from the Wellington guy, who had called her back last night, then made calls to the others. She connected with two, and once again dealt with the teary backlash of them asking why she was bringing it all back up again.

When she got to the last one on her list, it was from an accident a year ago. When a guy answered the phone, he said he was on his way out to work.

"Look. This is really crappy timing," he growled.

"I'm sorry. I just—I'm trying to follow up on a series of other accidents we have."

"Which is why I was on board with changing that traffic pattern," he snapped into the phone. "My daughter would be alive, and my wife would be almost whole again," he snapped, "if that accident hadn't happened."

"I hear you, and I'm sorry that the effort didn't go through."

"Politicians," he snapped yet again. "Nothing you can do with them. If you don't grease their palms, they don't give a crap."

"Do you really think it was a financial decision?"

"I don't think they could be bothered to look at it properly, and it just drove me batty."

After getting information about where he worked, she asked him gently, "I understand that your daughter died in that accident?"

"Yes, she was two years old," he said.

"I'm sorry, the death of a child is always terrible."

"My wife has never been the same either," he added, his voice hitching. "I thought, after a year, she would be much better, but I'm not sure one ever recovers from the loss of a child."

"No. I think most do, to a certain extent, though are never the same anymore," she murmured.

"In this case, I'm not sure recovery is even possible. Look. I'm late."

"That's fine. One last thing. You haven't had any contact with anybody else involved in these accidents, have you?"

He hesitated. "I don't know what you mean," he asked cautiously.

"I just wondered, if, through all this, a support group was formed or anything."

"*Huh*, no, but it's not a bad idea. At least other people in that situation would understand. I know my wife belongs to a couple online groups, but I generally avoid them myself. I'm not into sharing what's going on in my life with strangers."

"No, I can see that."

"It's hard," he said briskly. "Everybody expects you to react in a certain way, and, when you don't, it's like you're being judged."

"I'm sorry," she said again, "that's certainly not how I

want you to feel right now."

"Good. In that case, just leave us alone." And, with that, he hung up.

She wrote down his name and brought up the case to get a little more familiar with it. His daughter, who they had called Jillie, short for Jillian, had perished at the scene. His wife had been badly injured but had recovered. And like he said, recovery was relative in the case of something like that. Did anybody ever really recover? As somebody who had lost someone close and blamed herself, recovery wasn't necessarily impossible, but it was never the word that she would use. She had moved forward in life, but it's not like she ever had a chance to close the door on the loss of her brother.

There was no closure without a body; there was no closure without a case being solved. There was no closure without answers. And this man actually had answers, but what he didn't have was closure because his wife wasn't able to deal with it. So, although they had buried their daughter, a horrible event in their life, he had moved on as much as he could, and she hadn't. And that was a judgment in itself because, of course, she had moved on, but what had she moved on to? Kate frowned at that and brought up the woman's name. There was no contact information for her.

She wondered about contacting the husband again, and, realizing that she would have to, she quickly texted him. **I'll need to speak to your wife briefly. Could I have her contact information?**

His response came immediately. **Hell no. She's already racked over this. No more.**

Kate frowned and rapped on the desk in front of her.

As Rodney came in, he stared at her. "What's that look on your face for?"

"I'm trying to figure out how to speak with this man's wife, but he won't give me her cell phone number."

"It's not in the files?"

She shook her head. "No, it isn't."

"Did you check if it was registered?"

She nodded. "There's no cell phone plan that I have any way of uncovering for her."

"*Hmm*, any family, any friends?"

She looked again at the list and nodded. "I've got the mother. Let me see what she has to say." And, with that, she picked up the phone and called the mother's phone number. When a woman answered, Kate identified herself.

"Oh dear," the woman said, "my ... my daughter really can't handle another investigation into this."

"Okay, I was just hoping to get a few questions answered."

"Please don't call her. She's really unstable."

"Unstable in what way?"

"Overcome with grief."

"Even after a year?"

"One never gets over the loss of a child, Detective."

"I get that," she said quietly. "I'm not trying to upset her. Could you tell me how bad things are with her?"

"Her sight is failing for one thing. It's bad, and now all she does is cling to the memories of her daughter."

"Hang on a minute. Did you say she's losing her sight?" And her heart confirmed her head, and something, a knowingness, came through.

"Oh yes," the mother replied, "absolutely."

"Was it from the accident?" Kate asked hesitantly.

"Yes, she had a severe brain injury. Some of the blood vessels were damaged. It's been a slow process, and, over this last year, she's become quite … quite blind."

"So she had her daughter with her at the time of the accident?"

"Yes, my daughter was attending the university. She was an assistant professor, trying to finish her master's degree. My granddaughter was at a day care there. They frequently rode her bicycle back and forth, the baby in the carrier behind her. She was killed, and my daughter was injured."

"Do you mind me asking what your daughter's mental state is like at this point?"

"How would you feel?" she snapped. "If the darkest days of losing her daughter weren't bad enough, now she's lost her sight as well. And probably her husband. I'm sure their divorce is also imminent."

"I'm very sorry to hear that. I'm sure she must be riddled with grief."

"She's grieving for everything, for the loss of her daughter, the loss of the life she knew, for the loss of her sight, and now for the loss of her marriage."

"How do you feel about the divorce?"

"I don't really want to say. I know they were having trouble beforehand, but, with the loss of our little Jillie, it's just been too much. There was a lot of blame happening early on, but my daughter was in and out of the hospital for a long time, and she really couldn't handle too much arguing. She got very depressed and just sank into a well of grief."

"Outside of her eyesight, is she injured?" she asked hesitantly.

"I don't really know what you—"

"Does she have further permanent injuries, other than her vision?"

"No, if you mean broken legs or injured spine, no. She does have a sore shoulder all the time. She's never been very strong to begin with, and I know that lifting heavy objects really puts a strain on her back now."

"Right, and the driver was charged?"

"Yes, but it was a pretty minor charge, and I believe he's already out," she said in disgust.

"Was there a reason given for the accident?"

"I guess he needed new glasses. It was a momentary lapse of judgment, and he hadn't seen her coming. I don't know. I mean, obviously he was charged, and he ended up pleading guilty. I'm sure he's devastated over everything. But, as somebody who has a permanent loss from something like that, it never seems like it's enough."

"No," Kate said, "I'm sure it doesn't. Although the driver also has to deal with the fact that he killed somebody— and a child at that."

"Yes," the woman agreed. "If that were me, I would be terrified of ever getting back in a vehicle again."

At that, Kate sat back and wondered. She spoke to the older woman a little bit longer, and, when she hung up, she sat here, staring at the monitor, wondering.

Again Rodney looked over at her. "And?"

"Her daughter received some head injuries, some of which have caused her to slowly go blind over the last year. She's not only lost her daughter but also her sight, and now it looks like her marriage is about to collapse."

"Ouch, that's a tough one."

She nodded. "It is, indeed. The driver was charged and was remorseful. He needed new glasses, made a poor judgment as to distance and timing. He may have done jail time because her mother said he was out now. I'll have to confirm that. He was charged, and he pleaded guilty, and, apparently a year later, he's free and clear."

"But, if it wasn't due to negligence, then it was little more than a really crappy accident," Rodney replied.

"I know," she murmured. "When does one feel like justice has been served?"

"In this case, probably never because they've lost a daughter and a granddaughter."

"Right. And the marriage is not likely to survive much longer either." She got up and grabbed her jacket, then looked at him. "I'm going to run across and grab a pretzel."

"No breakfast, huh?"

She shook her head. "No, I went for a run this morning. I didn't have a great night and went for a run, then I just grabbed some coffee."

"Get food," he warned. "All that caffeine will turn your stomach into acidic mush."

She smiled. "Not likely but I'm starving. I'll be back in few minutes."

And, with that, she walked out the front door of the station and down the steps. As she crossed the street to the pretzel vendor, her phone rang. She looked down to see it was Simon. Rather than answering the call, she picked up the pretzel and stepped into the park slightly and called him back. "You called?"

"Yeah, where are you?" he said.

"I just picked up a pretzel outside. Why?"

"Because I'm hearing from her again. It's just really bad today."

"I may be a part of that," she said quietly.

There was a moment of silence. "What?"

"I think she's the victim of one of these accidents from a

year ago. She worked as a TA at the university, while working on her master's. They only had one vehicle, so she would ride her bike into school every day, her daughter strapped into a carrier on the back. She went to the day care center on campus."

"Oh no," he said.

"Yeah," she murmured. "The driver was in need of better glasses and apparently didn't see her coming. The woman and child were on a bike and had the right-of-way, but he was taking a right-hand turn onto the boulevard and hit her. The two-year-old daughter was killed. But this next part is why it's really interesting. The mother received a head injury and over this last year has gradually lost her sight."

He gasped into the phone.

"So I'm thinking that just might be your victim."

"Wow, so she's going blind."

"Going blind, lost her daughter, and her marriage is failing fast. Divorce is imminent, according to the woman's mother, and, on top of all of that, the driver is already free and clear."

"Which, if it were truly an accident—"

"Exactly. Just because there's a bicycle accident doesn't mean that it's murder and doesn't mean that somebody set out to kill them."

"Right," he murmured, "but that would explain the grief and the sadness."

"Yes, and the *why me* aspect."

"Of course because not only is it one blow but it's now three blows."

"Exactly. And more really, with her education and career off track as well. For some people it's just all too much."

"Hell," he said forcibly, "for anybody that's too much.

Look at your mother."

"I don't want to," she said flatly. "My mother is a mess."

"I know," he said quietly. "And you're still dealing with it yourself."

She snorted. "And I probably always will be."

"So, this woman. Do you have a name for her?"

"Pamela. Pamela."

"Pamela," he said slowly. "You know what? That fits."

"If you say so. I don't know what the mind of a Pamela looks like."

He must have smiled as it easily came through in his voice. "I don't know that people associate sounds with names, but it might help when I try to talk to her."

"You do that, and at least now you know where that connection is likely coming from."

"Yes, even that body odor had a feminine smell to it, now that I think about it. As if she exercises intently, possible as a form of stress release, and that's when I'm picking up on her. I'll rest a lot easier, knowing she's not imprisoned somewhere."

"Only in her own mind," she said quietly. "In a guilt-ridden prison of her own making and then the loss of her sight is giving her no light to crawl back out to."

"Not a visual I'd like to remember." After a moment, he added, "I wonder how I can help." And, with that, he hung up.

Kate stared at her pretzel, wondering at a man like Simon, whose response to the plight of this one woman would be to wonder if she needs help. Of course she needed help, but that he had wondered—and now knowing the next step in his mind would be to try to figure out what he could do to help Pamela—just blew Kate away.

He was a good man on so many levels. Now if only he didn't have this weird penchant for connecting with her victims.

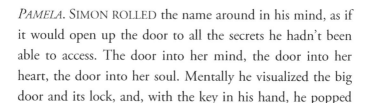

PAMELA. SIMON ROLLED the name around in his mind, as if it would open up the door to all the secrets he hadn't been able to access. The door into her mind, the door into her heart, the door into her soul. Mentally he visualized the big door and its lock, and, with the key in his hand, he popped the lock and opened the door and stepped inside.

"Pamela," he called out quietly, as he sat in his chair, trying hard to keep his energy contained, so he could suck in the vortex of her space. He felt a certain startled reaction from her.

"Who's there?" she whispered, fear in her voice.

"It's fine. I'm not here to hurt you."

"Who are you?" she cried out.

He felt her body jolt and jerk, as if she were trying to see in the shadows, and he realized she was brandishing a stick with her hand. He groaned; this was not what he wanted. "Easy," he whispered. "Take it easy. I'm just talking to you."

"Where are you?"

"I'm inside your mind." He stopped, not sure he could do this. Part of him wanted to cry out to his grandmother and to tell her that this was all wrong, that he wasn't the right person for this. But she wasn't here to listen either.

Pamela quieted. "What do you mean, you're in my mind?"

"You've been sending out messages. I'm a psychic"—he winced at the phrase—"and I'm picking up your distress."

She gasped. "What?"

"Yes, please don't worry. I'm not here to hurt you."

"That's not possible," she cried out, "to be in my mind."

"Maybe it is. Maybe somebody out there can help you."

"No. There's no help for me."

"I know what happened."

There was a stillness inside her.

"Your daughter. She was killed in a terrible accident."

Immediately Pamela started to bawl.

"I hear you, Pamela. And I understand. You were riding your bike, and you feel responsible."

"How can you know this?" she whispered in horror.

He took a slow deep breath. "It doesn't matter. I just want you to know that somebody out here can hear you, and that, when you're crying out, somebody is listening."

"That doesn't make it any better. My pain is private."

"Sometimes your pain isn't private. If you want it to be private, you have to change the way you're screaming out to the universe."

She stilled again.

And he realized just how absolutely stupid that sounded. "I get it. You weren't thinking. You're just reacting. And that pain that just won't go away lives deep down inside you, in your heart. I also get that. I'm just trying to tell you that, if you want to be alone, you need to change the way you scream and cry because there is a way to reach out, without having other people hear. And, if you do want to reach out and not be so alone, just know that you aren't alone, that someone is listening."

"This is bizarre," she whispered.

"I know, and I'm not really fond of it myself," he agreed, with a note of humor. "I also can't connect with everybody, and I can't answer all your questions because that's just not how it works. I don't have the answers," he said flatly.

She half laughed. "If you're a psychic, why are you talking to me in my head? You realize that everybody will think I'm mental?"

"Who is everyone?"

She quieted.

"Are you okay?" he asked suddenly.

"Maybe, maybe not."

"Meaning?"

"I don't know. I can't trust myself. Everybody says I can't trust myself."

"Who is everybody?"

"My family, my husband."

"Because of your grief?"

"Yes," she said softly. "Apparently it's not normal to grieve for this long."

"I think it's very normal," he argued quietly. "Nobody can give you instructions on how long it takes to become accustomed to the loss of somebody you cared about, and, in your case, you're adding guilt to the mix. So that becomes even harder to let go of."

"Am I responsible?" she asked quietly. "I must be. I was riding my bike, when it was hit by the car."

"Did you feel like the hit was intentional?"

"No, not at all. I just wasn't paying attention."

"Is that the truth? Were you not paying attention, or you just don't remember?"

"I don't know. It was terrible—whether I assume that or I just wasn't paying attention, I don't know."

"And it's quite possible. When the weather is bad, your head would have been down."

She sighed. "I also had taken a blow that day too."

"What kind of a blow?"

"My husband, he asked for a divorce," she whispered in a soft voice.

"Ouch, and yet you're still together?"

"Not for long. I think he's only stayed because I was," she hesitated, then used the word, "fragile."

"Fragile," he said.

"Yes, and I think he was afraid I would hurt myself."

Simon knew instinctively that she would have too. "I'm very sorry. It's hard to lose a child and your sight and your marriage."

"You know about my sight?" she asked hesitantly.

"A little bit, all I see are shadows coming from your eyes."

"Yes," she whispered, "shadows. Sometimes I wonder if they aren't the shadows of my life instead of the shadows that I see."

"Whatever metaphor you need to use, just know that you don't have to remain a victim."

"It's not being a victim, and I deserve all the guilt that I can take because I caused the loss of that beautiful child."

"And when would you ever get over it?" he asked curiously. "When would you ever be absolved of this guilt?"

"Never," she said passionately. "Somebody has to pay."

He winced because it sounded a little too close to some religious fervor that he wasn't comfortable with. "Who told you that?"

"Everyone," she said quietly. "Everyone."

"Do you belong to a religion?"

"No. Not really. And I wouldn't be allowed to go now anyway because I'm too unclean."

"Unclean?" he asked, questioning.

"Guilt. It stains my soul."

He shook his head, more worried about Pamela than before. "In my world, God absolves us of our sins, if we are truly repentant."

"That's because you aren't guilty. The guilty find no peace in our souls."

"I get that. I really do. But I wonder how much of that talk is coming from other people."

"Maybe. It doesn't matter because they're correct."

"Are they angry at anybody else in the world over this?"

"Yes. They are. It's been a very tough year, and everyone blamed the other driver. Everyone blamed me. Everybody's blamed life, God even, and I'm crying out."

Then suddenly Simon heard another voice.

"Who are you talking to?" some man asked Pamela.

She immediately fell silent. "I'm sorry," she murmured in a conciliatory tone. "I was just talking out loud."

Simon stayed silent in the background. He heard the voice again, via her hearing.

"That is a symptom of going crazy," the man snapped.

She mumbled an apology yet again, and finally there was silence. She whispered, "You need to go away before I get hurt."

At that, his eyebrows raised. "So you've been hurt, and you are a prisoner?"

"No." And then she whispered, "Well, yes."

Simon asked, "Which is it?"

"It's a yes, but you can't help me." And she slammed the door shut.

CHAPTER 19

K ATE WALKED INTO the office the next morning, her head full. As she sat down at her desk, she reached for her phone and immediately contacted Pamela's mother. "I need your daughter's contact information."

"No, please, I already told you that it's not a good idea."

"I can get it, but this will be much easier."

"No, no, no. You don't understand. She's too delicate for you to talk to."

"Maybe, but I need to confirm a few things. Now is she living with you, with her husband, or someone else? Where is she?"

The woman hesitated.

"This has to come to an end," Kate said sternly.

The woman gasped. "What do you know?" she asked. A fearful note was in her voice.

"I want Pamela's contact information, and I want it now."

"But you really shouldn't have any contact with her."

"That's just too damn bad."

The mother hung up.

Staring at the phone, Kate shook her head. "That won't work with me." She looked over at Rodney. "I don't know what to do with this," she announced.

Lilliana had just entered the bullpen with her cup of coffee in hand and asked, "What's up?"

Kate explained what Simon had said and that the mother was acting suspicious and wouldn't give Kate any contact information on Pamela.

"Are we really expecting her to be a prisoner?" Lilliana asked.

"I'm not sure if *prisoner* is the right term," Kate replied.

"Is she being held against her will?"

"Potentially."

"That's the definition of a prisoner," Rodney said in a dry tone. "Does Pamela have anything to do with these recent fatalities?"

"I'm not sure."

"Does anybody in her circle have something to do with all this?" Lilliana asked.

"Possibly."

"Get a warrant to search the property," Lilliana said. "Present all your evidence to the DA, get a warrant, and see what comes down. Because, if she's in harm's way, we have to do what we can to help her."

"I get it." Kate reached up to her temples, trying to rub away a headache starting there. She snatched up her phone and immediately called the DA for a warrant. When she tried to explain the circumstances, the woman snorted.

"Because a psychic said so?"

"And because the mother refuses to give me any information about the daughter."

"Try the husband again. Better yet, show up at his house."

"I can do that." She looked at her watch. "He's probably gone to work though."

"Go to his house, check it out, and contact him first. I'm

not getting you a warrant based on a psychic."

Kate slammed down her phone on her desk and glared at Lilliana. "I knew that would happen."

"Simon again, huh?" Lilliana spoke with a note of apology in her voice.

"She won't do anything based on Simon's advice."

"Of course not. It doesn't matter how much he might have helped in previous cases, every time his information could be wrong."

"And every time it could be right." Kate pulled up her notes and dialed the husband. "I need to speak with your wife."

"That's just too damn bad," he snapped. "My wife is resting."

"So she's at home?"

"Doesn't matter if she's at home or not. She's delicate."

"*Delicate* is not the issue. You can be there when I talk to her."

"I'm on my way to work, so that's not happening."

"Then I'll have to stop by your house."

"No way," he snapped. Kate heard the note of alarm in his voice. "I'm turning around and heading back home again. If I have to stay there and protect her from you guys, then that is what I'll do."

"Why are you trying to protect her from us?" she asked curiously. She put her phone on Speaker, so that her partner heard.

"You guys pounded her last time, asking all kinds of stuff about how she was trying to commit suicide or she's the one who caused the accident. I don't know, but she's terrified of the police now."

"Is she, indeed?" she said. "I wonder if she's terrified of

the police or terrified of you."

"That's enough of that," he roared in outrage. "You want to talk to her, you should talk to her lawyer, our lawyer."

"I'd be happy to, what's his name? I'll go ahead and contact him and have both of you brought down to the station for questioning."

Dead silence came from the other end of the phone. "Why are you doing this?" he ranted.

"I just said that I needed to speak to your wife. So you give me the information, or I'll get a warrant, and I'll come and search your house."

"You can't do that."

"Come to the station. Produce your wife, healthy and willing to be here, and we'll talk. Otherwise I'll treat your wife as a hostage and come with a SWAT team." And, with that, she hung up, winced. "A bit too much, huh?"

"Not too much," Rodney said. "When you think about it, if she's being held against her will, and nobody will let her talk to you, then it's a situation where she needs rescuing to some degree."

"Something is going on," Lilliana said, "and, yeah, it involves Simon, so I'm inclined to agree with him here."

"Hey, maybe this Pamela ties in the annual deaths in that area with the additional recent ones. I don't know," Kate snapped. "This lack of cooperation—from Brandon, from the faculty dean, now with Pamela's family—it's just so frustrating. But why would it have anything to do with these kids at the university?"

"Yeah? What about that Brandon kid?" Lilliana asked.

"Nothing new. I'm still waiting on the forensics reports on the two females." Just then an email popped up, a *beep* signaling her. "And here they are now. So, for Paula, there is no forensic evidence in particular, other than the bump on her head. Two kinds of blood were found on the carpet in the dorm room, verifying that was the crime scene—which we already knew—and tons of fingerprints were found. It's a student residence, so that is to be expected, and they have lots of parties. DNA from multiple people in the bedding as well." She winced at that. "So, who the hell knows if any of that leads us anywhere?"

"And what about the other one, whose blood is also on the carpet? Candy, is it?" Lilliana asked.

"Candy's case has one distinction. The same projectile at the side of the head, like with Sally, but also drugs were in her system."

"Drugs, that's new," Rodney said.

Kate nodded. "Recreational? It looks like quite a cocktail." She frowned.

"So they really did party," Lilliana stated.

"Alcohol too." Kate sighed at that.

"Would she have even been capable of riding a bike?" Rodney asked.

"I don't know." Kate picked up the phone and contacted Dr. Smidge.

When he answered, he was cranky and fed up. "You better not have any more victims."

"No, but I do have questions."

"I don't have any answers."

She smiled. "I'm looking at the cocktail of drugs and alcohol that you found in Candy's system. Would she have been capable of riding a bike?"

"Maybe, but not too far. She probably could have managed, if she got balanced and had some help. She could have gone for a fair bit, considering. It's amazing what the human body and the human mind can do."

"Would she have ridden out in the middle of traffic like that?"

"That's also quite possible, though—at the time of Candy's death, which would have been a few hours after Paula's TOD of about four a.m.—I don't know how much traffic there even would have been."

"If she was down there at that intersection and rode out into the middle of it, then it's quite possible she rode straight into a car, like somebody heading to work in the morning, not expecting to see a cyclist pull out in front of them."

"It's possible. I found some damage from a collision, but it's not bad."

"Would the drugs have killed her?"

"It's hard to say. It was definitely a cocktail."

"Are we thinking she took it willingly?" Kate asked.

"It's possible. There was no injection site that I could see, but her stomach was pretty full."

"Considering she died just a few hours after Paula, I have to wonder how related they are."

"That's for you to figure out. Paula didn't have any drugs in her system. She was killed by blunt force trauma to the front of her head."

"I had wondered if she had something to do with Candy's death, but it doesn't sound like it."

"Paula could have been the one who gave her the drugs, for all you know. I don't imagine Candy would have taken all of these on her own."

"You think the drugs were in her drinks?" Kate asked.

"It's quite possible that the speed was. I'm still waiting on a more detailed tox analysis, but that's enough to get you going."

"Yeah, it surely is."

"Paula had none of the drugs, alcohol only. And she had the same drink."

"So, they were drinking together," Kate murmured.

"It's quite possible that Paula slipped the drugs into Candy's drink and was either expecting to do more or would leave her like that."

"And then what? Somebody interrupted them? Or," Kate said quietly, "somebody decided to get rid of somebody who could turn the tables on the bad guys and could lie about her involvement."

There was silence in the other end. "You know what? That makes about as much sense as anything," he said tiredly. "Whatever happened to just having wet T-shirt contests and drinking until you puked?"

She laughed. "I think that still happens a lot too. But this group, in particular, has a nasty element."

"Right, well, you should be checking with the faculty to see if any other nasty elements abound."

"Yeah, I've sent several emails to the Dr. Agress and his executive assistant already. He was supposed to send me the files last night, and I haven't received them as of yet."

"Wow, so what is he hiding?"

"That's exactly where we're at." As soon as she got off the phone with Dr. Smidge, she contacted Dr. Agress.

When his executive assistant said that he was out, Kate replied, "Okay, in that case, I'll be coming with a warrant, sirens blaring, and we'll search all the files ourselves. We'll see how he likes that. Then I'll call the president of the university myself and let him know how uncooperative the two of you have been. Then we'll contact the UBC Legal

Department. Does that suit you better?" As soon as the assistant started to yell into the phone, Kate said, "No, ma'am, I'm done. We asked for cooperation. We tried to keep it low-key. If you continue to choose not to cooperate, I'll be sending in the media next." She slammed down her phone again. Then she sat here, pinching the bridge of her nose.

When Colby came in, he asked, "What the hell was that all about?"

She glared at him. "Dr. Agress is stalling me, refusing to cooperate, and so are the family of another woman who was involved in one of the accidents a year ago."

His eyebrows shot up. "What do you mean, Paul refused to cooperate?" She crossed her arms over her chest and told him. He shook his head. "Let me talk to him."

"Don't even bother. I've already talked to the DA about getting a warrant. As far as I'm concerned, I'm bringing the press too."

He winced.

"No, I've had it with this crap. We need answers before we end up with more dead people. I get that Dr. Agress's only concerned about the politics and the university's budget ... not to mention his job, but those dead students belonged to his faculty too, and he should be giving a damn about them. That the crimes didn't happen on campus shouldn't matter."

Colby held up a hand. "Now just stop."

At his rebuke, she glared at him. "Why? Because he's your friend?"

Instantly an awkward silence fell on the room, and she knew she'd crossed the line. She'd dared to bring up the reason he was telling her to back off.

He glared at her, his spine stiffening. "I'll talk to him, Morgan," he said in a hard voice. "Don't you cross me."

She crossed her arms, looked at the clock above his head. "Ten minutes. That's how long until that warrant comes through."

He took a long breath and then turned and walked out.

Slowly she sank back into her chair, closed her eyes, and waited for the noise to start up around her. Instead just dead silence. So she knew her team members were either shocked or pissed.

She rose, walked out of the bullpen with her cup, and filled it up with coffee. When she came back in again, they were talking normally.

Lilliana stood. "That won't get you any brownie points."

"If I was looking for brownie points, I would have become a chef. As it is, I'm helping the victims, and I don't give a damn who is friends with who." And she sat back down again.

Rodney leaned over. "He's a good man, you know."

"Fine. He needs to remember who his friends are and who they are not," she said.

A few minutes later her phone buzzed. It was Colby with an order. "Get in here."

She got up, and, pocketing her phone, she grabbed her coffee and walked to his office, where she leaned against the open doorway. It wasn't so much insolence as it was trying to appear casual.

He motioned at the chair across from him. "Close the door, Morgan."

She walked in, closed the door, then sat down and sipped her coffee.

"Why the hell aren't you quaking in your boots?"

"Because I'm right, and I know it. So do you, Sergeant," she said calmly. "You could protect your friends, and I could protect mine, but, at the end of the day, the truth has to come out."

He glared at her, and then his shoulders slumped. "I just talked to him. He was yelling and screaming at me pretty hard."

"I don't care. He's not being cooperative. We've got three dead kids, not even in a week, and, for all we know, this has been going on for ten years up there."

"He's sending over the files by courier."

"That's not good enough, sir. For all we know, he's not letting us see way more, protecting his rich donors. He wanted to go through the complaints first. I was supposed to have them last night, and, for *some* reason, he's stalling."

Colby stared at her in shock.

"Yeah, I assume he's pulling out the complaints that might reflect badly on any of the wealthy donors' *fine upstanding offspring*."

Colby picked up the phone, while she sat here, and called Dr. Agress back. "Hey, make sure you send *all* complaints. No cleaning of this pile is allowed."

She heard the dean's loud protest on the other end of the line.

"No. Listen to me. The warrant is already being issued, and Detective Morgan is coming up there. No courier. You should have been sending copies to another department as well. The legal department if nothing else. This is no longer secret. It needs to be dealt with. You give those complaints to her, all of them, or we'll have a bigger problem than you're prepared to deal with. If there's nothing to hide, then we won't need to keep them." With that, he hung up. "Go get them."

She nodded and walked out. As she returned to the squad room, she put down her coffee and grabbed her keys and her jacket.

Rodney immediately hopped to his feet. "And?"

"I'm going to get *all* the files from the damn Dr. Agress." And she walked out.

Rodney raced behind her. "I'm coming."

"You can, but I'll also stop and see where Pamela is."

"Did you find out?"

"Nope, but I'll go to her husband's house and then her mother's house. Pamela's got to be at one of those two places, or else she's been locked up somewhere. We need to find her because now that's become a critical issue too." She walked like a woman on a mission, but, when she got outside, she swore and threw up her hands.

"What's the matter?" he asked.

"I left my car at home."

"Perfect. I'll drive." When they got into his vehicle, he looked over at her. "We were all talking about how you burned Colby."

"And I shouldn't have."

"Actually, as it turned out, you should have. It couldn't have been easy, and I don't know how he took it, but I know he would respect you for doing what you thought was right."

"Maybe. I expected to get fired."

"You didn't get fired," he said quietly, "or did you?" He looked at her sharply.

She shook her head. "No. He contacted Dr. Agress, and then, after Colby and I talked, he called him a second time."

"Good, that means that he knows you're in the right and that you'll do the job, regardless of who it offends."

"That's one way to look at it," she said, with half a smile.

When they got to the the Faculty of Arts offices, Dr. Agress wasn't there, but his executive assistant was waiting for them. She looked at Kate and pointed to two boxes. "That's all of them."

"So how do I know that it's all of them?" Kate calmly faced her.

"Well, of course it is." The assistant looked surprised.

"You've lied to me before."

At that, the woman's face flushed and then turned white. She sat down in her chair. "You can check the files, depending on the scope of the warrant, but you can't take anything else away, except for these, without Dr. Agress's permission."

"I also want digital copies of all the emails."

At that, the woman's jaw dropped. "But there are hundreds of them."

"And I'm sure you have them all in a folder," Kate said.

"Why, yes, of course we do."

"Good, so zip them up and send them." Kate put her card down in front of the woman. "Send them all to this email address."

"Is that really necessary?"

"We have two dead students gone in three days alone. All three dead students happened in the last eight days. So, what do you think?"

At that, the woman pinched her lips together and started typing. "Yes, I understand." She sent the dean a copy of the message. "I don't even know if Dr. Agress has seen these."

"Has he?"

She shook her head. "Not most of them, no."

"Exactly, so maybe it's time he took a closer look at what's been happening under his nose."

"He's a good man," she said defiantly.

"I'm glad to hear that because I'm counting on him to do the right thing at this point." Kate stood here and waited until the woman was done.

"Okay, they've been sent," she said.

"Good. We'll take these boxes. They will be returned to you, if we don't find anything we need. If I find anything incomplete, I'll be back. Please make sure that you're complying with what you've been asked to do."

The woman nodded.

"And, if it's not what we're asking you to do, you need to understand that going against the law right now won't go well for you."

The woman looked at her resentfully. "I owe my allegiance to the dean, who gave me this job."

"Yeah, I get how you might think that. But, with three university kids dead already, it would be awfully nice if somebody at this university would give a damn about their deaths." And, with that, Kate swept up one of the boxes in her arms, as Rodney grabbed the other one. Then they turned and walked out. Once they were outside, he nudged her shoulder.

"You really do have a flair for drama." He practically beamed.

She frowned. "No, it's not that. I just have a nose for the truth, and it really pisses me off when people intentionally skirt around the edges of it to get to a place that's more convenient for them."

He laughed. "Personally I think that's what everybody does."

"Of course they do. But, when it's important and when they get in my way"—she shook her head—"I just see red."

"I get that." He put the boxes in the trunk of his car. "There's more here than I expected."

"It's probably a hell of a lot more than he wanted to give us too," she snapped. As they drove off the campus, she said, "Pull up here at the pizza joint, would you? I just want to take a look around."

They both hopped out, and he asked, "Is this the place where that ex-cop hangs out?"

She nodded. "Yes." She walked into the small restaurant, Rodney following her, got herself a coffee, and ordered one for Rodney. There was a different guy at the counter this time. She looked at him for a moment. "Are you the owner?"

He looked up, smiled. "Yeah. I've been here for twenty years."

"I guess you've seen all the accidents on this corner, huh?"

"Yeah, bad news. Some have been way worse than others. That poor woman with the baby last year? That one just broke my heart."

"Do you know what happened?"

"I have a theory of what happened."

"Let's hear it."

"She was upset and distracted. The weather was terrible. She didn't hear the car coming and rode right out into the street. And that was it."

Kate nodded. "I'm sorry to hear that. It's got to be tough."

"It was tough for those of us with scars. But a guy was sitting here at the time. His son had been killed in a cycling accident a couple years ago, same spot. He was pretty upset and said somebody had to do something about it."

She stopped, looked at him. "Do you have any idea who

that was?"

He shook his head. "No, he just mentioned that his son had been killed there earlier."

"Thank you. If I brought you some pictures, would you recognize him?"

He shrugged. "Maybe."

"I'll be back this afternoon."

And, with that, she headed outside, Rodney rushing to keep up with her. As they got into the car, she said, "Let's go check on Pamela. I'll start researching while we drive. As I remember, the only guy killed on a bicycle was years ago. He was twenty-two and riding home from the university. He lived close by, within a few blocks, I think."

"That would be him, I'll bet. What was his name?"

"Vance, I think, or something like that." She looked it up. "Yeah, it's Vance." She checked further. "There's a picture of him but not of his father."

"You should pull up his driver's license photo at least, if you can narrow down his name."

At that, she searched, and soon she said, "Turn the car around, Rodney." Without question, he immediately pulled a U-turn. "Take us back to that pizza place."

She walked in a moment later, and, on her cell phone, she had the picture of the man. "Is this him?"

The owner frowned, looked at her phone, and his eyebrows shot up. "Yeah, it's him all right. You know what? I see him around here every once in a while."

"Any idea when you saw him last?"

"Sometime just after that last accident. He was swearing pretty heavily about it. I heard a lot about the efforts to get the traffic pattern changed, but he said that it didn't go through."

"I know. A lot of people are saying that. Thank you for your time." She then turned and walked away.

"IS IT HIM?" Rodney asked, as Kate got back in.

She nodded. "It is, but I need an address. Apparently he lives somewhere around this area." She quickly mapped out the address from the driver's license data. "I don't know if it's current or not, but maybe it's time to find out."

Rodney nodded, and, with the address entered into her phone, she quickly gave him directions on how to get there. When they pulled up to a small apartment building only about six stories high, she looked up at him. "That's interesting. He lives close by, as if he can't leave the area where his son died."

"Think about it. If that happened to be his only child ..."

"I don't remember that from the case file, but it's got to be hard for them to live right by the scene of the accident—but maybe it's hard to leave it as well."

"And it probably burns inside in a pretty ugly way," he said quietly. They hopped out and then walked up to the address on the driver's license. There was no answer, and she leaned on the doorbell a little bit harder.

Rodney turned toward her. "What do you think?"

"We might have to knock on a couple doors in the neighborhood and see if they know who lives here."

Just then the door opened and a scraggly guy stood in front of her.

He glared at her. "What are you doing here?"

She recognized him as Bill, the ex-cop, the guy she'd seen at the pizza parlor. "Hi," she said.

He just glared, but no fear was in his gaze. There was no sign of having been caught or anything.

"We want to talk to you."

"That's nice, but I don't want to talk to you."

"We can call you down to the station, if you don't want to talk to us here." Kate hardened the tone of her voice. "I guess, looking around this area, maybe you don't want your neighbors to know that we have some questions for you."

"I don't give a fuck about my neighbors. I haven't given a fuck about anything for a very long time." She looked at him in surprise. He shrugged. "What's to care about? I lost my son."

"I'm sorry for your loss," she murmured. "You didn't mention that when we were talking."

"I don't tell everyone. Particularly not nosy cops. And nobody can get the government to change the goddamned traffic pattern."

"Was he killed because of the traffic pattern?"

"He was, and a couple of the others were too, but not enough for the city to actually care."

"What do you mean, *care?*" she said.

"As long as there's enough justification for the city to not do it, they never will."

"I see. So I guess you would do a lot in order to make that traffic pattern change."

"A hell of a lot," Bill said, with a nod. "But it's not likely to happen."

"Maybe it takes more accidents," she said.

"What? That's a hell of a thing to wish for." He stared at her.

"I'm not wishing for it, not by any means. I just wondered if people are trying to make it look like more and more accidents are there, hoping the city government would step up and make the changes."

He stared at her uncomprehendingly.

She turned to look at her partner; he had suddenly stumbled into what she was getting at. His eyebrows shot up. "That's an interesting idea," Rodney said slowly.

"You're talking nonsense," Bill said, then looked up and down the hallway. "Haven't you got anything better to do with your time?"

"Better than solving these crimes? No, I live and breathe them."

"You guys do a hell of a job, do you? Right," he said sarcastically.

"And yet the guy who hit your son was drunk and has served time for what was his third DUI."

"Did you hear yourself? *Third DUI.*"

She nodded. "I get it, Bill. The law sucks when it comes to a lot of drunk drivers. He got off, and, because he got off on previous ones, he was out again and available to hit your son."

"Exactly," he sneered.

"So, I would think you'd be trying to change the drunk driving laws instead."

"What's to change?" he asked. "Nobody gives a damn. If it's not their own child, nobody gives a crap."

There was so much truth to his tale, so much woe in his voice, that she had to wonder. "Have you seen anybody else hanging around this intersection? Anybody who looks suspicious?"

He stared at her. "What? Now you want me to start tailing other people?"

She crossed her arms over her chest. "What if somebody—potentially somebody like you, who lost someone—is trying to make this whole traffic pattern thing change in order to save lives?"

"Then go ahead. I'm all for it."

"But you didn't have a hand in that, right?"

Bill stared at her in shock. "What? You talking about staging accidents? Hell no, and anybody who's lost somebody wouldn't do that."

"I'm not so sure about that. People's motives can get pretty twisted when they're emotionally overwrought."

"Maybe, definitely a few people are pretty overwrought. I saw the lady whose kid got killed in that accident last year. She was absolutely beside herself because she'd been riding her bike with her daughter."

"I know about her too," she said quietly. "When did you see her?"

"She seemed to haunt the place for a while. But she'd been hurt herself as well and was losing her sight. She was in poor shape. It was pretty sad. I mean, you think about that, and it's not only the loss of life but also a loss of her way of life."

"Agreed," Rodney said at her side, staring at him. "We're just wondering if something a little more nefarious is going on, like over the last two biking accidents."

"You think that somebody might be still hanging around, somebody who was involved in it?"

She nodded. "But the cameras are very limited, and the observers aren't very helpful."

He snorted. "That's nothing new."

"I'm wondering about you. If you could tell me where you were during the accidents, then it would help us clear you as a viable suspect."

"I was in the damn pizza parlor. It happened right in front of me."

"And you can give me the actual details, can you?"

He shrugged. "I could, except that it's something so horrific, I really don't like bringing it back into my mind. I'm sure you guys think that's absolutely stupid, but reliving that just brings my son's death back for me."

"And I get that, but you might want to consider the reality that there could be somebody out there causing these accidents and hurting other kids."

Bill paled slightly. "Now that you mention it"—he stared off at nothing really and then turned to look back inside his apartment—"I did get an email from somebody that was a little odd."

"From whom?"

"They just called themselves a *concerned citizen*."

"Do you still have it?"

He frowned. "I don't know. I was pretty upset about it."

"What was it all about?"

"They wondered about changing the traffic pattern, after the proposal had already been rejected. Something about by *stronger means*."

"That is something I need to see," she said instantly.

He frowned at her, and she shook her head. "Please, this is not the time to fool around. There's already been a couple deaths in the last handful of days, I don't want more to happen and have more families torn apart."

"God, no," he said in shock, "but I don't even know if I've still got it."

"Can you take a look?"

"I guess, but I don't understand why somebody would be doing this. When you say that, what do you mean? Are they trying to cause accidents?"

"Exactly," she said instantly.

"But that's just sick. Who's sick enough to do that?"

"Somebody who's broken over the loss of a loved one maybe," she said quietly, "and that is something you should understand, Bill."

"Understanding the pain is one thing, but doing something so outside the law and causing the same pain for somebody else? No, I don't understand that at all."

"I get that, and I'm really glad to hear it." She quietly studied his face but heard only truth. "I still need to confirm your whereabouts, so we can move on." Then she gave him the date of the first accident.

He frowned. "My days pretty well roll one into the next. I live alone, and, outside of the time that I'm out shopping, either I'm here or I tend to haunt the pizza parlor. It's just ..." He stopped, looked shamefaced. "I feel connected to my son there."

She nodded gently. "Did you see the first accident?"

He shook his head. "No, I arrived just afterward."

"It's pretty traumatic to see a duplicate of the horror you already went through. Did you recognize anybody who was there at the first scene, when you *were* watching?"

"Yeah." He frowned. "A couple people, somebody who made my blood run cold. I've seen them before. They were usually just—"

"Go on," she urged, with a gentle smile.

Bill frowned. "I don't know for sure that it was the same person. Those damn kids were hassling her."

"Hassling who?"

"The blind woman. She comes around here once in a while too. I think it's the same one who lost her daughter.

It's not just me who hangs around those street corners. It would be better off if we hung around their graves, but it feels like they aren't there. It feels like we lost them here, so this is where we are."

Kate understood, but, at the same time, it was ghoulish. "And you saw the blind woman there?"

"And I only saw her because of those kids. They were being asses to her."

"In what way?"

"Trying to push her down, I think. She did go down, and she looked like she was injured. I wondered about going over and helping her, but she got back up, and the kids lost interest in her."

"Interesting." Kate's senses were on high alert. Candy had said something about her friend group wanting her to push a blind woman. "Could you recognize the kids?"

Bill shrugged. "They hang around here a lot," he muttered. "It's not like it's hard to miss them. There's a group of six of them."

"When you saw the other accident, the second one in a week," Rodney stepped in, "did you recognize the victim?"

He shook his head. "No, but she didn't look so good. Honestly she appeared to be high."

"High drunk or something?"

He shrugged. "I tell you what. The kids who come off that university, some of them are great and really intense. Some of them look like they're completely stressed out, and others look like they're off on their luck. And, at that accident, she looked like she was out of luck."

"Right."

"Another guy was there, and that group knocked him down too."

"Interesting, very interesting," Kate muttered. "We did hear complaints about some kids knocking around other people, who were injured and the like."

"Well, this woman from that group knocked somebody else down—he was disabled—but it wasn't as bad as what the group did to the blind woman. I know she was sobbing and trying hard to not appear any more vulnerable than she was. I was getting ready to go out and pound the crap out of those little shitheads."

"How many were there?"

"There is a group of them, usually a couple women with some guys, so about six total in their little gang, and they were hassling the one woman pretty badly."

Kate nodded slowly. "Yeah, let's see if it's the same group I was thinking of. She was supposed to knock down the blind woman."

"She didn't. One of the other guys did, but they were hassling her pretty good about something."

Kate pulled out her phone and brought up a picture of Brandon. "Does this look like one of them?"

"Oh, hell yeah, that's one of them." Bill stared at the photo. "That kid needs to be taken down a peg or two."

"Absolutely. Now, the question is, did he do anything more serious than hassling a blind woman around?"

"Meaning, he had to do something more serious for you to come?" he asked. "What the hell's wrong with this world?"

"Oh, I get it, but we're also hamstrung and have to work within the law."

"See? This is why I couldn't be a cop any longer. I just want to pound him into the ground and forget about evidence or finding him guilty. What I saw out there? That was just BS."

"And the guy who they did knock down?"

"Yeah, it was the one woman who did it, and you're right, she looked like she was being pressured."

"*Nice, nice* group," she said.

"That's when the cyclist jumped ahead, maybe to get away from them. I'm not sure. Anyway, the cyclist got hit by the car and went down, and, after that, they scattered."

"But you don't think the group had anything to do with that?"

"The cyclist definitely got hit by the vehicle, and I don't know why else she would have jumped ahead into the traffic, besides trying to get away from that group. Hell, I would have too. Unfortunately, in this case, it was fatal."

"Yes, it was. When you say they surrounded the person on the bike, do you know if they came up on one side or the other?"

Bill stepped down the hallway, positioned the two of them on either side of him. "If I'm the cyclist, I was up here, and they came up on either side of me."

"Was this before or after the blind woman?"

"It was all around the same time really. They weren't all hassling the blind woman. They were just crowding and jostling everybody. You couldn't really see who was doing what, and you sure as hell couldn't prove what they were doing to any legal standard because everyone was all so crowded together."

"Which is probably part of the MO," Rodney said.

"Then you don't know if it was an accident or not," Kate said.

"Maybe. The one guy, Brandon, looked like he raised his hand and punched the person in the red hoodie on the bike or did something, but it looked pretty odd."

"What about the woman riding the bike? Did you see her face?"

"No, except for the fact that she was coming in and looked a little woozy."

"Were the guys around her?"

Bill frowned. "Somebody was, but I think like four or five people were at the intersection. I mean, that's a popular place, as intersections go."

"It is, so, no, I'm not surprised that a few people were hanging around. Now if only I had some proof of it."

"Proof of what?"

"That they were all there at the same time and that they were hassling people."

"If you find the one guy they knocked down, I'm sure he'd have something to say."

"He probably would, but I also have to identify him in order to ask him."

"The one girl knew who he was because she was talking to him before she shoved him. They were *friendly* like."

"And you think that's why he was targeted?"

"Yeah. At least it's a reasonable assumption, and the other guys didn't look like they appreciated her being friendly at all."

"No, I'm sure they didn't." She looked at Bill. "So I guess you haven't heard."

"Heard what?" he asked.

"The female from the second biking accident?"

"Yeah?"

"She was Candy, the one in that bully group at the first accident this week, the one who didn't knock down the blind woman but did knock down the guy."

Bill stared at Kate, and his jaw dropped. "Yeah, but

like …" He stopped, frowned. "My God, that's really shitty. I feel like she got into something she couldn't handle. Now she's dead?"

Kate nodded. "Your theory is totally possible. Can I get you to come down to the station and give us a statement?"

He stared at her. "You know what? If you hadn't told me about that one, I would have said, *Fuck off*, but because of her …" He sighed. "Are you thinking it's those damn kids?"

"I don't know, but they are definitely up to no good. Now at least we have a direction to go on."

"They looked like the punk-ass kind who never get caught."

"They're also the *rich* punk-ass kind," she said.

He nodded. "Of course they are. I know a bunch like that gave my son a hard time a few years back. He was in his first year, and he just couldn't seem to keep it together. He was trying so hard to get aligned and to stay afloat, but he was just overwhelmed with it all. He put them in their place, but it never seemed to really take. When he was killed, for the longest time, I wondered if they had had anything to do with it, but I didn't have any reason to suspect that. And it was the drunk driver who knocked him out anyway," he said sadly.

"And I'm sorry. There's nothing worse."

"No, there definitely isn't." Bill looked at Kate. "Do you have any kids?"

"Not yet," she said.

"Sometimes I think you're better off without them because, despite other relationships in your life, you won't really understand what love is until you have that child. Then everything in your world flips. And, if you're unfortunate enough to lose that child, the pain is something so incredibly horrible that it's beyond anything you could ever imagine," he said, shaking his head. "I don't know how I was ever supposed to move forward from it."

"I'm so very sorry that you—that anybody—has to endure that kind of agony." She paused, tilted her head. "Do you mind coming down to the station now and getting this over with? I know it brings up very sad and painful memories for you."

He said, "It's important, isn't it?"

She nodded. "It's not only important but we have a time element working against us."

"You think those kids will come back and hassle somebody else?"

"It's very possible, and that doesn't mean they'll kill anybody, but—"

"No, but they might kill if it was in self-preservation."

Kate nodded. "And I think that's quite possible. But we do need your statement, so I have something to give to the DA when I ask for a warrant."

"Crap, you're right." He walked inside his apartment, picked up his laptop. "I'll look for that email you wanted. Can I get a ride with you guys?"

She nodded. "Sure can, and we'll even drive you home again."

At that, he smiled. "In that case, I'm in."

Together they trooped out to Rodney's car.

———————

THE DAY WORE on, yet Simon struggled to get anything done. He'd decided to stay home just because things were ... breaking apart, for lack of a better description. But, at the same time, maybe it was him breaking apart. He felt Pamela in the background, though she hadn't cried out or called to him. So he didn't really feel like he should be interrupting her, as she managed her pain, and that just felt stupid too.

Did you leave somebody alone in order to suffer in silence like that? He didn't know, but it sure didn't seem like that was the right thing to do. But, at the same time, it was a hell of an intrusion to *not* talk to her, when she obviously knew that he was there. Plus, if she'd wanted to talk to him, she could have tried. But, so far, she was avoiding all of it. And he understood. He didn't want to get into her life if he didn't have to. But she felt so much pain, and he hadn't realized he was so susceptible to that.

Men always talked about a woman's tears. And, sure, Simon hadn't followed through with relationships with a few girlfriends for exactly the same thing. Of course, at that thought, Kate came to mind. A thought that he determinedly pushed back out again. And it was hard; it was really hard not to think about her. He also didn't want to go outside to check on his rehab projects, only to be struck with more of these visions that made him look like such an idiot. His professional life was very important, although holing up in his apartment wasn't exactly a smart move either.

Just then he got a phone call from Kate.

"Hey, things are looking up," she said.

"Great. Did you find Pamela?"

"No," she said softly. "We're working on it though."

"She is being held against her will," he said.

"I get that, but something else moved forward."

"Crap, that's your world though, isn't it?"

"Unfortunately it really is. I'm only one person. And just the five of us on the team are dealing with a lot."

"Right, so it's up to me to find this woman, huh?"

"No, I do have a little bit of information, but I don't have a whole lot. And her husband's not being cooperative."

"Of course he isn't," he snapped. "Why would he be?" He hung up on her and sat down and determinedly contacted Pamela. "Pamela? Are you a prisoner?"

This time he heard her tears, but he didn't know if she heard him. "Tell me where you are so I can come rescue you."

"No," she whispered. "I deserve this."

That truth slammed into his heart.

"Because of your daughter?"

"Yes, because of my daughter."

"But other people can't blame you for something that was an accident."

"I should have taken more care," she whispered. "I should have been looking after her."

"That would be nice, but that isn't the way life works." At that, she started crying, and he didn't know what to do. How do you even begin to deal with that level of guilt and pain? "We can get you out of there, and you can talk to somebody, get some help."

"I don't deserve any help," she said.

"Are you at your home with your husband?"

"No," she whispered. "He didn't want me there anymore."

"Why?"

"He said it was too hard to see me and to not see Jillie."

Simon winced. "That's hardly fair."

"Nothing is fair, not now."

It occurred to him that maybe she was being kept for a reason that wasn't necessarily bad. "Have you been suicidal?" There was silence at the other end, and then she cried some more. His heart sank. "You've tried to kill yourself, haven't you?"

"Yes," she whispered. "I don't want to live in this darkness. I don't want to live in this pain."

He sank down into his chair. "Are you at your parents' house?"

"It doesn't matter. This is my life now."

"You can't be sitting there, sick with grief every day for the rest of your life. This won't go away. All the better that you learn to find the tools to deal with what's happened."

"Who are you to say that?" she snapped.

"Somebody who doesn't want to see you waste your whole life because of one mistake. Surely you can envision doing something that would make you feel like you deserve to live again."

"There's no way to bring her back," she said sadly.

"What if you worked to help people? What if you worked to do something to help others?"

"I tried to change the traffic intersection, but that failed."

He stared ahead blankly. "Were you involved in that too?"

"Yes, not in a big way, just in a little way."

"Ah. Then I guess you're blaming the traffic for the driver."

"At the time I was ready to blame anybody, anything that would take some of the blame off me. But there is no getting away from my involvement."

"Who told you that?"

"Do I need to be told what I already know?" she asked curiously.

"*Right.*" He pinched the bridge of his nose. "The thing

is, what you did was still an accident. You didn't mean to do it."

"That doesn't make it any different. It doesn't make it any better and doesn't absolve me of the loss. She was everyone's true delight. She was tiny. She was perfect. She was this angel we all loved."

"And I get that," he said sadly, hating her pain. "I really do. But you can't be held accountable for the rest of your life. The guilt alone is too heavy of a burden, without adding in the loss of Jillie. The best you can do is live your life in a positive way to help others and to make sure that you don't get caught up in something so massively toxic like that again."

"You don't get second chances in life," she said.

"How would you feel if the traffic pattern did get changed?"

"It would make me feel better, but it's still too little, too late, all because I know I can't bring Jillie back."

"Maybe not. But what if you could save another little girl?"

"Then I would do anything. But I also know that nothing I can do will change it."

"Maybe. Have you had anything to do with that group who was working on it?"

"No, not really. I tried to get people interested in trying again, but everybody was pretty well depressed about it, and I haven't heard back."

"Right. That's something I could look into."

"And what good would that do?" she asked.

"Maybe nothing, but, until I try, until I look into it, I wouldn't know."

"You do that"—a note of bitterness filled her voice—"but it won't help though." With that, she disconnected.

It was weird because he was talking with her, and he didn't know if anybody was listening to her or not. Then Simon remembered the other man who spoke so harshly to Pamela. Simon tried to contact her again. "Are you still in danger? Who was that man yelling at you the other day?"

"He's part of my family. He was yelling at me because he loves me."

"Ah, is that a little bit of twisted love?"

"Love is love. When you're like me right now, you take whatever you can get. Because of what I've done, I'm unlovable."

"You've got to stop saying that," he snapped.

"That's true," she said sadly. "Like I said, there are no second chances in life."

"But there are." Simon was getting really annoyed at her.

"No, you're just living in dreamland."

"And what are you living in?" he snapped.

"Reality," she whispered. And she disconnected again. Even though he tried hard, it blew him away that somebody who supposedly didn't have any abilities and didn't know how this worked was capable of shutting him out, even though he seemed incapable of shutting others out. How did that work? It seemed like everybody else was better at this, and they weren't even psychics.

Frustrated, he sat back down again and sent Kate a text.

I contacted the blind woman again.

Good. Did you get an address, a location?

No, but she's not at the husband's apparently.

So she's at the mother's then. The mother said something about her, but also said that she wouldn't let anybody in to see her.

We need to track her down.

I might have a better idea. I'll get back to you in a few minutes.

CHAPTER 20

BACK AT THE station Kate led her guest into an interview room, where they went over Bill's statement.

"On the drive over," Bill said, "I found the email too." Bill flipped around his laptop, so she could see it.

She read it in surprise. "Interesting," she murmured. "Can you forward that to me?"

He nodded, then flipped the laptop back around and quickly sent it to her.

Rodney looked at her. "Who is it? Do you know?" When she frowned, Bill spoke up.

"Honestly I think it's the blind woman. She made a couple references in there. And I know that she came to the process late."

"And it kind of fits." Kate considered what Simon had said about the information that he had.

"That email certainly isn't criminal either," Rodney noted.

"No, of course not," she murmured. "It just makes it all that much more important that we figure out what's going on with her."

Bill shrugged. "I haven't seen her in a long time. She came a lot to the intersection, and then she didn't come anymore. Until this week. At least I thought it was her."

"Did you ever see her with anybody?"

He nodded. "A couple times she was with an older man. Her father maybe?"

"Or maybe her husband?"

"No, I don't think so. I would say older."

"*Hmm,*" Kate murmured, "that's interesting."

As soon as they finished writing up Bill's statement, which was recorded as well, and she'd arranged for a ride back home for Bill, Kate walked to her computer and quickly looked up all the relatives around Pamela.

Rodney said, "We've got an address for her mother. I confirmed it."

"Good, I thought we did. Local?"

He nodded. "Yeah, they're in town."

"Then let's go have a little talk with her."

"Do you think they'll let us in?"

"It depends. It also depends if I can get Simon to help at all." Rodney raised his eyebrows at that. She shrugged. "I know. I know. I just feel like something very strange is going on here."

"We have a lot of parts and pieces. Eventually we'll get all of it."

"True, I just don't understand why though. I wish we could also find the other person from that incident where Candy pushed down her guy friend instead of Pamela, as Brandon wanted Candy to do. All that happened at the same time as the blind woman—presumably Pamela—got pushed by somebody."

"The two women in our group of bullies are dead, and the four rich guys aren't likely to talk to us again, especially if we don't have more information to use against them."

"And I don't want to bring them in just yet. We don't want to tip our hand."

"Depending on what we'll be accusing them of, it's already too late."

"I suspect that's why we already have two dead young women on our hands. And I don't want there to be a slew of young men either." Rodney stared at her. She shrugged. "I don't know whether Brandon thinks he can't trust anybody or if it's just the females."

"So you think he's cleaning up?"

"I do," she said quietly. "But I don't know that it's related to any of these other accidents—those yearly occurrences."

"No, maybe not. We also don't know for sure that the recent deaths are even related to each other."

"I know, yet ... these two—Candy and Paula—are definitely related, being in the same gang and all, and that's what we have to keep our eye on. Plus, Candy and Sally were probably killed with the same ice-bullet contraption. So right there it seems we have a cross-over from our annual deaths to these most recent ones. I still think we have two killers."

"Or," Rodney suggested, "one killer with two MOs."

Kate groaned. "I just want some answers." And, with that, she looked over at the two boxes of paperwork from Dr. Agress's office and groaned again. "We haven't had a chance to go through this collection either, and we need to. Colby will have my head if I don't get through this, after all the fuss I made."

"Let's do it now. We can push back the visit to the mother's place for an hour," he said, checking his watch.

"Let's see if any names here pop at least." After only a few minutes, Kate sat back. "Looks like Pamela had lodged several complaints against the group of kids." She shook her head. "Yeah, even before her horrible accident."

"Seriously?"

She nodded. "Yes, apparently they harassed her a couple times, badly enough that she was quite nervous around them. They even scared her little girl at one point, when Pamela and Jillie were walking on campus, heading home."

"Assholes," he muttered.

"I know, and we have it here in black-and-white."

"Do you think that's what Dr. Agress was trying to hold back?"

"I don't know. Either way it's not good news for Brandon. But, so far, outside of being an asshole, we don't have anything bigger than that."

"No, what we need is a confession or some forensics. And the trouble is, because Brandon says he's having an affair with both of them," Rodney stepped in, "his DNA could be all over the place, and we have a logical explanation for it."

"Yes. I don't know about the other guys' particular sexual relationships, his three gang members. However, they all confirmed that the 'relationships,' such as they were, had been a shared mess between them."

"How is that even normal?"

"It's not normal, but self-expression, exploration, trying to outdo each other? It all fits." She gave a wave of her hand. "Maybe not common sense or smart choices, but again it's nothing we'll get Brandon or his buddies on as criminal."

"Unless he did do something to those two young women."

"I am interested in the fact that Bill said that he saw Brandon step up to the first victim—Sally."

"But do you really think nobody would have seen him shoot her?"

"If he held his hand out and just popped her one in the general direction, I don't know what it would take, what kind of a firing mechanism it would involve to shoot those ice bullets."

"Hell, a BB gun, an air gun? Something with some force but it wouldn't necessarily have to be a pistol."

She looked at him. "It could be one of those small ones that are easily hidden in the palm."

"We just have to find that weapon."

She nodded. "And because the ice pellets melt, no forensics would allow for a match against a weapon."

"And again, we have to catch him with it. Which means a warrant for his place, but we don't have enough for that yet."

"No. That's another reason to go talk to Pamela." She looked at the rest of the information Dr. Agress had been forced to turn over. "Dozens and dozens of complaints are in here. Even if we just stick to the years when Brandon was around"—she pulled up just the last year's worth of complaints in one folder—"I bet thirty complaints are in here."

"Not necessarily all against him though."

"No, but I bet a lot of them are." She sat at her desk to sort through them. "Out of these twenty-four complaints in the two last years, sixteen are against Brandon or his group."

"Wow, and the four male bullies are still there."

"Because none of the accused were ever dealt with. We need to make some phone calls." And she grabbed her phone and handed him the list to split.

As it was, Lilliana walked in. "I can help."

Owen followed behind her. "Me too."

And, with the four of them, they split up the list and made phone calls to the sixteen complainants in question.

When they all put their phones down about forty-five minutes later, they just stared at each other.

"These guys are sheer assholes." Kate almost growled.

"The gist I got," Lilliana said, "after comparing notes with Rodney and Owen, is that they surrounded their target, threatened them, pushed them—in one case knocked them down the stairs. In another case they knocked a woman over, and she broke the heel on her shoe, so she tripped on a lower step. Another one fell on the sidewalk in bad weather and slick mud. She already had a condition that made it difficult for her to walk, and she didn't have a walker or anything with her that day. All the complaints were withdrawn, or they refused to follow through, and it took these phone calls and some pressure for them to confess that they were threatened. I got two people who wouldn't even say that much. They wouldn't talk about it, and they got very scared."

"In other words, the threats are of an extreme nature." Kate grimaced, shaking her head. "Whenever we get these assholes charged, we need to contact these people and let them know that they don't have to be afraid for their lives from this guy or his pals again."

"Not until the whole group of them is locked away," Lilliana said. "You don't dare right now. Their fear of that group is keeping them alive. If Brandon ever sees his victims again, I wouldn't be at all surprised if he wouldn't take it a step further."

"I think he did. I can't reach this guy, Trent." Kate tapped at the last number on her list. She brought the name up in the database. "And that's why. He's dead."

"How did he die?"

She sat back, quickly reading. "Interesting."

"What's interesting?"

"He supposedly fell off the top of a building."

"And we're calling it suicide?"

"I don't know." She frowned at the information. "The first responders found no suicide note. The investigators found no typical suicidal actions beforehand. He was thought to be a bright student and happy."

"So, what do we—"

Kate pulled out her phone again and dialed Trent's parents. When she identified herself to Trent's mom, Kate explained that she and other detectives were taking another look at her son's death, as it might pertain to others on campus. The mother said, a simmering rage in her voice, "You need to look at those assholes."

"Who is that, ma'am?" Kate asked, instantly putting the phone on Speaker.

"He was being tormented by a group of people on campus. Because he had Tourette's, they were always bugging him and mocking him, and there was nothing he could do."

"Did he say what they were doing to him? Like did they physically attack him?"

"Several times. He would never press charges because they kept swearing they would make him pay if he did. I don't know what the threat was, but it was always bad enough that he wouldn't turn them in. I begged him to talk to his dean, and he finally did put in a letter about it, a formal complaint, but it never went anywhere, as far as I know."

"Did he withdraw that complaint?"

"I don't know. It's possible," she said, her voice heavy. "I know those guys tormented him mercilessly."

"Did he ever go up on the rooftop before?"

"Yes, all the time. He loved to watch the stars up there. And, no, I don't believe for a moment that he committed suicide," she snapped, her voice once again revealing her grief and anger. "It wasn't his style."

"No, of course not. And he was a good student too, wasn't he?"

"Yes, he was. He'd already overcome so many things in his life. But these kids, they just wore him down."

"And that's partly why there was suspicion of suicide, correct?"

"That and the fact that he was on the roof. Nobody seemed to think that anybody would go up there."

"It's beautiful up there, I imagine," she said calmly.

"It was, indeed. He used to send us photos of it all the time."

"And did you ever send those photos that he sent you to the coroner, to prove that he was up there a lot?"

"No." She hesitated. "Would that have made any difference?"

"I can talk to him about it." Kate noted Smidge's name on the autopsy report.

"I'd appreciate it if you could. I really can't stand to think that they all think my boy would commit suicide."

"And I'm sorry. I know college can be deadly at times," she said.

"Not that deadly. He had a new girlfriend, and he was planning on coming home right after the holidays. He was hoping to talk her into coming too."

"Any idea what her name was?"

"Of course. It was Candy. He was really sweet on her."

"Wow. When did he start going out with her?" Kate asked the question, as she checked the dates on the student's death. It was only a month ago. "I don't know. Honestly it's all rolling into a nightmare of details that I don't want to remember anymore," she whispered. "He was so sweet on Candy, but he said that she was in with a bad crowd and that he would try to get her away from them."

"You do realize that bad crowd was the same crowd hassling him, don't you?"

"She was part of that?" Trent's mom asked.

"Yes, she was one of the group."

"I don't think he ever would have gone out with her if he had known that," she replied in shock. "I mean, they made his life hellish. Not just bad but unbelievably bad. I just can't see him wanting anything to do with her because of that."

"Maybe she kept it from him."

"Yet, according to Trent, she wanted to get away from that crowd, like they were bullying her too."

"I think they were. Yes, Candy's mom also said something about Candy wanting to leave that group too."

"Too bad she didn't leave earlier with my boy, then my son would still be alive."

"Candy's dead, as well." A few minutes later, Kate hung up the phone and sat here, her face buried in her hands, as she thought about everything. Then her head popped up, as she faced her team. "Candy's body was found on the bike in the intersection. I only know that she had a bike, as we confirmed that with the university, based on a bike permit, and we found her other possessions in Paula's dorm room, but I wonder if that's all of it? Did Paula collect it? Brandon? If he did, what are the chances he still has something of hers? A souvenir, so to speak."

"It'd be great if we found something with Brandon,"

Rodney said, "but, since they were in a relationship, he'd have a logical reason for anything we did find."

"I guess, but I do wonder how stupid he is." Kate paused. "Or how overconfident."

"He's stupid for sure, but it doesn't mean he's that stupid," Lilliana said. "Yet my vote's for overconfident."

"I know. And a warrant would help us find the gun and possibly some of Candy's stuff. We've got so much going on here now, and, although it's starting to break, we're just not quite there yet."

"I think we need to talk to Pamela and see what we can get out of her," Rodney said.

Kate nodded. "Oh, I agree. I definitely agree with you there. Let's hope that we can find her and that she will talk to us." Kate stood, straightening slowly. "Man, this case is twisted."

"They're all twisted, one way or another," Lilliana said. "It's just a matter of carefully untwisting it so that we can figure out exactly what we've got going on."

"And that's the problem. There's so much confusion." Kate shook her head.

"Seems to me that you need to find this Pamela, ask her questions about all this," Owen said. "Then go at this bully Brandon again and see if you can get a warrant for his house."

"I wish I could get that warrant right now"—Kate sighed—"but that just won't fly yet. We don't have enough."

"But you're close," Lilliana said. "Think about it. You've got a lot. You just need that final clincher that says he's guilty. Just that one piece, other than the word-of-mouth talk from other people."

"And that's where the problem is. Because, so far, everybody with real insider information is dead."

"Except for his cohorts," Rodney said.

"Which one of them is the weakest link, you think?" Kate turned to face her partner.

Rodney frowned. "You know what? I'm not sure. But, if you think one of them is a weaker link, you can bet Brandon does too."

She winced at that. "Maybe we'd better locate all of them and bring them back in for questioning at the same time but in separate rooms." She stopped, frowned. "Yet I've got to get up to Pamela's place now."

Rodney spoke up. "I'll call them in. You want all four guys?"

"Just the three for the moment." She considered it carefully. "See if we can catch them in a lie and shake something loose."

"Got it. Are you okay to find Pamela then?"

"Yep, and let's hope that I can talk to her."

"Yeah, and let's hope that, when you do, she has something to say."

Kate nodded. "Bingo." And she grabbed her wallet and keys and her jacket, then turned to the others. "I have to go and pick up my car first. Wish me luck."

At that, Owen shook his head. "You sure you should go alone?"

"Why not?" She didn't know him anywhere near as well as she did her partner Rodney, but he was a good guy, a good family man, and a good detective.

"I'll come with you," Owen said.

Lilliana nodded. "Not a bad idea."

"If you guys are all in, then why don't I go with Kate, and you guys can call in these a-holes," Rodney said.

"Sure," Owen replied, "that works. So, which three do you want?"

"Not Brandon. The other three." With that, the list of names and contacts was handed over, and, as Kate headed out, she looked at her partner. "I wasn't expecting all that."

"I wasn't either, and that's one of the reasons I'm with you now. Because if they feel like a second person is warranted, I don't want to be sitting on my ass, making phone calls, while you're out alone, facing whatever the hell's happening next."

"I'm just surprised."

"Don't knock it," he said, with a cheerful smile. "Might not ever happen again."

She burst out laughing at that. As they got into his car, he said, "Let's head into the Heights."

"Is that where they live? Wow, swanky. They must have money then."

"Exactly."

As they drove out, she sent Simon a text. **Heading up to Pamela's mother's place, hoping we can talk to her.** She got a response back right away.

Good luck.
Any insights for me?
Twelve.

She frowned at that. "Hardly room twelve in a house," she grumbled. She looked over at her partner. "Simon says room twelve."

He rolled his eyes at that. "That's weird, unless she's in a motel or something."

"Yeah, well, I don't know what that's about either. Let me read his message again." And then she corrected herself. "Oh, wait. He just said *twelve.* I'm not sure that it's *room*

twelve." Frowning, she studied his texts and shrugged. And then sent him a quick text. **What's the number for?**
That, my dear, is your department.

She snorted at that. "He has no idea about the number."

"He really just gets raw information, doesn't he? He can't put it together in any logical sequence, so it's hardly even helpful."

"Yeah, you're preaching to the choir here." She shook her head. "Remember? I don't really believe in half this stuff, and then he gives me something that seems random and stupid, but then it fits. So, yeah, *twelve*. I don't know what to do with it, but, hey, I'm trying to be open-minded."

"I think you're doing really well, considering." Rodney glanced at her. "This is pretty crazy stuff for anybody."

"This whole case is a mess. I hate to say it, but I'm wishing for a nice little open-and-shut murder of an old rich guy by his young gold-digging wife or some BS like that." She laughed at her words. "It makes a whole lot more sense when it's flat-out murder, crisp and clear, instead of these kinds of cases."

"These are hard but more fun in the end, and they're also the ones that you remember."

"Maybe, but it's hardly something that you want to remember."

"No, but these are the ones that stick with you. Look at how many people we've got involved now."

"Too many," she whispered.

He looked over at her, then smiled. "It's okay, you know."

"Maybe it is. Maybe it isn't. I don't know. It just feels like it's all about to break wide open, and I don't know which way it'll go."

———

SIMON URGENTLY CONTACTED Pamela. "Help is coming. You need to do something so they can find you."

"No. I told you. I can't be saved."

"And that's crap. I don't even know if you've done anything terrible or not, but you can't keep existing like this."

"I have to suffer the consequences," she whispered.

"Or do you want to do something that your daughter would be proud of?"

There was a hesitation and then almost a hiccup in her voice. "What do you mean?"

"You don't have to spend your life in there, being this prisoner. Help is on the way."

"Nobody will find me," she said.

"Why not?"

"I can't tell you."

"Look. I know that you're blind and that you can't see. But that doesn't mean other people can't see you."

"Yes, but I'm also injured from the accident. It's not a pretty sight."

"Nobody gives a crap about pretty on the outside. It's more about pretty on the inside," he snapped. "Either you'll do something to help this woman find you, or you'll be stuck in this position for the rest of your life."

"I could probably leave if I tried. I do go out sometimes. but you don't understand."

"There is no way I can understand unless you tell me something so I can," he said in frustration, "and, so far, you're not doing that."

"No. Because—" And then she stopped.

"Because what?"

"I just feel like it's better if I'm here."

"So, then you're not a prisoner."

"I don't know. I've never tried to leave. They keep the door shut, and, when I try to open the door, it's locked."

"So—"

"I think they just do it for my, ... you know, to keep me alive."

"So you don't try to commit suicide?"

"Yes," she said in a fretful voice.

"How often do you get out of there?"

"Every once in a while." But something odd was in her voice.

"Meaning?"

"I do go out and meet some people every once in a while."

"And does your family know about it?"

"No," she whispered. "And I shouldn't be telling you either."

"Why not?"

"You wouldn't understand. Unless you've ever loved and lost, you wouldn't understand."

"Oh, I've loved and lost. I understand a hell of a lot more than you might think I do," he snapped. He could sense that she was fading away from him again. "Have you done anything to hurt other people?"

"Why would you ask me that?" she said, her voice wary.

"I don't know. Maybe because you're scaring me."

"I scare myself," she said quietly.

"What is going on?" he roared, and she immediately shut down. He stared at his phone in his hand, wondering if he should call Kate. But what would he tell her? That this was a slightly crazy lady, who may or may not be locked up. And then he realized that Kate really needed to talk to Pamela.

Kate really needed to get some information from this woman.

"Listen, if you want to get loose," he called out to Pamela quietly, "this is your chance. This is your chance to redeem yourself."

She whispered back, "There is no redeeming me."

"There is, if you want it bad enough. Cops are on the way because they need to talk to you. They need to talk to you about your accident and the other related accidents."

There was a jolt to his system, as he realized it was her jolt. He nodded. "Yes, and they are the ones who can help you."

"No." She sounded almost frantic.

"Yes," he snapped. "It's time."

Almost as if she gave in, she whispered, "Yes, it's time." And she cried.

He didn't know how to convince her this was the time for some real change, even just some little improvement out of the mire of guilt and agony and self-hate that she and others had built around Pamela. Simon could only hope that Pamela got the message he had intended. He sat back, prepared to wait, and hated every minute of it.

He had a gnawing sense of something wrong, something not quite right. But he had to trust that Kate was on it. It's just that he knew—to his own folly—that sometimes just being on it didn't mean jack shit. Things still went wrong. He thought about the little bit he knew about this woman and the things that he'd heard from Kate, and he realized it was still a wild open field of chaos.

He shook his head, walked over to his kitchen, and put on a pot of coffee. It would be a hell of a long day. No way he would rest until he knew how this ended up playing out.

And he could only hope that Kate would come and tell him at the end of the day. But he knew that, if things went wrong, she wouldn't get free from this for hours yet.

CHAPTER 21

KATE WALKED UP to the beautiful house. It was a huge brick estate. With Rodney at her side, she stared at it in surprise. "It's easy enough to see why they think they won't necessarily have to deal with the law," she murmured.

"And yet we're still not exactly sure what's going on here."

"No, but it is damn well time to find out." She knocked on the door, and, when a maid answered, Kate identified herself with her badge and asked to speak to Pamela's parents.

The woman frowned. "If you'll excuse me, I'll let them know that you're here."

"Please do," Kate said in a cool voice.

"How many times have we come across maids in our work?"

"This may be the first time for me, but, of course, you're acting all blasé, like it's business as usual."

He laughed. "Wouldn't that'd be nice ... to have a maid, you know?"

"Laundry, buying groceries—and cooking—that's what I would have mine do," she said.

"Did you ever unpack?"

"Hell no," she said.

"I suppose they could do that too then." He chuckled.

"Nah, that'd be a waste of time. I've got out just what I use."

Then the massive front door opened again, and they were allowed to enter the foyer. As the maid turned to look down the hall, Kate watched as a well-dressed—almost overdressed—woman scurried toward them. Kate smiled at her. "Are you Sarah, Pamela's mother?"

"Yes. Why are you here?"

Kate held up her badge and identified herself. "I told you that we needed to ask Pamela some questions."

"No, you don't understand. Pamela is not in any shape to answer questions."

"Then you need to explain just what that means," her partner said.

"She's not all there now," her mother replied. "This all had a terrible effect on her nerves."

"So, is she of a nervous disposition?" Kate asked, pressing. "Because that doesn't mean the same thing to me as it probably does to you."

The woman frowned at her. "Look. I told you already. She's not capable of talking to you. That's all there is to it."

"No, it's not. That is not all there is to it. We need proof that she is alive and well," Kate said flatly. "And we're not leaving until we get it."

The woman looked at her in shock. "What are you saying?"

"You heard me. Now where is your daughter?"

She shook her head. "You don't understand."

"I think it's you who doesn't understand, and frankly you're not helping your case."

At that, a booming voice called out, "Who's at the door?" Kate braced herself as the father came around the corner. He glared at them. "What on earth are the cops doing at my house?" he said, with a sneer.

"We're looking into the well-being of your daughter. We have a few questions for her," Kate said simply.

"This is outrageous. I'm calling my lawyer."

"You absolutely may call your lawyer, and, if that's your preference, we'll see you down at the station bright and early tomorrow morning, with your daughter in tow, please," she said.

He stopped. "Did you hear me say I was calling my lawyer?"

"Did you hear me say that that was totally fine? You're certainly allowed to do that. It doesn't quite make sense, since we're merely looking into the condition of your daughter. But, hey, if you feel you need to have legal representation for something like that, it's your prerogative. However, you will show up at the station with your lawyer, your wife, and your daughter, tomorrow morning at nine. Understood?"

"I have no intention of showing up."

"In that case, we'll be issuing a warrant for your arrest," she stated in a steady tone.

He took a deep breath. "How did it get to this?" he asked, obviously trying for a much more genial approach.

"It came about because you refused to even discuss why we're here."

"I have this thing against the cops." He waved his hand in front of her, as if able to swat her away. "Seeing you set me off."

"I'm not concerned about what set you off," Kate replied in a harsh voice. "I want to speak with your daughter."

"You can't do that," he said.

"And why is that?"

"My daughter's not here," he said.

Kate looked over at the wife and witnessed her bottom lip trembling. "I see. Where is she?"

"She's off with her friends. I don't even know where she is these days. She is an adult, Detective."

"She is, indeed, an adult, and yet we have a strong suspicion that she is not free to come and go. As a matter of fact, we have reason to believe that she is essentially your prisoner."

He looked at her in shock, and she watched his lips firm up, where there had been a little bit of a nervous tic in the corner of his mouth. She nodded. "So we're here to get proof of life and assurance that she is free and clear to move around on her own."

"Good Lord. What do you think this is, a prison?"

"You know, for some people, that might be a prison they are completely happy in, but we'll hear it from her, thank you very much."

"And, as I said, she's not here," he replied, his voice harsh.

"So you say, and, since we have a suspicion regarding the welfare of your daughter and find you wholly uncooperative, we'll get a warrant and return. In the meantime, we'll still see you and your entire family down at the station in the morning for questioning. Thank you for your time. Now we'll need to speak with your maid."

"You can't."

"Obstruction of justice." She beamed. "I love it. At this rate we'll arrest you and take you down to the station in handcuffs. I'm sure the neighbors will love to see that show."

"Oh, Gerard," his wife whispered.

"They're bluffing," he snapped.

"We're not bluffing. Produce your daughter so that we may speak with her, and all of this can blow over."

"And if we don't?"

"I just told you." Kate's voice remained equally firm. "Absolutely no way will we walk away now, *until* we can speak to your daughter and can ascertain that she's not come to harm."

"Why didn't anybody give a shit about my daughter when she was in that accident?"

"It was my understanding that the driver was charged."

"So?" he said. "Do you think that makes up for the loss of our grandchild?"

"No, of course not. Does keeping your daughter prisoner make up for the loss of your grandchild? Or the fact that Pamela was also a victim?"

"She should have never been riding to work on that ridiculous bicycle," he sneered.

"Ah, is that how it works for you? Because her husband had their only car, and so she had the bike?"

"What are you talking about?"

"You don't get to punish her just because you hold her responsible."

"Maybe she's punishing herself."

"Maybe so," she said flatly. "I'd like to see for myself, so where is she?"

He glared at her. "I'm calling my lawyer."

"I think I'll call mine as well." She pulled out her phone and called the DA. As soon as he answered, she said, "I need a warrant," and went on to give the address.

"Pretty high-falutin neighborhood. What's it for?"

"Suspicion of kidnapping, unlawful imprisonment, obstruction, and we'll likely have more to add once we go through the place. They're refusing to produce any proof that their daughter is alive and well. We have it on good authority that she is being held against her will and is not free to walk around."

"And this daughter is how old?"

"She is twenty-nine."

"Okay, give me five." And she hung up. She pocketed her phone and just stood here, waiting.

Gerard stared at her in shock. "You're serious."

"I am absolutely serious. Finding out that you're imprisoning somebody makes me that way in a hurry. And pissed off, by the way, but that's okay. Why don't you really call your lawyer, and we'll see what he has to say about all this."

"Look. We got off on the wrong foot." He tried to calm things down.

"We're still on the wrong foot," Kate said calmly, "because you have yet to produce your daughter."

"Then I guess you'll have to get that warrant."

"That's fine. It's in process."

"Not once my lawyer gets a hold of you," he said.

Rodney shifted at her side.

"I'm sorry, are you threatening me?" she asked.

"Just your job," he said calmly. "Do you think a slime like you gets to keep a job after you threatened me?"

"Do you think a slime like you gets to keep anything after we find out you've imprisoned someone?"

He stared at her and looked over at his wife. Her bottom lip was trembling even more, and the tears in her eyes were clearly evident, as she silently pleaded with her husband.

"So now the real question at this point is this." Kate turned to look at Pamela's mother. "Do you want Gerard to let your daughter go and tell the truth, or are you just protecting all this that your husband has done, so that you don't lose out on your fancy home here?"

The woman gasped, and then she burst into tears.

"Don't you say a thing," he snapped at Sarah.

But she bawled uncontrollably.

"You see, Gerard? It's not that easy." Kate turned to him. "When you start pulling tricks like this, it impacts everyone."

"My daughter is not of sound mind," he said.

"So everybody keeps telling me. Until I see her, and we get her evaluated by a specialist, then nobody will have an answer to that, will they?"

"You have no right!" he yelled.

"Your daughter is an adult, and you have no right to keep her here!" Kate stood taller, her legs braced apart, and her arms crossed over her chest.

"What are you, some kind of a bitch?" he asked, but she was completely unfazed.

Kate smirked at him, which seemed to anger him more. When her phone rang again, she grandly smiled, as she read the text. "The warrant is in."

"Wait, wait, wait. You're not allowed to enter my house."

"Did you hear what I just said about a warrant?" She held up the document on her phone. "And your maid already gave us access inside. The warrant just clears the rest of it for us. You certainly may call your lawyer now, if ever, if you wish, and this is the number on our warrant." Kate read it off to him. "He can do an investigation on this right away, as I'm sure you want him to. In the meantime, you will excuse us, but we'll be bringing in extra personnel to take a look at your house."

"You surely can't do that," he said.

"Yes," she said flatly, "we can and we are." She heard the sirens pulling up out front. She looked at Rodney. "You want to let them in? Then we'll escort Sarah and Gerard out of the way."

"Where? What do you mean?" Gerard yelled.

"Downtown, where you should have gone in the first place. In the meantime, we'll talk to your maid."

"No, no, no, no."

"Yes," she said in a hard tone. "You haven't been the least bit cooperative so far, and I have no intention of doing it any other way." His jaw firmed. "I know," she quipped, with a wave of her hand. "My job's in jeopardy. My life's in jeopardy. *Blah-blah-blah-blah.* Bullies like you just never quit."

Kate turned, then looked at the wife and smiled. "You know something. I think we'll start with you." As she led her into a different room, Gerard was yelling, "You can't talk to her."

"Oh yes, I think I can, and I will," Kate snapped.

He yelled out, "Sarah, don't you say anything."

As she got the woman into the kitchen, Kate faced her. "Where is your daughter?"

But the woman shook her head. "You don't understand."

"No, I don't, because nobody is cooperating. That's why you have all those flashing lights outside, lighting up your neighborhood, not to mention sirens still blaring. I bet your neighbors are annoyed. All I'm concerned about is that your daughter is safe and sound."

The woman's eyes welled up.

"No way. The tears might work on others. They won't work on me."

At that, she took a slow breath. "I don't know where she is."

"Now that, I almost believe." Kate studied her.

"That's because I really don't know. I only wish I did."

At that, she turned to find Rodney, standing behind her. "Let's do it. Search the house, top to bottom."

He nodded, then took off with the officers who had just arrived.

She motioned at Sarah to sit. "You can just sit there, while the search is going on. How many rooms are in this house?"

Puzzled, she closed her eyes, as if counting before saying, "Thirteen."

"Thirteen rooms?" Sarah nodded. "And how would you judge which room is which, like, for instance, which would you call the thirteenth room?"

"Oh my goodness, that would be the second maid's quarters."

"Second maid's quarters." She shook her head. "So room twelve would be the first maid's quarters or something like that? Your maids live-in?"

"Yes, been with us for years."

"So you're hoping that you pay them enough to be loyal?"

She stiffened and glared at Kate. "There's no reason to be insulting."

"That depends on what you've been doing to your daughter," she said.

"Nothing, absolutely nothing."

"Meaning?"

"Everything we did is because we love her."

"And yet you won't even acknowledge where she is."

"Because I don't know," she cried out passionately.

"And why do you not know?"

"Because I haven't seen her lately." She glanced nervously out of the kitchen toward the front entrance.

"You're afraid your husband's done something to her?"

Her eyes widened. "No, of course not."

"Yeah, yeah, yeah." Kate looked around the kitchen and noted a door on the side. "What's in there?"

"Nothing, it just leads to the basement."

"Right." With one of the other cops walking in to assist Kate, she said, "Sit here with her, please, while I go check out the basement."

"No, you can't," Sarah whined.

Kate turned, gave her a hard look. "Not only can I, but I will," she snapped. "I've had quite enough of you two and your lies and your delays." And, with that, she headed downstairs. Kate flipped on the light switch. She stopped and looked around at the main room in the basement, leading off to a lot of other rooms, smaller rooms. Kate called out, "Just what all is going on down here?"

"Nothing," Sarah replied.

"*Right.*" Kate walked from one room to the next, checking each, while calling out, "Pamela, are you here?"

Only as she got to the other end of the basement did she hear a voice cry out. She opened the door to see a young woman of maybe fourteen. "Hi, who are you?"

"I'm here as maid," she said in broken English.

Kate stared at her in shock. *Surely she's not the maid who has been here for years.* "Are you alone here?"

She shook her head. "No, two more."

"Great, and how long have you been here?"

"Years."

Kate pushed down the anger. *Remain calm.* She looked around the small room and saw that it had a single bed with a dresser and some clothing. "So, you look after this house?"

She nodded.

"Do they pay you?"

She slowly shook her head.

"*Great,* now we have human trafficking to add to the whole mess." She quickly sent that message to the DA. Then she escorted the young woman upstairs and sat her down in the kitchen. Sarah cried when she saw her. "Oh, your legal and criminal struggles are *just* starting," Kate said. To the uniformed officer, she added, "Keep watch on both of them, please."

At that, Sarah bawled and bawled.

"I still haven't found Pamela though."

Sarah looked back at her, tears in her eyes.

Kate went back downstairs again and followed the other hallway to several other small rooms and the two other maids, who were too scared to call out in answer to Kate's yells. She told them both, "It's okay. We'll get you out of here." She wasn't sure they understood her. But still Kate found no sign of Pamela. She searched high and low and then came back up with the two females, who were also left in the officer's charge. As Kate looked outside one of the kitchen windows of the large home, she noted a floor over the garage. "Is anybody in the rooms above the garage?"

Sarah shook her head.

"But, of course, I don't believe you, so whatever. It doesn't really make a difference what you or your husband say." Kate walked outside and looked at the garage, opened it up, stepped inside, and managed to make her way upstairs. But nothing was there. It looked like it had housed people at one point in time, but nothing was here now. As she turned away to leave, she caught an odd sound. She listened to it and frowned because she couldn't quite place it. Then she remembered something Simon had said.

She called him. "Hey, I'm at the parents' house. You won't believe some of the stuff we found here, like human trafficking. There are fourteen-, fifteen- and sixteen-year-old girls here who have been working at the house as maids *for years*—without pay."

"Jesus. Funny how Pamela hasn't mentioned anything like that."

"I'm hearing a weird sound, nothing that I can really pinpoint. But there's no sign of Pamela."

"I was afraid of that. I was hoping she was there, but you know how hard it is to get any information."

"I know. I know. And because we found these girls, I'm not upset about it. Believe me. I still feel like Pamela has to be here somewhere."

"She's not being very cooperative, and she's scared."

"Yeah, her parents are pretty scary, but it's still not helpful. We have to find her and to figure out what's going on, before we can help her."

"Let me talk to her again," he said.

"No, just tell her to give me a sign, some kind of a sign, so I can figure out where she is, if she's even alive. Do you know for a fact that you're not talking to dead people?"

When she heard him on the other end almost choking, she said, "Okay, fine. I'm hearing a weird whirring sound."

"Whirring," he said thoughtfully.

"Yeah, you know? Like something going around and

around."

"She's riding the bike," he said suddenly. "She's on the bike. It's all she has for sound."

"What do you mean, it's all she has for sound?"

"I don't know. All I can tell you is that it's all she has for sound."

But, with that, she pocketed her phone and turned, beginning her search. By following that sound, she got to the far end of the garage and found a door inside a closet. She popped open the door and stepped inside. In there, in a room in utter darkness, she flipped on the lights to see a young woman on an exercise bike. She appeared to be crying silently, as she pedaled the bike faster and faster and faster. Kate stepped over in front of her and reached out a hand to touch her arm.

The woman shrieked and stopped pedaling.

Kate waved a hand in front of her eyes, realized this was, indeed, Pamela.

"Pamela, my name is Detective Kate Morgan. Can you hear me?"

With her arms wrapped around her chest and shivering, the woman nodded.

"Can you speak?" she asked.

And the woman nodded again, then stilled.

"Now, can you tell me who you are?"

"I'm Pamela," she said in a faint whisper. "Simon told me that you were coming."

THE MESSAGE ON Simon's phone was short and terse.

We got her. We're taking her to the hospital to be checked over.

He sank back down on the bed in shock. "Thank God," he whispered. "Finally something decent happening in Pamela's life."

At least he thought it was decent. He didn't know. Something was still nagging at him. Something that he should have noted but hadn't yet. He sent back a message. **Thank God.**

He received a happy emoji in response. With that, he grabbed a coffee and sat back down in the corner of his couch, wondering if all the incessant background noise and the smells on steroids and everything would stop. Now that Pamela had been rescued, surely the connection wasn't necessary anymore. At least he hoped so. It's just so hard to know what was going on.

As he sat here, he noted a cleanliness to the air that he hadn't felt in quite a while. Not so much that it was a problem, just that it was different. He smiled. Yet something was going on, something frustratingly nagging Simon in the back of his mind that he couldn't seem to get to.

And, as he settled on the couch, lying here, he just let his mind empty. This was the most bizarre case he'd ever had. But then he'd only had very few of them. Smiling, starting to feel a whole lot better, he got up and had a quick shower, pulled off the sheets, then made the bed with fresh, clean bedding.

When he came out again to the living room, he sat back down on the couch to study the beautiful view in front of him. And then it hit him. He didn't know what it was yet, but that feeling of wrongness was building and building and building. He grabbed his phone to call her, and Kate answered right away, her voice much happier now. "Something's wrong," he said.

"What are you talking about?"

"I don't know, but something's wrong. I'm sure of it."

"Like what?" she snapped.

"I don't know, but it has to do with Pamela."

"Okay, if you say so. We're still at the hospital, and she's getting checked over right now. She hasn't done any talking yet."

"Right. Does she have a phone with her? Or a laptop? Anything?"

"She has a phone, but it's got no battery in it."

"Interesting, that doesn't ring true."

"What are you saying?" she asked curiously.

"I'm not sure. I'm not sure at all. I don't know what's going on."

"But something must be."

"Yes, and I know I shouldn't be saying this, and I have nothing to back it up, but ..."

"Come on. Just spit it out," she said impatiently.

"I don't trust her. There. I said it."

"Jesus, you're the one who sent us there to rescue her."

"I know. I know. I just ... Something's wrong."

"Good enough. I'll see what I can figure out." And, with that, she hung up.

Now there wouldn't be any hope for sleep at all for Simon. Because whatever the hell was going on had to do with Pamela. He just didn't know if she wasn't telling the truth or if something else was happening. And he wished to God he did know.

CHAPTER 22

KATE STUDIED THE woman being checked over in the hospital. Rodney was beside her, a big grin on his face. She whispered to him, "Simon says something's wrong."

He looked at her in surprise. "Does he know that we got her?"

She nodded. "He does. I'm looking forward to interviewing the parents."

"Yeah, me too. I can't believe we found those poor girls down there."

"I'm still shocked to know they've been there for years, I just ..." Like Simon, now Kate was wondering what was going on. "As long as Pamela's okay here, I'd like to go back and interview her parents."

"They're at the station, waiting for us."

Leaving guards to keep an eye on Pamela, they headed back to the station. Separating the parents, she walked in on the father, introduced herself again, put down the tape recorder. "I'm recording this interview."

"You can do whatever you want. I'm not saying another word until my lawyer gets here."

"I understand. Human trafficking is a pretty serious crime. But, for the moment, I'd just like to talk about Pamela."

He snorted. "You don't have a clue about Pamela."

"No, I probably don't. Something's definitely wrong."

"*You think?*"

"Was she normal before she lost her daughter?"

He hesitated, then said, "All we could figure out is that's what brought this on."

She nodded. "When you think about it, it was pretty traumatic." He didn't say anything. She wasn't even sure how to direct the conversation to help resolve the anxiety building inside her. Then she realized she had one avenue. "Given her depression over what happened, when did you realize she was a danger?"

He groaned. "She's always been a little off. When she hates, she hates with a passion."

"And so, she directed that passionate hate to the person who killed her daughter?"

"Yes, of course, but she couldn't get at him because he was sent to jail."

"And now?" She wrote herself a note to check on the status and the location of the driver.

"I believe he's served his sentence and was released. Might want to check on their welfare instead of bothering us."

She froze and looked up. "You think your daughter might harm the driver who killed Jillie? And how would your daughter have managed to do something like that? Particularly given the way you were holding her hostage."

"I'm not talking. I don't have any proof."

"No, but you have suspicions."

He groaned. "I've got a hell of a lot of suspicions. I've got even more than that. But *uh-uh*. Not until my lawyer gets here. Then we can talk."

"You mean that you want a plea deal for the trafficking

in exchange for information on your daughter, is that it?"

He just gave her a thin smile and buttoned his lip.

She nodded. "We'll talk when your lawyer gets here." She got up and walked out. She reached for her phone and tried to contact the driver with the expired glasses who had killed Pamela's daughter. There was no answer. Contacting the family, she asked for an update.

"What update?" the woman said. "He was killed several weeks ago."

"I'm sorry to hear that. How did he die?" But she knew; goddammit, she knew. "He was hit by a car while riding his bike."

"And he was riding a bike, why?"

"Because he had killed a child. With a felony on his record, he didn't get to drive again," she snapped, "at least not for a very long time. And then the irony of it all is that he ended up in a car accident."

"And where did that occur?"

"Up by the university," she said.

"I don't remember seeing an accident report about that."

"I don't know why you didn't see it." She added, "If you want to find it, it wasn't right at the university. The accident was just a few blocks away."

"Right." Kate pinched the bridge of her nose. "Do the investigators know who did it?"

"No, not at all. It was a hit-and-run."

"I'm sorry to hear that," Kate murmured.

"He made a lot of mistakes in his life, but killing that poor child was an accident. He wasn't paying enough attention, and he needed a new pair of prescription eyeglasses for sure, and, of course, he deserved to be punished for killing someone, but he didn't deserve to die."

"No, ma'am. I get that. I am sorry for your loss. Thank you for your time." Kate hung up the phone, and, staring down at the information, her stomach got queasy. "How though? Just how the hell did that happen?" she whispered to no one.

At that, she turned on her email and checked for the *concerned citizen* email that had been sent to Bill, the ex-cop, the guy who had lost his son. Kate read it intently. Nothing was on the surface, but something was underneath. An intimation that something needed to be done, something more. Was that it? Was killing Jillie's killer it? Was that what needed to be done? Was it that these people needed to be dealt with in kind? And, if the city wouldn't do anything to fix it, then the survivors would do something?

Not that the city would come and fix the intersection after they had already refused once, but Pamela—and her proxy—actually wanted these people to pay for killing their loved ones. The oldest motive in the world: revenge. As Kate sat here, staring, Rodney came into the bullpen, crowing in delight.

"The mother is no longer quite so cocky."

Kate looked up at him. "And?"

"Apparently Pamela was making phone calls, trying to get somebody to kill the guy who killed her daughter. In her opinion, Pamela didn't feel he did enough time."

"She was trying to hire somebody, right?"

He looked at her in surprise. "Did you already hear that from the father?"

"No. But he did intimate that Pamela wasn't right in the head, and that's why they were keeping her locked up."

"So she had a cell phone, but it had no battery, so she couldn't contact anyone."

"I bet she's not that stupid. Do we still have people at the house?" she asked.

He nodded.

"Have them search her room for a battery for that cell phone," she said.

"You think she's behind this?"

"I'm not sure, but we're close. We're very close."

"She couldn't have done it on her own. Not being blind. Not the way they had her locked down."

"No, she wouldn't have, especially with her failing sight. And I don't know that she even knows about the other victims, the loved ones they left behind. It could be that she set something into motion that somebody else took up, and it eventually took on a life of its own."

"Jesus, but who?"

"We don't have a shortage of suspects. Unfortunately we still have too many, but I'm thinking of the father who sent us the email. The ex-cop."

"But wouldn't that have just sent him on Pamela's trail?"

"Yes, I'm just not sure who else knew though." With that, she picked up the phone and called him. "Bill, it's Detective Kate Morgan. I'm calling about that email you got again. Did you tell anybody about it?"

"Sure, a couple people."

"Anybody in particular?"

He laughed. "Yeah, for sure. You were talking to him today."

She ended the call, telling Rodney, "I have to go."

Rodney called out, "Hang on. I'm coming."

She nodded. "Let's move fast."

As it was, Rodney drove, and they headed out to the pizza corner. "Seriously, it's him, the owner?"

"No, I don't know anything yet, but he's one of the people Bill told about the email."

"Why would Bill do that?"

"Because when he got it, Bill was pretty disgusted. He wanted everything to be within the law," she murmured.

"Do we believe him?"

"Hell no, I don't believe him. I don't believe anybody at this point."

"So," Rodney begins, thinking out loud, "Pamela, in her pain, reaches out to the ex-cop and to at least one other person, hoping she can get someone to take action on her behalf? And what? Once this guy gets started, he's not ready to stop?" He glanced at Kate, then put his gaze back on the road.

Kate shrugged. "Maybe he just figured it was a perfect time for him to get revenge for all those accidents that happened over the years in front of his business. And now that he'd the courage to do something, he would clean the slate and a few other things."

When they walked into the pizza store, the young kid was behind the counter again.

"Where's Aaron Carlton?" Kate asked.

"He just went up to his place. He should be back in about five minutes or so."

She nodded and ordered a slice of pizza. "How's he been lately?"

"Ha! He's been on a high, actually happy for a change. I figured at one point in time he might have sold the business or something, he seemed so cheerful."

"Interesting, sometimes life is like that."

"Maybe. It's all good though because you know he's had a pretty shitty life at times too."

"Yeah? Why is that?"

"His sister was killed a few years back, maybe four or five years back. Not right now, like all the others, or the ones that are all of a sudden happening. It was like a few blocks up and around."

"Another traffic accident?"

"No, another cycling accident. He and his sister used to ride together all the time."

She nodded.

When the door opened, and the owner walked in, he took one look at them, and the smile dropped from his face. Aaron turned, and he booked it.

Kate took up the chase. She heard the kid yelling behind them. But she didn't stop. With Rodney on her heels, the two of them split, Kate going one way around the block, and Rodney going the other, and, by the time she came out on the far side, she saw the owner racing toward a vehicle. He was frantically punching a key fob to get it to start. She tackled him at the car, and he slammed her cheek into the sidewalk, grazing it over the concrete into a nice road rash. But she had him.

He immediately screamed, "Police brutality, police brutality!"

She quickly handcuffed him and pulled him to his feet. "Really? And what about all those kids you killed?" Aaron stared at her. "You know the ones, and the guy who needed glasses... the one you killed ... for Pamela."

Aaron didn't say anything.

"But you liked it, didn't you?"

"What's not to like," he said calmly.

"Yeah, you're in control, right? You get to say who lives and who dies."

He shrugged. "I had a list." He glared at her.

"And was Pamela the one who started it?"

"Yep, I'd thought about it before. I mean, I really did think about the whole revenge angle, but I didn't get past that. Until she contacted me, and then I was just like, *She's right, and we have to do something.*"

"What about all the others?"

"What others?" he asked.

"These last two at the intersection, for starters—Candy and Sally."

He shrugged. "I didn't have anything to do with that."

"The two females who were just killed days apart?"

Aaron shrugged. "No, that wasn't me."

Kate stared at him hard but believed him. *Brandon.* She turned and looked at Rodney.

His eyebrows were up, as he studied the shop owner. "How many did you kill?" Rodney asked.

"There was another recent accident here a few blocks away, and that person is in the hospital right now," he said.

"And why him?"

"Because he's a pedophile." Aaron shrugged. "Why the hell should he live?"

"So, you used your vehicle in order to take down some-body else?"

"That's the thing. Once you start down this pathway, you realize just how much you can clean up in the world," he said enthusiastically. "That's a reward all in itself."

"And how many other bike accidents did you and your vehicle have a part in?"

"Well, first, for five years now, I tried hard to make it look like the city needed to fix the traffic pattern. So, in memory of my sister, I killed someone near the university annually. But that didn't work out because the city refused. Then later, when I found out Pamela was reaching out, suggesting doing more, I contacted her. We met a few times. It was a fluke that we happened to be there at Sally's accident scene. Besides I had this list and worked my way through it. And since then, slowly I've been picking off various people."

Kate still didn't have the killer who took Candy's and Sally's lives, the one they'd been looking for this past week or so. Instead she found Aaron, who had killed multiple others annually. She shook her head. "How do you choose your victims?"

"Some are related to other accidents. And some are related to just being shits."

"You said you didn't kill Candy or Sally, the last two at the intersection."

"No, I didn't. I honestly watched those two happen, but something was weird about them."

"Yeah, something was weird about it. What though? Did you see the shithead guys at the time of the accidents?"

"Jesus, those students? Yeah, I saw them." He shook his head. "What a mess."

"Why?"

"Because they were either high or stoned or something. I don't know. But they were obnoxious. They were hassling Pamela and another guy at the same time. She asked me not to make a scene, so instead I added them to my list but didn't get a chance to carry through there. Anyway this obnoxious guy was a bully to everyone. ... I saw it happen over and over. Mostly he picked on women or injured people. Although, not too long ago, maybe a month ago now, this one guy was being bullied for talking to the one female, the one who died at the intersection a few days ago."

"Candy?"

Aaron shrugged. "Don't know her name. But she was part of that bully crew. Not the red hoodie chick."

"Right," Kate confirmed. "Candy."

"Regardless that other woman was there too—the second woman in that bully group. Both of the women who seemed to be part of the bullying group are now dead."

"How do you know that both Candy and Paula belonged to Brandon's group?"

"Because they were both talking to that one guy ahead of time, right before the one female pushed him down."

"So Candy pushed down some guy. Did you recognize him or see them try to push the guy into the traffic afterward?"

Aaron stopped, stared out at nothing. "You know what? At the time I wondered what was going on because it looked odd, but so many people were around that I figured no one could tell—or *would* tell. But the fact of the matter is," he said, with a nod, "the ringleader almost tapped the guy on the back of his head. And, if they were all part of the same group, that would explain why so many people were around, and, of course, they could have hidden anything they wanted to do with that kind of a mob, simply by distracting people." He nodded. "Yeah, the little shits"—he grinned—"they killed that guy."

"Okay, and what do you know about the dead females in that group?" she asked.

"*Hmm*, whatever. I mean, they had their reasons."

"That's it? These bullies send the women to their death, and that's it? *Whatever?*"

"Yeah, whatever. But I didn't see them *do* anything."

"Now if only you saw a little more than that."

"You could always find the other blind woman," he said.

"There are two? Both bullied by Brandon's gang?"

Aaron nodded. "She's younger, like a student—eighteen, nineteen, twenty."

"I'd like to talk to her," Kate said. "I'd really like to get her statement."

He volunteered the other name. "Pamela, who you already know about, is one of the blind women, and the other one was Catherine, I believe."

"And why are you being cooperative all of the sudden?" Kate asked.

"Why not? I'm proud of what I did. I intend to confess, but I'll be telling the jury exactly what I did and why. It's all good."

"And which blind woman hired you?"

"Neither. The younger one didn't have any money. Besides, she was pretty desperate. But it was Pamela's idea, and we planned everything out together."

"How did you get in touch with her?"

"Back then Pamela had more of her sight, so she was still using a laptop and had a cell phone. I did try to contact her a couple months back, but I couldn't get a hold of her." He frowned. "I wasn't even sure if she was still alive."

"Yeah, she is, but she might not be happy about it just now."

He laughed. "When you make a decision like this, you need to be proud of what you are doing. You need to do it for the right reasons because you'll have to live with it for the rest of your life," he said.

Now, if Kate had said those words to him, there would have been a warning and a different tone in her voice. But, in his case, he seemed legitimately proud of everything he'd done. She shook her head, spoke to Rodney. "I need to go talk to this other woman, Catherine."

"It's all right," Rodney said. "I've got a cruiser coming for Aaron."

She nodded and looked at Aaron, handcuffed, leaning on his car, but she turned to address her partner. "Now we need to find that other woman, and maybe we can get this wrapped up."

"Maybe," Rodney said. "But I wouldn't count on it just yet."

"I know. Brandon's pretty slippery."

At that, her prisoner said, "Yeah, that'd be the big guy, the asshat who thinks he's big man on campus."

"Was he the one … What did you see him do?" she asked.

"He's the one who reached up to the woman in the red hoodie." And he put a hand to her, as if to demonstrate, albeit with the handcuffs, "And went *boom!*"

"Did you see him shoot something?"

He shrugged. "That's what it looked like. The person jolted, like she had been shot, but then carried on. With the hoodie, I didn't know it was a woman, until I heard the news later that day. Anyway, the group of bullies were helping her stay on the bike. She carried on and rode out into the middle of the road, even though they were yelling. I think to everybody else it would look like they were trying to stop her or to warn her. But you know and I know differently. I don't think that's what it was at all."

"What do you think it was?" Rodney asked.

"I think they were cheering her on."

"I wouldn't be surprised," she said sadly.

Just then the cruiser pulled up. She looked over at Rodney. "You coming with me?"

"Hell yes. Let's go talk to this last person."

Catherine's last name and address were on several of the complaint reports. Thankfully they found her at home, sitting with her family. When they walked in, the family looked relieved to see them.

"We've been trying to figure out what to do about this," Catherine's father said nervously. "She said these guys have been hassling her at the university a lot."

"They won't be doing it again," Kate said flatly. "I do need to get your statement though."

And her statement was very similar to what they had just heard from Aaron. Luckily she had a friend who witnessed this bullying too.

Kate nodded. "I will need to get that in writing. Can you and your friend come into the station tomorrow?"

"Sure, I can bring them down," her father said. "Thank you."

Kate nodded. "Sounds good. Now we need to go talk to these guys." At that, she turned to look at Rodney.

He smiled. "The three are showing up tomorrow morning."

"Good. Let's get Brandon in too now."

At that, the young blind woman called out. "It's Brandon. That's the guy's name."

"Yes, we know who he is. Not to worry. He won't be doing it again." She hoped for the best when she said that, but she also knew that lawyers could make her life difficult.

WHEN KATE WALKED into the station the next morning, she was more than happy to see Brandon was here with his lawyer as well. She tried not to smile because it hurt her face where it had met the pavement yesterday. She looked over at Rodney. "This should be fun."

"Only when it's over. Should we talk to his buddies first?"

"Yeah, I think so. We can see if Walter, Jonathan, and Tony are smart enough to get themselves a plea deal."

"I don't think any of them get it yet," he said.

"At least one dead victim is from their bullying—Trent, Candy's potential boyfriend. Plus the two women—Candy and Paula." Kate held up one finger and shook her head. "No, Aaron talked of killing a woman. Never confirmed who she was. It could have been Paula, since she didn't have the same ice bullet wounds as Candy and Sally."

"Right," Rodney agreed. "So we count Sally instead of Paula in Brandon's kill column. So maybe three deaths on the bullies."

"At least." Kate shook her head. "We can always throw Paula's death in the mix. See if we can get them to disclaim that death, kinda incriminating themselves on the other three."

They walked into the first interview room to see one of the guys standing against the wall, an insolent look on his face.

"Three counts of murder, Walter, that we know of so far."

He looked startled, and then his face paled.

Kate nodded. "Did you think you would just continue playing God, deciding who gets to live and who gets to die?"

"Do you really think Brandon gives a shit about you guys?" Rodney asked, as he pulled out a chair and gestured for the young man to sit down.

She shook her head. "Did you really think that Candy had to die?"

"We didn't have nothing to do with Candy," Walter said nervously.

"Well then, one out of three isn't bad, right?" Kate asked, all serious.

"It's still two counts of murder," Rodney said.

"I didn't want to do it," he blurted out suddenly, looking frantically back and forth between them.

"Of course not. I supposed Brandon made you do it, right?"

"You don't know what he's like." Walter sat down, as the words poured from him. "If you want to be anybody on campus, you have to toe the line with him. You have to do what he says."

"And why would you want to be anybody on campus?" she asked curiously. "I mean, particularly with him."

He stared at her. "Because he's ... he's the wealthiest on campus. He's the one with all the connections. He's the one who can get you a job when you're done. He's the one who has the family ties." He slumped toward the table, his head in his hands. "It's all about who you know."

"So, in order to get a job—when this wasted college experience was all over—you were prepared to sell your soul in the process? That's not the way university life was for me."

He scrubbed at his hair with both hands. "But we didn't realize what we were doing. It didn't start off that way. It just slid into this, ... this horrible chain of events that we couldn't get out of."

"Tell me what happened at the intersection with Sally, the one in the red hoodie."

Walter looked at her in surprise and then frowned.

"Brandon had this new gimmick ice-cube thing that he got somewhere off the internet. He read about a case on campus a long time ago, and, while we were drinking at the student pub, we searched for it and found it for less than twenty bucks. Brandon ordered it. We took it to the pub and shot these little ice bullets into our drinks. He thought it was a great toy and always has it on him," Walter said.

"We were walking down the sidewalk, outside of the campus, heading for our pizza joint, when he walked up to this woman on her bike and, all of a sudden, just said, "There you go." As the girl moved forward, Brandon reached up, and he popped her behind the head. But it was just ice, so we didn't think anything of it, but the girl wobbled forward and then slowly did this weird hit into the car, and lots of screaming and shouting and whatnot happened, but Brandon just laughed."

"Yeah. Any idea where that tool is?"

"Probably at his place," he said.

"What happened to Paula?"

He winced at that. "I don't really know what happened with Paula," he said quietly. "I just know that it was bad news. That whole deal was bad news."

"Why is that?"

"Because Brandon pitted the females against each other."

"And yet the one, Candy, had a boyfriend?"

"No," he corrected quietly. "She was supposed to make it look like Trent was her boyfriend, and then she was supposed to break off with him and torment him even more."

Kate sat back and stared, her heart aching at such a nightmare. "So did you do anything worthwhile at university, or just prove what a prick you were?"

He flushed at that. "I'm not proud of everything I did," Walter said. "But I had nothing to do with killing those people."

"What about Trent, ... the boyfriend?"

He flushed at that. "I didn't throw him off the roof."

"Yeah. No, of course not. That would have been Brandon, I'm sure."

He nodded. "Exactly. It was Brandon. I wasn't even there that night."

"Lies, all four of you were there. And Paula? Did you just wait until she dosed Candy with the drugs? That much blood with no visible wounds means a nose bleed to me, and that goes along with the drugs. Then, after you put Candy somewhere safe, you hit Paula hard, so she couldn't say anything to anyone. What's the matter? Was she crying with remorse and making you nervous?" Kate taunted Walter. "And, when Candy didn't OD, you took her out to the same intersection and dumped her and the bike and popped her one too."

He flushed again but nodded slowly. "I didn't hit Paula. That was Brandon. I want a plea deal." He leaned forward. "I can help you."

She nodded. "I can see you trying to figure out how to get out of this, but I'm here to tell you that there's no chance. You're too far in the hole. There are too many deaths. There is no forgiveness. But I'll see." And, with that, she got up and walked out. Outside, she was almost vibrating.

"Take it easy," Rodney said, exiting the observation room.

"Take it easy?" She spun on him.

He held up his hand. "Come on. There's more to be

done. Let's see what these other two have to say. Then we'll go talk to Brandon."

After interviewing Jonathan and Tony, and getting more of the same confirmed, they finally stood in the hallway, exhausted and sick at the unnecessary loss of life.

"Just one more, Kate," Rodney said. "Just one more."

She walked into the interview room, where Brandon and his lawyer had been waiting for a very long time. She slammed down her file. "Three counts of murder and we're looking for more."

The lawyer immediately jumped up. "Detective, you are mistaken. My client has done absolutely nothing to warrant a murder charge, much less three. I can't believe you've wasted our time—"

"Oh, wait. I misspoke. Make it four. And maybe we should listen to what others who were present have to say."

"It won't matter what anybody else said," Brandon replied in that lazy insolent voice. "Because it's just their word against mine."

"Unless they were observers of you committing murder."

"If they were observers, then they were guilty too, weren't they? So all they're doing is trying to save their ass and pin it on me."

"That is quite possible. But do you think we don't have any evidence?"

"You've got nothing," he said, with a sneer.

The lawyer hopped to his feet. "I'll be taking my client out of here, Detective. You've clearly got nothing."

"Yeah." Brandon hopped up.

Kate noticed something in his pocket. "Rodney?" She motioned at her partner. "Wasn't it nice of him to bring in the murder weapon?"

Immediately her partner stepped forward, one hand already gloved, and removed the item from Brandon's pocket. Rodney held it up and nodded. "Forensics will love this. That along with the drugs in Candy's system, that you used to keep her compliant. You parked on the boulevard, helped her onto the bike and into the center of the road, likely laughing the whole time. She collapses, and you pop her with this as a final coup." He held up the ice-bullet gun.

"Hey, that's mine," Brandon protested, eyeing his gun the whole time Rodney had it. "You don't have any right to that."

"Oh, that's all right," Kate cajoled him. "I mean, you've got nothing to worry about, correct? You had absolutely nothing to do with any of those murders. You didn't kill Candy. You didn't kill Paula. You didn't kill Candy's supposed boyfriend, Trent. And you didn't kill Sally, the woman in the red hoodie at the intersection. I guess Candy just couldn't do the job, huh? So you had to prove to her that she was in it, whether she liked it or not."

"The stupid bitch," he said, with a sneer. "She was so weak."

"It's not a show of strength to kill and to torment helpless people," Kate said. "You've been running a reign of terror on that university long enough. And we're here to tell you, it's over."

"Nothing's over." Brandon smirked, looking at his nails. "You've got nothing on me. Besides, you have no jurisdiction over me. The university is policed by the RCMP."

"That last part is correct. But we do have jurisdiction over you, as the people you murdered were killed at the intersection outside of the university grounds or at off-campus housing—neither of which is policed by the RCMP but by us. You can bet we're working together on the charges you'll face for your other lovely nasty bullying attacks at the university. As for evidence, we've got the murder weapon for one," she said, with half a smile. "We've got statements from all your sixteen reported cases of attacks on students, then of your threats thereafter to keep your victims silent. Plus now we've got the testimony of your cohorts in the crimes. You remember them, don't you? Walter, Jonathan, Tony?"

Brandon glared.

"Did you really think all your bullying and your threats wouldn't backfire on you eventually?" She turned to look at the lawyer. "Don't even think about bailing this guy out, We've got four counts of murder in the first degree."

He immediately shook his head and started to speak.

She held up her hand. "I'm not even talking to you. He's going down, and he's going down for a very long time."

Brandon sneered. "My family will buy my way out."

"I can't imagine why they would even want to." She looked at him, like he was a slug. "You're nothing but trouble. At some point in time, all of them will just cut their losses. Cut their losses and walk away because you're just one of those, you know, unlucky sperms that made it through when it shouldn't have," she said, with a sneer of her own. "There's always more where that came from." And, with that, she turned and walked out.

She heard Brandon screaming inside. She had left the recorder running, just in case he said anything helpful, but, as far as she was concerned, it was done and over. She walked out into the bullpen and dropped the stack of files on her desk. She faced the rest of her team. "I know I need to stay and do a ton of shit, but my stomach is churning with the reality of what our society is producing, so I'll be taking off for the day. I'll be back in the morning to handle the rest of this shit."

After sharing a high five with Rodney, she turned and left. As she walked across the street, ready to find a cab instead of walk, she saw Simon sitting there, waiting for her. He noted the road rash on her face with a grimace, but he didn't say anything about it. She looked at him. "It's over. It's sad and really sickening, but it's over."

He stood and opened his arms. Grateful, she walked into them. When they closed around her, he said, "I'd suggest a swim to cleanse all this away, but lacking a pool, how about a walk to remind ourselves of some good things about the city."

"You know something? I think that is a great idea."

Then hand in hand, they strode off to enjoy the rest of the day.

This concludes Book 3 of Kate Morgan: Simon Says... Ride.

Read about Kate Morgan: Simon Says... Scream, Book 4

Simon Says... Scream: Kate Morgan (Book #4)

Introducing a new thriller series that keeps you guessing and on your toes through every twist and unexpected turn....

USA Today Best-Selling Author Dale Mayer does it again in this mind-blowing thriller series.

The unlikely team of Detective Kate Morgan and Simon St. Laurant, an unwilling psychic, marries all the unpredictable and passionate elements of Mayer's work that readers have come to love and crave.

It's taken some time, but Detective Kate Morgan's various relationships are gelling at work—and even at home. Until Simon starts screaming in the middle of the night. Worried and not sure she's up for this, Kate distances herself from him. When a tortured female body shows up, Simon's visions are of no help, until he describes one specific injury, ... the same injury on Kate's latest case.

A case getting weirder as more is uncovered. A similar tortured death happened more than a decade ago, where the killer was caught and served time. As a suspect he looks good for this current case because he's now out and back in society. Except he has a solid alibi …

This isn't the only victim though, and, as the Vancouver PD Homicide Unit digs deeper, Kate's team finds several more cases—all with connections to the same suspect. But Kate's still not convinced.

Too much more is going on, and she's determined to get to the bottom of this, before someone else dies a painful death …

First Sunday of September, Wee Morning Hours

A SCREAM FROM hell woke up Simon. He bolted from the bed and spun around in a panic. In the dark and nude, he tripped over his clothing on the floor as he raced for the window. He didn't know where that scream had come from, but—

"Jesus Christ, what's the matter?"

He stopped, turned, and slowly reoriented himself.

Kate sat up in the bed and stared at him. "Simon? What's the matter?"

"An unholy scream." He held up his hands, so she could see them trembling.

"From where?" she asked, sliding out from under the covers.

"The hallway? Your neighbor?"

She quickly pulled on her panties and jeans, then a top over her bare chest, as she walked to the front door. She stepped out into the hallway, coming back in again.

He stared at her. "I think"—he took a deep breath—"I think it was inside my head."

She groaned. "Not another one."

He gave her a lopsided smile. "Hey, Kate. This isn't my doing. Remember that."

"Hey, Simon. This isn't what we wanted either. Remember that."

"I know." He nodded. "And it's been a long time."

"It has, at least a couple weeks." And, with that, she gave him an eye roll.

"I know. Sorry."

"It's all right," she noted, "but it would be good if you could explain a little more."

"There's no explaining," he murmured. "This is just insanity."

"I get it," she agreed. "I really do."

"Good, because this is just too much."

"You don't know where or when or what or who?"

"No." His expression was grim. "Just the most horrific scream."

"A woman?" Kate asked, and he nodded. "In pain or fear?"

He looked at her, frowned. "Pain."

"I get it. Somebody being tortured." She sighed heavily.

He slowly nodded. "I think so." He paused. "I wish not, but I think so."

She nodded. "Oh, *great*. Here we go again."

Find Book 4 here!

To find out more visit Dale Mayer's website.

smarturl.it/DMSSSScream

Author's Note

Thank you for reading Simon Says... Ride: Kate Morgan, Book 3! If you enjoyed the book, please take a moment and leave a short review.

Dear reader,

I love to hear from readers, and you can contact me at my website: www.dalemayer.com or at my Facebook author page. To be informed of new releases and special offers, sign up for my newsletter or follow me on BookBub. And if you are interested in joining Dale Mayer's Reader Group, here is the Facebook sign up page.
https://smarturl.it/DaleMayerFBGroup

Cheers,
Dale Mayer

Get THREE Free Books Now!

Have you tried the Psychic Vision series?

Read Tuesday's Child, Hide'n Go Seek, Maddy's Floor right now for FREE.

Go here to get them!
https://dalemayer.com/tuesdayschildfree

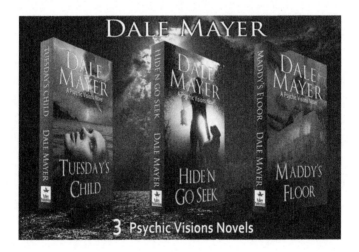

About the Author

Dale Mayer is a *USA Today* best-selling author, best known for her SEALs military romances, her Psychic Visions series, and her Lovely Lethal Garden cozy series. Her contemporary romances are raw and full of passion and emotion (Broken But ... Mending series). Her thrillers will keep you guessing (By Death series), and her romantic comedies will keep you giggling (*It's a Dog's Life*, a stand-alone novella; and the Broken Protocols series, starring Charming Marvin, the cat).

Dale honors the stories that come to her—and some of them are crazy and break all the rules and cross multiple genres!

To go with her fiction, she also writes nonfiction in many different fields, with books available on résumé writing, companion gardening, and the US mortgage system. She has recently published her Career Essentials series. All her books are available in print and ebook format.

Connect with Dale Mayer Online

Dale's Website – www.dalemayer.com

Twitter – @DaleMayer

Facebook – facebook.com/DaleMayer.author

BookBub – bookbub.com/authors/dale-mayer

Also by Dale Mayer

Published Adult Books:

Bullard's Battle
Ryland's Reach, Book 1
Cain's Cross, Book 2
Eton's Escape, Book 3
Garret's Gambit, Book 4
Kano's Keep, Book 5
Fallon's Flaw, Book 6
Quinn's Quest, Book 7
Bullard's Beauty, Book 8
Bullard's Best, Book 9

Terkel's Team
Damon's Deal, Book 1

Kate Morgan
Simon Says... Hide, Book 1
Simon Says... Jump, Book 2
Simon Says... Ride, Book 3
Simon Says... Scream, Book 4

Hathaway House
Aaron, Book 1

The K9 Files

Lovely Lethal Gardens

Psychic Vision Series

Psychic Visions Books 1–3
Psychic Visions Books 4–6
Psychic Visions Books 7–9

By Death Series
Touched by Death
Haunted by Death
Chilled by Death
By Death Books 1–3

Broken Protocols – Romantic Comedy Series
Cat's Meow
Cat's Pajamas
Cat's Cradle
Cat's Claus
Broken Protocols 1-4

Broken and... Mending
Skin
Scars
Scales (of Justice)
Broken but... Mending 1-3

Glory
Genesis
Tori
Celeste
Glory Trilogy

Biker Blues

Morgan: Biker Blues, Volume 1

Cash: Biker Blues, Volume 2

SEALs of Honor

Mason: SEALs of Honor, Book 1

Hawk: SEALs of Honor, Book 2

Dane: SEALs of Honor, Book 3

Swede: SEALs of Honor, Book 4

Shadow: SEALs of Honor, Book 5

Cooper: SEALs of Honor, Book 6

Markus: SEALs of Honor, Book 7

Evan: SEALs of Honor, Book 8

Mason's Wish: SEALs of Honor, Book 9

Chase: SEALs of Honor, Book 10

Brett: SEALs of Honor, Book 11

Devlin: SEALs of Honor, Book 12

Easton: SEALs of Honor, Book 13

Ryder: SEALs of Honor, Book 14

Macklin: SEALs of Honor, Book 15

Corey: SEALs of Honor, Book 16

Warrick: SEALs of Honor, Book 17

Tanner: SEALs of Honor, Book 18

Jackson: SEALs of Honor, Book 19

Kanen: SEALs of Honor, Book 20

Nelson: SEALs of Honor, Book 21

Taylor: SEALs of Honor, Book 22

Colton: SEALs of Honor, Book 23

Troy: SEALs of Honor, Book 24

Heroes for Hire

SEALs of Steel

Collections

Dare to Be You…
Dare to Love…
Dare to be Strong…
RomanceX3

Standalone Novellas

It's a Dog's Life
Riana's Revenge
Second Chances

Published Young Adult Books:

Family Blood Ties Series

Vampire in Denial
Vampire in Distress
Vampire in Design
Vampire in Deceit
Vampire in Defiance
Vampire in Conflict
Vampire in Chaos
Vampire in Crisis
Vampire in Control
Vampire in Charge
Family Blood Ties Set 1–3
Family Blood Ties Set 1–5
Family Blood Ties Set 4–6
Family Blood Ties Set 7–9
Sian's Solution, A Family Blood Ties Series Prequel
    Novelette

Design series

Dangerous Designs

Deadly Designs

Darkest Designs

Design Series Trilogy

Standalone

In Cassie's Corner

Gem Stone (a Gemma Stone Mystery)

Time Thieves

Published Non-Fiction Books:

Career Essentials

Career Essentials: The Résumé

Career Essentials: The Cover Letter

Career Essentials: The Interview

Career Essentials: 3 in 1

Printed in Great Britain
by Amazon

73802974R00220